Microcosmia

Microcosmia is an original work of fiction, protected under United States copyright.

Microcosmia

by

Ron Sanders

© 2007

ISBN: 978-0-6151-6359-8

ronsandersartofprose@yahoo.com

Also by this author:

Freak

Carnival

Signature

Moth In The Fist

The Deep End

ronsandersatwork.com

Microcosmia

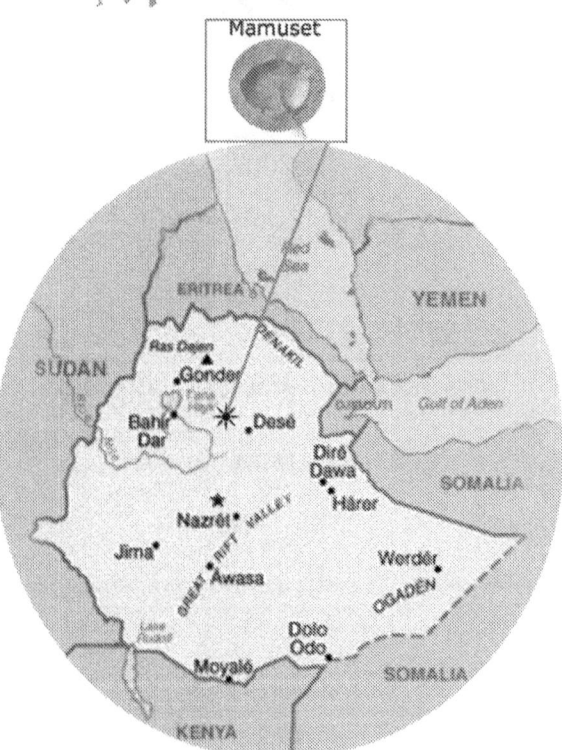

Mamuset

Chapter One

John

The old man rose through the darkness inch by inch, his fingers wriggling on the cold marble sink like maggots on hot china.

A muted *click,* and a bright pink light was blinking urgently on the bathroom's ceiling. Security's in-house monitors flashed back and forth, phones rang in staggered time. Resuscitation equipment kicked to life. A second later every alarm in the mansion was howling.

Old John stood clinging to the crystal faucet heads, horrified by his own reflection: sunken blue marbles for eyes, wasted nose plugged by dangling tubes, a gummy black gash of a mouth. In the strobelike light his lips writhed in slow motion, his eyes appeared to throb in their caves. Unable to turn away, he watched himself dissolve.

"Kaw," he croaked. The room sank six feet. He tightened his grip and fought for breath. *"Kaw!"* A scarlet froth broke from his nostrils and oozed down the tubes. The left side of his face seized and relaxed. Seized again. His right arm kicked.

"Kawr!" he gasped. "Kawr, Kawr!"

John's body rocked like a newborn foal. A long black drop trickled down his hollow cheek, seeming, in the panting light, to jerk as it rolled. His image swam in and out of focus. He coughed, *hard*. A second later blood was streaming down the backs of his thighs. With all his strength he filled his crepe paper lungs and cried,

"Karl!"

The big Austrian slipped between the door and jamb without appearing the least flustered, though he'd dropped everything and sprinted the moment he realized John was off his respirator. He calmly killed the alarm with one hand, turned the wall plate's polished nickel knob with the other. An array of cream-colored spears emanated from recessed fixtures in the ceiling and walls. Overhead, a fan's heart-shaped blades began swimming without a whisper, stirring a deep pink pile under-foot.

John staggered back from the sink, fluttering like a lame pigeon. With that same air of casual efficiency, Karl used a pink-on-cream bath towel to plug his master's trembling bot-tom, simultaneously lifting him free of his bloodied and soiled pajamas.

He lifted him effortlessly.

At one hundred and three, John Beregard Vane weighed a mere sixty-eight pounds, so it was easy as pie for Karl, a former fullback forty years his junior, to scoop him into the Big Bedroom. Karl tenderly placed him on the silk-canopied bed, padded to the ruby-dusted bay window, and mechanically spread the room's black shrouding curtains, all the while speak-ing as though the old man were a child.

"You are so bad to move, John! This I tell you many times. You must never leave the bed without you call me first. It is no trouble for me to come. But you are such a bad boy to move. What are you thinking? What will I do with you?"

Karl, now washed in bright California sun, crept back to the bed and pulled the cover to Vane's chin. On the ventilator's side-caddy were several bowls of pink roses surrounding a plush stuffed Winnie. Between the bear's splayed knees was a ceramic pot labeled HONEY, and inside this pot rested the room's fire engine-red rotary telephone. Karl pulled up a chair, reached into the pot, and lifted out the receiver.

"Kar," John moaned, his head lolling on the pillow.

"Doctor be soon, John. This I promise."

But John's head only rolled harder. In mid-roll the head stopped and faced the ceiling. The rooster neck arched, the tiny Adam's apple shuddered. "Chrisha," the old man gagged. "Chrisha, Chrisha."

Karl leaned closer, frowning. "John, this I now insist. Doctor Steinbaum here soon."

John tossed his head wildly, clutching the cover's hem and kicking his feet. "Christian," he gasped. "Christian!"

Karl placed his big palm on John's brow, lifted a withered eyelid with his thumb. He didn't waste time on the pulse. He set the receiver on its cradle, immediately picked it back up, and dialed a new number without looking. "Simms! Wake! Find Cristian now! Bring here! And go hurry!" Karl's pale blue eyes narrowed, his lips working hard as he sought words to explain the situation concisely and with finality. A storm brewing nigh on thirty years was about to break and take everything that mattered with it. He unclenched his toes, steadied his breathing, and pressed his lips against the mouthpiece.

"This," he hissed, "is it," and gently replaced the receiver.

Like a bright ballerina on a softly shaken carpet, a golden hump of spume was swept laterally by the tide. Wave by wave the delicate mold progressed, at last dissolving on the sand. Farther along, a new hump was born.

Twenty yards back, a quiet young man was observing this charming process as an event analogous to his own bullied existence. Like all depressives, he believed his personal fate was determined by a particularly cruel tide.

Cristian knew he too was being watched; he could feel it. He didn't budge, he merely rolled his eyes. A glistening brown woman, wearing only a thong bikini and half a pound of cocoa butter, was studying his profile. Her hair was golden blonde, her bikini the pink of cotton candy. She was flawless.

"I know you," she mumbled. "Don't I know you?"

Cristian wagged his head. "I would have remembered. Definitely. Eternally."

She leaned forward, palms on knees, intuitively going for the cheesecake close-up. "You're in movies? A sitcom? Now where did I..."

Cristian's finger shot to his lips and his eyes darted warningly. "Nothing solid yet. But my agent keeps me hopping. Maybe we met at casting. There're just *so* many pretties."

Perfect hands went to perfect hips. "*Who's* your agent?"

"Ah-ah-ah." He wagged that same finger. "Don't ask, don't tell."

The woman's mouth fell open. Her nose turned up. "As if I need..." She straightened. "Just you...don't you worry!" She took a few steps and whirled. Cristian could read her lips. His cheeks and ears burned. *"Honey...Honey port...Honey pie. I...know you!"* He watched her sashay up to her friends, looking back every other step. The women huddled. Their faces popped up, vanished, reappeared.

It was time to go. Cristian grabbed his gear and tramped across the sand, intermittently peering over his shoulder. The women were now squealing hysterically, their bobble heads grouped behind a sleazy gossip newspaper. He made his way along a lightly-traveled access road below Pacific Coast Highway, cursing all nosy women and their stupid supermarket rags.

Cristian Honey Vane's ill humor, under Southern California's golden therapeutic sun, was as conspicuous, and as incongruous, as his paranoia. He'd never lacked a thing in life. His health was good, his mind sound, his father staggeringly wealthy. He was moderately famous.

The fame came not from talent or hard work, but from bearing the surname of one of the richest men in the western hemisphere. It was a hollow fame. And although Cristian hated media attention with every fiber of his being, he was forced to acknowledge that he, and all resident *Vanes,* born "Vane" or otherwise, were fair game for periodicals preying on the rich and famous.

Not that his image was in such great demand; he wasn't exactly handsome, nor was he particularly ugly. Cristian Honey, the enigmatic, camera-shy bachelor, was invariably captured mulling in a reasonably photogenic gray area, where Vane-watchers of either gender could love him or hate him, depending on the breeze. The rags delighted in spinning him both ways, portraying him as a hard-drinking womanizer to one audience and as a closet homosexual to the other. He was neither. Through no fault of his own, master Vane was that rare paradox, the *compassionate misanthrope*. Compassion was in his nature. The misanthropy resulted from nurture. Considering the bloodsuckers who made up his "family," it was amazing he hadn't ended it long ago.

Cristian's boom box died on a dime. He shook it, punched the compact disk player a couple of times, and began rooting through his backpack. Inside were tennis shoes, half a cheese sandwich, a bottle of warm beer, and a reminder to bring extra batteries. He was just knocking the bottle back when his attention was arrested by a racing engine on the highway, quickly followed by a shriek of rubber on curb. The front end of a hot-pink Town Car appeared behind an emerald patch of carpet-weed, and a moment later the red round face of Paris Simms popped into view. There was nowhere to turn, nowhere to hide; Simms was already frantically waving his arms. With a jerky little cry he rolled down the grade, scraped himself up, and pawed at Cristian's arm. Cristian shook him off. "You'd better have eight D cell batteries, Paris, or we're done here." He slapped on his sneakers.

Simms's cheeks and forehead glistened below the bright pink limo cap. "H—" he managed. *"H—"*

"Heart attack? Hangover?" Cristian shook the driver's pudgy shoulders. "Damn it, man! How many syllables?"

"No, Cris...*hurry*. It's your father." Simms wrapped his arms around a leg. "It's time. We've got to go."

"It's *always* time. We've *always* got to go." Cristian grabbed his stuff and the men staggered up to the highway like a couple of drunks.

The cream leather seats were handsomely polished, the

interior gleaming with that all-around sheen only an intensely bored driver can produce. Usually the trunk would be agape; sanitized receptacles awaiting backpack, beach blanket, and sandy sneakers. The rear seat and carpet would be covered with fresh towels. An ice cold Grolsch and one of Cristian's custom-made, exceedingly thin cheroots would be perched on the folding silver tray. Cristian would slide his bare feet into a new pair of sandals and sit low behind the compact pink limo's tinted glass, quietly cursing the staring, grinning public.

But this time the trunk was closed, the interior unprepared.

Before his driver could waltz him in, Cristian twisted back an arm and wrestled him around, poising his rear end for a very rude entry. Simms squirmed out and slid to his knees, clinging. "Cris, let's *do* it, man! Please…don't fight me. Just get in."

"Fight you?" Cristian hauled him upright with one hand, peeled off his cap with the other. "Paris, you know I'm a lover, not a fighter." He shoved him in and kicked the door shut, placed the cap squarely on his own head and stepped around the car.

"I'll drive, you ramble."

John Beregard Vane's American descent can be traced to one Bemford Pye V'aine, a wealthy colonist with interests in Connecticut potash, Jersey pig iron, and Chesapeake shellfish. Thanks to Bemford's policy of disseminating deliberately conflicting accounts, the details surrounding his rapid acquisition of American capital will forever remain mysteries. What we *do* know is that Bemford, while still in his early thirties, was a ruthless industrialist, slave trader, and speculator playing both sides of the Atlantic. A virile and egocentric man, he kept eleven sons and four daughters in tatters while buying out every business he could get his hands on. Whenever he encountered resistance, V'aine hired gangs of hooligans to shut down competition. But he was no kingpin. The moment things got dicey he took his money and ran.

John

He ran west, always investing as diversely as possible, always moving on once he'd wrung all he could from a town.

His final breath came at the age of eighty-nine, in the high desert outside a frontier settlement named V'aineville. V'aine held commanding interests in over half that community's profit-showing businesses. He owned the town.

A week before his death, knowing it was his time, Bemford Pye cashed the town out—sold every business, withdrew every cent. He converted his entire worth to bullion and disappeared in the dead of night with a buggy and horses. His remains were discovered a month later. But not a gram of gold.

Bemford's surviving children, save one, thereupon entered the world in search of lives. That remaining one, young Milo, stayed behind into his late teens, caring for the ailing widow in the ramshackle, silver birch-columned three-story known as Old Spiderlegs. The woman's dying wish was to be buried on-property, in a favorite outlook just at the shadow line of the Mighty Eagle Mountains. Her burial, spurned by the entire population of V'aineville, was witnessed by outlying officials and local reporters, and no one was more surprised than Milo when gravediggers encountered a space filled solid with Bemford's bullion.

The young heir changed his name to Vaine, picked up his father's reins and went west, buying and selling, cornering and calculating. He'd learned from the old man: Milo made sure he owned a piece of everything. Eventually his teams of agents formed a web over the waking continent, keeping a toe in every seaport, in every major city, on every railway. Wherever the land was fairest, there would the spider drag his web.

Unlike his father, Milo made an obscene spectacle of wealth; traveling like a prince, spending like a sailor: wives, children, estates, offices—all facets of his booming mien. His tremendous ego made him take tremendous risks, and he was, overall, tremendously successful. The Civil War was a godsend. Milo bent with the wind, profiting handsomely in Winchesters and whiskey, in cartwheels and coffins. The spider walked the line between North and South with vigor and with dash, all the way to the California lode. When he died, also well into the years, his was one of the first great migrating families to own a major piece of the sprawling bean fields that would one day become Los Angeles County.

A grandson, Timothy Thomas, devoted himself to business while his siblings spent themselves into obscurity. Timothy foresaw the age of technology, and with it the Great War: the United States government became his biggest customer. Eventually prestigious beyond self-censure, T.T. nevertheless dropped that gaudy *i* from Vaine as he groomed himself for a Senate run, and his insular adult son, John Beregard, for the top executive office of his global business empire. Timothy, busted purchasing votes on a Monterey stopover, had his head blown off by a disillusioned supporter.

John never married. And not until past seventy did he produce a child. In his prime his heart and soul were given entirely to business. Important men shared his time.

Vane got an early hand in movie studios, in amusement parks, in public transportation, in fast food. Everything was fast in California, and getting faster. Vane stepped on the gas. Like Milo, he maintained a system of agents at home and abroad, and, as computers took a greater part in the dissemination and retrieval of information, engineered a corporation that, in an electronic haze of checks and balances, ran itself—he instituted *Automated Investment Management*, taking the brunt of guesswork out of investing. The *AIMhigh* corporation was a maze of integrated computers walled behind a fairly large, elegant office front in Hermosa Beach. Its lobby's walnut double doors featured carved profiles of facing eagles breaking into flight. AIMhigh in time became a solid institution employing over a thousand professionals devoted solely to the financial and emotional affairs of John Beregard Vane.

And John built a palatial residence on the California coast, a monument to money. He named the estate *Raptor's Rest*, and made its imperial house a showcase of luxurious living.

To paint himself human, John purchased masterpieces for public exhibition. To paint that human a saint, he donated small fortunes to any institution willing to carry his name. Apparently the public was ready for a socially awkward, harmless old billionaire with an insatiable desire to impress. John caught on and, for a while there, the master of Raptor's Rest was on top of the world. But as interest waned the old man's fragile ego went right on down with it.

Although Vane tried hard to recapture his moment in the sun, advancing age and displays of desperation only made him look foolish. His mind crashed, and with it his health. And one particularly bumpy day he handed the reins to Karl, the Austrian fullback who had served him, with loyalty and with love, for almost forty years. Those many years ago, John had been standing at knifepoint in Kapfenberg when Karl, hobbling from a tavern on his career-ending shattered ankle, decided to take out his self-pity on a completely surprised pair of muggers, breaking the face of one and rearranging the spine of the other. One of those inexplicable friendships soon blossomed, and Karl and John eventually grew inseparable. And so great became Karl's love for John that John needed merely speak it for Karl to make it so. Therefore, throughout Vane's later deterioration, those lavish displays meant to impress the world continued to accumulate, and with a growing accent on the bizarre.

In his early seventies John took a prescribed vacation south of the border to recover from a series of nervous breakdowns. He returned a year later, sicker and loonier than ever, with an infant son he'd named Christian Honey after a messianic hallucination en route (the first name's offending *h* was dropped by the boy at the onset of intellectual maturity, the mortifying middle name buried completely until dug up by gossip rags). On his arrival at Los Angeles International Airport, old John tearfully re-christened AIMhigh *The Honey Foundation*, ordered whipped cream pies all around, and collapsed in the arms of Karl. The eagle would soar no more. He was taken home to die.

Raptor's Rest, a 318-acre estate overlooking the ocean, nestles in a broad line of salmon hills rising majestically above Pacific Coast Highway. Centered on a manufactured plateau, the Vane mansion is a six-armed pillbox virtually unnoticeable from the ground. From the air it appears as a gray and white asterisk with a gleaming hub. The asterisk leans to the sea, on a crazy checkerboard of green and brown.

The Rest boasts six professional tennis courts.

Nobody plays.

Someday spectators will surely admire signed glossies set in gilded frames hung beneath the banner names of tennis greats and celebrity sports anchors. But for right now those frames are empty. Never has a coiffed commentator or bare-kneed luminary posed jauntily amid the figs and periwinkles.

There's a gorgeously manicured eighteen-hole golf course with a spiraling series of lakes, and a clubhouse containing all the amenities of a five star hotel. Yet that clubhouse is of little use other than as a winter stopover for swallows. And not a soul, other than staff, has set foot on the course since its construction.

A long wooded private drive leads from Pacific Coast Highway to West Portico, the mansion's ocean face. Only permanent occupants and V.I.P. guests are authorized to use this road. Art lovers and Vane admirers, on that glorious day they finally show in droves, will make their way by monorail on a little shocking pink train embellished with fancily-painted flames. The rail's station is just inside the highway gate, in a small clearing made up to resemble a Guatemalan arroyo. The station itself is a whimsical recreation of a miniature cantina, with a flashing neon sign above its swinging pine doors declaring, cryptically, *Welcome to Rosie's.*

The rail climbs over groves of pink plantains into the denuded hills, curves above the *La Bonita Hog Farm and Sausage Works,* circumnavigates the sprawling *Dulce Leche Honeybee Terraces*, and concludes, after a dizzying glide through the Central American Flag Garden, on the mansion's opposite side at East Portico's equally whimsical *Cinnamon Station.* There delighted patrons will board a luxurious ten-wheeled tram, and so be delivered to the Corinthian-columned ramp leading directly to the spectacular *los Visitors' Lobby.*

Once inside they'll encounter the stirring self-tribute to John Beregard Vane; philanthropist, visionary, and durable bed-ridden addict of the Home Shopping Network. Vane's *Hall Of Many Treasures* boasts the world's largest cubic zirconium collection, and is crammed with everything from Thighmasters to chia pets, each article mounted and enclosed in its own velvet-lined niche. The Hall's *Wall To The World* is an ongoing mural of the Raptor himself, posed with captains of industry, heads of state, and his hero, the Juiceman. John, far too weak to stand, is invariably pictured sitting, an unlit Havana in one hand, a banana daiquiri in the other.

After a safari-like tour of the eye-popping *Vane Collection* in Wings Northeast and Southeast, emotionally exhausted enthusiasts will one day embark upon an even grander return route; around the fantastic *Mi Cara Firewalk*, through Vane's gilt-and-granite salute to great Guatemalan generals, and over an intricately tiled pink-and-cream wading pool for nonexistent children. The great man's immense bedroom window offers a superb view of the monorail's entire wending course. Sundays the little flame-covered train, stocked with gaily-dressed members of the groundskeepers' families, makes several circuits for the ailing master. It works just fine.

Those four wings not dedicated to public art exhibits are assigned to the men and women who actually reside in the mansion.

The Southwest Wing houses the permanent Residents and their families. The Northwest Wing contains rooms for Help and Regulars, for the Raptor's personal physician and nursing staff, and for Honey's officers, both legal and security.

Between these arms, spread wide to brace the sea, is the magnificent ocean view West Portico, known by Residents and Regulars as the *Sunroom*. This unique structure is built entirely of curved glass panes twenty feet high by ten feet wide, utilizing chromed steel braces and struts. The room's Plaza doors, smaller than their surrounding panes but similarly shaped, are fashioned of fused cut crystal. The Sunroom, illuminated throughout the day by natural light, is lit by four humongous Waterford chandeliers from the moment the Pacific takes its first bite of the wild California Sun.

Abutting the Sunroom is the *Foyer*, richly paneled and carpeted, featuring matching marble hearths on either side of an elegant, sausage-shaped arch leading into the *Ballroom*, the Rest's great glass-domed heart.

This Ballroom is a stunningly beautiful chamber of polished cedar, designed to accommodate a small orchestra and hundreds of immaculately dressed dancers. Over ten thousand petite pink roses thrive in ornate marble troughs arranged in a sweet, room-embracing hedge. The great dome's outer surface is ground to produce prismatic effects with the passage of sun, the inner surface feathered to scatter the radiance of a hundred solid gold candelabra at night.

But not a string has been plucked, not a keyboard played. Never has a couple graced that gleaming cedar floor. The Ballroom waits yawning, its candelabra cold.

The North Wing belongs to John, the south to his son Cristian. Taken together, these two wings effectively bisect the mansion and are therefore considered a unit, the *Grand Hall*.

The Grand Hall's northern extreme contains the luxurious bedroom of the master, the rather austere quarters of his man Karl, and a number of rooms holding state-of-the-art test equipment and resuscitative devices.

Cristian's bohemian suite occupies the southern extreme. Adjacent rooms include a library, a small gymnasium, and a miniature observatory half a million dollars in the making.

Stacked leaning between these extremes are the numerous genuine masterpieces and street-bought oddities which have transformed the splendid Grand Hall into an unruly and garish garage.

Even deep into Vane's madness the Honey Foundation continued to blindly take orders from his Austrian manservant, vigorously accumulating great works of art through a ruthless team of auctioneers. Meanwhile Karl, forever loyal to his master's senile whims, purchased countless rubbishy curiosities from hucksters on the Venice Beach strand, and grudgingly invited into residency any unsung street freak who took the old man's fancy.

One by one these parasites contributed to the ever-swelling cast of *Residents* and *Regulars*. And piece by piece those many dear exhibits were mingled with all the worthless purchases, amassed side by side and heaped one on top of the other throughout the mansion. In the Grand Hall, in the Foyer, in the kitchens and bathrooms, near-priceless marble busts teetered between lava lamps and plaster waterfalls. Psychedelic posters and black velvet Elvises shared the walls with Monets and Eschers.

Into this growing maze came a pallid, skinny young woman in a beat-up canary-yellow Pacer.

Megan Griffin arrived in response to an ad in the *Argonaut*, one of several local papers utilized by Karl in his awkward search for a nanny. Once she realized the full measure of her staggering new circumstances, Meg got right to work on that flagging bedridden John. She *insisted* she was the boy's actual mother. She nursed the idea…smuggled the idea…hammered the idea into his head: she and John had been intimate while cruising the Thames. Cristian was their love child. The Central American encounter was a fantasy, a filthy lie concocted by that devious schemer Karl.

Megan replaced her paisley granny dress with a long black strapless gown, let her raven hair grow to her waist. Everything about her became funereal, as though her very demeanor might encourage John into the grave.

Her one mistake was not covering her scent.

Within a year she'd been tracked down by ex-husband Richard, who let the cat out of the bag even as he made his own play. Richard flattered John shamelessly. Long hours were spent bedside, recounting tales of personal hardship and a fatherless existence. One night the Raptor, terribly moved, tentatively called Richard "son." Right then and there Richard knew. He was in.

Richard's awarded living chamber quickly turned into a teak-paneled, aquaria-filled weasel's lair, where an endless parade of not-too-bright blondes were perpetually promised pieces of his assured inheritance. These used women, drunk and despondent, became temporary fixtures in the Foyer and Sunroom. Eventually, inevitably, they found their way to rehab, the gutter, or the morgue, and so passed forever from the mansion's memory. Yet while in residency they made damned good spies: far from being the simple wry debauchee he appeared, Richard was in fact a cold-blooded compiler of gossip.

But then, one dreary winter's eve, a bizarrely-dressed young psychopath blew in unexpectedly and made straight for the marrow, setting the stage for a chain of increasingly ugly power plays between this dauntless trio of vultures, the Big Three.

Jason Jute, or J.J., or simply Jayce, had been turning tricks for lines and drinks in a Santa Monica Boulevard parking lot when one of his backseat customers turned out to be a bitter young former AIMhigh attorney. Jayce became both live-in lover and partner in crime. With fraudulently notarized papers demonstrating Jayce's incontestable claim to the Vane blood-line, the two quickly established a corner on John; one threatening Megan and Richard with bogus legal actions, the other with very imaginative feats of mayhem. Old John, relentlessly regaled with Jayce's manufactured father-and-son anecdotes, miraculously began to remember. Two pairs of hands would joyously grip his; the tears would flow like champagne round the bed. But two clear blue Austrian eyes, staring coldly by the door, would remain dry.

To stack the deck in his favor, Richard began importing some of the rowdier members of his old crowd. Jayce responded with a gang of his own, comprised mostly of flashy, hard-boiled perverts. Their war became an immature contest of airs—a superficial show of sophistication on one hand, of ostentation on the other. Richard and his friends favored tuxedos and business attire. Jayce's group dressed with a flamboyance designed to shock and inflame.

As word of the setup got around, the mansion became a magnet for ruffians and runaways, for hookers and drug addicts, for all manner of street people. Raptor's Rest grew into a hang-out, a home, and finally a battleground overrun by conscience-less marauders—dealing right from the premises, giving birth in bathrooms and tool sheds, warring amongst themselves in a setting luxurious beyond their imaginations. For the sake of party space they dragged statues, suits of armor, and bulky artifacts outside. Priceless items from the Vane Collection were left to the elements. Karl, reduced to a hulking eavesdropper, protected canvas and marble with raincoats, with garbage bags, with slabs of aluminum siding.

The threat was clear. But the more adamantly Karl objected, the more frantically the Raptor resisted. It was John's first taste of family. Only when Karl began to seriously fear for his master's safety did he make the situation clear to the Hermosa Beach office. A security team arrived, along with a small army of Guatemalan housekeepers and groundskeepers.

When old John learned he was about to lose his family a stroke nearly killed him. For his health's sake, Residents and Regulars were permitted to remain, and the security team kept aboard on a permanent basis. The Raptor, convinced by Megan that Dr. Steinbaum was the angel of death, forever banned the man from residency. And Karl, fingered as a nark by Regulars, was ordered to keep his nose out of family affairs. It was a close call, but the scales had fallen from John's sinking blue eyes. Only the Big Three could be trusted.

Megan, Richard, and Jason, although fiercely competitive, maintained control by coalescing, allowing the general population to institute a pecking order as their natures dictated. The lowest peckers gravitated to wing extremes, occasionally cropping up in the Clubhouse, Pro Shop, and monorail station. This is where the security team was most effective; smoking out homeless and substance-dependent parties using the estate as a crash pad.

Security was much less effective with Residents and Regulars.

In the first place, John positively forbade their harassment. In the second, Security soon formed an uneasy alliance with the Big Three—the recipients of outrageously generous allowances. A prison-like economy went on indoors, with favors and penalties filtering from hub to extremes. Security earned far more working for the Big Three than for Honey. And sometimes they could get downright vicious.

Curfew in the mansion began precisely when the Big Three were all turned in; anyone caught hanging about risked a godawful stomping. But every morning, punctually at three, the pink-and-cream gnomes appeared as furtive silhouettes against the greater darkness, whispering espanol into walkie-talkies, cleaning and folding by the yellow spears of pencil-beam flashlights.

As the months passed into years, the wings' turf challenges were resolved through gang truces and Security beatings.

Children were born and grew into their teens, relatives came and went.

And still the old man refused to let go.

On his centenary only the hardest of diehards celebrated with him. They included the Big Three, seventeen really bad-news Residents, a few of the scrappier Regulars, two masochistic transvestites brought in for kicks, and a roving pack of wasted bikers.

And so moved was John that, at the stroke of midnight, he demanded the residing legal team draw up papers adopting everyone present.

The celebrants, documents in hand, swaggered into the Foyer for drinks and petty squabbles.

And to wait.

Three long years more they waited, roasting birds in the Ballroom during the holidays, inviting in truckloads of buddies for beer bashes on hot summer nights.

But now the wait was over.

When Cristian reached the long private drive's summit he was greeted only by silence. The tall rolling gates, with their matching wrought-iron descending eagles, were already wide-open. Not a soul was about. The polished cobblestones were clear all the way to West Portico Plaza, a circular tiled court under an enormous live oak. The limo was hearse-creeping along when Security guards, surreal in pink and cream, appeared out of nowhere. A hard face cut by dark glasses sprang at Cristian like a snake. "Move it, Fat Boy! What do you want, an escort?" When the face recognized Cristian it immediately became professional. "Sorry, Mr. Vane, sir. You're cleared to go right through." The face disappeared.

"*Please*, Cris," Simms moaned. "Just for decorum's sake."

Cristian put the transmission in Park and climbed over the driver's seat. Simms tumbled up front, slicked back his hair, and cruised up to the Plaza with as much gravity as he could squeeze out of a crawling hot-pink limousine. Before the car halted, the Sunroom's crystal doors swung outward to reveal Megan in black, tiny on the glass bubble's lip. An anxious crowd rolled behind her.

John

Cristian took the rounded steps one at a time, mindful of the occasion's solemnity. He paused meaningfully at the entrance, but Megan reached right into his forced aplomb, embraced him possessively, and dragged him inside. His arms and chin fell lifelessly. Every face was dead on him. Cristian looked up to find himself surrounded by a pack of nervous hyenas.

He was home.

Chapter Two

Megan

As a lad Cristian was walked through these animals like a toy poodle through rottweilers, reminded again and again to distrust smiles and promises, to refuse treats and favors. Residents were introduced as aunts and uncles, Regulars as friends of the family, business associates, or art lovers. Each had capered for his affection, and perhaps he'd have leaned to one or the other, if not for the steely hand of Karl. For the longest time, even into his twenties, he believed that Karl was his true father, and that Karl's own father was that festering nightmare in the Big Bedroom.

His only experience with Woman, discounting those unsettling glimpses of Richard's strumpets collapsed in their fumes, was Megan.

Meg throve in the mansion; she *blossomed*, if that can be said of evil things. She became, in fact, extraordinarily beautiful, but not in a way that draws healthy men. Her face, a bone-white, eerily pretty, almost Oriental mask, possessed an *ap-*

parent ability to absorb or reflect light according to mood. Sometimes circles appeared beneath her eyes, vanishing even as you stared. Her cheeks might be bruised one moment and alabaster the next. And her lips, poison and plum, could swell like leeches on a pig, or thin to two slowly pursing lines.

Cristian's paternal influence came through Karl, who had Megan pegged. But he couldn't keep her in check forever: the Raptor, more senile by the day, nevertheless realized his son would suffocate without something resembling a mother. So old John instituted rotating possession periods. Cristian was reared alternately by both a mother figure and a father figure, permitting neither to establish a permanent chokehold on his soul. Theirs was a war of iron wills. Once in a while, however, John drifted back into the real world long enough to demand the two put up a parental front. On these occasions they could be seen coldly escorting the boy, each holding a hand as though he were a wishbone, paying no attention to Richard and Jayce, or to the ever-changing field of junkies, petty thieves, and lounging whores. They merely strolled, quietly and mechanically, sharing a hatred so deep it was rumored to cast its own shadow.

Karl's amazing self-control allowed him to respond to all things Megan with icy silence. He instructed the boy more as staunch lumbering mentor than as dedicated substitute father. Meg, for her part, possessed in spades the innate cunning of her gender—all those subtleties and sympathies and soft ways guaranteed to warp a sensitive youngster's development. She practiced this ages-old witchcraft on Cristian with bloodless precision, from a possession period's saccharine commencement to its histrionic demise.

Right off the bat Mommy exposed Karl as a very, very bad man—a monster, an inarticulate felon whose every word was a lie devised solely to destroy young Cristian. This scheming pervert kept a sick old man prisoner in the Big Bedroom; the same Sick Old Man Cristian was periodically forced to view; a man like a dying fish in a diamond bowl. Karl's one great goal in life was to poison little Cristian's mind with hypnotic stories and "facts" out of his dirty books, and so blind him to the warmth and love only a mother could provide. Megan fought ice with fire: she smothered the boy—massaged him and caressed him and hugged him and kissed him; did all those naughty and emasculating things Karl warned of. Cristian was always "Mommy's little man," his upturned face ever nestled between her tight white breasts. And as the youngster approached puberty, he found his face urged deeper, and felt those bruising lips fuller, and lingering.

The boy's confusion and emotional scarring did not escape Karl. Unable to break through John's delirium long enough to clearly describe Cristian's danger, he could only respond with a greater emphasis on schooling. Karl's possession periods became spartan affairs, Megan's periods, in retaliation, brazenly sexual. Cristian Honey Vane grew into a morbid teenager trapped in a haunted house with an iron grip.

During these critical formative years, a second woman further muddled his impulses. This lady didn't like Mommy at all. She would show at the mansion irregularly, usually during one of Megan's possession periods, and argue shrewishly while Karl, cold umbrella that he was, corralled the boy in a Foyer corner and monitored the action like a cobra.

This lady, always dressed in a very severe woman's business suit, didn't want Mommy to hold Cristian too tightly, or to speak with him about Karl or the Sick Old Man. She could get really mad, and one day she made the staring men in the pink and white suits drag Mommy off. Once they were gone she held Cristian the way Mommy did, while Karl told him it was okay, okay, okay.

But it just wasn't the same. Cristian eventually concluded that the suited lady was Karl's wife, though she'd appeared young enough to be his daughter. Megan, stomping in the next day, solved the paradox. The Other Lady, Mommy explained, was a witch working with Karl, who was a kind of man-witch. They both lived in the Big Bedroom under the Sick Old Man's bed. They wanted to steal little Cristian's soul. They wanted to keep him hypnotized in a big box in the Big Bedroom, and take him out every day for miscellaneous tortures. But they couldn't work their evil so long as the Sick Old Man was alive. Mommy was here to protect him. Richard and Jayce, all the bogus aunts and uncles, all the "Security" men, and all the little brown people in the pink and cream costumes were zombies, manipulated by the man-witch and that skanky, over-dressed Other Lady. The Sick Old Man's passing would be marked by a terrible battle of Good and Evil. It was up to Cristian to hang onto Mommy, to look at no one but Mommy, to trust no one but Mommy. Together they would destroy all the bad people and live happily ever after in the mansion.

That great battle had been slated to come any day.

But now Cristian was twenty-nine, and he was numbly enduring Megan's penultimate Sunroom embrace. All traces of blue were gone. Her lips were plumper than ever, her cheeks dappled with rose. And this embrace was nothing like the chilly enclosure that had accompanied him on his uncertain path to manhood. It was a vital hold, full of tremendous anticipation. It was the grip of a woman with good news.

"Oh, Cris, oh…oh *Cris!* It's John. He's—I'm *so* afraid."

Cristian gently pried himself loose. "We all are."

A pair of middle-aged men, blocking the Foyer entry-way like bodyguards, quietly watched him approach. They took their sweet time stepping aside. Megan hung back, her moist eyes hard.

Richard's sideward pace was as suave as his expression. He smiled wanly and offered Cristian a facetious nod, swishing a bourbon on the rocks in one hand while tapping ash off a Parliament with the other. Richard was now fifty-one, having lived in the mansion since he was Cristian's present age. But he no longer despised the younger man. He'd learned to observe the sole blood heir to the Vane fortune with cynical admiration, as an aloof fellow predator; one who would certainly receive the bulk of the inheritance, but would nevertheless deal the choicest cuts to those who knew him best. Besides, Richard had some really sticky stuff to sling against Cristian, against gay Jayce, and against that conniving witch Megan—and some inspired accusations to hang on Karl, if need be. He was sure Cristian would be positively relieved to have Honey's legal dogs turn over control of a few mega-holdings, rather than spend the rest of his days denying perfectly credible tales of homosexuality and parental abuse. The Rest's self-proclaimed Top Dog was trolling for a large piece of the corpse, and for a nice chunk of hush money on the side.

The other man's step aside brought to mind the sideways advance of a slowly circling Sumo wrestler. Jayce was one of the scariest creatures the West Coast had spawned: obscenely tattooed and extravagantly pierced, with a face creatively slashed and sutured under a spiked platinum Mohawk. Scarier still was today's choice of attire; a billowing silk apricot blouse draped by fifteen pounds of quarter-inch anodized steel chain, a blood-red miniskirt over leopard leggings and spurred platform shoes. On anyone other than Jayce the overall effect would have been supremely comical. But there wasn't a damned thing funny about the man. Jayce hated Cristian, hated Richard, hated Megan, hated his gang almost as much as he hated himself. But no one on earth did he hate more than John Beregard Vane. He'd spent over two decades kissing up to that depressing cadaver, and he, like Richard and Megan, felt he'd done a sight more than the fair-haired son to earn the lion's share.

Cristian's impact on the crowd was that of a stone on still water. Residents backpedaled into the Foyer, stepped on darting children, collided with Help. Help, in response, backed into furniture, spilled into the Ballroom. For once, Cristian made sure he didn't miss a single darting residential eye. He'd deliberately blocked out names and particulars, remembering Residents simply as Uncle Bungle, Aunt Fat, etc. They'd raised their families in the mansion. Their children and grandparents used the Sunroom and Foyer as dayrooms. He spread them all like a hot knife through butter, only to pause tellingly on the Foyer steps before strolling across the Ballroom into the Grand Hall. Cristian zigzagged between the leaning busts and bric-a-brac until he met a pair of cold blue eyes.

Karl unfolded his arms. The Big Bedroom's heavy walnut door featured a gorgeous woodcut of an eagle in repose, its head buried between its wings. The Austrian lowered his head somberly and rapped twice.

Half a minute later the quickly-reinstated Doctor Steinbaum appeared. He glowered at Cristian, then at the faces of Residents peering round the Ballroom's Grand Hall arch.

"Go ahead," he sniffed. "I guess it's too late for you to do any more harm." The men avoided eye contact. "But behave yourself. I'll stay well back against the wall; I'd be derelict if I left you two alone."

The Big Bedroom's antiseptic smell only exaggerated the underlying stench of extreme age: Karl had scrubbed the floor and bedposts with isopropyl alcohol while awaiting the doctor's arrival, and Steinbaum had applied a merthiolate solution to scrapes incurred in the old man's bathroom fall. Karl had closed the curtains, leaving only a crack. Very little sunlight found its way in.

John looked like he belonged on a slab instead of a bed.

He appeared exactly as a cadaver—blue and white, stiff and supine, with deep blotches on his face and arms. The only proofs of life were the oxygen tubes fitted to his nostrils, a pair of chattering machines connected for ventilation and dialysis, an intravenous drip attached to his left arm, and a collection of thin wires leading from his chest to a portable monitor beside Pooh. Even as Cristian stared, that emaciated chest quivered, slowly rose an inch, and collapsed. The event was accompanied by a small pinging sound, and by a corresponding spike of light on the monitor. It seemed to Cristian, standing quietly in the dim room, that almost half a minute passed between pings.

Steinbaum leaned back against the door and watched impassively as Cristian crept to the bed.

The old man came off pretty much like last time, except for a couple of details only apparent to the three men now controlling the room. In the first place, that nauseating bruised-albino look was now profoundly underscored by purple patches that appeared to well and snake. John was hemorrhaging even as his son stared. In the second place, it was the first time the old man's lips were not moving. On past visits John's mouth had worked convulsively, even during deep sleep.

As a child, a spellbound Cristian had observed that mouth in perpetual motion; sometimes operating thoughtlessly, sometimes reminding him what a good boy he was. Sooner or later John would begin to ramble. The rambling would diminish to jabbering, and the jabbering to silence. But still that mouth would writhe.

Now Cristian considered the mouth with morbid curiosity. He had no familial interest in the repulsive creature beneath him. Long ago any natural concern he might have harbored had been replaced by disgust and impatience.

The eyes rolled behind the lids. At last the mouth quivered. The eyes opened as if John had been kicked, and his chest filled with air. The eyes found Cristian.

Cristian watched the lips pull apart until there was only a black hole girded by gray, freely bleeding gums. The eyes became desperate.

"Please," the corpse managed. "Say."

There was an urgent exchange just outside. Cristian heard Karl open the door and realized that members of the Foundation's legal staff were working their way in. A strange hubbub blew down the Hall. Karl squeezed around Littleroth's enormous posterior and closed the door.

"I *promise* you, Father," Cristian whispered, his eyes locked on John's. "I promise to do you proud."

John shuddered head to toe. His back arched and relaxed. A few seconds later his right arm rose and hovered a foot off the bed.

Karl, standing tearfully in the corner, punched a button on a wall plate. A fixture high on an adjacent wall immediately emitted a bright white beam that bathed John's chest. As Karl continued to jab the button the beam rose slowly, an inch at a time, at last focusing on the old man's twisted features. He depressed another button. The room's lights dimmed until the Raptor's purple face, flapping like a fish out of water, was cleanly lit for recording.

Sickened, Cristian took a deep step back. Littleroth oozed right around him, his usually heavy hands a blur; vacant one instant, occupied the next. In a single sinuous motion, he flipped open his briefcase, swept it onto the bed, and extracted a fistful of papers. He wiggled his fingers. A gold pen materialized out of nowhere. Thyme, video camera poised at eye level, waltzed around Cristian effortlessly and melted onto one knee. Bryant seemed to glide to the bed's far side, where he produced a small DAT recorder from a vest pocket with all the facility of a magician plucking a rabbit from a top hat. He one-handedly played the instrument's controls like a keyboard while whisking the recorder's microphone to within an inch of John's spewing lips. All three men had moved smoothly, and in concert.

The ghoulish precision made Cristian turn away, putting him nose-to-nose with Karl, instinctively advancing on these brutally efficient men surrounding his master. Cristian watched as a dark cloud cut off the light in those cool blue eyes. In slow motion Karl's chin dropped onto the younger man's shoulder. Cristian, reflexively extending his arms, found himself in an intensely uncomfortable embrace. He awkwardly patted the closest thing to a father he'd ever known. The room rolled backward. Karl's arms fell to his sides, his chin to his chest. Both men listened to the small bedside sounds; the scuffing and shuffling, the whispers and whirrs, the painfully executed scratching of pen on paper. Karl stormed past with a little choking cry. There was the sound of paper being violently torn, a few mangled words.

Cristian unclenched his fists. Taking the deepest breath of his life, he turned back to face the room.

Chapter Three

Limo

Littleroth, Bryant, and Thyme navigated the Grand Hall, stamped resolutely across the Ballroom, and executed a no-nonsense parade rest on the Foyer steps. Cristian, for once the mansion's dominant presence, took his final walk under the Ballroom's gaping glass dome in an oblique shower of rose, his sneakers squeaking on the polished cedar floor.

He walked with affected slowness, halting two steps down to gaze pensively through the Sunroom's segmented glass face. Under the live oak's broad umbrella squatted the candy-striped carousel where he'd sat, rain or shine, as Karl's shy attentive pupil. The carousel's conical roof was of buffed copper. Its raised circular floor simulated a chessboard, utilizing contrasting squares of bleached Chinese ash and polished Burmese teak. No horses remained on the structure. A glass-enclosed library, a tall central gas lamp, and two steel folding chairs made up the floor plan. In the distance could be seen one length of the estate's wrought-iron fence. There were no walls, nor any trace of shrubbery; nothing to obscure a fraction of the eternal Pacific.

He stood casually, his hands folded on the small of his back, and waited. A child's scream was followed by a quick double smack. A Resident's son kicked a Regular's daughter. The little girl shrieked and the crowd dissolved.

Cristian turned.

Uncle Goggle and Aunt Jabber peeled apart, allowing the bruised loveliness of Megan to slither through. She swayed hypnotically, wringing her pretty white hands and hyperventilating. Then she was all over him; clinging, smothering. *Handling*. Meg was Mommy again.

"Oh I know it, sweetheart! I know it, know it, know it …I can see it in your dear blue eyes. You poor, poor, innocent thing." She dragged him down the steps, pulling his face right into her chilly white bosom. "It's all better now, baby." Megan closed her eyes and hummed in his ear, nibbling the lobe. "Congratulations," she breathed, "to the richest and sexiest young man in America."

Cristian grasped her shoulders and gently pushed her away. He looked around the room, said frostily, "Okay. The party's over. As of right now you're all off the Vane payroll."

The Foyer's interior became the conical guts of a kaleidoscope, the Sunroom's face a segmented screen. The crowd blew apart. When the room came to rest the Residents were all lopsided; out of focus, out of options. Faces sought others in slow motion.

As the rooted centerpiece, Megan had not spun along. But her color had changed. Her face had run the entire range of blue, only the cheekbones and chin showing white. Something wild peeked from behind her eyes, retreated.

Cristian backpedaled up the steps, placing John's blood and Honey's reps in direct opposition to the crowd. Lumped in with the others, Megan went scarlet. This was a woman new to Cristian. His eyes flickered as her voice climbed an emotional ladder, stomping on rungs along the way:

"What the *hell* are you *talking* about? This isn't about *money*. It's about *family*." She stood with one arm akimbo, a forefinger directed at the Big Bedroom like the finger of Death.

But, unlike Death, Meg's expression was defiant, as though a resuscitating charge crackled from that finger, penetrated the door, and shimmered around the departed. After so many years of urging John into the grave, Megan was realizing that, without him, she was utterly alone.

"That...*man*, who clung so *bravely* to this world, would have been *outraged!* How *dare* you speak of *money* in the midst of all this grief? Are you on *drugs*? Have you lost your *mind*? I think you owe us all an apology here. No, *damn it*, I think we should *demand* an apology!" The maternal charade was over. This performance was for the house.

"It's a family of ghouls," Cristian said through his teeth. "Don't tell me this isn't about money; you buzzards have been measuring my father's pulse for almost thirty years." He descended the steps with forced casualness, kicking a bright yellow beach ball across the Foyer. "That's all history now. You won't get a deed, you won't get a dollar.

"Control over father's holdings will be maintained by the Honey Foundation. The only difference is, I'm its new chief executive officer, and as such have final say over all transactions of moment. Meaning my word on this estate is final."

Anodized chains rattled on one side of the room. Jayce pushed through his crowd until he was right in Cristian's face, cocked his head, and whispered, "Cut the crap, Crissy." Without looking away, he motioned his nearest partners nearer. "Can't you see you're spooking the happy campers?"

But it was Richard who broke the pack, smiling pleasantly while swirling the cubes hard against his glass. "C'mon, *Honey*. This is hardly the time for levity."

Cristian held Jayce's stare as long as he could. "It's no joke, *Dick*. Father willed me the whole ball of wax. That means his properties and worldly possessions, along with every notarized item in his art collection. His stocks and bonds and futures, his holdings both foreign and domestic, the exclusive use of his personal name in each and every enterprise...in sum, *everything*."

He raised his hands and retreated a step.

"As you are all rabidly aware, it was Father's wish that the disposition of his estate wait until the very last moment. As you're also aware, several documents were drawn up relating specifically to that last-minute decision.

"Each of these documents contained a different configuration, describing various holdings for potential heirs; both for individuals and for groups. His signature on any one legally voided the others. Several of these documents were quite complex, involving some very creative provisions and cross checks. By making certain all potential recipients were legally obligated to these conditions, Father was guaranteeing that no party or parties would piss away his hard-earned fortune on mindless, gluttonous frenzies." He sneered as he looked round the room. "Imagine him thinking that.

"As you all know, there were also a few relatively simple documents, pertaining solely to three brutally-determined lampreys who've spent the last twenty-odd years convincing a sick and senile old man that they loved him dearly. These wills left all that was his to the aforementioned unmentionables.

"There were, additionally, two documents transferring everything Father possessed to either his manservant, Karl Günfel, or to his only genuine son, Yours Truly.

"Karl did the unthinkable. He tore up his personal will before my father's dying eyes and told him he loved him." Cristian looked out through the Sunroom, addressing the carousel. "John Beregard Vane has signed over the entirety of his estate to me. That miserable little ceremony, hardly a quarter hour cold, was witnessed by Littleroth, Bryant, and Thyme, along with Father's lifelong physician Dr. Steinbaum, by his man Karl, and, of course, by me. The signing was recorded every which way.

"You are all more than welcome—indeed, you're enthusiastically invited—to view this document prior to your being genially ushered from this estate by myself, or, myself failing, by whatever amount of purchasable muscle will see the job through."

"Wait a minute." Richard punched Cristian's chest with his drink-fist. "What's all this crap about stuff taking place behind closed doors? Don't play with us, asshole."

Jayce threw all his weight against Cristian. He and Richard physically moved him back up the steps, slamming him side to side. "What do you mean, 'off the payroll,' prick? Since when is anybody on your 'payroll'?"

"Call it a fact or a figure of speech." Cristian steadied himself against the top step. "You are now both on my property, and that's all that matters, legally speaking. If you don't, of your own volition, remove yourselves, I will have Security forcibly remove your selves for you."

"I," Richard gnashed, "want to see this evidence of a 'will' brought before a court of law. You orchestrated the whole affair, worm, and it won't stand."

Jayce looked one to the other, bristling at the phrase *court of law*. He backed off gradually, appearing to deliberate, then made a great show of signaling the Foyer barman. When he looked back his eyes had softened. "I suppose the cocktail onions are still on the house?"

"Help yourself."

Richard smashed his glass on the steps and the Residents erupted like pigeons in the shadow of a tabby. Three security men immediately stomped over. He shook them off. "Gorillas! Touch me again, and I'll not only have your jobs, I'll have your ugly puppet heads!" The crowd broke into small circling packs. Richard shouldered his way into the Ballroom.

Cristian was trembling head-to-toe as he walked back down the steps and straight up to the small knot of Security. Their captain, with Honey from the beginning, had always treated him like a degenerate little snot. He waited in the stance of a gunslinger, his *Honey* cap tilted aggressively, the pink and cream uniforms coalescing behind him.

"William, I want your guys to clear this estate of all these bloodsuckers. Their claims and arguments are illegitimate. They are, as of this order, trespassers." He snatched a framed photo from the south hearth and slung it like a Frisbee. "That means all the brats." He slung another. "All the old goats...all the 'in-laws'...everybody!" Cristian raised his voice so that it scathed the house, one hand on a hip, the other pointing at the Big Bedroom in a childish impersonation of Meg.

"Allow me to clarify! Only myself, officers of Honey, and the occupants of that room, living and dead, are legally authorized on these grounds once the turds have been flushed.

After that, you and your men can all go home: you're relieved. You can discuss severance with Honey. The Foundation will, in my name, guarantee compensation and placement for every man who has served this estate so well. I'll take care of Help, indoors and out." He stuffed his shaking hands in his pants' pockets and lowered his voice. "Now, I want to thank all you guys personally for your invaluable service here. It's been a real pleasure and a great privilege."

William stared back fiercely, his men's eyes boring into the back of his skull. Cristian turned on his heel and raised his arms like a choirmaster.

"All right! Listen up, listen up! I want everybody packed and out of here by the time I get back. You are no longer residents of this estate. Mister Bryant will be handling any claims levied against the Foundation, and I'm assuming there will be many. But that famous 'adoption party' was a total sham, and you know it. Those wonderful signed documents attesting to your legal claims to the Vane name are about to come crashing down. You're all about to receive a very rude introduction to reality. Brace yourselves.

"This is now *my* house. And I've learned a great lesson here, thank you very much. To wit:

"Should I perchance someday reach my father's advanced age and state of deterioration, I will make damned certain there are no bottom-feeders around to flatter and delude me. They say longevity is inherited. If that's so, I'd rather die young, with drama and with dignity, than be a helpless victim of senility and the slime that feeds on it.

"Honey will accommodate you in the process of relocating. This means that moving vans will be arriving shortly, and will be providing transportation for you-and-yours within, and not exceeding, the L.A. county line." He looked at the toys on the furniture, at the new handprints on the walls, at the clothes draped casually over vases and busts. "I want all this personal crap *out of here*. Understand that any articles left behind will be accessible only through Honey. Once you have all passed out that gate you will not—repeat, will *not*—be coming back." He faced the Plaza to hide his shakes. An arm jerked up, pointing at the Pacific.

"William and his men will now assist you in sorting your property, and they will escort you *out* of this house and *down* that drive and *onto* that highway. I'm sure they will conduct themselves professionally, but they are hereby relieved of all those behavioral restraints previously imposed by the Foundation.

"You are as of this announcement no longer welcome to the assistance of Help. If you harass them in any manner whatsoever you will appear in court. They are still under the wing of Honey, and will be placed elsewhere.

"The kitchens and bars are hereby closed, as are all amenities of this house. *You,*" he screamed, *"are evicted!"*

Cristian exploded out of the Sunroom onto the drive. His hands did a quick drum roll on the limo's roof. Simms, passed out on the front seat, nearly knocked himself back out rising. One arm embraced the wheel while he searched wildly for his glasses. "I'm up, I'm up!"

A fist crashed on the roof. "Now pay close attention here, Paris! I love you more than anyone else on the planet, man, but if you don't get your fat ass out of this car, *immediately*, I will not be responsible for my actions. I'm two seconds away from genocide." He jackknifed his body inside and tore the keys from the ignition. As he was backing out, a wide shadow fell on the Town Car's side.

"A pretty speech," Littleroth wheezed. "But before you go a'jaunting, I've got a present for you." He extracted an elegant pink and cream cell phone from a breast pocket, flipped it open. Inlaid jewels flashed in the sun. "Your life just got a whole lot busier, Cris." Littleroth bowed wryly. "Mr. Vane." He pointed out an intricate series of golden buttons beneath a liquid crystal display. "From now on you will be communicating solely through Denise. You can dial her directly by touching this lozenge-shaped button here, and she'll link you to the various Foundation departments. Additionally, you may reach me whenever you have a legal question by sequentially touching buttons one, four, and five, followed by the asterisk. Denise will explain the screen and these ports, and how the device interfaces with the Lincoln's computer. All incoming calls will be recorded, and you'll have the option of recording outgoing calls.

Just press the pound key and wait until you hear a triple-beep repeated twice. Then press it again. This phone has a miniature disk drive. What you record can be downloaded, the disk erased and reused. If you need help, go to the dash menu or ring up Denise." He snapped the instrument shut.

Mr. Vane took it as if it were a loaded gun. "Right." He slammed the phone into its dash mount, slid onto the driver's seat, and pulled his shades from the passenger-side visor. "But I'm dead-serious about kicking out those creeps. Enough is e-nough. You handle it personally—bust some chops, call in uni-forms if you think that'll expedite things. Get the hell away from the car, Paris."

Vane fought to relax, the shades' lenses dancing with the sun. After a long minute he said curtly, "I'll be in touch," and placed the car in drive. He drove with both hands squeezing the wheel, watching the still round figures shrink in the rear-view mirror. It took all his willpower to follow the pretty little cobbled road clear to the gate without accelerating. Once he was out of sight he floored it, hammering his fist over and over on the dash as he deliberately thrashed the limo's undercarriage on the road's paved gutter. But that wasn't good enough. He bashed fenders against tree trunks, tore up the transmission us-ing the low gears and gas, whipped the car side to side with sudden dramatic yanks on the steering wheel. Vane ate up the whole right side in one long slow-motion swipe of birches. At the Highway gate he found himself leaning hard on the horn while repeatedly slamming a fist into the roof. He drove straight into the gate, backed up, smashed in the front end again. When Vane backed off the third collision, he left most of the limou-sine's grille embedded in the horizontal bars. It was then he re-membered the dash switch that electronically triggered the gate.

He bullied the beat-up pink limousine through traffic; deaf to shouts, blind to gestures, responding to blaring horns by hitting the brakes or gunning the engine. Eventually his auto-matic pilot took over, making adjustments broad and fine. The Town Car fell in line.

The cell phone chirruped in its mount.

Vane glared at it. It challenged him again.

He determined to follow the six-rings rule. Six rings,

he'd been told, was the average time a caller would wait before concluding no one was home.

After fourteen rings the sound was eating at him like a dentist's drill. Vane tore the phone from its mount and seriously considered hurling it out the window. He took a deep breath before flipping it open.

"Yes?"

"This is Miss Waters, Mister Vane. Are you all right? We've been having problems connecting."

"I'm fine, Miss Waters. I was just stretching my legs."

"I understand, sir. But it's very important to keep your phone handy at all times. The information-flow can become quite heavy."

"I was under the impression that Karl would monitor the critical calls, and that you, Denise, would field the general ones. It's still pretty early in the game for me to be handling big decisions, and I've frankly had a pretty tough day."

"Of course, sir." The voice was cautiously sympathetic. *"We're all deeply saddened by the loss of your father. However, your mention of Mr. Günfel leads us straight to the point of this call. He won't be able to handle Honey's major decisions. I'm going to have to coordinate with you."*

The phone grew slippery in Vane's hand. "Why? What's wrong with Karl?"

"He's become incapacitated, the poor dear. He took your father's passing very hard, and seems to have experienced some sort of cardiac event."

The drilling began in Vane's temple. "So he'll be all right?"

"It's very fortunate that John's personal physician was on hand. He assured me that Mr. Günfel is resting comfortably."

"That's good," Vane said hollowly. He rolled his aching eyeballs. "Look, Denise, I'm about to make an executive decision here. Whatever your salary was, it's doubled. I know nothing of Honey's machinery; who handles payroll, et cetera. But if there are any questions about your raise, route those questions straight to me, and I'll personally ream the son of a bitch. Today I learned all about dealing with tapeworms."

"Mr. Vane! I'm...I'm..."

"Along with your raise, Denise, comes a quantum leap in your duties."

"Of course, Mr. Vane, sir."

"Your first responsibility is to address me as Cristian, or as Cris. You can even call me 'hey you' if you'd like. Anything but 'sir.' It appears we'll be communicating a lot from now on, so we'd might as well be solely on a first name basis.

"Additionally, *Denise*, you are for now basically running the show. Your title is to be commensurate with your pay raise. For the time being let's just say you're the acting president of Honey, and I'm the Foundation's roving CEO. You're taking over the station previously assigned to Karl by my father. Anyways, it's no secret that Karl always went through you, and, to my knowledge, you're the person in the best position to make quick decisions." Perspiration was heavy on his brow. Vane flicked on the air conditioner, but didn't think to raise the windows. "It's going to take some time to get me up to speed, Denise. It was Father's design that I obtain full control of the Vane empire, at home and abroad...but, to tell you the truth, I don't know squat about accounting, stocks, legal proceedings, or international finance. Karl did all the inside work for Father, but he was hesitant about discussing details. He schooled me in a lot of things that are wonderful when it comes to handling abstract matters, and I'm certain that, psychologically, I'm in a much stronger position to deal with moral and ethical concerns than had he not been there for me. But as of today I'm beginning to realize he had no intention of preparing me for real-world success."

"You really think Mr. Günfel disliked you that much?"

"No, Denise. I think he loved me that much. In his own way, I think he was setting me up for the slow explosion that's taking place inside me right now. I think he knew I'd find myself caught between two worlds, and I think he knew that when my moment of decision came I'd make the right choice."

"Now hold on a minute, Cristian. Things aren't as terrible as they may seem. You're in a rough spot, and you need some space. But let me tell you something about business, darling. It's a lot like mathematics. If you separate your emotions

from your work, and are perfectly logical and alert, your figures will always add up. Success is slow metastasis. Show up, be patient, be honest, be dispassionate. Success forces a man to grow up. So before you go exploding all over the place, I want you to do a little meditating or yoga or whatever helps you relax. Do some swimming and jogging at the Rest. Enjoy your hobbies, make your peace with your father's memory, and get rid of all those horrible people who've been feeding off him. When you're all better, come back to me, honey. I'll show you all the things Mr. Günfel forgot to teach you about business. I'll make it fun. Teacher and pupil."

Vane massaged a temple. There was something inappropriately familiar in the woman's tone, something that dug. "Please," he whispered. "Don't call me 'Honey'."

No reply.

"I'll bring an apple," he said tentatively. "Shiny and sweet." He listened closely.

"You're a dear." The response was neutral. *"And when you've got a handle on all this you can start running it any way you want. I'll play secretary, and I'll keep you up on the ins and the outs. You really don't want a woman fronting the Foundation for too long, Cris. There's what I might term a Good Old Boy network that goes back over half a century. It's international, it's cold as ice, and it's deadly waters for skirts and compromisers. You might even enjoy swimming here, sweetheart, but it's no place for a woman."*

"Thanks, Denise, but no thanks." He wiped a hand over his face. "I'm taking everything you've told me seriously, and I'm banking on you all the way. I'm glad I took your call. I was *this* close to running over this damned phone."

"Don't do that, Cristian! Please! That little device is your lifeline. It's our physical link to getting business done, professionally and personally. If you lose it, or if you blow up and run over it after all, just look up Honey in the yellow pages. Ask for me directly."

"Okay, Denise. I feel...better. Thanks for talking me down."

"Wait, Cristian! Don't hang up yet. I need some info from you. Just a quickie."

Vane controlled his breathing. "What now?" he asked quietly.

There was a hard pause. Something made him focus. He pushed the phone against his ear.

"Listen, Cris...did your father ever mention a woman he had a thing for...oh, maybe some thirty years ago, before... before you were born? She would have been a light-skinned Latina, an...entertainer he met in Central America. This was way before he started seriously slipping."

Vane thought a minute. "No bells."

There was a longer pause. *"It's not all that important."*

"Then why bring her up?"

"Another claim jumper. That was her sob story. Some nobody out of nowhere saying she's a lost relative of one Cristian Vane." Waters laughed without humor. *"This one takes the cake. Says she's actually your mother, that she and your father...well, you know, were intimate at some junction in their lives when they were both desperately needy. And she says—get this—that your father paid her off when he found out she was pregnant and later took the child back across the border and tried to bring him up with a nanny, but that this nanny took over John's failing mind in order to control the boy's inheritance."*

Vane's mind dissected, sincerely tried, but came up with only shadows. "No..."

"Anyways," Waters gushed, *"at least I can cross that one off now. I was sure you'd know if there was even a grain of truth in it."*

"Sorry," Vane said. "Zilch."

"Good. Because for a while there this crackpot really had me going. Every time she mentioned you it tugged at my heartstrings. I could have sworn she just loved you all to pieces. And do you know what she had to say about you, Cris?"

"No," Vane muttered. He was becoming annoyed. "How could I?"

"She said you were way too nice a guy to go out in the world without guidance. She said the world would eat you alive. And she said she would be watching over you wherever you went, and would support you in whatever you did, because you

*were all that mattered. And she said she'd dreamed about you
her whole adult life. Phony or not, I understood where she was
coming from. She sounded like she had very strong maternal instincts."*

"Miss Waters, I'm really not in the mood for a sermon
on the undying love of mothers, thank you very much. I never
had one, and I think I turned out pretty okay, all things considered. A mother who loved me would have been behind me
right now. Instead I get a blank space followed by some conniving imposter dressed like Dracula's daughter. And now this.
A real mother would have stuck with me all the way, supporting
me. Not just physically...spiritually. And she'd be proud of me,
whether I went on making billions or gave it all to charity. Miss
Waters," he said with finality, "I know all about these people.
Believe it or not. I grew up with them, in a very posh cage. So
you can tell this soulless, underhanded slut just what she can do
with it, *okay?* I don't need her. I don't need you. I don't need
anybody."

"Okay," Waters whispered. *"Okay. Just relax, Cristian.
Enjoy your drive. I promise not to call you unless it's important."*

Vane crammed the phone in its mount and switched on
the radio. With soulless Muzak in his ears, he took the 10 in-
land, got off on La Brea, and passively headed north. He had no
idea where he was, no idea where he was going, no idea what to
do when he got there. He only knew he had to keep moving.

But inevitably he did stop, halfway into an intersection
on a dark unfamiliar street.

To a casual observer Vane might have been a dead man,
sitting slumped behind a wheel with the engine humming and
the transmission in PARK, his bloodless face running red, amber, and green. Drivers honked repeatedly, screamed obsceni-
ties, sped around him. The cell phone rang insistently, but it was
as numbing as Muzak.

A glockenspiel chimed in his left ear: HEL ᴸᴼ ₒ? The
voice tried again, louder. "Hell—LOW—oh? Hey-ey-ey-*ey-ey-ey*
...*MISTER!* Are you, like, *okay?*"

Vane rolled his head until he came nose-to-nose with a
skinny girl in her mid-teens. He closed one eye and squinted

with the other: fine brown hair crackling in spears of neon, flat nose pushed to the side, tiny teeth way too perfect to be real. Three eyelid piercings, two tongue studs, a row of bunched hoops hanging from one sagging lobe. Some weird things done with makeup; a deliberate Halloween mask for a face. But most disturbing was the deep blue liner under her eyes. Old memories stirred his pain.

She was posed inquisitively; one palm on the limousine's roof, the other displayed like a waitress with an imaginary tray. "Well, y'know, you can't just *sit* here. You're blocking traffic, man." The girl looked around nervously. "Are you frying, mister, or what?" She peered cross-eyed through the windshield, leaned back, lightly shook his shoulder. Vane heaved a sigh.

"Oh, thank goodness! It's alive. Alive!" She flapped her hands. "Look, man, you've just *got* to get me out of here. There's these like *super*-grungy guys who've been following me, and I'm totally freaking out. So can I get in? I mean, can we just *go?* Oh, pretty, pretty, *pretty*-please?"

There was a light clopping to his right. A splash of cool night air. The voice popped into his other ear. "Dude, it's like what're you doing, anyway? Taking this thing to the great queer body shop in the sky?" A door slammed. The smell of cheap perfume hit his nostrils. Plastic nails danced up his wheel hand and tapped on the gear-shift. "It's like this long bar," the voice said. "You have to move it over, from the little P to the little D. Then the car goes forward."

He raised his head and her eyes sparkled. Tiny teeth flashed between heavily painted lips. Vane grinned back. "No wonder I wasn't going anywhere." He took a long peek in the rear-view mirror. "What'd you say about being followed?"

The girl jumped all over the car's accessories, punching buttons and spinning knobs. "Wow, man! Who do you drive for, anyway?" She pecked the console's computer keyboard with rainbow-glitter nails, saying, "Dear Mom. It's like, *wow*. I mean, I'm being kidnapped by this handsome limousine driver. His name's…" She paused in her play-typing.

"Cristian."

"…Cristian, but I just call him Limo, 'cause Cristian

makes him sound like some kind of geeky priest or something. He drives this great big thrashed-out pink car for Elton John and George Hamilton, with a gay bar in the back and *everything*. He may have kidnapped me, mom, but I stole his heart. We're up in Hollywood on Cahuenga, and we're gonna go pick up some, like, *major* movie stars and party heavy all night. So don't wait up. Love, Prissy."

"Prissy?"

She stuck out her tongue. "Priscilla. What is it with parents, anyway?" She jammed her plastic sequined pumps against the glove box. One heel was loose. Prissy wiggled down her butt and got comfortable, the short red dress sliding up her skinny white legs. A second later she was all over the place; bouncing up and down, yanking on the visor's vanity mirror, opening and closing the glove box, corkscrewing her torso to work the radio. "Yuk! What are you listening to, anyway? No wonder you're so spaced out." She looked him over while poking the SEEK button, her mouth turned down. "Can't your boss afford one of those cute limo driver hats?" Prissy found a rock station and broke into an awkward little dance with her upper body. Vane had to laugh. She looked daggers for a second, then laughed right back.

He put the car in gear and squared his shoulders. "So where do you live?"

"It's not far. A few more blocks, up on the right." Following her directions, Vane pulled the big pink car into a hotel's parking lot.

"You live in a hotel?"

She stared sarcastically and showed him her palm. "C'mon, man. Are we tripping here, or what?"

Vane drew a blank. He slowly pulled out his wallet and exposed the bills.

Prissy took a fifty and a twenty. "That's just for now. Wait here." She stepped out and sashayed up to the office, enormous purse slung over scrawny shoulder.

Vane turned down the radio and zoned out. He was just starting the car when that same small voice popped back in his head. "Okay, let's go. But put up the windows and make sure everything's locked tight. Even so, I told the manager to keep an eye on this boat." She rubbed her thumb against the first two fingers meaningfully. "And I told him you'd be remembrandt in the allet-way, if you get my drift."

Vane touched the dash switch that armored the vehicle. Windows hissed shut, doors locked in conjunction, red lights winked on latches and dash. Remembering the cell phone, he plucked it free and stuck it in his right rear pocket. Vane double-checked the locks before following Prissy into room seventeen. It was as he'd expected: bed, dresser, television, bathroom. He sat on the bed. Prissy closed the door and hung her purse on the knob.

"I can't ever get the porno channel, but there's plenty of magazines in the dresser if you need 'em." She kicked off her shoes, unbuttoned her blouse, and stepped out of her skirt. The bony body looked deathly pale in the room's dirty yellow light. Vane glanced at the old scars and fresh scabs.

"How old are you?" he asked quietly.

She peeled off her panties. "I like to keep the bra on."

"I'm not surprised."

The girl fumed: foal on fire. "Look, mister. You've already paid, so you'd might as well get what you paid for."

"Fifteen? Fourteen?"

"Jesus!" Prissy stomped to her purse, tore out a California identification card, and gave it a fling. She sat hard as he bent to retrieve it, a scabby hand on his thigh.

Vane tilted the card to catch the light. It appeared genuine. One Priscilla Ellen Hartley would be nineteen come the sixth of February.

"Why is ID always so important? Why ruin the illusion?"

"Men are funny like that," he muttered. "For some reason the thought of spending a healthy chunk of your life in state prison tends to sour the experience."

She unzipped his fly and reached in. "Is that what soured it for you?"

Vane fell back on the bed. Depression enveloped him like fog.

"It's okay," Prissy whispered, releasing the catch on his trousers. She pulled off his shirt and sneakers, expertly slid down his pants and shorts.

Vane drifted along in that fog; without meaning, without mooring. After a while he thought he heard his voice say, "No, it's not. It's never okay." He was so far gone he didn't realize she'd been busy for over a minute.

The goofy face popped back into view. Prissy pulled herself up using his knees for support, yawned, and reclined on an elbow. "I can get the manager to find the porno channel if you want."

"Forget it."

The room died. After a while she said, "What's killing you, man?"

"I don't know. Things change." He clasped his hands behind his head. "I lost my father today. That could be part of it."

Prissy dipped a thumb and forefinger into her bra and pulled out a small zippered pouch. From this she extracted a sloppily rolled cigarette and disposable lighter. "I always come prepared." She lit, hit, and passed the joint. It was a new experience for Vane, so he copied the girl's actions; drawing deeply, holding in the smoke as long as he could.

That tiny voice said, "I'll need some money. I'm going for two dimes."

"Sorry," Vane mumbled. "I don't have any change."

The girl laughed and picked up his trousers. "You're cute." She fished out his wallet, removed a twenty, and stuffed the wallet back in his pants pocket. "Hold onto this for me." Prissy gave him her little pouch and kissed his cheek. She already seemed to have matured five years since their meeting. "I'll be right back." She pulled on her skirt and blouse and, barefoot, stepped outside and softly closed the door.

Brand new impressions seeped into Vane's fog. Something was playing with the tension in his neck and shoulders, something was tightening and loosening his eardrums.

Odd.

The ceiling light was throbbing with his pulse, the room breathing right along with him. Vane stared up at that fly-specked bulb for years, too drained to react. Finally the bed rocked again, and a slender hand pried the pouch from his fingers. He sat up.

Prissy took a tiny glass pipe from the pouch, pulled a white chunk about the size of a hearing aid battery from one of two miniature Ziploc plastic bags, carefully placed the little chunk in the pipe's steel bowl, and flicked her Bic. She closed her eyes and rocked gently while drawing, then lovingly handed the pipe and lighter to Vane. Again playing copycat, he sucked slowly until the rock had expired. Prissy plucked the pipe from his fingers and continued to draw, turning the bowl under the flame to get every molecule of residue.

Vane's lips were numb, his loins liquid. His brain relaxed and sharpened, relaxed and sharpened. He laid back. Prissy pulled off her blouse and slid out of her skirt. Her lips found his. Her tongue rolled over his chin and down his body, fluttering like a wet butterfly. The butterfly rolled back up. Vane brushed her moist hair from his face, wiped the dew out of his eyes.

"You've been driving too long, Limo. You need to learn how to cool." Prissy sat up, swaying languidly. She found her pouch and second little Ziploc bag, then helped him to a sitting position. Vane was allowed to hit the pipe first this time. He fell back as she killed the bowl.

The bed rocked. Prissy picked up the television's remote control unit and a sudden voice blared, "—*contacted Jet Propulsion Laboratory in Pasa*—" She muted the sound, stepped to the wall plate and switched off the overhead light. The room was now lit only by deep reds and blues. The bed rocked again.

The scrawny body smacked into his. "Let *go*, Limo!" Vane let his head roll, felt her hot breath wash against his lips. He half-parted his lids. Prissy's eyes were closed, her lips preening. As the shadows played over her face, the flesh round her eyes appeared to bruise and heal, bruise and heal. Her lips became a pair of writhing purple leeches; pursing, pouting, reaching for his throat like the sweet undead.

Not since he was a teenager had Vane felt his body come alive. His tingling fingers clenched and unclenched, his hands found her breasts. The drowned face rolled back up. Fingers came wet in his hair, pulled his lips to a breast, slowly drew his face deeper.

The similarity to Megan was maddening. Vane fought to break away, but she bit hard on his lower lip, climbed on top, and guided him in. The room was a pounding, squeezing cube. Vane's brain went fuzzy, contracted, released. It all happened very fast. When the jack blew out of the box he was left empty and cold, anchored but adrift. Slowly the fog lifted.

Prissy flopped off and rubbed his sweaty belly. He heard her voice in a dream, *"Thanks, Limo. That was sweet."* She walked her fingers up and down his chest. "You've deflowered me, baby. I've never had a trick get off while calling me 'mommy' before. It was kind of cool."

Vane's head rolled on the pillow. His expression was frightening. "Shut up."

Prissy shivered, her eyes gleaming between the half-closed lids. She looped her arms around his neck and smiled cozily, flattered by a sweetheart. The phrase *shut up* came as the emotional equivalent of *I love you.* "Yes master," she whispered huskily. *"Yes*, Daddy."

"I mean it," Vane said. "You're playing with forces you couldn't possibly understand." He sat up on the bed, hauling her up with him. She nibbled on his earlobe. He pulled away.

"Give me another twenty," Prissy said, clinging. "You'll cheer up fast enough. Or make it thirty. I can score right in this hotel if the money's right."

"Forget it. I can't think as it is."

She pushed him away with disgust, cussed him up and down, and two seconds later was hanging all over him again. Vane couldn't peel her off for the life of him. They leaned against each other quietly, using flesh for emotional support. The televised images, blowing around the room, made grim shadow puppets of their heads. Vane was experiencing an exaggerated sense of the sordid, unaccustomed as he was to the sticky underbelly of society. All he wanted was a long scalding shower.

"Why do you live like this?" he wondered aloud. "Why don't you find a decent guy and settle down?"

Prissy laughed harshly. "Like *you*, Limo? Don't judge me, man. And don't give me any of that holier-than-thou crap about finding a 'nice guy'." She pulled away. "I know all about men, probably more than you do. There are no 'nice guys.' A man is either horny or he's not. If he is, then all his 'niceness' is a load of BS. He'll say and do anything to get what he wants. And if he isn't horny, then what good is he? You think I want to listen to him bitch and whine about how there aren't any 'good girls?' You think I want to listen to him snivel about what a great guy he is, and about how the slut who left him didn't appreciate how he busted his ass, day in and day out, *for her*, baby, only *for her*?" She swung her legs off the bed. "In my line of work I hear more bullcrap than a bartender. I've heard it all. Mostly it's the daughter thing, dig? Like, I'll be laying there with some freak who's paying top dollar to get off on a chick *just because she reminds him of his daughter*, and then this bozo's gonna lecture *me* about how I should be a 'good girl,' and go back to daddy." She looked like she wanted to heave.

Vane hunched gloomily. He'd been preparing to tell the girl precisely this. "Everybody," he fumbled, "needs a father. Someone who can guide you. In decisions. In love. Someone with experience."

Prissy squeezed his hands. Her eyes were dancing. "Let me tell you about fathers, Limo. Let me tell you about men." She hooked a foot under his leg and stared at the ceiling. Backlit strangely, Prissy became a wise, caring tutor, a mother figure poised naked on a grave. And bruised, so very bruised. Her head fell forward and her eyes reached into his.

"There have been two loves in my life, Limo.

"The first was my father.

"Daddy was an alcoholic with a bad streak. I mean *bad*. He used to kick the crap out of my mother, every single blessed night of the year; twice on birthdays and holidays. He worked at the foundry in our little town in Paso County, New Mexico, and each morning he brought a thermos filled with Jack Daniels to the job. That's what the other workers called him. They called him Jack: Jackie D. Somehow or other he managed to bluff his way through work every day. Eventually even his friends despised him; first for the way he had to get his paws on anything female, second for the way he went ballistic on anybody who objected. The heavier the tension got at work, the heavier it got at home. Then one day he got fired for breaking the foreman's jaw. I remember seeing mama, swollen and bleeding, crying and spitting out teeth. I remember her falling on me to protect me, screaming in my little face while Daddy kicked her in the head and spine. I must have been—what—maybe thirteen, maybe fourteen, and I remember seeing his bleary eyes sort of shining, and his mouth twisting as he looked down at me.

"Y'see, Daddy was getting ready to teach me all about you poor, misunderstood men.

"He grabbed mama by the hair and hauled her off me. I think she was unconscious, but things were too weird at the time to tell. Then he took me by the front of my blouse and just kind of fell on me. I think his original idea was to pick me up, but he'd wore himself out thumping on mama. He rested there on me, and I was, like, gagging on his whiskey breath, and also I couldn't breathe because he was so heavy and I was so tiny."

Prissy's grip on Vane's hands became passionate. Her eyes burned in the surreal, glancing light. "And I said 'please, Daddy.' I said *please*, Limo!

"I think I must have meant no. But it was *Daddy*. And he wasn't touching mama any more. He was touching me!

"And I remember seeing his fist rise above me and just kind of hover there. And I remember screaming, 'I love you, Daddy, I *love* you!' And seeing that fist, big as a Christmas ham, come slamming down."

Prissy hugged herself, shivering. "Poor Daddy broke my nose so bad it took three surgeries to fix it. But I was young, and he was sorry, and it all came out okay." She beamed prettily. "See?"

Vane clasped his ankles. The rock's effects were passing. Part of him wanted to say he understood, he was sorry, but the reds and blues had done their number on his soul.

"There was so much blood," Prissy said rapturously, "that I couldn't see his expression. I had to see with my other senses. And they told me Daddy was real busy. His hands were all over me. He tore off my pretty blouse, and he tore down my pretty panties. He had me pinned, Limo. And he loved me real. Then, when he was done, he clenched his fists and started whaling on me again.

"And I remember waking up in his arms. He was crying, man, and he was telling me how much he loved me. There was blood all over the place; on the walls, in his moustache, on our faces. He was crying like a faucet while he told me how much he loved me, and every third breath he proved it with his fist.

"In the hospital they let me and mama share a room. We spent a lot of time holding hands between operations, talking about how life was going to get better. Daddy had busted up something in mama's spine, and she went through these freaky trips where she'd get all spastic and foamy. The doctors would rush her out and wheel her back in, then wheel me out and whisk me back in. They gave me some new teeth and fixed a funny clot in my head. We were there, like, *forever*, man.

"All this time mama kept getting worse, no matter how many tubes they stuck in her. She started to drift. I made like I was all concerned and stuff, but secretly I was on a total high. I knew she was gonna die, and then there wouldn't be anybody between me and Daddy."

She paused to study Vane's face in the creepy light. He stared back woodenly. The TV's images bounced off the walls, froze with the screen, bounced some more.

"One day a Jehovah's Witness came in and scored *big time* with mama. She clamped on his rap like a pit bull on a postman. He tried me too, but I wasn't buying. I gotta hand it to those guys, though; he hung with mama like a real trooper. When they wheeled her out for the last time he was still telling her how lucky she was.

"Now there was nobody around to dump on Daddy. I laid there dreaming about the day I'd get out of that morgue— about how I'd tell Daddy that I was pregnant by him, and about how happy he'd look when he loved me real.

"But then, just when I was getting ready to be released, this social worker bitch comes in and breaks it to me. Poor Daddy'd stuck a gun in his mouth and blew his freaking brains out. So this social worker throws me in this halfway house with a bunch of total losers, like she's doing me a favor or some-thing. I split and was just cruising on the streets, but I got caught and thrown in juvie. The old broad bails me out. More favors. Next thing I know I'm living in this big condo in Marina del Rey with my new foster parents. It's no mystery why they didn't have any kids of their own. Their idea of a good time was balancing checkbooks over chai latte. I was always Poor Prissy. Sweet Prissy. They liked to show me off to their geek friends, liked to show them what great parents they were. I was out of my mind, Limo. One night I told 'em I was gonna go admire the stupid sailboats or something, but I stuck out my thumb and got a ride down Lincoln to the freeway. After a couple more rides I wound up in Hollywood, cold and hungry and pregnant. That's when I met Jeremy."

"Jeremy?"

Prissy hugged herself again. She closed her eyes and began gently rocking back and forth. "The second love of my life. Jeremy's a biker-slash-philosopher. He pulled me out of the gutter and put me to work. I could make him a grand a day by going down on the daughter freaks, Limo. It was easy. All I had to do was look lost and helpless. They'd launch into these long teary raps about what wonderful fathers they were, and tell me over and over again how much I reminded them of their darling daughters. The hornier they got, the higher I jacked up the price. Jeremy schooled me on the freaks. They're scared, he'd tell me, and they're all tore up inside by guilt. But they're horny as all get-out, or they wouldn't be there." She shrugged. "They're guys.

"Jeremy began slapping me around after each trick to make me work harder, and the harder he hit me, the deeper I fell in love with him. When I started to show, he got super-pissed. He thought I wasn't being up front with him on account of I didn't tell him I'd been knocked up by Daddy. He beat me better than ever, but kept me in circulation. I learned to use makeup creatively. When the bruises got too loud I'd do my face up like a sissy punker. The johns really dug that. They wanted to punish their little girl for looking rebellious. Some of 'em could get pretty Neanderthal. But none were ever as good as Jeremy."

Her eyes looked directly into Vane's. "I'm not boring you?"

He closed his mouth and forced a casual shrug. "You must know by now I'm no talker."

The girl considered this. "I guess that's cool, when you drive a limousine for a living." She beamed. "I'll bet you never made a grand a day steering that big old pink hearse around."

"I wouldn't know what to do with that kind of money."

Prissy ran a hand along his thigh. "You could spend it on me."

"And it would all just go to Jeremy."

She smiled sweetly. Vane was again taken by the way she seemed to be maturing before his eyes. "One night," she went on, "one of Jeremy's best clients complained that little Prissy wasn't so little after all. The guy was so mad about Jeremy's business ethics that he said he was gonna spread the word around town that Jeremy was a scammer. Nothing my man could say or do would make that creep change his mind, so Jeremy put him down. He had to, Limo. It was either that or go out of business. And Jeremy couldn't let that happen. He had these, like, *major* bills to pay: Jeremy was in way-deep with the Mexican Mafia. So he rents a van and a bunch of tools and takes this guy's body out to the Mojave Desert. He lines the inside of the van with these heavy plastic drop cloths, gets naked and stashes his clothes up front. Then he climbs in the back with the saws and the sledge hammers and gets busy.

"He worked all that day and night. Jeremy told me he had to do an eight-ball of meth and a quart of Kentucky bourbon just to get through it. But after he was done he had a hundred and eighty-five pounds of primo lizard food. He poured the ex-trick down a gully, took out the drop cloths, covered them with gas, and let them burn. Now the van was good as new. He'd brought along one of those big fifty-five gallon drums, filled to the brim with soapy water. Jeremy said he sat in that drum for three hours soaking out the gore. Then he put the tools in the drum and innocently cruised out of there like some lost hippie looking for a Dead concert. Halfway home he stopped, poured out the funky water, and dried the tools and drum in the sun. While the speed was still keeping him jazzed he scrubbed out the drum, oiled and polished the tools, and even had the van detailed. When he got home I made him tell me all about it. He laid it down, then calmly reached back and slugged me in the tummy just as hard as he could.

"In the emergency room they told me the baby had been killed instantly. Now you see why I love the man, Limo? He's a real problem solver. The doctors also said my spleen had to go, but that I'd get along fine without it. Did you know all the stuff you've got inside you that you really don't need?" She ticked them off on the fingers of one hand. "Gall bladder, appendix, tonsils, one kidney, one lung..."

"You can lose your arms and legs, too," Vane countered, "and life'll still go on. But I'd rather keep what I've got."

Prissy nodded cozily. "I'm hip to that, baby. I'm keeping what I've got too. Do you know what a good man can do with a propane torch and a pair of needle-nosed pliers?"

"Shut up, man! You're wearing me out."

Her eyes gleamed. "So now you're all mad at me."

"No, I'm not mad at you. I'm just starting to see how stupid I am to feel sorry for myself."

"Yes you are, you totally limp loser. Mama's boy. You're all pissed off, you pink limo pig faggot. You're just not man enough to deal with it."

"Oh, for Christ's—"

She slapped him right across the face. *"Then get pissed!"* The blow was not only accurately placed; it was well-timed. Vane never saw it coming. He grabbed her right wrist with his left hand, caught her left hand in his right, and shook his head. No one had ever struck him like that.

The girl kept right on throwing her arms, but his weight and upper body strength had her pinned. It was an interesting position. Sitting on the bed with her heels under her thighs and her arms gripped at ten and two o'clock, Prissy was completely helpless. All Vane had to do was lean forward and hold on. He had leverage.

She spat in his face, lurched back and forth and side to side, did everything she could to free herself. When she finally relented, smiling demurely, her voice was sweet as treacle. "Doesn't anything make you mad, lover?"

"Not mad enough to hit a woman."

"Not mad enough to hit a child?"

"Or a child."

"Even if that child lied to you? Even if that child set you up?" She batted her eyelashes comically. "What if you were looking at hard time for having paid sex with a minor? And what if that minor copped your license plate number so her man could add you to his list? What if this minor had the hotel manager photograph you entering the room with her? And Limo, what if all the stuff I just told you about were parts of a big plan that goes down every night, starting on that very corner where this what-if chick got picked up by a certain limousine driver? It's like goin' fishing, baby; the names on Jeremy's List could fill a small phone book. Now, think about it, honey. How many paychecks would you be willing to turn over before you got *really* mad? Cons don't like new-meat molesters, Limo. Not at all. So wouldn't it kinda bug you if some strange chick did this to you? Wouldn't it make you just a *teensy* bit upset?"

Vane gripped her wrists fiercely. "Your ID says you're of legal age." He shook her limp arms. "My father's company hired tons of Guatemalans. I've checked out green cards and I.N.S. papers. I know good California ID when I see it."

"And so does the Mexican Mafia, darlin'. They've had plenty of experience creating false ID for illegals. And Jeremy makes sure his girls get the best cover possible. Like I told you, he's a real problem solver." She shook off his hands.

For a moment Vane saw red. When his mind cleared he found himself with one hand in her hair and one fist poised to obliterate that crooked, ready smile. Prissy was teetering on the lip of climax.

Vane unclenched his fist and pushed her away. It was not an act of passion, nor of passion controlled. The night was over. He got off the bed and picked up his trousers.

Five rainbow-painted trowels tore down his back. He turned.

"Don't go, Limo! I need a ride, baby. Bust my ass out of here!" She was now on all fours on the bed, her head lolling, the fine brown hair clinging to moist spots on her face and shoulders. Her eyes were black caves, her mouth a livid, groping sea anemone. A string of saliva, red and blue, hung from her lower lip. "Do me right, driver daddy. Lock me down and roll. Bash my funky face in, baby. Beat me sweet."

"Little lady," Vane said politely, pointing back and forth like a special education teacher demonstrating for a particularly slow student, "*I* don't know *you*. *You* don't know *me*. We've never even met. You're going to have to get your kicks, figuratively and literally, from somebody else. I'm out of here."

Prissy collapsed on her side. She drew up her legs and thrust her hands between her knees. The tears began, gently at first. In half a minute she was a blubbering wretch.

"That won't work either," Vane said solidly. "I've endured the charade of femininity since childhood. The whole self-serving gamut: tender concern, maternal warmth, petty jealousy, and, of course…lachrymosity. As a matter of fact, crying's the worst thing you can do to make a man care. We're organizers. All it does is make the situation unmanageable."

The girl began to wail.

"What're you crying for, anyway?" he said nervously. It must have sounded like a cat was being tortured in room seventeen. "Finally you're in the company of a man who treats you with a little respect, and you act like the world's coming to an end. You should be happy, girl. Your whole head's turned inside-out."

She lunged and threw her arms around his waist. The wailing diminished to sniffles and gulps. Vane stood still, fighting the urge to put an arm around her shoulders. He let his trousers unfurl from one hand, used the other to pluck out his wallet, and let all the bills rain onto the bed. It was a flutter of mostly tens and twenties; a few fifties. Maybe four and change. "I've got to go. I'd like to say it's been nice."

Prissy snatched up the bills with one hand, still clinging with the other. "Mine?"

"On the condition you don't give it to Jeremy."

"If it's mine I'm using it any way I want." She stuffed the bills into the open body of his pants. "I'm hiring you. It's my turn to be the trick."

"Hiring me for what?"

"Just to *be* here with me. Let your boss wait. Tell him you're at the beautician's or something."

Vane fell back beside her. "But no more drugs for a while. Not so long as I'm here. Deal?"

"Deal. Let's just talk."

They stretched out and snuggled. "Tell me," Prissy ventured, "about the real Limo."

Vane was silent for a minute, watching the dumb interplay of images on the screen. "Well, for starters my life is no-where near as interesting as yours. I live in a great big house with a whole lot of people I don't really know, and nothing much ever happens." He was struck by the accuracy of this little revelation. "Except for today. My father died and everybody moved out."

After a while Prissy said dully, "That's interesting."

Vane was catching on: the girl was less than a fireball without fresh drugs in her system. It was also becoming plain that sobriety didn't do a hell of a lot for his own personality. "What a couple of losers."

"Monsters," Prissy agreed. She leaned across his chest, scooped up the television's remote control unit, cranked up the volume and began surfing the high channels, muttering, "This room gets crappy cable." Finally she settled on a broadcast apparently highlighting the glorious wildlife of Africa's savannah. She curled up and nestled in his arm. Both were glad to let the set do the talking.

The announcer explained that all Africa was not the wild land of savage beauty portrayed by Hollywood. The film cut to an aerial shot of an achingly dry desert, which he described as the Danakil Depression in northeastern Ethiopia. Now a small plane's camera, receding at around a hundred feet, exposed a crescent of smoothed hillocks. A few seconds later an even wider view revealed an immense impact crater with a very low, highly-weathered rim. The crater was partly bisected by a ridge continuous with the outer desert, giving the site a shape something like the letter Q. Only its hellish location could have kept such a tremendous natural phenomenon unknown to geologists.

The viewers were informed that an American spy satellite, monitoring suspected Eritrean troop insurgences in the un-mapped Danakil, had stumbled upon this huge crater and the thousands of nomadic pastoralists calmly starving to death within. Nothing would compel these people, the *Afar*, to leave.

The voice said the area, and the crater by extension, were known to the Afar as *Mamuset*. He explained that this could be translated as both *came* and *waiting*. This was all the proof the voice needed: the half-dead Afar had an appointment with Jesus.

The film cut to a close shot of a nondescript desert location. The camera panned across numberless people dead and dying; desperately malnourished, parching in the sun. The next shot, also nondescript, was of relief workers passing out rations from the backs of a few dusty pickup trucks. Sagging in the distance was a large canvas Red Cross tent, the nether arm of the cross extended downward with paint to create the symbolic cross of Calvary. It was all very pathetic.

According to the announcer, a drought of unprecedented magnitude had decimated the Horn of Africa. The ensuing famine was already the worst on record, with a projected death toll in the several millions. Typhus and cholera, along with the slow but steady march of AIDS, had so weakened the pastoral population that many victims were succumbing without struggle. Taped sounds of weeping and moaning burbled over a brief clip of a little boy and his sister smothered by flies. The boy was dead, his sister clinging. Right behind this came a wide still featuring an entire family in rigor mortis, their cadavers being fought over by hyenas.

"Only on cable," Vane muttered.

Prissy shuddered and clung tighter. "What's going on? What...why are they showing all these suffering people?"

"It's a religious organization," he explained absently, "looking for subscribers. They want to bleed viewers dry, and they're savvy enough to be as graphic as possible. You don't break hearts with picnic scenes."

The frozen horror was replaced by a worried-looking man posing before a large group of famine victims. He was dressed for safari.

"That guy there," Vane continued, "is a kind of barker for the organization. It's his job to soak the rubes by appealing to their consciences. The actual problem is very compelling, yet it takes a real performance to hold a crowd. It's just human nature. Everybody's a rubberneck at a pile-up, but it's the rare individual who'll become passionately involved. The barker encourages them to stay. He plays upon their guilt, making it difficult for them to return to the workaday without feeling ashamed. Cash solves the whole problem. The contributor has done something. Now he not only sees himself as that one in a million who cares, but he can go back to chasing profit, pleasure, and status without all those damned skinny black beggars making him feel guilty.

"Scamming's always most effective when it's done in the name of religion, like on this program. The believer at home is caught between a real big rock and a real hard place, almost as if his conscience is staring him in the face while his deity watches over his shoulder. What's he gonna do? Offend his God in order to save a few bucks? But I'll guarantee you the barker and all his cameramen get first-class catering, depths of Africa or no."

They watched the man pass his microphone like a censer over the passive black faces, all the while shaking his head and pouting. The camera zoomed wide and remained on the paltry mission while additional footage, of desert outside the crater, was superimposed.

These new images were appalling.

Whole tribes were shown wiped out by famine, bodies and personal belongings strewn amidst thatch huts. Camels and cattle lay rotting as far as the lens could capture. A new voice came over, explaining that a combination of factors had produced a situation that could impact the region for decades. Danakil, one of the hottest places on Earth, was in the grip of an exceptionally intense eleven-year cycle. No stranger to drought and famine, the region now appeared to be the focal point of an event much wider than any recorded in East Africa's history. Kenya, Sudan, Somalia—all were being affected by rapid desertification. The Nile was shrinking visibly, while the Sahara gradually ate away its perimeter like a slowly welling pool, etching arable earth into sand. Even Saudi lands, far across the Red Sea, were slowly losing fertile ground to desert sand. Doomsayers could wail all they wanted about acid rain and the ozone layer, but the pouting man with the microphone, once again at center stage, knew that a far greater Hand was at work. The man on the mic freely admitted he wasn't smart enough to know why his All-loving God would so cavalierly allow His precious children to suffer so. He only knew it was absolutely none of his mortal business. Two things, however, he was ready to claim with complete certainty. One was that man's wickedness was somehow to blame, the other that the sinful viewer could immediately take the edge off at least a part of that wickedness by pulling out a credit card and dialing the toll-free number now throbbing orgasmically across the screen. He pumped the viewers to dig *deeper*, that these innocent babies might smile in the omniscient Eye of God. The camera zoomed onto a logy old woman holding a pair of dying infants to her burned-out teats. The infants were little pot-bellied black skeletons, mouths wide and eyes shut tight. Their tiny fists beat the stifling air in slow motion.

Vane felt Prissy's nails digging into his chest. He turned his head to find her quietly crying. "Why," she whined, "why doesn't somebody *do* something?"

"I could change the channel."

"Don't joke, Limo. That won't save those babies."

He picked up the remote and muted the sound.

"My dear, what you just saw was a taped recording, not a live broadcast. I guarantee you those children are out of their misery by now."

From the primal womb rose a piercing, nails-on-a-blackboard wail that gradually tapered to a long suffering sigh. Vane's hair stood on end. Something in that very basic, very feminine plaint had gouged a nerve in his heart fortress. Prissy seemed to fill out as he stared, until she appeared fully opposite the scrawny, back-stabbing runaway he thought he knew. At that moment Vane thought he had a lot to learn about women, when in reality he had lot to learn about testosterone. The sequence could have been the reverse—he could have encountered a mature woman and watched her morph into a teenager. Nature was hypnotizing him, stirring his hormones, trying to convert him from a procrastinator to a procreator. And now, watching agape in the crazy light, he could have sworn her lips plumped as her cheeks ran alabaster and blue. He was looking at Megan; he was looking at Mother the way she intended, as prisoner for life.

Vane slammed a fist on his thigh and swung his legs off the bed. "God damn you *all!* Just leave me fucking be!"

Prissy blinked rapidly. "Dude, it's like what're you rapping about? Who shoved a bug up your butt, anyway?"

He stepped into his trousers, pushing the trapped bills through the legs and out onto the carpet. He let them lie.

"Limo?"

Vane turned, said, "My name's not Limo," and caught her hand before the intended slap could reach his face. He threw down the hand and shrugged on his shirt. "And you should know me better by now." He watched her closely while dressing. Stepping round the bed, he found himself paused in front of the TV, mesmerized for perhaps half a minute by images of children and adults rotting in the savage African sun. There was a general *look* to these people; the look of worthless animals resigned to their fate. He was reminded of photographs of Jews liberated from Auschwitz and Treblinka. Staring skeletons. Faces too wasted to express gratitude or relief. The innocent Afar were freaks in a two-dimensional sideshow, exploited by an evangelical gang of trespassing profiteers. Vane, grimacing, ran down the channels until he reached a cartoon. Some kind of bear and a hound dog were bashing each other with mallets.

"This is more your speed, *Priscilla*."

There was a familiar burring under the bed. Prissy showed him her tongue and leaned over the side. A moment later she resurfaced holding Vane's cell phone.

"*Wow!*" she said, fascinated by the blinking pink jewels on the sculpted cream case. "It's so *pretty!*"

Vane stomped over and plucked it from her hand. He flipped it open, placed it against his ear. Prissy's jaw dropped as she watched the phone's colored lights winking in response to the transmitted signal. In the throbbing red and blue darkness Vane looked like some kind of futuristic explorer preparing to beam up. At last he closed his eyes and winced.

"Here," he said, handing her the phone. "It's for you."

He turned on his heel and drew open the door. Without another word he stepped outside and was swallowed by the night.

Chapter Four

Christian

Vane burst through the sugarplums, spat out a mouthful of leaves, and collapsed on the beautifully groomed hilltop overlooking Oceanside Cemetery's most exclusive real estate. Before him was an immaculate garden sheltering spotless crypts of the departed well-to-do, behind him a weedy green expanse holding endless rows of simple white crosses for faceless American servicemen. The part behind him was accessible to any old Joe with a car and a window sticker. Reaching the exclusive side meant getting past roving armed security, seven feet of ivy-draped chain link, and sensor-equipped warning signs embedded in triple-looped razor wire. It took all his water-damaged ID, and a phoned confirmation from one Denise Waters of the famous Honey Foundation, for permission to wander the grounds barefoot and without supervision. No one was comfortable with the raggedy unshaven drunk, staggering between the tombs and statuary, scaring the hell out of everybody.

But now it was twilight. The place was thinning fast.

Christian

Vane rolled in the grass, embracing a half-full fifth of gin—one
more grudging concession by the Cemetery Director. Honey's
name worked wonders: the Foundation's ubiquitous hand was
deep in nitrates, in floral concessions, in marble and pine. And
of course there was The Monolith.

Oceanside is visually dominated by an enormous manufactured plateau. Upon that plateau squats a stone fortress fit for
Pharaoh, from the air resembling nothing so much as a west-
leaning asterisk. The structure's name, inscribed in Roman cap-
itals on projecting friezes, is *Raptor's Rest*.

Superficially at least, the Rest is an outstanding re-
production of the palatial Vane mansion. The mausoleum rises
above a canopy of willows, elms, and magnolias like a castle on
a cloud, awing elite visitors, but remaining sheltered from the
boulevard's prying eyes by a long rank of eucalyptus sentinels.
Like its namesake, the Rest is surrounded by an ornate wrought-
iron fence. A long serpentine brick path climbs from the cobbled road to the fence's magnificent wing-shaped gates. Beyond
those gates the path is all polished tile. Only persons cleared by
Honey are permitted within hailing distance of the mausoleum.

Four privately owned, pink rose-lined lanes abut the
Rest. They are not to be traveled, even by Oceanside's workers,
without permission from the Foundation. They are named *Rosarita Road*, *Bonita Boulevard*, *Alvarado Avenue*, and *Christian's
Crossing*. But every day a crew of highly trained Guatemalan
groundskeepers in hot-pink jumpsuits is led across the Crossing,
scanned through the gates, and dispersed to scrub the structure
and mother the grounds. Not a scrap of litter, not a wayward
leaf, not a pigeon dropping dares mar the final resting place of
the man who refused to die.

Many years ago these groundskeepers, and anything else
reminiscent of the lesser world, would be rushed elsewhere
whenever young Simms pulled in the limo for a visit from Meg
and Chris.

Christian spent many a Sunday in this place, released by
Megan to play for hours while she reclined with a paperback, a
sack lunch, and a thermos of Bloody Mary. Blissfully alone, he
would creep shadow to shadow, drawn to the mysteries of hollow and stone. The mausoleum possessed the structural famil-

iarity of home, but without all the ugly aunts and uncles and funny foreign ladies, and especially without the Sick Old Man. Most of little Christian's nightmares revolved around that bed-ridden, soundlessly jabbering monster.

And once Megan was dozing and the shadows were cool, Christian would steal away to his favorite spot in the neat old building. You didn't attain this groovy place by just blithely following the many blind halls while admiring polished granite facsimiles of busts and vases. You had to know when to em-brace, rather than shrink from, the darkness. Then, if you were really adventurous, you reached the top of a staircase. Below lurked a blackness no amount of peering could penetrate.

The walls surrounding this staircase were intricately carved to resemble the walls of a grotto. On his first three visits Christian sat on the stone perch he'd named Top Step, whistling in the dark, tenderly running his fingers over the fascinating stonework. But on his fourth visit those fingers encountered the fat plastic cap of a dimmer switch. The room the boy illum-inated by degrees was a low artificial cavern, populated by the stone figures of unfamiliar mythological creatures milling about a large filled pool. In that pool a pink marble Neptune was cap-tured in the act of rising, his triton raised protectively over an oblong granite box. The box was open, waiting.

Blocking the pool stood a tilted, highly polished black marble slab, its inscription at eye-level for little Christian. He read it over and over, until that very personal message was burned into memory. The inscription read:

John Beregard Vane

Just below this, the numbers *1898* were followed by a long dash. No numbers succeeded the dash. Beneath numbers and dash was a disturbing paragraph. The paragraph was dis-turbing in that it rambled, and in that it proved, handsomely, that a stonecutter will do anything for money.

Pioneer and captain of industry. Loving father. Creator of empires great and small. Employer of the unemployed, legal always. Patron and presenter of the arts, established as such and otherwise. Adopter of those who are all his always legal children. Legal father of Christian Honey Vane. Loves Christian Honey, legal always. Signed John Beregard Vane. Christian Honey. Christian Honey. Papa loves his hot li'l pink honey pot. God is not a Christian.

The boy would dash back up the steps harboring a mental photograph of the crypt, then slowly, bravely tease the dimmer until he again stood in pitch. He'd weave through the silent halls to the marble staircase, take the steps three at a time to the roof. Christian would creep to the railing and peep down on the cemetery's parking lot, where Karl's personal kelly-green station wagon would be parked in its usual secluded space. Having caught the glint of sun on Karl's binoculars, he'd lay low and watch planes approaching L.A.X. until the sun fell and he could count their lights in a long descending line.

Now Vane, having relived all those buried childhood memories on a single drunken reel, found himself unspeakably blue. He pushed himself to his feet, empowered by another mouthful of gin. The stuff was tough to swallow, harder to keep down. It was medicine nonetheless.

The last of the bereaved were filtering from the rose garden into the reception hall for drinks and farewells. It had been a frightfully unattended funeral for such a well-known and influential man, and, as far as Vane could tell, only one of the Rest's Residents was interested enough to show. The mourners were mostly sequestered clusters of Guatemalan workers and family members, confused and intimidated by the proceedings. John Beregard Vane had been their indestructible symbol of America.

Prior to the awkward assemblage of workers, a bizarre scene had unfolded on the polished tile path leading to the mausoleum's entrance steps. At least it had seemed bizarre to Vane.

A woman had exited the reception hall pushing a broken old man in a wheelchair. The woman was so solicitous, and the old man so wretchedly hunched, that Vane at first refused to accept these remade figures as Megan and Karl. He followed carefully, tree to tree, as they slowly traveled that long winding path to the beautiful gates. Vane watched Megan swipe her pink and cream card in the scanner, then somberly push Karl up the tiles to the bleached granite steps. Karl, wrapped in a heavy shawl in the magnolias' leaning shade, remained crumpled in the chair while she massaged his neck and shoulders. Occasionally she would stare long and hard at the mausoleum's roof. Her gaze would fall to thoroughly inspect the grounds, her face running blue in the shade. Finally she inclined her head and spoke a few words in Karl's ear. Karl's trembling hand rose and fell. Meg kissed the top of his head, turned the chair and rolled him out the gate, her eyes locked on the trees obscuring Vane; all the way down the winding path, along Christian's Crossing, up to the rose garden, and into the building.

After a respectful pause, a starchy middle-aged woman appeared, leading a wide parade of conservatively-dressed men and women from the reception hall to the Rest. Her dress, her carriage, her expression, were all business, and somehow all familiar to Vane. In a woozy flash he remembered: it was that lady who'd interfered at the mansion when he was just a kid. He wiped his lips and took another careful swallow. The old man was dead, and here she was, meddling still. This woman, her pink-and-cream breast-badge flashing with each step, walked the solemn ranks to the mausoleum and delivered a very businesslike eulogy beneath the main arch. The men and women were then admitted in groups of ten. These were the still-active members of the Honey Family. Vane, watching carefully, saw not a hint of commiseration. With John gone and his tumultuous heir out of the picture for the last three days, the infighting must have been fierce.

The Honey Family exited John's grotto with looks of barely contained amusement, making Vane break into a fit of uncontrollable snickering that left him just short of vomiting. He looked back up through watering eyes.

The stiff woman ushered everyone back out the gates and down the cobbled path to Christian's Crossing. She watched the relieved Family clamber anxiously up the path. When they had all filed into the reception hall she wheeled and hiked back to the mausoleum gates.

It was getting dark. She pulled a cell phone from her handbag and punched out a number, spoke a few words. Seconds later floodlights lit the Rest dazzlingly, fully illuminating even those deepest recesses of false windows. She spoke into the phone again. The floods' beams slowly expired, and the mausoleum's muted internal arrangement took over. Pale green light emanated from partial chimneys spaced between arches, exposing columns and cornices. At cornices marking wing entrances, pairs of electronically-lit gas candles admitted cheerless orange prominences. A row of sunken lights pulsed softly on either side of the path, from the cursive gates all the way up to the granite steps.

The woman replaced her phone and swiped a card. The gates separated smoothly. She went down on one knee, placed an envelope neatly on the path, rose, and took a last look a-round. Vane blearily watched her recede, an intense, lava-like burning in his esophagus. He squeezed shut his eyes and swallowed repeatedly. By the time he reopened his eyes the woman was gone.

It was now fully dark. Vane stumbled down the grade, the grass cold and wet between his toes. He paused twice, taking cautious swallows of gin.

He really didn't want to be here, wasn't even sure why he'd come; the last few days were pretty much a blank. Shell-shocked and borderline-suicidal, he'd hitched a ride to Venice Beach, mooched meals in the churches, made friends with a variety of street people, slept on the sand. Blending in had been a snap.

The Town Car's discovery in a sleazy hotel parking lot was big news on the local stations. Anchors probed every species of disgusting activity, talk show-hosts basked in urgent calls from madams and drug counselors, tabloid dailies trumpeted endless accounts of foul play. A banner headline in one of these papers first made him aware of his brutal kidnapping and eight-figure ransom. That rag's front page featured a photograph of a much younger, much happier Vane, comfortably juxtaposed with an airbrushed photo of his father on the Aegean, a banana daiquiri in one hand and a fat cigar in the other. From this paper he also learned of John's funeral date, and of the heart-stopping cavalcade of celebrities slated to pay their final respects. Paparazzi were warned to back off or risk arrest.

Now Vane, crouching unsteadily at the gate, ripped open one end of the envelope and tore out the single, neatly folded page. Under the pink HONEY letterhead was the missive:

Cristian,

I've left your father's crypt accessible for the night. The groundskeepers will seal it tomorrow. My heart goes out to you.
I realize you're in a tough spot, and need time to be with your thoughts. Take that time, knowing I'm handling your interests well. But you must grab the reins, no matter which course you feel is best for HONEY. And for you.
Call me, Cris. Please contact me the moment you feel rested and ready.

Yours,

Denise Waters

Below were business, home, and cell numbers. Vane lost his balance cramming the letter in his rear pocket, turned an ankle and bent back a toe. He shook his hurt foot in the air, whispering curses at the edifice. The next thing he knew he was flat on his back, arms folded across his chest. His instinct had been to save the bottle rather than his bottom.

Vane had no idea how drunk he'd become. He rolled onto his stomach and clawed up the steps, jacked himself to his feet at the top. This was his first view of the mausoleum at night, and not since a teenager. The Rest's ghastly orange-and-green interior whispered a sick Halloween welcome-back. The black granite entrance was a faultless recreation of East Portico; in John's damaged mind his mourners would be salivating Visitors, anxious to explore the treasures within. Vane followed half-seen walls until he reached the great polished-stone staircase leading from the simulated Ballroom to the structure's roof. He was tempted to go for it, but the imagined effort blew him right off the idea. Suddenly nauseous, he hugged an icy column, slammed along a familiar wall, and so came upon the illuminated crypt's stairwell. Vane teetered on Top Step, blinking. When he was a boy the lights had been many, and of a buttery hue. Now they were few and irregularly spaced, emitting a muted hot-pink glow. He staggered down, bouncing against the left-hand wall for balance.

The place was just as he remembered: frozen figures of satyrs and nymphs, poised behind polished stalagmites and columns. The Minotaur and unicorn, graceful and proud. And, carved from the faux-marble walls, those same detailed trees and vines in bas-relief.

But now it was a stage set in Hell. The new pink lighting lent the figures a burnt hue, made the central pool a low vat of blood. Neptune still rose to protect the Raptor's hold, but with the greater accent on shadow his eyes were empty orbits, his angry dignity a frustrated snarl. Likewise those smaller figures, once dancing in blissful ignorance, appeared as miniature lechers and whores, sneaking around pustule and pit. Capering animals had become infuriated beasts. Trees bristled with poison, vines coiled and reared.

Vane stumbled to the black marble slab and forced a swallow, shuddering as a night breeze ran down the steps and up his spine. He traced his father's engraved name with a finger, cleaning the area of dust and prints, and let his eyes surrender to the pool. The bolted-shut stone coffin appeared to be floating, waiting. Vane's voice boomed in the stillness.

"Old man? Y'*home?*" He stepped side to side, his bare feet peeling off the damp floor with bright flatulent sounds. "Is me, Crishun." He rapped a knuckle on the slab. "You know," he snarled, "your pink little…hot little…your…*honey*." He spat the word. "I come, I guess, say goodbye." Before he could gather a breath, his eyes and knees crossed, his spine caved. He looked around desperately.

"*Christ*, old man! But you…forgive me." One hand found the pool's flat stone rim. Hardly aware of his actions, Vane stood the bottle upright and fumbled urgently with his fly. "Oh God, oh God, I'm so…so *sorry*." He kept up a garbled monologue, trying to drown out the sound of his stream contributing to the pool. At last he drew back, almost losing his feet.

"I die," he vowed, "swear be least one freaking restroom…visitor!" He snatched up the bottle, took a careful swallow and studied the contents. Two fingers left. His eyes sizzled while the crypt did a slow pirouette. He puffed out his cheeks and tightly shut his eyes, again suppressing the urge to vomit. Tears squeezed between his lids.

"*You*, old man, richest sons bitches…planet. What *good* you do? What your…*goodness*?" Vane clung to this one point like a man clinging to a life preserver. "What *good* it? What good you *do* it?" He stared at the hollow-eyed, gaping statuary. A satyr grinned back viciously. "All this…*crap?* Why…why you couldn't *better* something? Some…*body.* Some…*where!*" He raised the bottle.

At the liquor's smell a hundred alarms went off in his brain. Vane released the bottle's neck as though he'd just picked up a rattlesnake. The bottle did not break, but rolled loudly into a wall niche.

"Old man, what *goodm* I? What good you do *me*? You had…time. You had chance. You should…I should…*greatness*, old man." Vane gulped the cold air. "You want me follow footstep. *Why*? So I one-up you on…this?" He waved an arm at the room.

This? the crypt echoed.

"I been busy last few day old…doing nothing." Vane sat hard on the pool's broad lip. "I hadda get away. *Hadda!* I hung at beach…no money. Slept there, panhandled, ate sack lunches…churches. Met all kindsa people, people who didn't… *y'know what, old man?* Life *sucks!* Big surprise you. But people …*live*. Simple rules! Ethics! Friendship! Don't just…don't just *buy* everything. They 'dapt. They…*sac*rifices. An' *grow*. In own ways…stronger. Not just…not just…*older*."

There was something else bugging him, something else he'd come to say. One minute he was searching for the words, the next he was on his knees, searching for the bottle. Once the neck was in his fist he felt better. Vane reeled back to the pool and took a breath so deep it nearly knocked him out.

"*What good money really do old man?* I mean, did it clot…blood and crap squeeze out ev'ry…or'fice you useless old body? Make you better man…better man…*wiser* man. Better,

better, better…*father*? When I say what *good* it, I mean what good it *do*? God *damn* you, old man, *where's the goodness?"*

Vane staggered around the pool into the ogre garden, took a gulp, spat it right back out. "ALL CRAP!" he spewed, and smashed the bottle on a shrinking fawn. As he pitched face-first onto a spiny stalagmite the place erupted. He rolled onto his back.

Vane's collapse was the call for a general uprising. That same satyr leaned over him, grinning maniacally. A buzzard the size of a roc enveloped them both in its wings. The face of a Cyclops appeared, eclipsing a crazy montage of spurting shadows and throbbing pink lights. Two whore nymphs laughed madly, tearing at their eyes. When their hands came away the sockets were bare, the eyes rolling down their melting faces. Vane tried to scream, but the satyr's claws were at his throat. Systematically shutting down the twisted light, the shapes came together above him, silhouette marrying silhouette, until there was only a black expanse with seams bleeding pink.

Chapter Five

Karl

A pair of dust devils on collision course tore across the flat desert floor, leaving matching plumes on either side of the old road linking Massawa and An'erim. Just at the point of impact, the devils gained the road, banked hard, and shot, as a single driving force, to meet a long convoy lumbering west in groups of five and ten.

The convoy consisted of forty large trucks—flatbeds, reefers, and tractor trailers—and a fading tail of buses, vans, and pickups, all led by a battered silver Land Rover with a sawed-off roof. The Land Rover, named *Isis*, contained Cristian Vane and his translator-guide Mudahid Asafu-Adjaye. As Mudahid had repeatedly, adamantly, and occasionally with passion pointed out, his name was pronounced Moo-DAH-heed. But no matter how many times Vane tried, it always came out Mudhead.

Like most civilized souls in East Africa, Somali-born Mudahid was a Muslim. Though he persisted in wearing the headpiece and traditional robes of his faith, a rebellious streak allowed him to refuse to face Mecca five times a day, to drink and smoke on occasion, and to eat whatever he wanted whenever he felt like it. To be sure, in his heart Mudahid was no Muslim at all. Nor was he an outright hedonist. He straddled the fence, leaning one way and the other, his conscience forever snagged on the barbs.

As a young man he'd been a longshoreman and itinerant handyman, making his way around Saudi Arabia, the Mediterranean, and the Horn of Africa. Back then he ran guns, trafficked in opium, did anything he could to survive. And he'd worked for lords of crime, and twice had to kill a man. Eventually he lost his stomach for it, found Islam, and embarked upon life's second half as a wandering wannabe cleric and dark dreamer.

The key to Islam is submission, a revolting thing to a man. But the flip side is that submission can be an endurance test, an attractive thing to a man. That was Mudahid's edge. He embraced sacrifice and prayer like a man in solitary confinement with a barbell. And Islam made him strong, and kept him strong. He fasted and thirsted, he bowed and scraped with the best of them. He prayed himself dizzy and tithed himself dry, made his required pilgrimage to Mecca, was jostled and bruised in the Great Mosque corral.

Then one day during the holy month of *Ramadan*, in the prime of middle age and peak of health, Mudahid, too weak for discipline and too strong for suicide, for no apparent reason broke down; pigged out, drank himself silly. He expected the consequences to be overwhelming self-hatred and abysmal depression. When he came out of it feeling more a man and less a mannequin, he began to rethink himself. He'd spent way too long mechanically worshipping Muhammad, an unknown messenger, and Allah, an unseen deity. It was time to meet Mudahid, a character certainly deserving a life of his own.

Now Mudhead, at sixty-two years of age, was testing his ability to believe in anything. That waffling spirit had served as a magnet for the morbid personality of Cristian Honey Vane on the docks of Port Massawa.

Other qualities made the two men gel.

Mudhead, whose English was quite broken, was able to

almost incidentally encapsulate Vane's lonesome trains of thought, and so make simple sense of seemingly complex problems. This process could also be self-illuminating. As Mudhead explained his compromise with religion on that night of their meeting, over whiskey and burgers in a very-underground Port Massawa dive: "Mudahid Asafu-Adjaye can be Muslimman, still keep self. Can be Muslimman plus drink, smoke, fool around, gamble, even eat pork in pinch. Other Muslimman starve first. But Mudahid Asafu-Adjaye not robot. If Mudahid Asafu-Adjaye can pray five time day, Mudahid Asafu-Adjaye can sin five time day."

Vane saluted him that night, and gave him his new nickname. And Mudhead came to accept it as his own, though such a name could be considered a great insult in the Islamic world. The familiar use of the name *Cristian*, however, was a hurdle too high for a man so steeped in the Koran. Vane from then on was simply *Bossman*.

Their glaring contrasts were complementary: Mudhead, black as coal, kindled Vane's California glow. His spotless white robes were startlingly formal against his employer's dirty T-shirt, khaki shorts, and grungy blue canvas deck shoes. His tiny round rimless glasses seemed almost a deliberate counterpoint to the American's broad dark shades.

Mudhead's rigid personality brought out Vane's latent gallows humor. Vane, in rebelling against his own dumb luck, allowed Mudhead to find justification in rebelling against his own blind faith.

Vane rejected his wealth-determined status by impulsively *bending* whenever leadership was called for. Mudhead grimly teased Vane into being a goofy kind of B'wana, and Vane, out of his element, teased him right back by playing along.

This relationship was exclusive; the men Vane hired were illiterate blacks who spoke not a word of English. They watched coldly as the friendship of Vane and Mudhead grew, seeing openness as weakness, and closeness as a mutual death throe. They hated Vane's guts, while secretly measuring his stamina and adaptability. So alien were they to his way of thinking that he'd have believed their icy demeanor was simply their style, had not Mudhead informed him otherwise.

There in the roofless Land Rover, Vane automatically leaned into his friend, who was once again completely under the spell of Sinatra. Vane's ample CD collection was both blessing and curse; Western music kept the African occupied when Vane needed to be alone with his thoughts, but dragging Mudhead away from the headphones was like pulling a man out of rapid eye movement sleep. Now Mudhead shook him off and leaned away. After a few more seconds he removed the headphones and popped the cord out of the jack. He waited for the closing storm of *All Or Nothing At All* to fade out entirely before switching off the player. Mudhead then nodded vigorously while pointing out a double gleam preceding the approaching dust devils. Vane raised and repeatedly crossed his arms. The driver of the following truck, a flatbed stacked with rolled canvas tarps, made a complicated gesture out the window with his left arm. The convoy slowed to a halt.

"Jeeps?"

"Police," Mudhead said shortly. "Mudahid advise Bossman handle discreet."

The devils braked laterally to block the road, plumes of dust billowing behind them. Four cops stepped out of each jeep like men looking for a brawl. These were some of the blackest blacks Vane had ever seen; Mudhead, by comparison, was a fair -skinned specimen of East African descent. They plodded around the Land Rover, slowly and with great deliberation; like sumo wrestlers sizing opponents. All were very solidly built: barrel chests, high rears, protruding bellies. The police uniform was a spotless white headpiece, bleached polo shirt and shorts, black belt, and knee-high white athletic socks under highly polished steel-toed Army boots. Only the boots and belts did not scream white. Each belt held a holstered Luger, nightstick, mace canister, dart gun, walkie-talkie, and leather-sheathed seven-inch knife. Vane could feel their unmistakable contempt for his Aryan fairness. He and Mudhead were motioned out of the Rover.

The senior policeman, by his brass chevrons a captain, stepped directly in front of Vane. Two more from his vehicle, along with the other jeep's occupants, began walking truck-to-truck, ordering trailers opened. The captain's driver, a young bull of a man, stood smartly behind his superior, spine straight and hands gripped behind the back. It was a very military stance.

The captain was older than his men by twenty years, and heavier by a good fifty pounds. Planting himself as squarely as he could, he looked the sunburned American dead-on. Vane, who had removed his dark glasses prior to stepping out of the Land Rover, had difficulty with the black pools of the captain's shades. It was like looking into the twin barrels of a shotgun. Worse, the man's expression was that of a cruel and very personal bully. Vane instinctively lowered his eyes, looking back up cautiously when the captain turned to follow the movements of his men. Those custom-made sunglasses, which appeared quite expensive, bore a gold engraved figure running the length of each arm. The general impression was a prone griffin, but the figure's head belonged to an animal unfamiliar to Vane. All the policemen wore sunglasses with this gold design. The captain's shades, however, had the distinction of bearing three tiny diamonds above the winged figure's raised tail.

"Good afternoon, officer," Vane enunciated, minimizing the English nuances. "We're on our way to an area called Mamuset in the Danakil. The tract was purchased by the Honey Foundation, an American entity dealing directly with Addis Ababa. We have state clearance for roads, railways, and airfields. The papers are in the glove box."

The shotgun barrels swung back until they were aimed directly at Vane's absurdly blue eyes. The thick lips split apart.

"Relax, *Honey*." The voice was a basso profundo rumble. "This is not a traffic citation." Vane inclined his head respectfully, gritted his teeth and kept silent. The sunglasses swerved to his left.

The captain spent much longer on Mudhead. A loathing incomprehensible to Vane arced between the two men until the air seemed charged. At last Mudhead turned away like the meeker of two strays.

The face swung back.

The captain, addressing the sky, said, "I am not interested in your papers, Honey. You may be surprised to learn that we are not overwhelmingly impressed by rich Americans here. We do not follow their exploits with delight and envy. So you will perhaps show no offense if I do not seek your autograph, or beg to be photographed in your famous presence."

"I appreciate that, sir."

The great black head drew back. "Is it true that all Americans are so...chatty? *Must* they comment on an officer's every statement, as if his words, heartfelt and well-intended, were merely tidbits to pass with the Beluga and Dom Perignon? Honey, in Africa there is time without end, but not a moment to waste on the droll and mundane." As calculated, the captain's command of English greatly heightened his presence. The tactic must have been terribly effective on his inferiors. "Perhaps the fight for survival, which is inherent in all creatures here, precludes us from the pleasantries of easy conversation. We in Africa do not 'run with the mouth,' as you Americans like to say; we come directly to the point and are done with it. This deferential reticence may seem crude and primitive to you, naked as it is of dalliance and whimsicality. Our respect is for culture, for age, and for authority.

"*Culture*, because it is ingrained in all of us. The men and women you will encounter on this continent are steeped in ways that control every aspect of their personalities. They are not gaily-jetting free spirits.

"*Age*, because a man who has attained his later years obviously possesses the physical and psychological wherewithal needed to survive his full span. He knows the ways of Africa and he knows the ways of men.

"*Authority*, because therein a man learns his place. If he intends to stay alive in Africa he respects authority absolutely. He knows that his Beverly Hills playmates cannot help him here. He is quietly respectful. In this way he survives another day."

The captain took a labored breath.

"Evidence of your coming, and of your willingness to tamper with systems timeless and beloved, has far preceded you. I speak not of the new paved road bridging your purchased land and An'erim, but of this great pipeline across our homeland, Awash to Mamuset. For five months now we have watched this dirty plastic headache growing like a tendril."

He squeezed his hands together and rocked side to side, bettering his temper. "Now, Honey, I *realize* this must all seem an ugly dry waste to you. I *understand* you feel you are doing us an immeasurable favor by flooding a hellish crater of value to no one. Or maybe our wretchedness breeds myopia. Could it be that a swimming hole in the desert is sorely needed? In either case, I am certain your North American fans will get a real 'kick' out of it. They will surely see you as a most clever and sophisticated little Honey."

The captain stopped rocking. "Over those five months I have been your closest ally. Believe it or not. The land at Mamuset is essentially a fraction of my precinct, so I have protected your monster from the decent indigenous people who wish it destroyed, and who despair over your blasé trashing of a landscape that has filled the eyes of long-forgotten ancestors with a kind of love that I'm sure you would find laughable, were you able to comprehend it at all.

"I did not protect this pipeline out of concern for you and your endeavors. Indeed, I have spent many nights with those decent people, sharing their fantasies of polyvinyl chloride mayhem.

"But I *have* protected the Eyesore. I have done so because it is my job."

The captain turned slightly to the south, as though visualizing Mamuset's new water source over seventy miles distant.

"I spoke with engineers at Awash only last week. They informed me that the pipeline is complete and already under operation. As your arrival coincides with its completion, I must assume you are here to stay." His sunglasses blazed as he turned back. "You may be surprised to learn that you, and all your trespasses, are my personal assignment. I know *all* about you, Honey; I know far more than I would have freely sought to know. I know that every detail of your operation is covered, and cleared, by a State Department lackey in Addis Ababa named Mohammed Tibor. I am also aware that Tibor runs under the reins of this powerful American organization that shares your name.

"I am further aware that your account has been won by Banke Internationale in Addis Ababa. The figure rumored would make a conglomerate of sheiks shriek with envy. I am no spy, Honey; I flounder in the endless wake of paperwork your presence generates." He nodded. "There is great rejoicing; not only at the bank, but in our government—the enterprises of a powerful American are dug everywhere into Ethiopian soil. The red carpet hungers for his feet. There is even speculation his appearance may prove an auger toward happier relationships between his country and mine. There seems nothing to stand in his way here."

He hammered his fist on his palm. "*Every* aspect of his operation is *legal* and one hundred percent *aboveboard*. As a man of law I see this and am pleased. But as a son of *Ityop'iya* I see this and am haunted by nightmares of losing myself.

"In these nightmares I become a crazed black beast seeking the throat of anything rich, blond, and foreign. These are very troubling dreams, Honey; they will not allow me a moment's sleep." The captain dismissed him with a turn of the head. "Fortunately, there is bicarbonate of soda." He glared at Mudhead, praying the African would speak. A minute later he strolled off, head held high and hands behind his back.

Vane's whole body caved. "Thank goodness he went straight to the point."

Mudhead spoke out of the side of his mouth. "Bossman be glad. Captain like."

"It's that stinking rich, devil-may-care charm. So what now, Sacagawea? It sure doesn't look like he likes you."

Mudhead shrugged. "Mudahid Asafu-Adjaye know too much."

"You've got something on him?"

"Not thing he sure. Bossman see fancy sunglass, little gold lion on arm?"

"Sure. Nice shades."

"Shade *not* nice shade. Man wear shade belong Armaan. Armaan strongman. Do what want, take what want. Anything go down Ethiopia, Armaan get piece."

"Oh, cut it out, Mudhead. They're cops; cops in the desert. Just wearing a uniform doesn't make a man a Nazi. If the government of Ethiopia was as corrupt as you think, they'd just cut our throats, take our stuff, and be done with us."

"Bossman," Mudhead said solemnly, "in Africa throat sometime cut little bit at time."

They stood in the sun for the better part of an hour. At last the captain strolled back to Isis with a hide-lined clipboard in his big hand.

"An interesting manifest. My men have thoroughly inspected your cargo, and I find myself much perplexed. Frozen whole foods in the refrigerated trailers. On two of the flatbeds are what appear to be several hundred canvas tents or the like, tightly rolled and stacked along with pallet upon pallet of some kind of..." he underlined the description with a forefinger as he read, "...'hollow square steel bars with regularly spaced holes drilled on all sides.' Additionally, we have uncovered, in one forty-eight foot trailer, a pair of speaker cabinets, each at least a dozen feet high, and a maze of sophisticated sound equipment crammed between very powerful amplifiers and generators."

He looked back up. "You are perhaps planning a concert for the Danakil, Honey? Afar-aid? And are we invited to the party?"

Vane ground his teeth. The captain glanced at Mudhead, absorbed in a ruminative study of the sun.

"Excellent. We will bring our own beer. Now, I have not mentioned the school buses full of students from the universities in Gondar and Addis Ababa, nor the vans stocked with nurses and doctors. The former are typical fresh-faced liberals excited to be members of your entourage, the latter respectable professionals with credentials from institutions in at least four countries. There are also to be noted a tanker truck porting a thousand gallons of gasoline, and a truck hauling a propane tank the size of a small submarine. Running almost as an afterthought is the train of pickup trucks loaded with bags of cement.

"Again, everything is aboveboard."

The captain backpedaled six feet and stood with his legs wide and his hands clasped casually behind his back, one corner of the clipboard showing at his hip. His great belly preceded him, the muscles of his heavy legs bunching and relaxing as he effortlessly raised and lowered himself with his toes. Despite the massiveness of his midsection and rear, there was nothing *fat* about the man, at least not in the sense Vane had known back home. The captain was like a huge blind bullfrog using its senses to target gnats.

They stood in the equatorial sun forever. Mudhead appeared unaffected, but Vane's eyelids were drooping. His shoulders sagged, his back screamed for a break. He was sure he'd faint any second.

The captain clicked his heels sharply. "Your cargo is in order, sir. I hope our humble country will not be too great a disappointment." His men strode to their jeeps, staring back with open hostility. The captain came up nose-to-nose. Sweat was pouring off Vane's face.

"Enjoy your stay, Honey. You may photograph, but not touch, the lepers. Avoid those afflicted with elephantiasis, typhus, AIDS, and either the pneumonic or bubonic form of African plague. Carrion birds are not for hunting. They perform a very important function in our *ecosystem*. Kindly confine yourself to bird watching." He half-turned, stopped, and turned back, this time standing nose-to-nose with Mudhead while addressing Vane.

"Also, Honey, I would be derelict were I not to warn you about your crew. As you are new here, your ignorance is excusable." He sprayed saliva in Mudhead's face with each exhalation. Mudhead did not move.

"The men driving your trucks are exclusively Shankili. This is very singular. Yet I cannot hold you responsible for your hiring practices. I am sure that to you all Africans look the same.

"All Africans *are not* the same.

"A continent this immense produces a tremendous variety of types, all with enduring allegiances. A newcomer's indigenous confidant would be fully aware of these differences. He would make sure his employer hired only reputable drivers.

"As this is not the case, I would find it entirely forgivable were his employer to take drastic measures."

The captain turned. He took his time walking back to the jeep. When he was comfortably aboard, his driver threw it in first, then floored it while playing with the clutch. The second jeep followed suit. Pounds of dust blew over the American and his guide. The double-plume tore off into the desert.

"*Shankili*?" Vane coughed.

Mudhead's expression was hurt. "Shankiliman drive good anyman else. Bossman ask Mudahid find many driver. Each man tell friend. Friend tell friend. All show on dock, Bossman hire." He dusted himself down. "Bossman not be impress by police. Captain scared, or never mention Shankiliman." Mudhead thought about it a minute, seeking an apt comparison. "Africa tribe, caste, class, equal America neighborhood, religion, race. Ethnic group. Man over time learn neighbor way; become neighbor. Neighbor have enemy, that enemy now enemy man number one. Everyman have allegiance."

"Gangs," Vane muttered.

Mudhead raised an eyebrow. "Muslimman no gangman. Holy brotherhood. But captain try say Africa root run deep. Prick modernman, wake savageman. Allman same only democracy. In Africa Lubjaraman smell Wambetsuman. Wambetsuman *feel* Oromoman. All look same Westernman. But all same, all different."

"Thanks for clarifying."

They climbed into Isis. "No problem, Bossman. No worry Africa mosaic. Westernman think too much. Try pet lion. Lion bite Westernman nose off. Westernman wonder how he offend lion." Mudhead shook his head gravely. "Africaman see lion, give lion space. Lion respect man, man respect lion. This what captain try say Bossman: respect authority, captain not bite nose off. Save captain trouble. So here be respectful Africaman, not disrespectful Western richboyman. Then everyman have space. Plenty space Ethiopia."

"True," Vane sighed as they bumped along. "Plenty of space."

In certain places the old road was so potted even the Land Rover had trouble. At impasses the volunteers made shade while the doctors huddled. Drivers rolled out the Caterpillar and other earth moving equipment. During these breaks Mudhead would clamp on the headphones and blow his mind with psychedelic rock while Vane took long walks with his notebook and binoculars. The drought's signature was everywhere. Acacia and mimosa were in shock, their fronds and spines blanched and desiccated. Dik-diks peered out of the scrub, much leaner and less energetic than expected.

Once they were back in gear Vane would take a bushel's worth of snapshots with his Nikon, his wanderlust still blinding him to the miserable state of his surroundings. But an ugly silence grew outside the convoy's persistent rumble. Along the Kobar's rim, small villages lined the road like beggars; they were merely thatched ghost towns. Inhabited sites became rarer, tribesmen increasingly lethargic, crops nonexistent. Soon human remains showed amidst the bones of cattle and sheep. The air, suffocating the desert like a great blanket, grew perceptibly hotter as they approached the Depression.

Vane dozed off and on, the great master plan burning on the back of his eyelids. In his imagination he looked down at Mamuset as though at a snapshot, raptly revisiting his one long glimpse from a rented Cessna.

Prior to that flyover he'd been following the conduit's progress along its tortuous seventy miles-plus course, taking notes and making rough drawings in charcoal. The pipeline below was of PVC tubing with a six foot bore, cemented in lengths varying from eighteen to thirty-two feet. The whole affair rested in a seemingly endless, constantly zigzagging ditch, supported by cross-struts positioned every twelve feet, and protected from sun and blowing sand by a series of tent-like canvas sheaths. The canvas, so as not to scream the rich American's presence, was dyed in tones of the great Ethiopian desert. In places frequented by herders, the Honey Foundation had provided equally inconspicuous prefabricated bridges capable of supporting both nomad and stock.

There in the bucking Rover, Vane's mental snapshot gra-dually took on depth and perspective, becoming an expanding relief map, a revolving fish-eye chart viewed from all sides, and finally a topographical model partitioned by grid lines extend-ing well beyond his visual periphery. He looked down on a huge, partly-bisected crater, its floor as absolutely flat as the de-sert without, scrunched in the heart of a dead, nearly featureless plain. The ridge making up the crater's rim, smoothed over the ages by heavy seasonal rains, was at present barely a hundred feet at its highest point, less than forty at the lowest. Those life-giving rains were no-shows for several years now; the Mamuset crater was dry as a kiln in Hell. But when the region was active it would annually fill into a startlingly anomalous lake. One section of the rim facing the Red Sea had eroded in several pla-ces, allowing the site to drain, like everything else in the area, to the east. During his flyover Vane had observed his excavators aggressively rebuilding that section with cement and steel.

North and west of Mamuset are the broad highlands of Ethiopia. Brutal desert stretches to the south, ancient volcanic peaks and the fifty mile-wide swath of Eritrea, backed by the Red Sea, to the north and east. Southeast is a glistening, 2,000-square mile bed of salt, Lake Assale, in places over three miles thick. Farther south runs a dirty blue worm known as the River Awash. The whole wretched area north of that worm is the Dan-akil Desert, home of the Great Danakil Depression. In this place all waterways die; rolling water simply surrenders to earth and sun, never reaching the Sea. Daytime temperatures can reach 145 degrees.

Vane caught himself drifting. He refocused on the cra-ter. His memory took a shy peek inside...*there were thousands of scrawny black people in there, staring up fearfully at his buzzing little Cessna!* Jesus. Were they hiding from him, or were they waiting for him? And who the hell was he to come sneaking overhead, anyway? He relaxed as he saw all that hea-vy equipment, mere toys from his altitude, efficiently creating the project's foundation. He was their savior, the great white miracle worker. Vane wanted to be sick. And again he saw the intermittent stream of planes, camels, and small trucks bringing survival supplies and medicine. Not enough, not nearly enough. His skin crawled with the closing miles. With the pipeline oper-ational and the project actually under way, he was finally out of distractions and forced to face reality: at some strange forgotten point he had determined, for some strange forgotten reason, to take a healthy sample of a foreign population and experiment with its destiny as though the conscientious, spiritual, plans-and-dreams members were mere laboratory rats.

It had looked good on paper. All the parts came together

smoothly to form a seamless, entirely workable blueprint. The imagined participants followed instructions without question while Vane, the invisible benign overseer, boldly forged ahead in complete disregard of the human element.

But now he was sweating. Young Christian had been raised to believe that it was his obligation to dream big, and that, so long as he remained true to this inherent commitment, he could go out with a bang or a fizzle, and bring the rest of the planet right along with him. Yet, because of that very upbringing, he couldn't genuinely *care*. To Cristian Honey Vane, people were just bugs; flitting here, crawling there. To his great credit, he didn't see himself as anything greater. He was simply another bug, doomed to be crushed and recycled. The difference was in his schooling. He could crawl along with the best of them, while another aspect of his consciousness looked on indifferently, noting patterns and postures. In this sense he was very *un*buglike.

Somewhere along the line Vane had, by some fuzzy extension of that distant schooling, begun to envision his bugs as permanent tenants on a large level field, and seen himself as a similarly situated insect. And he had begun visualizing this imaginary field as though from a cloud.

The field was partitioned as an enormous grid, from the cloud appearing as a mesh screen. Vane's imagination could zoom on the Grid, telescopic and wide, allowing him to check fine points or study overall. And so his utopia was constructed from on high, in advance of his presence.

Vane's coign of vantage was about thirty degrees off the horizontal plane, looking almost dead east. From this vantage point the Mamuset experiment lay before him as an expanded chessboard. That imagined chessboard appeared to stretch without end, its most distant squares showing tinier and tinier still, until they faded to black in the low rim's hazy embrace. (It was easiest to systematize such a vast projected community using the typical chessboard arrangement of alternating light and dark squares, rather than visualizing all squares an identical shade).

The Mamuset community would have five thousand *Squares* in all.

A block of a hundred Squares comprised a *Sector*. These

fifty communal Sectors of one hundred Squares apiece would take up the eastern half of the crater, as defined by the partly-bisecting hilly ridge. An equivalent tract to the west would be given over to cultivated Fields. Mamuset, the community, would therefore be a single site divided into five thousand equal sub-sites. Those sub-site Squares would each be fifty feet by fifty feet, or twenty-five hundred square feet. Vane had to step back, figuratively, to comfortably imagine Sectors. But at each corner of each Sector he visualized a blank Square.

These were *Utility Squares*. There would be four per Sector, one at each Sector corner. Each would serve a quarter of the Sector, or a total of twenty-four Squares. The quarter-Sectors would be known as Quadrants, or *Quads*. And, since each Sector would have a Utility Square at each corner, the common corner of four Sectors would be a grouping of four Utility Squares: Utility Quads, or *UQs*. Mamuset would contain fifty UQs, or two hundred Utility Squares, in all.

Utility Squares were to be storage areas. Each Utility Square would house the twenty-four sets of implements for its Sector's Quad, along with water reserves, fodder, fertilizer, seeds, etc. Strings of solar panels situated on arbors above U-tility Squares would charge banks of batteries for *Street* lamps. Streets were the ten-foot-wide, crisscrossing ways separating Squares. Mamuset would require no fences; each Square would have a Street on every side.

The success of this entire concept relied on a crucial, untested notion: *If a man's neighbors were to copy his competent efforts step-for-step, then a number of equivalent copies of his project would be produced.* Additionally, *if these neighbors' efforts were, in turn, copied by their neighbors, a multitude of surrounding copies, mirroring the best efforts of the original, would be produced.* The ripple effect would, in theory, eventually produce a community of copies that were functionally and aesthetically as stable or unstable as the prototype; Mamuset was to be the sum of thousands of independent attempts to mimic a single effort. Practically speaking, if ground zero was the ideal, the standard would be a diminishing return relative to that prototype, with the outskirts harboring those copies of highest imperfection.

In time the rough edges would be smoothed. The Ideal would spread ever outward, until the plain was absolutely level, not only spatially but qualitatively. Cristian Vane's completed project would be a perfect multicellular organism, cooperative, disinterested, functional; an organism evolved in real time on the example of a prototypical Square.

And Vane would be the architect of that prototypical Square.

He knew he could do it, because he'd spent weeks creating and recreating one on a godforsaken field in Arizona, under the watchful eyes of six hired engineers, a trio of Arizona State professors, and a Texan fitness trainer-nutritionist. Those engineers and professors, using Vane's raw ideas, had hammered out a step-by-step plan, and educated him on everything from structural dynamics to pH systems and micronutrients. They designed a basic domicile for the intense conditions of Danakil, and referred Vane to Army specialists who gave him the skinny on survival techniques in arid extremes. And he'd boned up on physical and emotional tolerances, studied nutrition and personal irrigation, learned basic first aid procedures and cardiopulmonary resuscitation.

The radical differences in adaptive constitution were striking; despite their gaunt and moribund appearance, these desert people were far hardier than he. The big leap for the indigenous population would be learning to settle down. They were born to wander. Vane saw it as his challenge to entice them to settle, and as his mission to save them from themselves.

He had a mind-boggling fortune at his disposal, and was unshakably ensconced in a philosophy of education by reiteration.

He'd been schooled by Karl, an unexceptional, but terribly persistent man. Karl's method had been to present a new fact each new day, and incorporate that fact into an old lesson. He began with the mansion, his *house*, and moved on to the solar system, with every lesson including *house*. If teaching an adjective or noun, that adjective or noun would have to pertain, even by extension, to the mansion. It was a *great house* on a *greater world*, in the *greatest universe* of all. Karl, quite naturally, exploited the carousel library. He advanced systematic-

cally, grandiloquently describing how all things revolved a-
round the mansion, until, one typically awkward day, he stumbled upon Copernicus.

Humility did not come to the former fullback without a
fight. There, in that candy-striped carousel under the broad live
oak, he impressed upon little Christian that, although all men
are but motes in the insufferable scheme of things, certain individuals are bound, by propitious circumstance, to take a larger
role than that assigned to the common man. These predestined
individuals have a duty to repay this gift by working beyond
their selves. It is *they* who map the universe. It is *they* who
make the world turn, while the bugs run over it, ignorant of its
greatness.

Unfortunately this was not Aristotle tutoring young Alexander; in this case the sculptor was unworthy of his clay.
Defining the universe became the toughest job of Karl's life. He
proceeded, understandably, from the clear and present to the
humbling bounds of perception, only to find that, like all men of
average intelligence, he was utterly incapable of grasping the
concept of *infinity*, a word introduced by Socrates and blown to
pieces by Webster. Yet his damnable persistence kept him at it.
It became central to his cause that his little pupil, destined for
greatness, fully understand that single, paramount concept. The
boy had to be infused with the all-encompassing cognizance
that would elevate him, psychologically, above mere bugs.

Of course Karl's pursuit of infinity was hopeless. His
normal, healthy brain, designed by nature to deal with the physical world via the senses, automatically revolted at abstract-
ions.

But the man was *persistent*.

He began haunting book stores and municipal libraries,
demanding to see *space maps*. When the stupid people lost patience with his awkward verbiage, Karl resorted to gestures and
expressions to convey his meaning, but received nothing profounder than children's pictorial charts of constellations. Still he
went back for more, coming away with material that was ever-
more sophisticated. These new tomes only confused him further. Karl eventually came to the conclusion that, wherever it
was, Infinity was a place nobody was in any kind of hurry to get

to any time soon. By now his poor, persistent brain was beginning to smolder.

When inevitably he recognized he could scratch an abstraction no further, his attention did a complete about-face and hurtled toward home where it belonged. Karl trudged back to the carousel library for the last time, stomping on bugs all the way.

His new pursuit led him to the zodiac, and thence to the celestial sphere. Nights he would wonder aloud, staring upward lost in thought, muttering crabbily while the boy watched him dreamily, sleepy eyes falling. Karl was flustered by the idea of people and animals making up the constellations. In the first place, he found such descriptions absurd: those stellar patterns could have been anything, they could have been nothing. In the second place, they were curiously inactive for beings. He finally concluded, rightly, that they were just a lot of dumb stars encumbered by the perpetual silliness of human imagination.

The celestial sphere was a concept more comforting than the Copernican system, for simple Karl's soul was yearning for the geocentric. He'd come to realize that no inns await the spacewalker. Azimuthal maps were even closer to his heart. But curvature frustrated him in ways he couldn't understand. The very mathematical, very martial, very *flat* structure of a football field had been branded on his subconscious. That reliable gridiron had been the sole focus of his youthful ideals and discipline. Thinking hadn't been so important then. The coach took care of all that nonsense. What *had* been important was persistence.

When Karl first seriously studied a world wall map he had an experience akin to a spiritual revelation. The lines of longitude and latitude were like a pair of gridirons, one overlaid perpendicular to the other. From this vantage it was easy to dispense with the confounding nuisance of true spatial dynamics, and visualize the grid as proceeding in four directions to that funny place called Infinity. Furthermore, he reckoned that any depiction of a grid could be understood to be simply a fraction of a larger grid. This concept could even be illustrated by including a little arrowhead at the terminus of each longitudinal and latitudinal line, thereby depicting continuity. Excitedly, he drew these arrow-tipped grid lines over and over in the dirt with a stick while little Christian watched on hands and knees. Karl had done it. He had mapped the universe.

More important, he'd begun to extrapolate inversely, making his grid, sans arrowheads, representative of an ever smaller area. Finally the grid became, by diminution, no longer perceivable as a grid at all. Karl shared his frustration with Christian, incidentally encouraging the boy to ponder the imponderable. He ranted and raved over paradoxes for weeks in his futilely persistent way. Christian, wanting to please, stayed out of his way and timidly approached Euclid for perspective.

Karl fried his brain trying to visualize a grid smaller than small, then smallest of all. At last he tromped up to Christian triumphantly, tears in his eyes. He jabbed the stick in the ground and plucked it free, revealing a single point. Karl had done it again. He had defined finitude.

From then on, Christian's place in the universe was the centermost square of any grid. But the cosmos did not revolve around him. It went beyond him, in four directions. Those points were the principle points of the compass. Karl demonstrated how the mansion, as a physical extension of the boy, could also be placed in the central square. He used a bright red hotel off a Monopoly board to represent the mansion. And during that same demonstration he took a jar full of beetles and attempted to place one in each surrounding square. Some of the bugs froze in place, others scampered off in all directions.

Enraged by this revolt, Karl stamped savagely, smashing the insects and obliterating his grid. Christian took this very hard, carnage being a far more powerful lesson than math.

For the next demonstration, Karl first suffocated the beetles. These *good bugs* stayed put. But Christian cried again, and himself destroyed the latest grid in the dirt, running, for some reason, to the ready arms of Karl's nemesis Megan.

And so the tutor learned from his pupil. Karl watched the boy from the live oak's shade, knowing he was unequal to his task. But he knew one thing else.

He would persist.

Chapter Six

An'erim

"An'erim," Mudhead coughed.

Vane sat up and reached for his binoculars.

An'erim, a military outpost abandoned by the Italians in 1941, was all but history; faded, collapsed, corroded by time and seasonal torrents. Over the decades the cement-and-brick buildings on the white mound of naked rock had dissolved like sand castles, leaving a single burned-out, roofless structure of crumbling stone at the mound's base—sitting right where the wretched old road ended and Vane's handsome new, paved road began. Clumped about this heap were a few ragged army tents, a pair of lean-to sheds, and several dry huts constructed of thatch on flexed and bound sticks. Stepping up the mound's east face were regularly spaced hovels, each a bit larger than its predecessor, the largest of all sagging on the crown.

Vane twirled a languid hand.

"Crazyman church," Mudhead explained. "Christ In Box."

Vane cleaned his sunglasses on his T-shirt. "That's downright sad. What a feeble statement."

"Worse. Corpse farm."

In the open squatted a battered jeep, the rusting centerpiece for a dusty display of rickety wooden wagons. Leaning inward, like charred sticks stacked in a campfire, a number of jet-black men and women waited in a crowd of naked children, mesmerized by the approaching convoy. These were classic famine specimens; the adults emaciated and lethargic, the children all outsized heads and distended bellies. One man now broke from his spell and loped like a great gangly water spider to the standing structure's doorway. He thrust his head around a hanging canvas sheet. A tanned arm swept the sheet aside, and a blond man looked out with an odd expression. He was in his late forties, lean, wearing a light sleeveless khaki jumpsuit and dirty tennis shoes. His face swung from Isis to the trailing vehicles and back. He stepped out slowly. As the Land Rover pulled up he approached with his hand extended.

"Good afternoon, sir, good afternoon! And welcome to the Church of Christ Compassionate." The blond head cocked. "American, are you? I'm not used to such treats. Name's Lyle Preston."

"Cristian Vane." Their handshake was neutral.

Preston smiled. "Christian? What a marvelous surname."

Vane did not return the smile. "An unfortunate homophone, Mr. Preston. I'm afraid I don't share your views." He stirred the dirt. "Yes, I'm an American. I'm on my way to a tract I've purchased in the Danakil Depression. Except for some desert cops, you're our first sign of civilization." He looked around. Those structures stepping up the slope were strange little buildings of scrap tin, appearing as unstable as houses of cards. Each bore a large white cross painted on either side of a single doorway. The large structure on the summit had a sunken spired roof. Leaning west on that roof was a cross constructed of long sticks tied into bundles.

Preston seemed distracted. "You say you...you *purchased* land in the Depression? Whatever *for*, sir? And all these trucks...I—for a minute there I was hoping..." He licked his cracked lips. "As it stands, those policemen you ran into are not exactly our link to survival. They are Muslims of the worst sort." He made this statement frankly, indifferent to Mudhead in his bleached white robes. "Still, we are holding our own, Mr. Vane." Preston raised an eyebrow. "You wouldn't, perchance, be related to the 'California Vains'?"

This was the tabloids' pet name for those shady packs of Residents captured incidentally in Rest photographs.

Vane bowed ironically. "The very same. I didn't know you received those gossip rags out here."

Preston returned the bow. "And you arrive as...what—a speculator? You're surveying? You've obviously brought a lot of equipment. There is little to mine in the Danakil other than salt, and the Afar have preceded you in that regard by a factor of some centuries."

"Let's just say," Vane just said, "that we're engaged in charitable work. Similar to yours, but with dissimilar motivation."

"*Really?* What motivation could one have in this place other than saving the Lord's children?"

Vane, bowing deeper, clicked his rubber heels. "I can only respond, Mr. Preston, by repeating that I do not share your religious convictions. My motivation in addressing these people stems from a concern for their bodies rather than for their so-called souls."

Preston tilted his head side to side, his expression one of intense concentration. Suddenly his eyes were on fire. "It's *you!*" He got right in Vane's face. "You're the one responsible for all those caravans! That light plane! The road pavers! You ...Mamuset. How blind of me!" He rocked back as though measuring Vane for a punch. Little by little the tension passed from his frame. "Well, well, well. I've wanted to come face to face with you, in the worst way, for the last six months."

Vane recovered his balance. "What's your problem, man? I don't even know you."

"But I know you." Preston unclenched his fists and closed his eyes. When he looked back up he was all conciliation. "Perhaps you misapprehend me, sir. Perhaps you misapprehend our church. We do dearly love these people."

Stuck for words, Vane rolled his shoulders and tried to relax. After a moment he said levelly, "I respect that. You're a survivor. I sincerely applaud your temerity."

Preston plunged his hands into his jumpsuit's pockets. "Please follow me, Mr. Vane. I am your host, so you must allow me the honor of being your guide. And as for temerity, let us just say that a real strength arises from conviction." He tipped his head. "And I would suppose that an analogous strength comes from…inestimable wealth."

Vane's blood was still up. "Great wealth, Mr. Preston, used with great moral conviction, can produce great results." He waved a hand irritably. "*Real* results, far surpassing those produced by great religious conviction. Concrete results."

Preston's smile was patronizing. "Greatness, sir, is not of this world."

"*I,*" Vane said curtly, "disagree." He rolled his shoulders and changed the subject. "Mister Preston, what are these structures, and especially that larger one situated above us? I take it to be, by the cross on its roof, your physical church, as opposed to 'Church' in the sense of your organization?"

"Not so." The men began climbing a worn path. "That edifice is the most important building in this compound." Preston measured his words, eyeing the path thoughtfully. "We in the Church of Christ Compassionate have made several small compromises in our work here, Mr. Vane. The spiritual composition of contemporary Ethiopia includes Muslims of both the orthodox and the self-serving varieties, latter and modern day Christians, and countless animist communities caught up in barbarous indigenous practices. Those people we serve are primarily animists, and they have real problems dealing with monotheism." He waved an arm. "The structures we are passing— these minor hovels and sheds—represent certain portals in a gradual climb to salvation."

"These sheds are steps in a gradation?"

"…only in a physical sense."

"Then I take it this grade—this physical ascent—represents the climb out of their dark, primitive religion to your bright, sophisticated one?"

"You have an annoying obsession with symbols."

"I don't erect 'em," Vane muttered. "So what's the compromise of your Church?"

"The compromise is that we compromise at all. Ideally the road back to Nazareth should not be an untested one, but this bleak country necessitates certain illuminating stops along the way. These people are being saved here. It is not the road that is important, Mr. Vane. It's the destination."

"Saved whether they like it or not? Saved whether they understand it or not?"

"They," Preston said with exaggerated patience, "are being saved. A road need not be traveled by a limousine to be traveled successfully."

Vane's eyes slid away. "Nor need it be lined with psalms and promises." They halted at the summit, independently studying the desert beyond. It was clear to both men that they simply didn't get on. "This structure, then," Vane went on distantly, "is symbolic of what?" He caught himself. "And I'm using the word *symbolic* in deference to all we've discussed, Mr. Preston, and not out of disrespect. It's where they learn of monotheism, of Christianity? Of Jesus?"

"Yes. Yes and no. It's where they leave behind not only their primitive beliefs but their clinging selves."

The view was spectacular: perhaps a mile away sprawled a huge, almost circular depression dotted with clumsy wooden structures and markers, backed by a hundred square miles of rolling desert. Even from this distance Vane could see an occasional wandering black stick-figure.

"This," Preston said, indicating the leaning structure's caving doorway, "is the Way of Christ. It is where those wayfaring men and women, starved and smitten by plague and stone, have risen, through the ultimate sacrifice of Jesus, to surrender their sins into the loving Arms of our father God in Heaven."

"Amen," Vane said drearily. "So this is where they're brought to die?"

"*No*-o-o…*this* is where they are brought to be born!"

Vane noticed a winding path leading from the distant cemetery's entrance to An'erim's far side and continuing, presumably, to an exit at the rear of the structure. "In one door and out the other." He and Preston sauntered back down the path, small in the dust and sun. It was Preston who broke the silence.

"*Mister* Vane...the famine of '83 and '84 was responsible for the deaths of millions in Ethiopia, despite independent charity groups, and despite the best humanitarian efforts of Europe and America. Massive quantities of food and medical supplies went nowhere. Some of the kindest, most-caring individuals one could ever pray to meet bled and wept themselves dry in a passionate attempt to control it. Only time and the love of God preserved this place. But the cycle goes on, and our Maker does not apply His healing touch willy-nilly. I am certain the disaster unfolding about us right now will dwarf even the Great Plague of London. And I am sure, too, that every man doing the Lord's work here, no matter how paltry the effects of his labors may seem, is doing infinitely more than all you sunshine altruists combined, and more than all those governmental bodies merely seeking to apportion surpluses."

Vane halted mid-stride. "Preston, blind aid is, in my opinion, the practical equivalent of blind faith. In one sense I agree with you wholly. But now listen to this, and mark me well, as I'm not likely to repeat it. I am *not* a sentimental hands-wringer, here to kiss the poor darlings and make them better. Nor am I, as everybody seems to think, a bored rich boy playing chess using the dying for pawns. What I intend to do here is not about me, it's about Principle. I realize that, as a mere mortal, I can't significantly affect the big picture. There are famines in India and China and in other parts of Africa. Always have been, always will be. I can't fix this planet. But for the short time I'm on it I can use the tremendous opportunity of my inheritance to make a difference, if even in a small way. Who knows; maybe I can set a precedent, maybe I can serve as an example. Or maybe I'll fall flat on my face. But at least I'll have *tried*."

"And maybe, Mr. Vane, maybe you'll take down a whole lot of people with you. Life is not an experiment in free will at all. It's an extension of God's will. Besides," he sniffed, "not everybody has the opportunity, or the audacity, to tamper with ordained systems."

"All the more reason for those who do to energetically apply themselves. As long as their motives are good."

"The motives of man, unless they are solely aligned with those of God, are inherently selfish. It is man's very selfishness that prevents him from seeing himself as selfish."

Vane conceded the point. "It's a shame. It's always a shame. But you solve problems by addressing them realistically. Not by pontificating and proselytizing."

"Your appreciation of this 'problem,' as you put it, defines the narrowness of your scope. This 'problem' allows you to philosophize about a modern tragedy. This 'problem' allows you to minimize a calamity rearing upon the Horn of Africa like a tsunami."

"An 'Act of God,' Mr. Preston?"

Preston ignored him. "Let me give you an idea of what life in Africa is really like.

"Back when our church was still setting up, a terrible drought took this land. We at Christ Compassionate witnessed an extraordinary plague of grasshoppers coming out of Sudan, darkening the sky for miles, as deep as it was wide. All crops had failed by this time, and little remained but stunted acacia and shriveled euphorbia, yet this terrible storm came on; ravenous, relentless. There was nowhere we could run, sir, nowhere at all. We cringed inside our trucks with the windows tightly closed, crammed into one another like pranking college kids stuffed in a phone booth. The day was absolutely black. Hour upon hour we remained there, buried under a constant stream of hammering grasshoppers. The sound was like that of an endless hailstorm. The insects would spatter on our truck's roof and their slimy corpses roll down the glass. Some had already died of starvation in their final blind descent, others appeared to be cannibalizing the dead.

"After the plague had passed we exited our vehicles into a nightmare world of barren trees and dead grasshoppers. The beasts had stripped the bark from the acacias in their frenzy. The ground was slippery with their bodies. A bloody, chitinous slime coated everything, clogging the trucks' grilles and vents, oozing over anything solid. And in the east the great frantic cloud could still be seen, its extremes dipping and rising surreally, like the slowly flapping wings of a gigantic passing wraith. As we drove on we came upon the bodies of wildlife, and then of people, buried under mounds of these dead and dying insects. Squirming green humps for graves. We could only bless the fallen and truck them to a common burial site between Mekele and Gondar, where an entire string of villages had been denuded by the storm. No hurricane has ever been so thorough."

"A rude Ethiopian baptism."

"This was before we had begun the long haul into the Northern Highlands. Our party, as you see it now, was originally distributed among various tribes, working most where they were needed most. But as the effects of the drought increased and famine became widespread, tribes began to break up into family units that wandered off on their own, in desperate pursuits of sustenance. This is one of the great tragedies of lack of organization, Mr. Vane. What little support the government is willing to provide for its pastoral population is rendered academic by said tribes' timeless habits and cultures. In a country so vast it is difficult to reach them, if they can even be located. Those who wander of course die, and those who remain under the umbrella of some kind of tribal leadership simply die a little slower. Many people have for time immemorial followed a nomadic existence based upon moving their camels and cattle from watering hole to watering hole. Most of those holes are now dried up. The beasts are skin and bones, the owners dull, wizened stick-men. Our Church intervened whenever possible. Utilizing a spotter plane, we were able to locate those sites best able to water their animals, and so led many thousands of these nomads in great caravans, using our vehicles as guides and maintaining tight radio contact. Otherwise we would certainly have become lost. The people were docile. Ages-old tribal conflicts were forgotten in their common need. For a time there I began to believe I could actually make a difference." Preston spread his arms. "The ultimate site to which all these needy people were led is perhaps three miles north of us."

"I know of it. A series of rank pools growing feebler by the day."

"Its present state is immaterial. When we first elected to make it the permanent site of our Church there was more than enough for brute and nomad, and all signs pointed to a huge assemblage of tribes living as one under the loving eye of God.

But these people soon began to diverge and follow their old ways, wandering off in their hundreds to watering places they have visited regularly, cyclically, over many generations." Preston stamped the ground for emphasis. "Mr. Vane, these people were well aware their traditional sites were exhausted! They knew—their elders knew—that they were committing suicide when they began their treks. But they went! To this day their customs hold sway over even the most basic instincts of self-preservation. *This*, Mr. Vane, greater than any logistical or financial struggle you may find yourself facing, will be your real undoing here. You will never be able to cause these people to behave in a manner that runs contrary to their adaptive programming. For *you*, educated and rational Westerner that you no doubt are, *sir*, will be confounded over and over by a phenomenon too simple for a plain man to comprehend. Time and again, Mr. Vane, you will lead the horses to water. But only in Jesus will their thirst truly be slaked." He rolled his shoulders squarely. "Their husks are expendable."

"Their 'husks' are *not* expendable! Man—you almost make it sound like you *prefer* these people in a weakened, more pliable state."

Preston drew himself erect. "That's either a clumsy attempt at levity or a direct insult."

"Then why aren't you taking a hard line with the government? Why aren't you clamoring for supplies? Why aren't you working to relocate these people? What's wrong with this picture, Preston? If you *really* cared you'd be directing them my way, instead of ushering them up to your little morgue. Your operation here isn't Godly. It's ghoulish."

Preston said through his teeth, "In case you haven't noticed, this country is at war with the nation next door. The government of Ethiopia will not be bothered. I couldn't begin to tell you how I've begged for assistance, or how many I've watched die; men, women, and children." He snapped his fingers. "But you become inured to it. You see God rearranging His clay and you cease attempting to stay His hand. Meanwhile, the Word gets around. Would you have these people arrive and not find salvation? Do you think their own government cares a whit for their salvation? What more would you have us do here?"

"Fight for them," Vane said. "Fight for their lives. Focus on their natural drives, their tenacity. Feed them and educate them. Encourage them to fend for their selves. Fear for their blood and their breath and every jot of nervous energy they can manage. Marvel at each twitch and tingle, at every gleam of perception. Worry about their hides. Let your god worry about their souls."

"Bravo, Mr. Vane. Bravely spoken. But feed them what? Dirt and promises? You see what we have to work with. I've argued like a lunatic for supplies. When I saw your convoy I thought for sure my pleas had been answered." He shook his head angrily. "Instead I suddenly find myself with a rich hippie for a neighbor. No offense," he said, and his expression was anything but inoffensive, "but your intentions as I understand them, no matter how well-meaning, can only disrupt the work of our church and divert these innocent people from receiving the Lord's Word at the most important moment of their lives."

That did it. "The 'most important moment of their lives?' Y'know, Preston, people like you really make me sick. Men like you will step on anything and anybody to achieve their personal or corporate goals."

"And do *you* know what, Mr. Vane? People like you only make me love the Lord all the more. What do you know of goals? Look at you. Richer than Croesus and nothing to do but vacation in sunny Ethiopia with a boatload of goodies and an obscenely wealthy liberal's half-baked philosophy about rescuing the needy. Do me a favor. Pose for your pictures and pass out your parcels and take your entourage back where you came from. Take your silly Geldofs and your Harrisons and your Bonos with you. Go find another cause."

They had reached the bottom of the path. Vane turned on him. "No dice, Preston. And I'm not a Geldof. This isn't about my ego. If I were to walk out of here after what I've witnessed I'd be treating these people with the same contempt you're showing them. So get used to it: you'll be seeing a whole lot of me from now on. And I won't be citing scripture or building death holes for the living."

"And I tell you to go! This is not a playground for the nouveaux riche! I have solid friends in Addis Ababa, and they dwell high above sophistry and bribery. They are men who will move mountains to see the Lord's work done."

"I too have friends, Preston. So don't toy with me. I wasn't able to get state clearance, unrestricted use of roads and airstrips, and the go-ahead to set up my operation where and when I choose, simply because the Ethiopians think I'm such a nice guy. My account was won by Banke Internationale in Addis Ababa. As a consequence, my friends in this nation's capitol are, I daresay, a sight more interested in my welfare than yours." Vane looked away, ground his teeth, took a deep breath. "Look, I'll make a deal with you. You pick up your operation and come along with me. Forget your private campaign and become a team player. I'll provide transportation for you, these people, and whatever staff you may have. I'm not asking you to make any concessions. You can set up this same system if you want; I'll even provide you with sturdy structures to replace these tents and sheds. Regardless of my personal viewpoint considering the Big Picture, it is my understanding that human beings typically have a very deep, sometimes overwhelming spiritual need, as real as the libido. I'm assuming that applies no less to animists than to 'compassionate' Christians."

"It's called the soul. And *no*, you won't find it on an anatomy chart. And *no*, it's not hormonal in nature. It radiates from God."

"Some other time, man. One of these days you and I can sit down and have a good long gabfest about the meaning of life, if any. But for right now I'll make the offer again. Grab your gear and gather your group and join us in Mamuset, where you *can* make a difference."

Preston's expression was that of a man who didn't know which way to spit. He blew out his cheeks and exhaled explosively. "And when your resources are exhausted, what then? How next will you attempt to seduce these poor people? You may gratify your ego by buying their worldly adoration, but it will only be a temporary fix." Preston surprised Vane by double-twitching the first and middle fingers of each hand, the lowbrow gesture for quotation marks. "You accuse me of being involved in a 'private campaign,' as you put it, as if I, *personally*, have something to gain by doing the Lord's work in a place where it is so desperately needed. *This is not about me,* sir, and that is something that you, as a man of the world, are literally incapable of comprehending. This is about abnegation, about *denial* of the thing that is Me. I am doing God's business, as his grateful tool. My gratification is derived solely from the joy of humility. Some day, Mr. Vane, you will either lose your unbelievable wealth or outlive its appeal. Some day you will find yourself facing a death that right here and now seems only a prospect for losers. Then, when you seek and find the Lord, you will truly understand the meaning of enrichment. *Then* your efforts will be selfless and glorious. *Until* then, sir, you and I share nothing."

"You're giving up on me? I'm not worth saving all of a sudden?"

"Nothing sudden about it." Preston's gaze rolled truck-to-truck, settling on a thin sheath of fog around one of the refrigerated trailers. "Save yourself. Get rid of your wealth, your appetite, and your vanity. And when you have nothing left to lose and everything to gain, come here and join the Lord."

"That's just not going to happen. Because 'here' isn't going to be here. I give this place a month, Preston, half a year max. You talk about the 'Word' getting around. You don't think these people are hearing about Mamuset? I'll make a gentleman's bet with you. I'll bet these suffering people choose my house over your crypt. Man, I'll bet they leave in *droves.*"

"Get out of here!" Preston whispered nastily. "Leave these people be."

"Not a chance."

Their eyes locked. Preston hissed, *"Atheist!"* and drew a line in the sand with the toe of his sneaker. At the same moment Mudhead turned over the Land Rover.

"The deal still stands," Vane said evenly. He used his own shoe to delete the line. "We don't have to like each other. We don't have to agree philosophically. Pretty soon this site is going to be as deserted as those villages we've been passing. And it's *you* who'll be responsible, not your 'god'."

Preston took a step forward, his fists clenched. He pointed one at Vane's nose, said, "Don't tempt me!" and turned on his heel. He stomped to the crumbled building, threw aside the canvas curtain, and disappeared inside.

"Let's go," Vane said, swinging a leg into Isis. Mudhead put the Land Rover in gear. The trucks fired almost in unison.

The newly paved road was a tremendous improvement, but Vane couldn't stop squirming. Finally he sat up straight. "Damn the man! He's too interested in his silly ecumenical theatrics to realize he's doing more harm than good."

Mudhead searched for the right words as he drove. "Allman have angle. Difference is: Africaman angle survival. Whiteman not worry survival. Whiteman worry shine brighter everyman else. All time worry how otherman see. Big Camera always on. Whiteman try convince everyman else he most specialman." Mudhead gestured behind them with his head. "Even worry impress god. Think can fool god like fool everyman else."

"Everybody's an actor."

"In Africa," Mudhead said, "noman fool anyman. Africa too big. Africa yawn play-actor."

Vane stewed for another minute. "Everybody thinks I'm on vacation here." He kicked the dash. "Nobody'll take me seriously. Same thing back where I come from." He kicked the dash harder. "Called me a flipping Geldof! Where's the justice in this world? I don't want a goddamned medal, but you'd think people would be happy when they see someone trying to make a positive change. What's so wrong about trying to do the right thing?"

Mudhead once again chose his words carefully. "Justice whiteman plaything. All good idea come from democratman. All sound very nice, very cozy. Everyman same. Man same woman. Man love woman, man love man—all same democratman. Everyman have right. Crazyman have right. Thief have right. Child have right. Whiteman dog have same right whiteman. Whiteman dog democrat dog. Good dog. Democrat dog respect cat, learn meow. Whiteman lobby congress, open special school for sensitive dog. Good dog. Cat forgive. Good cat. All good. All 'justice.' Everyman happy. Now everyman like everyman else, whether everyman like everyman else or not."

Mudhead smiled without humor.

"Everyman crazy.

"Everyman full guilt if no see everyman same everyman else." He softly pounded his fist on the steering wheel. "But everyman no *respect* everyman else. Respect cheap as like. Cheap as justice. Democratman *must* respect everyman else. But phony respect." He nodded as he drove. "Phony as like. Phony as justice."

Vane rolled his head deliriously. "Well! *That* sure cleared things up! I ask a simple question and…aw…what's the use."

"Question not simple. Justice not simple. Respect not simple. Mudahid not respect simpleman, respect Bossman."

Vane tilted back his shades and studied Mudhead's expression. "Why? Why do you respect this crazy democratic white man?"

There was no pause from Mudhead. "Bossman take chance. Could stay home, play prince." He shook his head. "Bossman desertman. Skyman. Heart big as all Africa."

"Nonsense. You're the first man, Mudahid Asafu-Adjaye, to accuse me of having a heart. I'm an empty shell. Cold as a dead man's prayer."

"Not necessary be warm have heart. And Bossman shell fill fast enough. All said, Bossman rock world. Someday Bossman be Africaman."

Vane sank deeper into his seat. Well-meaning words couldn't undo reality. He'd run from responsibility like a hypochondriac from a handshake. And the world he'd run into didn't appear a whole hell of a lot better. It was simply different. He'd flattered his species, pretending that human beings, stripped of the encumbrance of *having*, would be devoted to intellectual and ethical pursuits. They would be fundamentally wise, eager only for spiritual enrichment.

All the people he'd encountered on this side of the world were just a poorer, grittier breed of buzzard. Stripped of their religious and cultural trappings, the only real difference was a lack of sophistication in chicanery. Anything could be had with a wink and a Jackson. Pirated cargo was sold on the Red Sea, unresisting orphans on either coast. Islam, on the surface affecting every aspect of this world's consciousness, was just as open to corruption as Christianity, as politics, as liberal ideology…

The pastoralists Vane observed were beyond ideas, hardened to a wretchedness he would have previously found unimaginable. The most pathetic dumpster diver the States could offer lived like a king compared to the blank-eyed skeletons staring back from pastoral Africa. So he drifted uneasily between philosophical extremes. He despised the flashy avaricious almost beyond words. But he was having a real tough time falling in love with the other side.

The other side was dumb, it was diseased, it was repulsive. He felt more akin to that hollow spouter Preston than to this dirty black horror that was too depleted to care.

Paving on the An'erim-Mamuset road, under construction for four months, was from both ends toward the middle.

That middle was all but complete.

Now the vibrations of Vane's trailers shook up the quiet afternoon as they slammed around vehicles entrenched for the long haul. Clusters of workers, looking like limp black coolies, sifted from burrows with spades and picks. They immediately set to: breaking up rocks, shoveling clumps and grit onto rousted dump trucks. These trucks began distributing dirt onto unfinished patches of road too weak to support the heavy tractor trailers. It was slow, hot work. The convoy crept along for a few miles, only to halt for an hour or more while the larger rigs pushed out trucks caught in sudden shifts of earth. There was no end to it.

Vane's Mamuset Highway was in no manner a direct route. Heavy equipment had worked it over those months, compromising often. Wherever the new road encountered tricky chasms it simply went around, despite great distances, or followed rims until their walls were low enough to cut ramps down one side and up the other.

At 0130 hours the convoy ground to an inevitable halt, mired by hunger and exhaustion. Mudhead, approaching to wish his boss a good night, was mildly upset to find Vane flat on his back on Isis's hood, staring dully at the stars.

"Mudahid not sleep," he muttered, "when Bossman fidget." He looked up. "Sky too big?"

"It's not the sky," Vane said after a minute. "I've been listening to Mamuset, Mudhead. Long distance. I can hear all those frustrated stomachs growling from here."

Mudhead rapped his knuckles on Vane's temple. "Bad connection. Bossman hear own stomach."

The American propped himself on his elbows. "God-damn it, this road was supposed to be ready! My people shouldn't have to suffer a single minute because the freaking road crew can't get it together. That's not fair; it's not fair at all." He blew out a sigh. "Now Mudhead, I want you to make a few enemies. Go roust all the drivers and tell them we're push-ing on or they're fired on the spot." He ran a hand over his face. "Wait, wait! That won't do. Offer a hundred U.S. dollars to every man who'll pull with me."

Mudhead's teeth and eyes gleamed under the stars. "No problem, Bossman. Muslimman not afraid step on sleeping snake. Hang on money. Mudahid know secret tongue."

In ten minutes the trucks and buses were idling, waiting for Isis to lead them on. The laborers, having scrambled back out from under the trucks, were huddled on the hillside. Vane turned around in his seat, trading stares with the driver in the rig behind. He knew he was trading stares because he could see two cold pools suspended behind the glass, trained on him without blinking or shifting. It was like being in a dark cave, watching something watching you back. The stare went on and on. Fin-ally the great windshield wipers swept the glass thrice. Vane waited another half minute. The wipers swept once more. He turned to Mudhead, who pumped the clutch and shifted into first.

"So how'd you get them up so fast?"

"Mudahid tap door eleven time. Driver look up, see Mu-dahid hand show seven finger total. Driver up fast enough."

"Eleven and seven? What's the significance there? Those are pretty lucky numbers."

Mudhead shook his head. "No, Bossman. Not to Shan-kiliman. To Shankiliman 5, 10 important."

Vane nodded. "I'm guessing that's because there's five digits on each hand and foot; ten fingers and ten toes altoge-ther?"

Mudhead frowned at his employer's lameness. "No, Bossman. 5, 10 sacred number. Magic number. Take number 5, add together number either side. 4 plus 6 equal ten. Keep moving. 3 plus 7 equal ten. 2 plus 8 equal ten. 1 plus 9 also. Amazing."

"A child's game."

"Pretty amazing child. Same go order. 1, 2, 3, 4, 5 equal 15. 15 divide by five. Sacred number. Go higher. 6, 7, 8, 9, 10 equal 40. 40 divide by 5. Sacred number. Or five in row start anywhere. 2, 3, 4, 5, 6 equal 20. 20 divide by 5. 7, 8, 9, 10, 11 equal 45. 45 divide by 5. All sacred number. 3, 4, 5, 6, 7 equal 25. 4, 5, 6, 7, 8 equal 30. Incredible. 8, 9, 10, 11, 12 equal 50. 50 cardinal number: divide equal by five *or* ten! 5, 10 very deep spiritual healing number, use center every Shankiliman ceremony, childbirth through funeral. But 7 alone, 11 alone? Bad number, two of worst. When Shankiliman see 7, 11, like see whole life odd number: birth odd number, death another. Bossman watch. Bossman before not notice sometime extra space between number 5 truck and 6 truck, between number 10 truck and 11 truck. This because Shankiliman alter order according to message pass down line. But now Shankiliman get message from up front! Truck now drive permanent group five. Also, Bossman see driver show hand every bad pass; show maybe four finger, maybe three, maybe two, maybe one. All depend how bad pass. Sign language deeper than superstition, Mr. America."

Vane laughed. "What if you've got a driver who's lost a finger? Talk about a chain reaction fender bender!"

Mudhead didn't smile. "No Shankiliman drive four finger. Maybe only one hand, all finger. Maybe no hand. Never both hand, one with evil number finger." He looked to the side guiltily. "All big joke to modernman in dirty black Africa. See superstition, magic, must laugh. Bossman see Mudahid as ignorant black Muslimman. But Bossman not know Africa. Here blood, terror, premonition equal logic. Whiteman see dead wildebeest under duoma, think see innocent nature in infinite give, take. See Afar woman, mushal wrap left, think she make fashion statement." He clucked schoolmarmishly. "Bossman, every beauty Africa cover horror unimaginable to modern, civilized Western Americaman. Mudhead try point beauty, but *Mudahid* very serious recommend Bossman be suspicious anything off-pattern. From now, when give direction driver, Mudahid translate so driver know Bossman odd number. Man to fear."

"Thanks very much. But I already know I'm an odd number."

"Look trunk."

Turning, Vane for the first time noticed that his driver had drawn a series of vertical slashes with a broad-tipped felt pen. He counted thirteen lines.

"That's an unpleasant number where I come from, too."

"Protect like guard dog," Mudhead said matter-of-factly. "Bossman sleep car, back seat. Mudahid sleep front seat. Bossman watch for odd number." Mudhead gripped the wheel tightly and stamped his left foot. "Bossman not laugh! Mudahid cannot be all-vigilant."

But Vane couldn't help himself, laughing out loud under the warm gorgeous sky. He grabbed a couple of Heinekens from the cooler, broke the caps on the dash and thrust a foaming-over bottle at his friend. "Cheers, Mudhead! Drink to the hot African night, for tomorrow we die. God willing, there'll be no DUIs tonight, but I want you to keep at least one mystical eye peeled for the rabid intangible. You never know when the desert will erupt with censer-shaking ghouls and witch doctors hitching a ride. But at least we'll be ready. If they're hitching with a thumb, pass 'em by. But all five fingers, load the bastards in. It'll be clear sailing all the way."

Mudhead frowned at the alcohol, then nodded five times quickly to the east and snatched the bottle. "Noman hitchhike desert, Bossman." He drove intuitively, his eyes glued to the rear-view mirror. Vane knew Mudhead was doing what he could to hold the gaze of the driver just behind them. The great rig's headlight beams swept left and right and up and down as its enormous tires negotiated the Highway's rough edge. The convoy moved with extreme slowness, in groups of five and ten, feeling its way around the ancient lava spills and rolling hillocks that bordered the flat plain of the desert with a pattern like that left by a retreating tide. The air grew hotter as they gradually descended into the depression, the sky wider and more intense than Vane had ever imagined. It seemed to be exploding with brand new stars as he watched.

An'erim

And the jackals stopped walking in the hills to stare at the miniscule worm of the rich boy's segmented convoy below, painstakingly making its way nowhere, all its itsy headlights, taken together, producing a slowly sweeping white mark feebler than the faintest star. The jackals, yawning at the moon, laid down one by one to watch the worm wasting precious energy as it pushed itself into that insatiable, bone-dry hole. It would take a while for the worm to expire, and a while longer for its strange metal skin to crack and expose the vital juices within.

But Africa could wait.

Chapter Seven

Mamuset

Precisely one minute and five seconds before the day's first ray burned across the Great Danakil Depression, a chord like thunder resounded over a dark sea of small hide huts. Strauss's *Also Sprach Zarathustra* had been employed theatrically, and with outstanding effect, by everybody from Presley to Kubrick. Although Vane was sincere about using it to make an astronomical point, the power of the piece, the near-audible crack of dawn, and his elevated station before an audience of thousands almost swept him up in his own ego.

Heads, popping out singly and in clusters, ratcheted wonderingly as the ascending theme blew out of a fourteen-foot speaker cabinet. Earlier that morning the cabinet had been toted in by a dozen men, pallbearers to a giant; up the new road's narrowing asphalt stream and down into the crater proper, around and behind the series of low tapering hills, and so up the final mound to a strategic spot opposite the crater's eastern rim. A soundless procession had crept behind, bearing computer and amplifier, batteries and hookups, wires and patch cables. Ever so gently, the cabinet was placed facing the uncountable sleeping huts. Vane's dream had always been to make his entrance a memorable one, but he was way too shy to appear without some kind of dazzling distraction. That shyness was evinced in his five a.m. tiptoe-approach up the southern rim with Mudhead, and in his careful peek at the unconscious village below.

It had been so very still under the stars; for a minute Vane was sure he'd arrived too late. In the darkness the little huts looked like ranks of tombstones. Only the still profiles of sleeping donkeys and camels prevented the scene having all the appearance of a desert cemetery.

He and Mudhead, accompanied by a pair of engineers, had first circumnavigated the crater in Isis, halting at West Rim to conduct tests at the *Reservoir*, a canvas-covered concrete retaining pool twenty feet deep and holding sixty thousand cubic feet of river water. Flow was controlled by a series of wheeled valves. Months earlier, a chunk had been dynamited out of the rim for Reservoir's steel conduit, and the new gap filled with cement. Vane's engineers were checking West Rim for stress fractures at points of ingress and egress. A well-worn path proved the Afar had been hiking over the crater's wall to collect their drinking water.

The Ridge, folding right up out of the desert to partly bisect the crater, had been planed to provide an access road for tractor trailers. Vane christened this road into Mamuset the *On-ramp*. Like a kid, he took delight in naming everything.

Ridge Highway ended a little over halfway across the crater, where the ridge itself terminated in a few uneven mounds. On the final in the series, a flat table some hundred yards square had been hewn from the hillside. The table faced east, and was known as the *Stage*. This was Vane's command center, with short wave radio, amplification system, microphones, and alarm triggers; all patched into an eight-foot-long motherboard. The Stage Wall featured a huge clock showing Greenwich and Danakil times, moon phases and barometric readings. It would be computer-driven. An enormous canvas canopy, the Big Tarp, was already in place over the Stage. The Stage's cradle, that final soft hill, was known as the *Mount*.

Behind the Mount were two great oblong excavations, designated Basement and Cellar (for perishables and beverages, respectively). Both were lined with cinder blocks, and were separated by an area the size of a football field known as Warehouse, the holding zone for materials and dry goods. The Highway's physical terminus was *Dock*, a concrete unloading platform abutting Warehouse.

Kitchen, one specialized component of that group of eager young university volunteers, had been hard at work since four that morning, boiling meat and vegetables out on the On-ramp over propane in fifty-five gallon drums. Those drums had then been carted back aboard trailers to await transport to Dock post-Strauss, where thousands of half-gallon *Bowls* would be unloaded and stacked. Bowls were numbered: Sector, Quadrant, Square. They were of high impact plastic, of Vane's own design, mass produced at one of Honey's Cairo factories and shipped through Suez to Port Massawa. Part of the Bowl mold was a foot-long, slightly curved handle, making the instrument resemble an outsize ladle. Opposite the handle was a flat protuberance for gripping with forefinger and thumb.

Fighting the urge to play air maestro, Vane now let his finger hover over the STOP button on the CD player's remote.

Recorded music was clearly a new experience for the Afar. They stood outside their little round huts under the lightening sky, their smiles growing as the music peaked.

So that the crescendo and first ray would occur in sync on a daily basis, the computer had been programmed to activate the player at precisely one minute and five seconds before each consecutive sunrise, as regulated by its internal calendar. Computer and amplifiers were powered by marine batteries. Those batteries would be recharging via solar panels arriving on the next convoy.

"Let's do it," Vane said nervously.

Mudhead, having raised the microphone to translate, peered aside dubiously.

Vane's throat clenched. A great unseen brush washed the desert red. Suddenly the African sun was a blinding blood-spotlight. "Good morning!" he blurted out. "And welcome to Mamuset!"

Mudhead's arm fell. "We fly Delta, Bossman?"

Vane blew out his cheeks. "This isn't easy for me either, man. I've got to come off as a nice guy, not like some kind of holy roller." Mudhead thereupon delivered what sounded like a scathing diatribe. More people crept around their huts, regarding Vane intently. The American's stomach knotted.

"What'd you just do, introduce me as the entrée?" He'd never been so aware of his fairness.

"Mudahid tell Afarman whole Bossman story. What say now?"

Vane chewed his lip. "It breaks my heart to have to do it, but I'm gonna have to order them to take down their huts. We need a flat playing field." He flexed his fingers and forced a few deep breaths. "This could get very ugly very fast."

"No problem, Bossman." Mudhead barked out a string of commands and the crowd immediately began dismantling their huts. Vane watched amazed as the hut city dissolved in an uncannily smooth receding sweep. In minutes the nearest huts were neatly rolled bundles.

"What'd you tell them, man?" Bundles were being tied to camels. "They're leaving! Jesus, Mudhead, you weren't supposed to threaten them."

"No threat, Bossman." Mudhead frowned. "No leave." He gestured broadly. "No problem!" Those same men were now clearing sitting spaces beside their camels. Distant huts were still coming down. "Mudahid tell everyman what Bossman say. Neighbor pass command to next neighbor. So on, so on. Mudahid tell like Bossman tell Mudahid tell."

"Yes! We're on! This's gonna happen—it's *got* to happen! Keep working 'em, Mudhead." He skidded down the Mount's northeast slope, hopped in Isis, and raced to Dock. Volunteers and drivers were already unrolling the eight 30 x 60 canvas spools that would make up the great Warehouse canopy. Vane handed all the young doctors walkie-talkies from the Land Rover, and ordered field reports radioed to Doctor 'Lijah, the group's pedantic and incomprehensible senior medical officer. He pulled a dozen hyper volunteers aside. Many were still in their teens.

"I want you guys circulating. Pick the healthiest men out

of these Afar and lead them to the Mount. I'm designating them 'Runners.' They'll be doing all the distributing, at least until everybody's able to contribute equally. Tell Kitchen to make sure these Runners get a couple of eggs in with their soup. See that the weakest people out there start on broth, and work your way up. Anybody reasonably fluent in Saho, now's the time to step up to the plate."

Three girls and a boy were nudged forward. "Okay," giggled one of the girls, "'Bossman'." A friend punched her arm. Vane shooed them in different directions and strode back up the incline with his juices flowing.

Soon a long line of Afar were snaking through the crowd, directed by doctors, nurses, and a constantly reforming mass of volunteers. These Afar men, strongest of the lot though they were, seemed lamentably lean to the privileged young American. He was surprised by their gentleness and compliance. Each was given a Bowl and shown how to scoop it half-full of broth. Cooks then used elongated colanders to fish out carrots, rice, beans, bits of meat, and two hard-boiled eggs per man. The men wolfed the solid food, greedily but gratefully, and carefully slurped the steaming liquid. Volunteers juggled Bowls of broth to the needier sites, marked by flags on long sticks. The anguish of those not being served was radiant; men and women turned their heads like wolves at the trailing aroma, children wailed as the broth passed them by. These people had been subsisting on Vane's cold dry care packages for almost half a year.

The sound of want easily pierced Vane's emotional armor. By the time he reached the Stage he was tearing at his nails. He forced himself to relax. They were only bugs. After a while he said coldly, "Order them to face this way." The African snarled into his microphone and heads immediately turned. A camel roared at the feedback's squeal. Children screamed and wept.

"Enough! Tell the damned Runners to scoop quarter-Bowls, food and broth. Tell them to pass them out indiscriminately. That way there won't be much lost when the crowd starts fighting over food. We can pass around second and third helpings later. Please don't shout. Just ask everybody to pass the Bowls back when they're empty."

Mudhead's spectacles flashed as he turned. "Africaman not fight food. Afarman gentleman. Accustom very little. Grateful even less."

"Be right, Mudhead. I've had nightmares about this moment. You know the kind. Feeding frenzies. Morsels torn from the mouths of babes."

"Africaman slow, not greedy. Too much space. Too much time. Not like...*State*. Americaman rush. Have more than need, but never enough. *Never* enough space. *Never* enough time. Whiteman greedy have all."

"Later. Wait till I'm in the mood for guilt-trips. But you're absolutely right about Whiteman disease. Now let's just hope you're on the money about Afar etiquette."

Sure enough, Bowls were neither hoarded nor fought over. The Afar sipped broth, plucked morsels with their fingers, shoved the food into their children's mouths, passed the Bowls along. Though children screamed for more, parents remained patient and dignified. They caressed, rather than scolded. The little ones soon calmed.

Vane needlessly supervised workers securing the pairs of titanic speaker cabinets on either side of the Stage, then ran down to Dock and ordered a replenishing of the drums. Volunteers were refilling the empty Bowls as they trickled back. His confidence continued to grow, but after running around confusing everybody he noted a certain rhythm—a milling, freewheeling progress involving Runners, volunteers, and recipients—taking place outside his command. Was there no one even aware of his awesome burden? He stood baking in the sun, staring at nothing, until the radio in his hand came alive. Doctors were reporting none dead, although the vast majority of his people suffered mildly from malnutrition. A panicky Vane was informed that this was not an unnatural state for pastoralists. He sprinted halfway up the Mount, forgot where he was going and why. Vane looked around. Dozens of people were stopped dead, staring at him. He depressed the transmit button on his walkie-talkie.

"Mudhead, I'll need a foreman out of the Runners to organize this mob before there's a riot on our hands. Pick the sharpest guy you can find and get back to me, and I mean pront-

o. I'm not hip to the currency in this part of the country. Just a-gree to whatever he demands."

"Can do. But keep wallet in pant, Ugly American. Try little respect."

"Can do," Vane said right back. "Don't give up on me, Africaman." He was hyperventilating. "Mudhead, what'd I get us into? What in hell's name am I doing here?"

"You break up, Joe Washington. Mudahid not receive last transmission. Try talk sense. Then maybe Mudahid understand."

"Okay. Before I have an aneurysm, I need some perspective. What was I thinking that night we talked in that stupid bar? What did I tell you? Everything seemed so clear back then."

"Sorry, Bossman. Lose you again. You break up all over place. Relax. Smell manure. Inspiration come. But at own pace."

"Ten-four, Mudhead. Keep the faith, Muslimman."

"Faith never go. Faith follow like shadow. Example: Mudahid have new foreman right here. Say hello Bossman, foreman." There was a sharp command from Mudhead in Saho. A high teenaged voice gushed a lengthy response that was all nonsense to Vane.

"Bossman? New foreman say name Akid."

"A kid he is," Vane pronounced. "And so shall he be named 'Kid.' Ask him what his demands are."

"Kid say salary open, Bossman. Kid like radio."

"Give him one, Mudhead. He'll need it. Put his on channel 3. You and I'll communicate on 2, and you'll be switching back and forth. Now we're beginning to build an organization! I feel better already. You're my Operations Director, and I'm your Commanding Officer. Kid is Lead Officer in charge of Manpower, and his workers are hereby christened the Crew. Kid'll be subservient only to you. You're the one responsible, as of right now, for all operations departments. We'll discuss your pay hike over pork rinds and Heinekens."

"Can be only one Bossman," Mudhead protested.

"Sorry, but you're breaking up. Start setting up the Stage Eyes and I'll get back to you."

Vane walked round and round the Mount; commanding here, instructing there, commenting, questioning, getting in everyone's way. He assigned Senior Medical Officer 'Lijah and all medical personnel to channel 4. As SMO, 'Lijah was to communicate *up* only on 2, to Mudhead or the Commanding Officer, and run the specialists on channel 4 exclusively. Way too busy for conferences or camaraderie, Vane charged up the Mount's southwest slope, across the Stage, and up the naked hillside to the summit, where he could look over his property. Mudhead, thirty feet below, was setting up two tripod-mounted digital binoculars. Vane was at a good vantage. Mamuset was now fully illuminated, the sun blazing up the sky. That untidy expanse of black bodies was already, in his widening eye, compartmentalizing. Two seconds later he was off like a shot.

Vane scrambled down to the Stage and huddled with Mudhead. The shade was suffocating. Even under the Big Tarp he was perspiring.

"Seven in the morning and it's already cooking. Now that their little huts are all rolled up, personal shade is going to be Issue Primo, no getting around it. Call Kid and tell him to get Crew humping out the Shade Packets. After that they can bring out the Square Kits." He stooped for a magnified gander at his infant world. The binoculars, solar-sensitive with digital reads, also functioned in the infrared when properly programmed. Solar-charged batteries powered a range of high-tech functions. Vane experimented with angles, with wide and telescopic zooms, with artificial shade, with white line contrasts, with Near and Far effects. When at last he was able to map quadrants and manipulate details he straightened his aching neck.

"You could almost pick a man's nose with these."

Mudhead grunted. "Bowl come back. Everyman eat. There Kid."

Vane squinted into the lenses again. "Where Kid? Everybody looks the same."

"Only Kid look like Kid."

"Make a note, Mudhead. We're going to need some kind of badge or armband or something for our Crew. We won't always have the luxury of searching faces."

Mudhead straightened slowly. "Maybe David star, Bossman?"

"Point well made," Vane said. "Point well taken. I'm going to rely on your uncanny ability, el Segundo, to distinguish the few from the many. After all, you're the Operations Director. Whatever works best for you is what works best for me." He wiped his palms on his thighs. "Okay. Tell everybody to segregate by family. We want isolated units, remember? That means we'll need as much space as possible between neighbors. Every group includes its stock and property, as well as any orphans they'll accept. But we want to discourage the old tribal mentality temporarily. The ideal arrangement is a unit of man, woman, child, and stock."

Mudhead shook his head gravely. "Like we talk...Africaman not happy independentman. No room ego."

"And like I explained a dozen times, Mudhead, this is still a kind of tribe. It's just organized differently, that's all. The name of the new tribe is Mamuset."

"And new chief Bossman."

"No. No chief. No rules. Just shining examples. Everyone has the same status in Mamuset. Each member equals One. That's if he's Joe Solo. If he's a member of a family, then his family equals One. Any way that family wants to work out the relationship of its members is its own business. If the unit doesn't work it can split up, if that's what's best. Then each fragment equals One. It becomes Mamuset's problem then, not the disintegrated unit's."

"One," Mudhead muttered.

"Unum. Everybody equals One. Everything equals One. Nobody's impressed into anything. And no one's left out in the cold. If your heart beats, you're worthy of the basics. There are no Afar, no Bossmen, no Mudheads in Mamuset, at least so far as status goes. Only Mamusetans. Everybody gets one share of Everything, and everybody contributes equally to Everything. If somebody doesn't want to contribute, then that one can be exempted, and even expelled, by the greater One. Ostracism. The only punishment, by overall agreement. Majority always rules in Mamuset. But not by vote. By consensus."

"So, O Bossman no better everyman. Show Mudahid where else idea work."

"Never been tried before," Vane said pleasantly. "No-body ever had the means, along with the lack of good sense and personal ambition, to experiment like this before. Sure it's doomed. But I've got almost unlimited funds, and almost no ego. Plus, there are no sycophants, competitors, or court jesters to muddy the waters. You and I, Mudhead me hearty, are in the crow's nest. So spend all you can while you can. This ship is going down."

"All same, Mudahid contribute paycheck Unum fund."

"Good. Money's gonna be worthless here, anyway. When it's all over we can settle up in the ruins. I don't forget my friends." Sweat was beading on his forehead, rolling freely down his neck and chest. "It's absolutely frying in this crater. Step One is shade, then we'll get started on the Grid. I can't have my people isolated in the hot sun." He wiped his eyes. Some of the Afar were so distant as to be lost in the hazy rise of East Rim.

"Let 'em all know I'm about to demonstrate a personal Shade Canopy's basic assembly. Explain that we'll be piecing together permanent structures after we've situated everybody and laid foundations, but that they should stay under their Can-opies, out of the heat, whenever they're not busy. Tell them they can put up their Canopies anywhere on their land they want, and take them down and put them back up just as they please. It's easy, man.

"Now—and this is crucial, Mudhead—you've got to make it *perfectly* plain: they're *all* responsible for passing in-structions along! I don't expect everything to be just what the doctor ordered, not right off the bat, but I also don't want any-body getting hurt. Those poles have pretty sharp points."

Mudhead peered glumly over his glasses.

"Okay," Vane said. "I'm gone," and skidded down the slope.

He pitched in, helping Crew create a sigmoid pile of Shade Packets in front of the Mount. Each Packet contained four hollow ten-foot aluminum poles and corresponding thread-ed stands, two 10 x 10 canvas sheets, four tether stakes, and four tightly wound nylon ropes. The Honey Foundation, dealing directly with the Egyptian Army, bought up warehouses stocked with surplus canvas tents, knapsacks, and the like. Those warehouses were then converted to factories for the manufacture of canopies and mats. Vane personally hired the most wretched souls he could find for the sewing and packing. The retained Egyptian foremen proved to be, in more than a few cases, unspeakably brutal and venal. Honey replaced these monsters with humane supervisors, but Vane insisted his hand-picked sewers and packers be kept on.

The Runners scurried all round with Packets under their arms, dropped the Packets off, and ran back for more. The deposited Packets were passed along man to man, smoothly, without a single visible glitch. Vane directed through his walkie-talkie with mounting confidence, impressed by the Afar's ability to pick up on ideas and instinctively follow through as a unit. Mudhead translated from the Stage as the Runners grew tiny and the Core units listened intently.

Mamuset was to be built upon Vane's example.

Adjacent units were to imitate his actions directly and precisely. Their neighbors were to do likewise, and so on. Each unit would be responsible for passing along instructions by both word and example. From this moment on, Vane proclaimed, the granted parcel of land for each unit was to be known as a *Square*. Mudhead had everyone repeat the word. The response from those within earshot came back roughly as "Squaw".

"Now," Vane said excitedly, "follow my lead." He maneuvered a Shade Packet between the piles and runners, walked out a further forty paces, and methodically erected his Canopy in the sun. Mudhead, watching impassively beneath the Big Tarp, described the proceedings in Saho as his employer laid one of the Canopy's canvas squares on the dirt, stretched it out flat, and hammered a foot-high pole stand through each of the mat's corner eyes, almost taking off a toe in the process. Vane then grabbed the second 10 x 10 canvas square and inserted a pole's nipple-end through one eye, paused to demonstrate the tying of a simple square knot, looped the knot over the nipple, and raised the pole. He slowly screwed the pole into its stand, the hot limp canvas clinging to his back. After standing the pole upright, he repeated the process with the remaining poles, ropes, and stands. His half-done Shade Canopy teetered in the sun.

Vane fought to keep his poles from caving to center while simultaneously reaching for a trailing rope, his struggles accompanied by shy laughter all around. Finally he snatched the rope, looped its knot to a stake, and hammered the stake into place. The other ropes and stakes quickly followed course, and then Canopy #1 was somehow standing taut, exactly ten feet above the crater's flat parched floor. Vane proudly stepped onto the equally taut canvas mat. The effect of his completed Shade Canopy was immediate.

He and Mudhead listened to the patter of laughter, near and distant, as families struggled with their Packets. Canopies began sprouting about them, clumsily as first, then with increasing efficiency. Rather than sit on their thumbs, the successful Afar rushed to help their neighbors; sometimes they were met with venomous stares or verbal threats. Vane thrilled at the way the Afar's eyes lit up when confronted by an interesting challenge. He got the feeling that, even without instruction, they'd sooner or later assemble the parts correctly, like clever children around a Christmas tree. He bowed to his neighbors, and they all bowed back. Everyone contributed to erecting Mudhead's Canopy.

By noon the Bowls, this time heavy with meat and vegetables, had made a second circuit. Vane's project was ready for a most crucial step. He chugged a Heineken and dragged his Square Kit out next to his Shade Canopy, unwrapped his Square Frame and Extensions.

Square Frames consisted of four identical telescoping aluminum tubes, fifty feet in length when fully extended, kept propped above the ground by adjustable plastic feet. The tubes locked at right angles, their female-end elbows accepting the male-ends of adjoining tubes. Four perfectly locked tubes created a perfect square.

At full extension, aligned perforations were exposed on these tubes, the holes positioned fifteen feet from either extremity. Bolts inserted through these holes would lock the arms of an unfolding internal steel lattice. From above, a fully assembled Square Frame would look pretty much like a bordered tic-tac-toe diagram. Properly assembled Square Frames would observe ninety-degree angles with exactitude, be absolutely rigid when locked, and be lightweight enough to be dragged intact by their builders. These Frames were temporary structures; inter-locking pieces for mapping the community's sprawling *Grid* of five thousand perfectly equal, interdependent personal sites.

Vane constructed his Frame as he'd constructed so many before, but this time without all the smarmy overseeing engin-eers, and this time with his indispensable buddy Mudhead tersely describing his efforts in Saho. When he'd finished he found due east on compass #1 and ran out a marker, then kicked, hammered, and hauled his protesting Frame until he'd managed to align one border. His neighbors very politely dragged their own already completed Frames out of his way. He couldn't make out the progress of distant assemblers, but the facility of their movements bugged him. Vane grudgingly watched his neighbors experimenting with their own markers, lines, and compasses, passing the tools back and forth like exu-berant idiot savants. "*Hey!*" he hollered. "Those things aren't toys, you know!" and almost passed out.

But at least *his* aluminum Square Frame was facing dead east. Vane wiped his face and got on his knees to attach his *Ex-tensions*; connecting rods designed to precisely bridge the gaps between Squares by locking with both crisscrossing lattice rods and Frame corner-studs. Each neighbor would contribute two-of-four per side.

As Vane worked, locking down Extensions on each side of his Square, he became increasingly annoyed by peripheral glimpses of his Core neighbors; their eyes hard on him, at first copying, then anticipating his moves. He felt the vital force on the opposite ends, locking down ahead of him, and suppressed powerful urges to yank his Extensions right back. Behind him, Mudhead's Square #2 was being ably constructed by compet-ing Afar youngsters while the African, fanning himself under the Big Tarp, farcically described the CO's mighty efforts in Saho—but even those little showoff brutes were making Vane hustle. Before he'd completed his extended Frame his neighbors were already locked down and pacing. They could barely con-tain their impatience. Vane knew he should have been proud of them...but were they *trying* to make him ashamed of himself? Dog-tired, his shirt clinging, he stamped up to the Stage, hacked the cap off a Lowenbrau, and collapsed on a folding chair.

"Afarman good student," Mudhead noted.

Vane glared. He pushed himself back to his feet and hunched at his binoculars. Including Mudhead's and his own, he counted twenty-one well-framed proto-Squares, each bordered by perfectly-straight Street outlines of four extensions apiece. Taken together, the laid-out Frames gave the impression of crisscrossed ladders lying flat. He adjusted focus. Work was scrambled farther along, and way down the line certain units were still struggling to set up their Shade Canopies. Some had given up completely. Huts remained standing only at the very foot of East Rim.

"It's a matter of gradations," he declared. "Our first set of instructions are still filtering back. The people farthest away are getting what must seem conflicting directions." He creaked to his full height. "I'm ordering additional walkie-talkies."

Mudhead fanned himself feebly. "Maybe tomorrow."

"Agreed. I'm plumb wore out m'self. Just tell those with completed Frames to bring their families and animals inside the Frames, and keep them there. And tell them to keep Shade Canopies away from Square centers, so they won't have to be moved when the real work starts. Get the Runners back in. I'll go tell Kitchen to start doling from the drums. And this time there'll be some *solid* food in those Bowls!"

He stumbled down to Dock, grabbed a full Bowl and sipped critically. He'd tasted better, he'd tasted worse. A young doctor handed him what seemed a ream of preliminary findings. Vane thumbed the pages. The words *typhus*, *diphtheria* and *cholera* leaped out at him. Suddenly he was clinging.

"Mañana," he said. "I've been up, like, some thirty-odd hours." He fought his walkie-talkie free of its holster. "Mudhead?"

"Bossman?"

"I'm shot, man. If anything comes up while I'm out, you take care of it. Don't wake me unless it's an emergency. I'm hitting the sack." Aching all over, he dragged his feet back to his Square, tripped over a tethered rope and landed on his face. Two poles crossed and his Shade Canopy dipped precariously. Before he could recover, the entire contraption collapsed on his

backside. Vane sprawled on his belly, flinching feebly. Somewhere a pair of camels roared in stereo, while the five thousand-
plus voices of Mamuset bubbled behind like a purling stream.
With the last of his strength, Vane pulled the burning canopy
over his face. Before the canvas had fully settled he was fast
asleep.

Chapter Eight

Afar

Precisely one minute and five seconds before the sun's first ray burned across the Great Danakil Depression, a chord like thunder resounded over an endless field of perfectly-squared Shade Canopies.

The day's pre-dawn convoy had already imported, along with tons of rice and barley, truckloads of tools and building materials. Mamuset, beginning this morning, was to be built from the ground up. Flatbed after flatbed flowed into Dock, hauling bags of cement and fertilizers, loads of fodder, lengths of polyvinyl chloride pipe. Pickups and forklifts moved it all into Warehouse. Also on this run were the initial loads of 15 x 15 solar panels, conveyed in six foot-high stacks on trailer roofs. A groggy Vane received some astounding news with his grits and coffee: his entire Highway, An'erim to Onramp, was fully navigable.

Much of the hangar-like tent of Warehouse was now crammed with pallets of dried food and fodder, interspersed with tools and building material. Basement was being stocked with perishables; Cellar with beer, wine, and dairy. Vane's technical team had programmed the generators to fire automatically whenever Cellar's temperature rose above forty degrees. The propane tank now squatted behind and to one side of Warehouse. On the other side rested the gasoline tanker, minus truck. Both were sheltered by peaked canvas.

All this came together in the dark while Vane was still unconscious, Mudhead demonstrating surprising effectiveness directing on his own. And the Afar were showing a real talent for getting things down with minimal supervision. Volunteers and specialists performed not only smoothly, but with zeal. At Dock the drums were already steaming.

Everybody, it seemed, was out to steal his thunder.

And now here came that arrogant drum-beater Mudhead, trudging up to the Stage in a godly fanfare of strings, brass, and tympani. Vane's welcoming smile was taut. "Tell them," he grated as the echoes blew away, "that the sun will rise at a slightly different time each consecutive morning, and that we Western men of science, having accurately gauged the immediate heavens, know exactly when that first ray will hit. Tell them they'll be seeing the first stab of sun every morning precisely at a particular point in the music, right on my down stroke."

Mudhead yawned. He threw his arms wide above the much-improved community, his white sleeves rising angelically. Vane's eyes narrowed. "Bossman move too fast. Too early physic 101. For now, keep foot on ground, head out cloud." He used those spread arms to pantomime embracing the raw, spotless sky. "Figure speech. Important thing now breakfast. How Afarman learn science on empty stomach?"

"They'll eat. And I don't think it'll be too great a draw on a man's strength to learn an interesting fact between chew and swallow. I mean, come on now, how much of your day did you just forfeit by hearing one simple fact?"

Mudhead yawned again. "Easy, Bossman. Take easy. Point is, how much Mudahid remember? If Mudahid have walking sick, if Mudahid have crybelly, how much attention Mudahid pay?"

"Uh-uh, man. The point is, if Mudhead hears the same thing every morning, how long's it gonna take before Mudhead remembers the thing?"

Mudhead considered this. He raised a forefinger. "*Point* is...what is point? How Mudahid know what time sun show help Mudahid be not sick, not hungry?"

"The *point* is:" Vane dug, "what if Mudhead heard other facts every morning, until these facts were stuck in his head? What if there were endless facts to learn, and plenty of them were important to Mudhead's everyday survival? What if Mudhead learned, say, how to avoid being sick, or which steps to take for recovery? What if he learned all about nutrition, and vitamins, and exercise? What if he became, little by little, a well-rounded student of his neighbors' problems, as well as his own, and an expert on how to solve them?"

"Then," Mudhead said, "poor Mudahid skull all full. Mudahid no time eat, no time watch sun, no time hear music." He placed his hands on his hips. "*Then*, Bossman, Mudahid no time Mudahid." He shook his head categorically. "Africaman have all time world, but no time play schoolboy."

"Ah, that's where you're gravely mistaken, Africaman. Life can be far richer than simple survival."

Mudhead, looking away, said levelly, "Rich life okay richman. What good music do dying desertman?"

"But what if that man learned about irrigation? What if he learned about the nitrogen cycle? How about if he were to learn all about soil management, fertilization, and crop rotation?"

Sudden revelation burned behind the tiny round lenses. "Mudahid see! Dyingman sing song about pretty garden when sun come up right on time."

"Now you've got it, Sancho. So just freaking *tell* them that the time of sunrise changes each day, and that the proof is in the Big Clock behind us, which will show a different reading every morning when the music peaks and the sun breaks in simultaneously. Then tell them it's not a trick, and that it's not magic. Say it's an entirely predictable, completely demonstrable fact. Explain that the solar system is like an enormous time-piece, and that we'll explore that in depth as we go along."

Mudhead approached the microphone, now positioned on a stand between the two mounted binoculars. "Mudahid," he muttered, "make sure all Afarman set watch." He snapped out a string of terse sentences. After staring humbly for a few seconds, the gaping Afar turned as one to face the blinding sun.

"Okay. You can tell them to look away now. I hope you mentioned that the goofy white guy is done making a fool of himself."

"Professor Bossman, Mudahid make sure everyman never forget lesson one."

"I've just *got* to learn Saho. Okay, man, let's get breakfast rolling. But this time I want my people to pass the Bowls on their own, without the Runners. Try to talk them into standing behind one another in rough lines. Explain, explain, explain: organization is gonna be *very* important around here! Ring up Kitchen and tell them to get the lead out. I've got some PR work to do." He patted his walkie-talkie. "Don't be a stranger."

Mudhead watched darkly as his boss scampered down the slope. Vane marched across his dirt Square and stopped pointedly in the marked-off abutting Street, then turned to wave while gesturing proudly at his neighboring Square. Mudhead did not return the wave. After a minute he began snapping out instructions. As soon as he was done he sank into his chair and reached for a humongous pair of headphones.

This was a major moment for the incongruous, freely perspiring American. Though his long-anticipated approach was perfectly nonchalant, his new neighbors crept backward a step for every pace, finally huddling under their lonely scarecrow of a Canopy. Their Square also contained an affronted-looking camel, a reclining long-horned cow, and one of the scrawniest mongrels Vane had ever seen. The camel stank from ten feet away.

Having crossed the Street template, he smiled politely and pointed down at the aluminum tube that was the Square's temporary southern border. "May I?" he tried. The family, a man, woman, and two children, grinned back nervously and clung that much tighter. After pantomiming opening a door, Vane gingerly stepped over the tube and strolled up, feeling like a visitor from another planet. He crouched casually, forearm resting on extended knee.

It was his first real close-up of an Afar group. Fleshless as they were, they didn't look nearly as moribund as he'd predicted. Skins presented an unexpected glow. Eyes were clear, teeth bright and strong.

Vane was absolutely stumped by the encounter's awkwardness. His fantasies had always included a kind of mute rapport; a toasty-warm exchange of sign language accompanied by spontaneous expressions of human universality. He now saw himself as a profound anomaly: a trespasser, a white ogre. And his great big plastic grin was killing him. The family, smiling back uncertainly, compressed itself further and avoided his eyes. Terribly embarrassed, Vane straightened slowly, turned like an automaton, and found himself nose-to-nose with the family's camel. The beast roared in his face. No funkier stench had ever, could ever...Vane threw his hands over his face and stumbled out of the Square. The gaunt dog ran circles round his feet, nipping furiously.

He staggered across the Street into his own Square, retching and slapping dust from his face. Once he'd caught his breath he blew a string of oaths into his walkie-talkie.

The dour figure of Mudhead rose behind his microphone like a white-swathed praying mantis. *"Yes, Bossman?"*

"For Christ's sake, wake up, Mudhead! Tell Kid we'll need all the Runners down here, and pronto! He's got to get the Crew hustling if we're ever gonna get the Grid mapped out! Hop! Hop! Acknowledged?"

Two embers flashed behind the mic. There was the longest pause. At last the African switched channels and began barking orders.

In less than a minute Kid came swaggering up, a long ratty emu's feather trailing from a rag tied around his forehead. He grinned conspiratorially and copied Vane's posture.

Vane slowly shook his head and raised his walkie-talkie. "What's Kid's problem?"

"Kid big man now. Kid Bossman number Two. Feather show rank."

"Tell him it's gorgeous. But there is no hierarchy in Mamuset. His position as Lead Officer is an honor, and nothing else. There is no higher status involved."

Mudhead switched back. Vane and Kid listened to the Operation Manager's flurry of Saho snapping from the radio. It was all Greek to Vane, but it made Kid's expression fall. In the next second the youngster's disappointed look had rebounded to the typical Afar toothy grin. He bowed deeply, plucked the feather from the rag, handed it to Vane. Vane, accepting, smiled and bowed in return. "Tell him," he said into his walkie-talkie, "that paleface will give it a place of honor on the Stage." Kid listened closely to the translation. He bowed even deeper. "And now tell him to cut it out. I feel like the freaking Queen of England.

"The important thing is to get rolling! *Try* to not get bogged down in details when you're hinting at the Big Picture, relatively speaking. O-*kay*, Mudhead? Also, make *sure* you explain the significance of Utility Squares. But keep it simple. Just say they're non-proprietary intermediate nexus communally appropriated in the service of Sector Quads, and leave it at that. Don't get into the math of it. Enlighten Kid on the Grid master plan, so he'll know where Utility Squares belong. Stay glued to Eyes, man, and if anything gets out of sync, *please* ring me right up. But we've got to get the whole goddamned Grid *down*, and without getting people bent out of shape because they're relocating Shade Canopies, or because maybe they feel they're being eighty-sixed off what they supposed was their duly-granted turf. Stress *patience*, Mudhead! Let them know they're not being shuffled indifferently. But for the love of God, don't bully them! All right? Just tell them their grievances will be addressed as soon as the dust settles."

"No problem..." Mudhead heaved a sigh *"... Boss-man!"* He stamped his foot and shouted, *"Now!"* The feedback's scream prefaced an electronic echo that tightened every tympanic membrane within earshot. *"For once Bossman clam up! For once Bossman listen! Then Bossman clam up more!*

"Everyman now Mamusetman! Mamusetman do what Bossman say. No riot. No lawsuit. No democratman Mamuset. Noman have whiteman right! Mamusetman dog. Feed Mamusetman, respect Mamusetman, Mamusetman stay, Mamusetman eat heart anyman threaten Bossman. Okay? Be good Bossman,

make Mamuset great house, no worry thing. Kick Mamusetman, cuss Mamusetman blue. Mamusetman respect Bossman, Mamusetman love Bossman." He coughed from the tension. *"Easy math."*

A full minute passed before Vane could get himself together. Every eye in the house was on him.

"Bossman?"

Vane cleared his throat. "10-4, Number Two," he said calmly. "But I'm going to spare the boot. Not my style...now, let's tackle this damned Grid! What's your read up there?"

Mudhead matched Vane's heavy minute with steely poise before casually eyeballing the vicinity. *"Total ninety-one basic complete Square Frame around Bossman Square. Hereman work, thereman work, everyman work, work. Someman lay Square Frame right, otherman walk wild side. All canopy up."*

"Ninety-one Square Frames!" Vane exulted. "All right! Only four thousand, nine hundred and nine to go! But instead of celebrating, we're gonna get humping. Mudhead, order Kid to follow your instructions to the letter. I'm staking my Square, and I want you right on that microphone, man; first describing my actions for nearby Squares, then switching to walkie-talkie. Translate explicitly into Saho for Kid: he'll have to dictate to all Runners. There'll be a pause after each step as he gives orders. During that pause you'll have to make sure through the Eyes that all hitches are reported back and resolved before anything gets hairy." Vane almost staggered under the load. "I can't do everything! Make sure Kid knows he's got to get on his horse. I want him running Square to Square supervising."

This command was pretty much unnecessary. Kid stamped around him in a tight circle, champing at the bit. Whenever Vane spoke his name the boy nearly jumped out of his skin with anticipation.

"Big doctor call, Bossman."

"Tell him I'm busy. It's not an emergency, or he'd be all over it."

"Lady Honey call."

"Denise? Jesus. Don't tell me she's worked out a direct through Addis Ababa..." He gave a negative sweep of the arm. "Pull the plug on that damned radio. No, wait, wait! Tell her I'll get back to her."

A look of deep resentment pleated Mudhead's brow. The expression was recognizable to Vane forty feet below and two hundred feet away.

"I'm sorry, Mudhead. I realize you didn't sign up for this. Just wing it; blow her off. Play Dumb Africaman, or say whatever'll get rid of her. I promise this won't become a regular thing. But right now we've *got* to get going! And remind me in the future to bring a pocketful of sugar cubes for Kid." His eyes lit up. "On second thought, put Denise through to Doctor 'Lijah." He rubbed his palms together. "Let's see if we can work a little magic."

Vane dragged Kid over to Stage Street, where the youngster began dancing and snorting like a boxer, waiting only a nudge. Vane held him back while Mudhead's basic directions came over the radio. Once schooled, Kid bounced Runner to Runner, shoving, shouting, and gesticulating madly. The Runners scattered like chickens.

"No gold bricks here!" Vane called delightedly. "Let's have us a look."

He climbed back up to the Stage, turning an ankle on the way. "Make a note, my friend. We're gonna have to cut us some Steps."

Mudhead bent to his Eyes. After a weighty silence he said tentatively, "Mamuset great big pie. Endless..." he mumbled, searching for the apt phrase, "...endless little neighbor tribe."

"One big tribe," Vane countered. "But in a way you're right." He peered through his own instrument. "Amigo, I'm guessing this whole concept must still seem pretty strange to you. But it's really important, to a Western man's way of thinking, to have everything organized and accounted for. Not only that; to *my* way of thinking it has to be both organized and *fair*.

"And as far as great big pies go...well, this operation isn't exactly on a budget, but the projected cost is staggering. In the months since my father died I've had to work it all out mathematically, with the Honey Foundation cutting every corner. So it's not about having some great big money bin I can just draw on to my heart's content. It's a tug of war with Honey all the way. That's what the call from Denise'll be about. You see, Mudhead, Honey has to mollify clients while it's funding this operation. We're leaking the word that Cristian Vane is involved in natural gas and bauxite sites in Ghana and Sierra Leone. That way the clients will think, hopefully, that all this money I'm going through will pay off in the long run. If nothing else, we're buying time"

Mudhead grunted. "So America moneyman pretty scared."

"Nah. They're hip to checks and balances. Banks all around the world rely on the Foundation staying healthy, so keeping me and the old Vane Empire strong and happy is just good business. Banke Internationale, with the commitment they've made, would fold in no time if Honey withdrew. That would be a small domino, but a domino nonetheless, and there are a gazillion enterprises that stand or fall on the Foundation. Honey is technically politically neutral, but it bends with the wind; supplying warring nations with arms, petroleum, grain, and pharmaceuticals. Karl, the man who was the vital link between Father and Honey, once told me that the Foundation could control the turns of power in Eurasia by way of coup, gas, bread, or overdose. Father himself, in his final senile years, knew nothing. All he could do was veto by power of insanity. And he expected me to get sucked into all that. Phew!"

Vane grinned goofily. "Okay, so I lied! There isn't a cloud in our financial sky. Mudhead...do you *realize*—do you have any idea—what a *billion* dollars can do? It's an almost unimaginable sum. A farsighted man with only a *million* dollars, in this part of the world, can live a long, obscene life. He can buy businesses. He can equip a private army. He can well-nigh topple a government if he applies his time, energy, and wealth wisely. And *still* retire rich, without having invested a birr!

"A billionaire can do that a thousand times over. He can have all he wants, and he can have it whenever he wants it. He can drive himself—he can rise early and buy everything in sight as fast as he can, and still die an old man with more money than he could ever count."

Vane decompressed a chestful of stress. "I'm worth *ele-*

ven and a half billion dollars, man." He raised a hand. "I say this not to impress you with my wealth. I only want you to understand the uniqueness of our position.

"I can order whatever I desire, and not have to take its cost into account. Add to this the fact that I have an organization behind me getting the best deals possible, steered by a very savvy lady who, for some reason, has decided to bend to my every whim, and you get a pretty round idea of our situation. A hedonist's fantasy, an accountant's nightmare."

"And Bossman?"

"And a bossman's opportunity."

Mudhead, standing erect, asked uncomfortably, "Opportunity how? Mudahid Asafu-Adjaye never ask, Daddy Bigbuck never tell." His arms embraced the crater. "Master Bossman?"

Vane cocked his head. "No...more like a self-contained community, I guess." He too stood erect. "Hey, man. Just what are you driving at?"

Mudhead shrugged and bent back to his Eyes. "Bossman could be king," he mumbled. "Maybe king all planet."

"Tell you what. The position's yours if you want it. I can make it happen. How'd you like to be king of the planet?"

Mudhead shook his head vigorously. "Mudahid still try figure Mamuset."

"Then you're a wise man, Mudhead. Let's keep it all close to home." He copied the African's stoop, and said through his teeth, "As soon as the Grid's down we can start moving upward, instead of just outward."

Mudhead made no reply. After a long minute Vane unbent slowly. "What the hell do you mean, 'Master'?" Mudhead didn't budge. Vane stumbled down to his Square and assembled his Core group. He used gestures to communicate while roughing up and leveling his foundation with shovel and hoe. Extensions were removed. Lunch came and went. Vane got back to Waters who, now in command of a bridged link to Mamuset, had been guaranteed unmolested transmissions by both Ethiopia and her warring neighbor Eritrea. Vane was expecting a lecture. Instead he received much-needed encouragement and a birthday greeting.

"I didn't...realize," he stammered, his mind fogging.

"Well. *Thanks*, Denise. Um...how old *am* I?"

"You're thirty, Cris. A good age."

"A good age."

Dead air. "See you later, sweetheart. If you don't keep in touch, I will." Waters kissed into the mouthpiece. "Many more."

Vane turned and found himself face to face with Mudhead. "Don't say it," he warned. "I don't get it either." Expressionless, Mudhead popped in a CD, put on his headphones, and kicked back in his favorite chair. Half a minute later his eyelids were fluttering.

A fresh convoy arrived at four. Crew removed thousands of stacked aluminum slats, along with endless bundles of white-painted pine stakes. Also trucked in were spoon-stacked wheelbarrows of forty-gallon capacity, stamped with Sector, Quadrant, and Square numbers. Included in wheelbarrow kits were shovels and pickaxes, rakes and hoes, mallets, workman's gloves, and bandanas. Each article was stamped and tagged: Sector, Quadrant, Square.

That night Vane reclined on a huge mound of packing under a sky black and richly lit, watching the flicker of families in the floodlights' haze. Chopin's Polonaise stomped and staggered behind him, playing tag with the mantra running round and round in his head: *Sector, Quadrant, Square.* He popped another beer and saluted the hot raven sky. From where he sat a man could dream of changing the world.

Vane had been led to believe, by every specialist he'd as much as shared a smoke with, that his crude attempts to change Mamuset would entail months of false starts, frustrating digressions, and bungled attempts at cooperation. So he was astounded to see the Grid expand like magic; sometimes the Afar seemed psychic. Lot-chosen supervisors, holding court in newly-cluttered Utility Squares, regally distributed numbered supplies to eagerly queuing Afar men. Excited boys cut a wide line of Steps up the Mount from Stage Street, then delightedly cemented the staircase over. Along with the inevitable footprints, handprints, and finger swirls, the wet cement received a long series of exotic designs created by old men furnished only with pallet splinters and hyperopic imaginations.

On the morning of the third day Vane and his neighbors replaced their aluminum Square Frames with white stakes pounded at guide-marks scored every twelve inches. The CO sat marveling on Top Step while the immediate area was rapidly and collectively staked off into a series of clearly definable Streets and Squares. The remaining aluminum Grid-skeleton, tighter and truer than he had any right to expect, spread all the way to the Rim.

By noon Crew numbered over seventeen hundred members. These men, young and old, were put to work digging Street ditches for the project's underground system of fresh water-and drainage pipes. PVC sections, still arriving on flatbeds, measured eight inches in diameter for Fields, six inches for Streets. Crew worked from the Mount outward as Extensions were removed, ripping ditches down the centers of Streets. Aluminum Square Frames were inexorably replaced by a solidly visual stakes Grid.

Watching an Afar with a pick and shovel was a mindboggling experience. The men worked sunup to sundown, intoxicated by the assembly line mentality; some racing waist-deep down Street trenches, some obsessively transforming Squares from metal-frame outlines to stake-dotted sketches in the dust-dry earth. Pine swept away aluminum in a growing frenzy. Everywhere you looked, it was all flying dirt; from Top Step the crater floor appeared under assault by gophers on amphetamines. Unlike Vane, who grew exhausted just watching, the unfit and quarantined men almost went out of their minds observing their fellows at work; at Warehouse even the elderly and infirm fought over spare and broken tools. Kid was the world's most obnoxious foreman, shouting himself hoarse, demanding and receiving the impossible from everyone in his path. He must have crisscrossed the crater floor a dozen times.

By late afternoon the Awash pipeline's great multi-armed breakdown unit, *West Comb*, was being bolted and sealed by Vane's engineers at West Rim's steel-reinforced Inner Slope. A corresponding series of descending *subcombs* lay in place, each successive subcomb's conduits, or *teeth*, having diameters decreased by half. A grid of cemented pipe lengths was waiting in ditches, Ridge-to-Rim. In the Fields, hordes of filthy, joyous men and women, as per Mudhead's eagerly-passed instructions, were busily cementing vertical PVC shoots into lines every ten feet, even as competing families, now accustomed to the copy-cat method, installed Laterals and Uprights in their Squares in what seemed the blink of an eye. Vane could barely keep up with his immediate neighbors. But he continued gamely shouting instructions into his walkie-talkie, dangling from his neck like a pendant with its transmit switch taped open, though fresh water lines were being laid down west-east Streets almost before he could get the words out. Engineers and volunteers quickly patched these lines to a comb on one end, capped and valved their Uprights in Square centers on the other. Parallel sewage lines were positioned directly on the heels of the fresh water lines, without a hitch or a bitch. Vane was staggered. Before the sun had set the system was all but completed.

Mamuset would take advantage of the Danakil's gentle easterly slope; all outflow would be centralized at Delta's East Comb, a breakdown unit identical to the fixture on West Rim. Used, contaminated, and otherwise unwanted water would be channeled out into the deep desert, where the water would soon evaporate and its particulates bake into dust. On the fourth day the Afar worked back toward the middle, measuring levels and inspecting joins, packing dirt round the lines, burying the system and rebuilding Streets. Just at dusk, the Reservoir was stress-tested and engaged. That night, under a gibbous moon, the soil of Mamuset had its first drink in years.

The fifth day found Vane and Mudhead eyeballing the site from Gondar's little mail plane. Vane's chessboard stared back up at him, fully mapped-out, each white-dotted section with its own tiny mushroom canopy. And on that chessboard thousands of black ants were hard at work, breaking up and turning their Squares' moistened earth with shovels and hoes. Not a man snuck a break. There were no loiterers, no pockets of loafing pals. Even the smallest children were hard into it, dragging parcels and crates from Dock to Warehouse like plainsmen hauling slain antelopes. The tiny plane's confines were almost unbearably tight. Mudhead, on the window, looked down with his trademark stoneface, squirming every time Vane brushed against him for a better look. The stubborn young American came *this* close to admitting he'd sold the Africans short.

And on that fifth day Crew completed their prepping of the crater's floor. By now all Sectors were cooperating via Utility Quads; the site's abundant water supply made cement-mixing possible at the thousands of individual Squares.

It was a big day for Vane, the day he'd dreamt of since that bleak moment he'd come to his senses on his father's hard crypt floor, weeping from nightmares of dead black babies in the dirt. In the wholesome muscularity of subsequent fantasies, he became the quintessential bronzed demigod, perfecting his model Square foundation with the patience of a saint and the intensity of a blacksmith. But no matter how willing the spirit, nothing in his dreams or training prepared him for this brutal task. Still he toughed it out, hour after agonizing hour, unable to bear the prospect of failing in public. He badly strained his back digging his foundation's foot-deep, 20 x 20 space, came up with a major groin pull, and twice almost collapsed from heat exhaustion.

Gasping horribly, a nearly delirious Vane forced in his excavation's four locking aluminum retaining walls, weaving on his blistered hands and knees, every joint on fire. And, though his gloved hands were raw and bleeding, though his thighs and underarms were badly chafed, he nevertheless summoned the cojones to align and lock the walls' corner post guides. His neighbors bent over backwards to drag along in time, but they were frustrated, champing at the bit...unintentionally mimicking him as he clung like a drunk to a propped-up, barely-vertical steel corner post...anticipating his moves, far too quickly, as he demonstrated assessing verticality with a plumb line. But once he'd found his second wind he showed all those impatient sons of bitches just how cleverly a steady-as-they-came Westerner could make critical adjustments on upright posts using only simple shims...showed them how they, too, could bolt down perforated steel corner posts if the damned cement ever set...showed them how a proud white man, out of his element and wheezing like a middle-aged marathoner, could still focus—how he could, no matter how tough the going, still manage the breath to explain, even with that pitiless black bastard's pushy translation searing out of U.Q. speakers, the

correct placement of these bruising roof posts...cross posts...
how the freaking corner posts' holes *would* accept a completed
domicile's foot-wide, twenty-foot-long aluminum "gills," and
how those gills could be opened manually and locked in place,
allowing the domicile, which was basically a one-room, four
hundred square-foot aluminum cabin, to, *finally*, "breathe."

Domiciles, explained a haggard Vane, or *Domos*, would
face south, allowing their roofs' sloping solar panels to take
maximum advantage of the sun. These panels would generate
enough energy to power a Domo's ceiling fan, and charge house
batteries with sufficient juice to burn four twelve-volt lights
over a twelve-hour period.

Vane now tottered to his Canopy and came down hard
on the mat, every muscle seizing, his back and neck in serious
pain. It was all he could do to recline regally, and to fan himself
without looking effete. But his performance was already old
news. In Core Squares Afar men were digging and locking with
delight, shoveling dirt in and out excitedly, begging neighbors
for a chance to contribute. Flung dirt arced through the air like
streamers.

Under a straight, tight Canopy next door, Mudhead sat
in a bored slump, duly facing Mecca while thrilled youngsters
dug out his foundation's space. Vane groaned to his feet and
grabbed his Upright's hose. Held it over his head. Turned on the
spigot. He howled with pain and shot out of his Square—the
water was scalding. Vane kept running, all the way up to Top
Step, where he fell back in his favorite chair under the Big Tarp.
He cracked open a well-deserved, lukewarm beer.

The odd mix of Afar work ethics—cooperative and
competitive—made the scene below a fast-forwarded 3D movie. He slowly shook his head as finished workers, pacing their
Squares in anguish, broke to assist their neighbors' neighbors.
Others, beaten to the punch, returned to desperately rake and re-
rake their own Squares. For half a minute Vane hated the Afar
almost as much as he hated himself. He forced himself up and
peered through his Eyes.

Nothing but unbridled excitement. Folks were running
like spiders, in and out of nearly completed foundation excavations. Experimenting men and boys, having fitted stray gills

into adjacent propped-up corner posts, were tweaking and spinning those gills intently. Again Vane was struck by their innate cleverness. He panned Sectors. The entire field was well-mapped and ready to go. Pickups, moving up nicely-aligned Streets, were dropping off stacks of gills to impetuous Afar. Other trucks transported eagerly-unloaded bags of cement. Vane leaned on his tripod; one useless Stage prop on another.

Mudhead was the crater's only other inactive party. Exhausted by all these clamoring children, he could only glare and mumble orders, stuffed in a Square resembling more a playground than a work site. His worn-out old eyes caught the gleam of Vane's mounted binoculars, trained dead on him. Staring back glumly, he made the old throat-slitting gesture with a forefinger. Vane cursed the vile day they'd met before hobbling down the Steps, his Core neighbors watching like dogs waiting for a ball to be tossed. He dragged Mudhead up to translate, then painfully galloped back down. He began blending cement and water in his wheelbarrow, pausing to carefully describe each step over his walkie-talkie. Mudhead's kids went wild with excitement.

Once he'd plugged his guides with dummy posts, Vane stirred, poured, and spread his cement. It was grueling work, almost as tough as the digging, but a kind of giddiness produced by the heat pushed him on—leveling, dousing, and smoothing—to the imaginary cheers of an engrossed and grateful crowd. Vane's cement foundation, under the fierce East African sun, was fully set in an hour, and that hour's rest, along with sufficient shade and irrigation, was enough to get him back in the saddle. Instructing with great care, he righted a corner post in its guide, checked and rechecked it with his plumb line, knocked in a pair of shims, and bolted the post in tight. His final check passed with flying colors. Vane wobbled around proudly.

Corner posts were popping up all over the place, a dozen in the wink of an eye. The bastards were racing him! In one Square a knight's move away, an elderly man already had three set up and was reaching for his fourth. Vane immediately scooped up his remaining three and ran puffing around his Square, plunging the posts in their guides, pounding in shims and bolts. After cursory checks for verticality, he ran dragging a twenty-foot steel roof post while barking out instructions for installation. He kicked his folding footstool to a foundation corner, but by the time he had the little aluminum monster in place a neighbor had already installed his first roof post and was excitedly eyeballing the next.

Vane bashed his knuckles raw and almost pinched off a finger tightening down his first roof post. He hung from the post for a few seconds before dropping to his foundation like a dead man, only to find that his surrounding Squares already had all four posts bolted in place. All his neighbors were squatting in a hard circle, watching; hyperactive children forced to sit still. And it hit him: taking his sweet time was his best defense. No one could copy the undemonstrated. Likewise, Mudhead couldn't translate without instructions. Vane dawdled with his roof frame, then took a good long smoke break before bolting in his cross posts with exaggerated care. He droned on and on over his walkie-talkie, pissing off Mudhead and confusing the hell out of his neighbors. Vane watched yawning while volunteers drove Square to Square; dropping off photoelectric panels, deep-cycle batteries, fan motors and blades, picking up crusty wheelbarrows for Utility Square washings.

He lit another cigar, casually toured his perimeter. From three sides of his foundation, he could peer down strange tunnels of Domo frames, seeing which posts were absolutely vertical and which required alignment. Most were dead-on. A fair measure of conceit helped fuel his stately, cigar-chomping march halfway up the Mount's eastern slope, but it wasn't enough to take him to the top. On one footfall like any other his entire body cramped up on him. Vane went down hard on his face. He writhed in the dirt like an epileptic until a small herd of doctors got their mitts on him. They irrigated and fanned him, kneaded his muscles and joints, crammed tongue depressors in his mouth. After a buzzing confab, he was ported to his foundation like a battlefield casualty. There Mudhead, having ordered everyone within earshot to hang mats from the Square's roof posts for shade, spread Vane out face-down in the dirt. He placed all his weight on the man's arched back, deaf to his howls.

"Boss...man...hold...*still!*" He hauled back on the

shoulders until Vane thought his arms would be torn from their sockets. Vane screamed like a woman while Mudhead balanced one foot on the back of his neck and the other on the small of his spine. The African placed an unopened bottle of beer in front of Vane's twisted face. "Bossman bite this." He pushed his way outside. In a few minutes Vane heard the famous *Tick* ...Tock...*Tick*...Tock...of the Chambers Brothers' psychedelic masterpiece *Time Has Come Today*, coming full-blast from the Stage speakers. Just as the interlude's scream fest began, Mudhead stepped back inside and grabbed an arm and leg. "*Now* Bossman holler."

That night the Afar slept on cement floors for the first time, using their former homes' hides as mats. While they were still up, conversing, Mudhead borrowed swarms of children to build Vane a sprawling bed of packing, hides, and blankets. When they were gone he stuffed Vane's face in those blankets and got back to work on him. The humbled master of Mamuset spent half the night on his back, absolutely motionless, staring at a shrinking candle.

When he woke it was way light. The computer had automatically opened the day with Strauss, over an hour ago, and Kitchen had already served breakfast; his own full Bowl and a mug of coffee were perched on his foundation's tilted lip. He'd never felt so limber, never so refreshed. Crossing his foundation was like walking on air. Vane pulled aside a pair of mats to greet the new day. He was astonished; in that single hour the unsupervised Afar had assembled their Domos from the ground up. Stretching across the crater's floor was a vast community of topless aluminum boxes.

They were not, however, identical boxes. Domos' gills are continuous only on two sides. Post extensions on the southern face produce a doorway requiring shorter gills, the northern face uses gills with louver-window inserts, along with a bottom gill designed to accept fresh water-and sewage pipes. The Afar could not have known this. Parts had been shuffled and traded experimentally; results were all over the place. But Vane, by ordering reassembly, bought plenty of time to properly set up his own gills. He was elated to have the first Mamuset Domo with walls correctly faced. Vane strutted in and out of his doorway while his neighbors cheered maniacally. Those cheers spread like wildfire. After a while even the most distant Afar, without the least idea why, were kicking up their heels.

Vane thereupon, while balancing on his folding ladder, bolted up his triangular north and south roof braces and face plates, horizontal spire post, eave ribs, and solar panels. Eventually guards, rather like inverted gutters, would be fitted across the roofs' spires, and protective strips snapped over channels between joined solar panels. Vane knew that someday rain would again find the Danakil. His brainchild would be ready.

At high noon he was hard at work inside a strange aluminum cabin, describing his actions over his walkie-talkie while he ran wires from solar panels to the fan motor bolted at the cross posts' junction. Vane screwed in the blades, wired the battery into the loop, and flicked the motor's switch. The blades began their gentle revolution. It wasn't much, but it was circulation. And once he'd locked open his Domo's gills the effect was heavenly.

The Afar whispered and tiptoed late into the night, though Vane slept with the dead. In a haze of moonlight they silently tore down and rebuilt their new homes, opened and closed doors, repeatedly walked inside and out. Thousands of gills whispered up and down in an odd communal Morse. Then, one by one, Domos threw out long slats of twelve-volt light, until the burgeoning desert oasis glowed like a little pool of stars.

Chapter Nine

Franco

For both Mudhead and Vane, the next day was an exasperating challenge in cooperation and translation. The dynamic functions of foot pumps and valves, the very Western concepts of aluminum sinks and stainless steel toilets—these were profoundly mysterious to the nomadic Afar. Measurements and tolerances required clarification in depth. For Vane it was frustrating, claustrophobic work; assembling parts by memory, repeatedly yelling instructions through his gills. Though he fiercely cursed Mudhead's penchant for garbling the CO's critical commands, and inwardly blessed the Afar's inherent call to mimicry, he still found room for hope and self-congratulation: the circulation created by his fan was nothing short of life-saving.

Folding partitions created compact toilet stalls, defined by Vane with considerable embarrassment. Arriving on that same run were loads of heavy foam padding, along with mountains of carpet pieces. Vane took his pick first, favoring solids in earth tones. He demonstrated from the Stage; unrolling and re-rolling a pad, layering carpet pieces like throw rugs to produce a civilized softness underfoot. The Afar, nodding and murmuring appreciatively, quietly stepped back inside their Domos, re-spectfully laid their pads and pieces, carefully covered them over with dirt.

Next came *Yards*: oblong Square divisions still marked off by stakes. Using smaller lattice guides, a Square's Yard could be subdivided into 10 x 10 corner squares for a coop, a hutch, a pen, and a camel pad. Other folding guides measured off rectangular side patches for the Square's gardens, both vege-table and flower. A south-side lattice produced a walkway and front yard, the north-side lattice a backyard and cooking/dining area. Any given Square's fence might be picket, chain link, sim-ple hedge, or whatever the resident's imagination could pro-duce. Or no fence at all. It was an aesthetic, not a security, concern. There would be no crime in Mamuset.

Once he had Squares up and running, Vane delivered a grueling series of lectures on micronutrients, tilling, and irriga-tion, commencing every morning directly after Strauss. Fields were sectioned for corn, tubers, beans, alfalfa, millet, and *teff*, a native grain. The chessboard effect was retained. And though Vane at times could be brutal in his grudging test of the com-munal will, the Afar just ate up his demands and begged for more. So he gave them more. To decrease the crater's salt con-tent, backbreaking applications of lime were instituted, coupled with diligent soil-turning and near-continuous flushings of Fields west of the Ridge. Vane kept waking expecting an up-rising. But each morning he found the Afar scrambling for the crippling privilege of hoeing hundreds of rows east to west. The dog was walking its master.

The project's first real hitch came on a morning like any other, after only a few short weeks of work. Calisthenics were completed. Breakfast, come and gone. Vane had *finally* conclu-ded his lectures on the multiplication tables, proper civil com-portment in a free society, and the great vitamin E controversy, with Mudhead's usual sarcastic mistranslations snapping from every Utility Square speaker. The relieved Afar, tools in hands, were scurrying off to Fields.

But on that otherwise typical, searing morning, the primary convoy arrived late, light, and manned by an evasive company of belligerent drivers. There was no excuse for it; by now the route from Massawa to Mamuset was entirely serviceable. And no matter how many times Mudhead tried to solve the mystery of the missing cargo, all he got was a raucous demand for cash up front and the promise of a broken jaw if he didn't quit snooping. The CO kept him at it until the drivers threatened to split with their loads intact. Vane had to take them seriously—light or not, almost a day's worth of food was at stake.

A call to Addis Ababa got him nowhere. And Honey, through 'local' contact Tibor, would only report unspecified difficulties in Port Massawa. Warehouses were non-responsive. When he stormed back to Dock, Vane found the drivers ganged around a stock-still Mudhead, chorusing their demand with mounting hostility. He pressed to his friend's side, and the ring closed round behind him. Through Mudhead and a series of universal hand gestures, Vane explained that he carried only petty cash, and that payroll operated out of a Massawa warehouse. The drivers turned away, preparing to make good their threat. Vane's very unmanly squeal of protest bought a minute. The men turned back. Vane studied the dozens of tractor trailers. Tons and tons of dried and frozen foods were in the balance. He thereupon offered, on his signature, double pay in Massawa if the men would only leave their loads behind. Their response was clear enough: they weren't planning a return to Massawa any time soon. Not only that, they didn't believe Vane for a second. Again with the ultimatum: cash in dollars American, in the fist and on the spot. The noose continued to tighten. A low growling sound, which Vane first supposed came from a refrigerator trailer, swirled out of a looming line of spiky shadows surrounding the drivers.

The Afar appeared to glide as they multiplied. Their common growl rose slowly, in pitch and in intensity, like a ring of cellos ascending in legato half steps. At last Vane cried out *"Stop!"* and threw his arms high. The sound cut off immediately, but the crowd's hundred eyes continued to glare. Vane hollered, *"Kid!"*

The youngster shot through the ring like a projectile,

142

dancing in circles, head down and fists clenched.

"Mudhead! Tell Kid he's in charge until we get back! We're gonna go find out what the hang-up is. You tell him to get Crew busy unloading these trucks...*now!*" He spat at the nearest driver's feet. "Then tell these reptiles they can pick up their walking papers in Massawa!"

Vane cockily strutted up to Isis while Mudhead translated. He fired her up, tore round in a tight circle, and braked emphatically. The African climbed in with decorum and braced himself. The Land Rover took off like a comet with a burning-rubber tail.

The fifty-mile stretch to Massawa did nothing for Vane; all his bluster and bravado were quickly replaced by funk and defeatism. The problem slammed his back against an imaginary wall. Before a single fact was in he knew he'd failed. Knew it.

It was a good thing he'd carried his inheritance to the desert, far from cameras and gold diggers. He'd never have handled the pressures of power and responsibility; his head would have exploded. And he'd have taken a whole lot of people down with him. Arguably a bad thing. And, after he'd blown, the rags would have reassembled the pieces to produce that insatiable egomaniac the public demanded—an ill-mannered, lecherous, walking time bomb triggered by a final play of soured greed. Tinsel starlets and cast-iron henchmen would have materialized, singing lurid tales of the pampered heir's physical and psychological abuses.

Better to live apart from all that. Better to forget. Better to be forgotten.

Mudhead watched his racing boss nodding with naked misery. He clung to the bucking Rover and smiled grimly, knowing that, all else notwithstanding, Vane was going to die an African.

Massawa, an ancient commercial port with a light military flow, was nothing like the place they'd worked out of only three weeks ago. Now the hills were crawling with earth-moving equipment, preparing what looked to be a series of battlements. A new airstrip flickered in the rising morning heat, her twin radar dishes mooning the sky. The rest of the place stank of decaying municipal control; in the trash piled along the major road's sides, in the abandoned cars and trucks looted of batteries and radios, in the new potholes and drooping power lines. Where once the harbor possessed an easy, almost sanguine ambience, there now existed a very ominous military presence. Jeeps full of hot-dogging black Muslims roared past, trying to goose a reaction out of Vane. Each soldier wore fatigues and combat boots, a camouflage Muslim headpiece, and very dark glasses. In addition, some wore streaming multicolored robes, flak jackets, and miscellaneous military paraphernalia of unfamiliar vintage and origin. All sported Uzis or shotguns, and looked far more like street thugs than soldiers. By contrast Vane looked sporty and naïve, Mudhead almost officious. They were the good boys on the wrong side of the tracks.

Nearer the water, Eritrean army vehicles monitored traffic by holding flow to a crawl in both directions. Civilians were halted with a randomness that appeared deliberately contemptuous; the roving sentries took particular delight in detaining the Land Rover, and in thoroughly checking and rechecking Vane's papers.

Eritrea's retaking of the Red Sea coast had deprived Ethiopia of her navy; at present, these seized Ethiopian ships were commanded by officers of Eritrea's army. Except for a narrow sea corridor, Massawa's commercial port was completely obstructed.

Several small aid-ships were locked in solid with the old Ethiopian naval vessels—they'd been immobilized for over two weeks (help for the sick and starving was dead in the water: the ethical distribution of humanitarian aid in East Africa, of little interest during peace, is of no interest whatever during war).

But a deep front existed. In fact, ships bearing the aid of major democracies were escorted up and down that narrow corridor with great ceremony. Their cargoes were unloaded, signed for, and warehoused. These stored wares were then divided and subdivided by Army officers and competing lords of crime. What did get through to relief organizations (mainly harried mobile distribution groups virtually cut off from facts and figures) was a miserable fraction of that reaching the fatted lips of Eritrean officers, and the fatting coffers of organized crime. While there was a perpetual outcry of disappointment and sus-

picion at the chain's far end, those groups doing the actual feeding and medicating believed aid was at an abysmal low due to
losses caused by conflict, rather than hush and piracy.

Port Massawa's ugly amalgam of crime and police had
produced a dank bully culture; in this world corruption was not
merely commonplace, it was the cornerstone and standard. Islam was a shadow; prostitution and murder were open means of
barter and resolution. No one questioned a thing, no one imagined questioning a thing. The government supported the port
by allowing it to remain open under military authority, and the
military supported the economy by regulating the flow of seized
tobacco, alcohol, and pharmaceuticals. Used syringes floated in
raw sewage amid cigarette butts and broken liquor bottles.
Massawa, once the jewel of Red Sea ports, had almost over-
night become a Third world ghetto, infested with every modern
disease the area could support. Yet in the hills there remained o-
ases, sheltered from the filth and misery, where the more successful bosses kept up retinues of Chinese gardeners and Turkish chefs. On these estates Eritrean officers and kingpins com-
petitively expanded their stables of whores, sycophants, and
spies.

Vane and Mudhead stuck out like sore thumbs in all this
squalor. The black Muslim sentries, standing loosely at intersections, were frankly contemptuous of the young driver's fairness, and of his elder partner's bleached robes and anal-reten-
tive appearance. They watched in eyeless appraisal; wearing
their ammo belts slung to the right in deference to Allah, doing
their sinning with the left hand alone.

Military vehicles seemed to come popping off assembly
lines as Isis approached the water. These vehicles' occupants
initially passed alongside with affected indifference. Then with
looks of hard inquisitiveness. Finally, with postures and expressions of outright hostility. Those black sunglasses were
everywhere. Vane and Mudhead faced straight ahead.

Harbor Massawa was a festering wound; a garbage-
covered pustule peppered with the rotting corpses of rats, cats,
and the occasional mongrel. Those ubiquitous gangster-soldiers
in fatigues and dark glasses fit right in. Jeeps full of them loi-
tered in subterranean drives and in the entrances to overgrown

alleys. Heads turned as one as the Land Rover rolled by.

A mile off the water was a barricade of worn military vehicles parked crosswise. Only one car at a time could be admitted. Vane put Isis in neutral.

"Not too late turn back," Mudhead said quietly, "Mister Vane." It was the first time he'd formally addressed his employer.

They listened to the hot engine. Finally Vane said, "It's always too late." Neither man moved.

A minute later Mudhead muttered, "Maybe Bossman right."

Vane, a tourist seeking landmarks, looked around casually. Two alleys back, a jeep crawled out of the shadows, hesitated.

"On right too."

A jeep crunched up on either side. Vane slowly turned his head to the left and stared poker-faced at the cold black masks with the impenetrable black glasses. An officer in the passenger seat said, in a thickly accented voice, "You will proceed to the checkpoint."

"We have clearance. We're civilian."

The man immediately stepped out and got in Vane's face. "You are *wrong*, sir. You have *zero* clearance here. You have entered a military zone in wartime. You are therefore under the jurisdiction of the Port's commanding officer. He alone determines affairs in Massawa."

Vane thrust out his chin. "I would speak with this commanding officer."

"This is already arranged. You are expected." Still staring Vane down, he said, "Proceed with this vehicle," and climbed back in.

Isis was escorted to the gap, where a gold Mercedes waited with engine humming. The Rover's doors were yanked open.

"No, not him. The American alone."

Mudhead was hauled out and smothered in a human knot. Before Vane could open his mouth he was flanked by four soldiers.

"I'll just be a minute," he said bravely. "No napping."

He walked close behind the officer, caught up in a tight crescent.

The man halted at the driver's door. After half a minute he stamped a boot. The car's rear door popped open, as though triggered by the concussion. The back was empty.

Vane slid across the seat. The officer shut the door firmly and leaned in his head. "There are alcohol and tobacco in that compartment. Indicate to the driver that you desire these things and he will flip a switch up front, releasing the compartment's door."

"Thank you."

"This automobile utilizes a very powerful air conditioning system, made necessary by our country's extreme temperature. The car's metal can become quite hot; at times even the glass will burn flesh. The deep coolness is for your protection, not for comfort. For this reason we require that all windows remain up. The doors will be locked for your safety." A pause. "Enjoy the drive. It is a short trip."

Vane stared straight ahead. The black face studied him curiously, withdrawing as the dark window hummed up. The door locked with a whisper. In half a minute the car's interior was a deep freeze.

The driver's head and shoulders did not invite conversation. The man wore no religious or military apparel, and stank of old sweat and cheap cologne. Half his left ear was missing. Vane sat back and stared out the window as the Mercedes quietly rolled toward Massawa's Old Harbor section.

His memories were of an idyllic montage, almost Mediterranean in feel. But now the harbor was a cesspool, dominated by what had to be the planet's largest, filthiest, and most decrepit three-island general-cargo ship, all set to burst at the seams. *Scheherazade* was a World War II eyesore, a fat mother hen wallowing in disrepair. Her name, acid-etched on the prow, incompletely obscured the ghost of her previous incarnation— *DEUT* was all Vane could decipher. Dozens of flagging derricks hung from her deck, leaning crazily over the holds and water, while seagulls swarmed about her like flies round a dog's mess, dropping their dull white thanks on her cargo and hull. The ship had not been cleaned in many, many years; below her mangled rail the white streaks of dung resembled icicles hanging from eaves. *Scheherazade*'s bridge had caved in from some past abuse of cargo, and was now a sad sagging shack with a soot-and-crap smokestack.

Vane mulled over his smashed bags and crates. Holds were overflowing with flour, rice, and fertilizer, parts and parcels poking up like flotsam. On deck, boxes and sacks were stacked willy-nilly, so that the tops of stacks formed a bumpy foundation for the next level. Everything was battened ingeniously; with ropes, with cables, with hoses and rags. Wide banks of flowing grain were intermixed with glacier-like drifts of bird dung and narrow dunes of fertilizer, the whole mess spilling across the deck into black holds and doorways. So grossly overladen was the ship that Vane could see only a narrow, zigzagging walkway between the heaving cliffs of cargo.

All around *Scheherazade,* Old Harbor lay festering; oily, stagnant, reeking with floating garbage. Gone were the typical rusting container ships, the native fishers, the tugs and transports. In their place were a dozen antique Eritrean naval vessels, slowly rocking with the tide. Docks were silent, overrun by strays and wharf rats. Contempt hung over everything; contempt for sanitation, contempt for life, contempt for the military, contempt for Eritrea. The camouflaged sentries were less conspicuous here; the ones Vane observed peering from cover were done balancing military protocol against energy expenditure. The heat always won. No man not an officer was willing to readily forsake shade unless addressing Mecca. So the black-eyed bogeymen, leaning half-out of shadows, watched insolently as the gold Mercedes passed, counting the days until the shiny prize would, by coup or subterfuge, be theirs.

Having spent most of the last five months in this section of Massawa, Vane was well aware they were headed for one of his principal warehouses. His blood rose when he finally made out the wide aluminum building, squatting deserted in the hanging sun. In a few minutes the driver pulled up to an open side door. The car's locks released.

Vane sat still. "Thanks again," he said quietly. The head did not turn.

When he stepped out the heat hit him like a haymaker. He kicked the door shut and the Mercedes pulled away.

Out of the frying pan and into the pressure cooker—Vane strolled through the warehouse's hot shadows, barely able to breathe, casting cursory glances left and right.

He'd been robbed.

The huge end fans were gone; torn from their stands. Split and reeking sacks of manure lay intermingled with torn bags of borax and manganese sulfate. A strange mustiness emanated from the mysteries behind looted shelves, where water or some other fluid had reacted with sulfates of zinc and copper. Vane casually probed an unfamiliar burlap bag with a forefinger. He leaned forward for a sniff. The texture was grainy, the smell neutral.

The warehouse's only innocuous features were two identical red leather barstools set on either side of a polished driftwood coffee table in an isolated pool of sallow light. A very stagy setting. Vane walked over and looked down. The table sported a sincere but lame spread of Americana: a six-pack of Coors long necks, a zinc-plated Zippo lighter perched on a fresh pack of Marlboros, a five-ounce bag of Fritos corn chips, and a small jar of Skippy extra chunky peanut butter. Carefully centered amid these articles was a wide glass ashtray with the legend *Ramada Inn* cut into its base.

Vane perched on a barstool and stared at nothing. Finally he plucked out a Coors, screwed off the cap, and raised the bottle to his lips. Foam blew out the mouth and ran down his arm; the brew was room temperature. He flicked the liquid from his hand and cursed quietly. After a few breaths he took a tentative swallow and studied the shadows. If this warehouse was any indication, seventy-to eighty per cent of his stores had been pirated. He drank deeper. It wasn't just a matter of replacing these stores. If Eritrea was being raped from within, anything coming through was as good as lost. He had to find a new corridor. But before that, if Mamuset was to survive, he had to get his property back.

Slats of light and shadow bisected boxes and shelves, giving the warehouse a lifeless, mechanical feel. Vane gently set down the bottle, squinted and perked up his ears. Not a sound, not a movement. Then, very slowly, a black contour melted out of the lesser darkness; deep sunglasses and epaulet-crowned shoulders preceding a broad chest crisscrossed by wide, camel-hide ammo belts. Vane watched two pale lips, obscene in a horizontal oval of cropped facial hair, convulse nervously until the coffee-stained teeth split for a genial smile. A heavy voice oozed, "I won't waste precious time with shallow salutations, homeyboy. Your arrival has forced me to cut short a local celebration. The party's life involved the exquisite disemboweling of three former employees who were, to their great misfortune, completely unaware of who butters the sides of their bread." The mouth's corners turned up a notch. "How do you appreciate my mastery of the idiom, Mr. Vane? I find that my toads are delighted and confounded by Americanisms."

"I guess it'll have to do. So who the Devil, as we Americans say, are you?"

A tall figure stepped into the dirty pool of light. The man very gently clicked his heels, and gave a bow so conservative it was more a reclining of the brow than a nodding of the head. "Colonel Franco a' Muhammed en Abbi...*Franco* to you, Cristian Honey Vane, son of the celebrated John Beregard."

Vane smiled sourly. "Franco? *El Caudillo?*"

The colonel bowed again. "You flatter me."

"And you're...what? Moroccan? Algerian?"

The square jaw cocked. "You were expecting...what? A man as dark as the African night?" He shook his head and clucked. "Outside the field, Mr. Vane, you will find no black officers here; not in Eritrea. Command is...ah...*imported*. An...international puzzle is being assembled—a fascinating structure, but," and he held a forefinger to his lips while mimicking paranoia, "these are matters for which your ears are far too green. Suffice it to say that I am Massawa's head official, the top of the dog. I alone coordinate the comings and goings of all before me, all around me, all beneath me. *No man* possessing a stake in Massawa is not indebted to me for life. I am chief of police; I am liaison between soldier and state. Knower of things, giver of favors, receiver of pleasures so abundant I grow weary of their getting. I am God here, Mr. Vane, appointed, indirectly, by a...Great Apportioner. And I know all there is to know, and I see all that is worthy of seeing. *Nothing* escapes me!" He sighed painfully. "And yet…I have come to suffer from—*ennui*. Bored with my petty anthill, I ask myself idle questions, such as: Why would Allah embrace pigs simply because they squat five times a day in swinish obeisance? And how is it that seemingly dignified men will snap at doubloons like dogs after treats? And, of course, what could possibly motivate one of the richest men in the world to come slinking through this serpentarium into my warehouse? Could it be that you too suffer from this great and noble disease, this *ennui?*"

"One of *my* warehouses," Vane corrected him. "And I didn't come slinking. I only came to see what's hanging up my supplies. My experiences here, along with your quaintly struggling explanation, have answered the immediate questions. The lifeline to Mamuset, the land I *bought*, the enterprise I pissed bullets for, has been sabotaged by the lead goofball in a troupe of opportunists straight out of the nineteenth century." He shrugged. "No, Mr. Abba Zaba, I don't suffer from ennui."

Franco cocked his head. Exhibiting no military bearing whatsoever, he drew back the other barstool and swung over a leg. He extracted a small writing pad and retractable pen from a breast pocket, thumbed the pen wide and, his expression intense, entered a quick note followed by a series of jabbed exclamation points. He looked back up, the intensity replaced by the warmest of smiles. "And you, sir, may address me as simply *Franco*."

"Well, Mr. Simply Franco, ennui is cured, simply enough, by directing one's energies into the constructive realm. Stop being so selfish and worldly. It's your little fiefdom that's killing you, not the Big Picture."

"I believe I have intimated as much."

"Then why persist in these bullying tactics? It's the way of small men. Imagine what you could accomplish if you were employed in the betterment of your surroundings." Vane rose. He stepped up to a pallet stacked with fertilizer, used his key chain's retractable exacto-knife to slit a bag, and caught a handful of pungent nitrates.

Franco looked on curiously. "You were expecting—what? Tons of camouflaged contraband, perhaps?" He shook his head sadly. "Mr. Vane, in Massawa we label our cocaine shipments plainly and with pride."

"Just a businessman's interest in his wares, Mr. Franco. You understand."

"The title is 'Colonel.' And they are *my* wares, Mr. Vane." Franco squinted at the rafters, measuring his words. "Ah, my belligerent civilian friend...you are aware that there is a mighty vessel anchored in Old Harbor, even now taking on supplies from these warehouses?"

"I saw it."

"This great ship holds the contents of all those warehouses and yards you keep insisting belong to you. Those warehouses and yards are now almost completely emptied, the ship almost completely filled. Depending on the outcome of our little chat here, that cargo will either be returned or go on the market. You may call this market black if it suits you ideologically. Whatever." An apt comparison eluded him. "I can see this is a pointed sore between us. The fundamentals of law you observe in your great nation are as applicable here as they would be on, say, the planet Neptune. For example, you presently feel distanced from certain articles which were once in your legal possession. What is your natural reaction? You will of course summon a policeman, who will quickly arrive to take a statement, receive a description of the articles named as stolen, and hopefully obtain a basic description of the guilty party. That is Step One; as understandable as the bleating of sheep at slaughter. I believe that, at all costs, this first step should be expedited with a clear head. And so, my friend, we shall now call us a cop. But which cop shall it be? I have several to choose from, and will personally guarantee that my selection's work ethic leaves you with nothing but admiration for our humble 'police state.' For you see, Mr. Vane, tardy and otherwise unsatisfactory officers in Massawa spend the remainder of their lives flitting from shadow to shadow, afraid of their friends and neighbors, paling at the least whisper of wind.

"But so much for Step One. We have now obtained a staunch *officer of the peace.* He has arrived, Allah be praised, expeditiously and with great sobriety, for he quite rightly considers his professional performance a matter of life and death.

He takes a statement: the wares of a rich foreigner are reported pinched by a dastardly criminal for purposes unspeakable. We even have a fairly accurate description of what you easily-violated democrats label a 'perp,' or perpetrator." Franco nodded cozily. "One of the 'perks,' Mr. Vane, of being a god cursed with ennui, is a limitless supply of pirated satellite broadcasts from the land of Laverne and Shirley. Hence my acumen in the rare hobby of Americanisms." He tapped a temple. "I am a legend.

"And our description of this audacious perp accurately embraces our whodunit: a tall, dreamy, vaguely handsome man with the medals of a hero and the nimbus of a god. Has he truly fouled the fair American? Our intrepid cop interviews relentlessly. None will say, none will say. But, almost inaudibly, a reverential whisper goes round. 'Franco,' it shudders, passing man to man. 'Oh, *Franco!'*

"This is more than enough for the outraged American. As none of these seedy, double-dealing African *gendarme* seem willing to bring down this dashing burglar-of-cats, our umbrageous visitor immediately seeks an attorney who will reduce the offender to quivering confession in a solid Eritrean court of criminal law.

"Again, no problem. There are several lawyers and judges to choose from in Massawa, Mr. Vane, and each will perform with the efficiency and expediency of our impressive policemen."

Vane raised his hands in mock surrender. "Okay, okay, I get the picture. I'm being held for ransom by the chief thug in a weaseling gang of Third world terrorists. There's no law, no decency, no justice in this dog-eat-dog jungle. But wait! That can't be right. Surely you've watched enough TV to know Captain America's on his way. I'll be saved, and you'll go down like all villains. The forces of Goodness always triumph. Top men in the cabinets of Eritrea and Ethiopia—you know their names—as well as in America, are deeply interested in the welfare of one captive corn-fed rich boy, and are perfectly aware of my whereabouts. Ironically, one of the drawbacks to being highly successful in a free country is an almost complete lack of privacy, especially when it comes to matters of state. Which is to say that the poor American rich boy, stuck in a pus-filled port on the Red Sea, is being watched, whether he likes it or not, by an invisible web of official nannies who, just like your sweating efficient policemen, do their job out of fear of a higher power. In short, Colonel Spaghetti-O, I can't pee on a pansy without some little man in a trench coat taking a sample. Why? Because my holdings are so extensive, and so commanding, that the least tremor in their foundation causes waves of panic in Wall Street and in the Pentagon. Cristian...Honey, son of John Beregard, *must* remain healthy, happy, and sane. And, most of all, free. Believe it or not, it's not just Hollywood and Burger King clinging to my shadow. NASA and JPL, and a few other groups of initials that would stagger even Y-O-U, are frightfully obsessed with my well-being. I would not be in *the least* surprised to find United States agents, even now, waiting without, while American satellites monitor our every move."

"If *so*," Franco retorted gleefully, "they will surely surrender royalties to my regime." The colonel posed for an imaginary camera. "I do hope your directors are as efficient as your spies. But I agree. There are curtains for me. Secret agents, as we speak, are preparing to burst in on jet skis that were once briefcases." Franco grinned and wagged a forefinger. "I will be shaken, Mr. Vane, but I will not be stirred." He snapped up the notepad and pen, and the instant his eyes met the page all aspects of chumminess and nonchalance were swept from his face. Vane didn't like the new look at all. Franco gave the impression of a civil monster; an official who could write off lives with a squiggle and jab, then return to business as usual. The colonel made a final slash and looked back up, a cheetah done feeding. He appeared to have trouble remembering the nature of their conversation. The glazed look slowly left his eyes. This was a different Franco. This was the garrulous interrogator bored with plain old torture. This was the man of ennui.

"Mr. Vane," he said flatly, "you will find in Africa elements that obviate each and every clever Western countermeasure you may attempt to invoke. In this country terrible things take place in the night, things that go forever unresolved. And not only unresolved; they may go unreported. You feel your operation is of great moment, and that you, yourself, are under continuous scrutiny due to your imperial station. But here in Africa you and your entire project can disappear leaving only a black hole surrounded by chicken bones and stacked pebbles."

Franco tapped his dark glasses with a gloved forefinger. "You've heard, perhaps, of the Mau Mau uprising in the 1950s? Monstrous acts were performed on decent people, atrocities that shook the civilized world...they were merely peccadilloes." He gestured continentally. "Within my reach are pockets of very uncivilized humanity, pockets crammed with primitives capable of doing unspeakable things to the most innocent of men. There are, additionally, demons and blood overlords to summon, maggots for hire, and 'political prisoners' who will do my darkest bidding for even a shot at release."

Vane shook his head wearily. "So how did I know this was all gonna come down to threats."

Franco copied the action, but with gravity. "These are not simple threats, my naïve American friend. Blood Africa is a place you cannot imagine. An ambitious man does not 'die' in Blood Africa. He reaches his apex and is then brought down. He is not *let* down. He is *torn* down, tissue by tissue, scream by scream. It is important to his successors that he be reduced not merely to death, but to dust; dust that has been sucked dry of every drop of blood, every scrap of dignity, every vestige of memory. Only then, when he has been ground into particles far too bleached for even the most anemic of vultures—only then can he truly be described as deposed."

"Colonel," Vane grinned, "I envy your position more with every syllable."

Franco inclined his head in acknowledgment. "Thank you, Mr. Vane. But I will do the joke-making here. I am attempting to describe the world you have pricked, like a tick on a Titan, so that you may better understand the futility of your aplomb, and the absurdity of this notion—this scenario wherein a pasty, hollow-eyed American is saved in the nick of time." He raised a hand. "No superhero rushes to your rescue. No sane man outside of Africa follows up on the unfortunate ingestion of a foreigner—no matter how well-heeled—by this cruelest of continents. If he does, he too will be swallowed. Africa is insatiable."

Franco leaned deeper into shadow, then suddenly loomed with bogeyman fingers wriggling playfully. "In *Af*-ri-ca," the bogeyman intoned, and was immediately replaced by the grave, sarcastic interrogator, "there is a universal belief that anger can take on a life of its own. It remains an aspect of the injured party, while at the same time extending beyond him. It reaches out to the offender in ways that are unbelievably brutal—ways that are wholly unimaginable to a soft white Westerner with his feeble barricade of black servants and Semitic boot-lickers." He dropped his hands in mock resignation. "All your beads and crucifixes, sir, will do you no good here. Shades walk among us, unaffected by walls or pleas for mercy. *My* shade, Mr. Vane, protects *my* wares, and will travel throughout the world to avenge *my* losses."

"I don't hide behind angels and jabberwocky, Franco. White religion is as removed from my thoughts as your black demons. So go ahead and call out your phantom legions; I'm getting my property back one way or another. You just don't seem to understand the extent of my influence. *Listen*, man: People of means, in high places, do not sit around in their offices arranging cinders and chicken bones. Nowadays practical concerns far outweigh superstitions. So get hip to the 21st century. Step out of the dark and work with me, instead of against me." He nodded civilly. "We'll forget this unpleasantness ever occurred."

Franco showed his entire dingy mouthful before bowing warmly. "Thank you so very much, Mr. Vane. You are wrong to believe these men in high places are above thousands of years of dark culture. They simply disguise it better.

"As to your proposition: I wish you to know I am wholly amenable. It was my sole desire that we reach this point of confluence. With your assets and my command it is fait accompli that our strengths should combine. Think of it! We are Napoleon and Alexander on the Elbe. We can take this forsaken land and bend it to our common will. We can be kings here, sir. King en Abbi and King Vane, masters of all they survey."

"A sure cure for ennui."

"A sure cure for mediocrity." There was a pause. Franco said apologetically, "I can see you have doubts…Cristian. You view your good friend Franco as entirely self-assured, and this makes you wonder—is this visionary perhaps blind to his flanks and rear? Am I throwing away my hat to a man already at war?" Franco, clasping his hands beatifically, sighed at the baking roof. "You are proper to ask, my best and most trusted ally." He nodded. "There *are* more than meet the eyes in Massawa. As omnipotent as I must appear to a man such as yourself—a man accustomed to having worms at his beck and call—it would be wrong, at this present, momentous junction, to not inform my dear friend and future partner that I am not sole bearer of the whip in this place. There is a foil—a pig of a dog of a bastard of a man...he resides in Massawa...who knows where? My men report him in various places at various times, ever scheming to undermine me. He heads a family—actually more a gang—of thieves and black profiteers, seducing the population with opiates and promises. His men are distinguished by a distinctive marking on turbans and kaftans. You will see it wherever there is carrion; a heavy black vertical line with a red dot on either side. It is the symbol of the vulture.

"This man wears a snow-white fez bearing this symbol, and claims to be a man of Mecca. He is no holier than I; only slipperier. He competes in the black market, waylaying cargo with his harbor rats, underselling my agents, frustrating our very government. But, were he to learn on the Massawa grapevine of our grand partnership—*then* would he quiver in his ugly boots! You need not fear him. Not ever! Not while you are on the side of Franco!"

Vane delicately cracked open another beer. "If I see him, I'll surely let him know."

Franco grinned and bowed. "Ah, Cristian! You are an apple in my eye!" He began to pace, his face twisting with excitement. Abruptly he stopped, and his jaw dropped to his chest. Nearly exultant, he cried, "It is done! *Done!*" The colonel wheeled and paced with greater energy, his hands escaping him in chopping gestures. "You, my friend, and all your underlings may relocate in Massawa. This will be a move of great ceremony. Our dual coronation will be televised over the entire Horn of Africa." The gestures became sweeping. "Yemen! Saudi Arabia! India, even! Maggot empires will see, will understand, and will grovel! Magnificence humbling Mesopotamia will roll before cameras trained upon our glorious union!" A thought struck him and he halted. Franco perched guiltily on his stool. "But do not brood on expenses, my loyal friend and confederate! The display will be financed by my beholden worms, by their relatives' businesses, and by their brats' futures. Do not fear, *mon ami*. I will bring you the sun. This party will be on Franco."

Vane deliberated. After a minute he said, "Y'know, man, I really have to hand it to you. I admire your cunning. Not only that, you've got genuine balls. Televised coronations, groveling subjects, mind-boggling splendor. What an imagination!" He could tell the colonel's eyes were burning behind the shades. "But I have an alternate plan." Franco's upper body tilted forward on the stool. "In this plan, my partner and sole confidant, you call forth your silly storm troopers, your puppets and your bogeys, and everybody lines up, with you at the very front. You've offered me the sun, I'll give you the moon. You and your stupid army can get on your Third-world knees and kiss my hairy white ass."

Franco's head jerked back as though he'd been slapped.

"An Americanism," Vane said.

Franco leaned forward again. His voice was cool. "*Then*, my American friend, it would seem we are at an impasse. Your old ideas are out of place here. You are a foreigner of no property in a state at war. It is not solely my good nature that permits you to exit in one piece, free to return to an enemy nation. It is because I wish to give you time to reconsider." He shook his head softly. "Anywhere you proceed in this part of the world, with your present point of view, you will be entirely frustrated. You cannot change people with money, Cristian Honey, you can only temporarily alter their behavior. Sooner or later they will turn on you, snakes that they are. This I know." Again he tapped his temple. "It takes a man of the world to know men of the world. But you, sir," he sniffed, "are far too innocent and spoiled."

Franco blew out his cheeks, rolled his eyes to the rafters. "All right, all right, all *right!* You have won me over, my wily compatriot. You have broken me down. I will now speak of things that are in your ears only.

"Eritrea, this pathetic little strip of land against the Sea has...how shall I say it—Secret Friends. To cut through the chase, I will tell you that these friends are not friends of your country, presently or historically. And of them I will speak no more. I will only say that they are supplying Eritrea with intelligent weapons, and with men trained to instruct our soldiers in their use, and also in sophisticated tactics of ground warfare. At the same time we are collaborating with certain...dark partners, who are busily working Addis Ababa to soften her sweet belly.

"The state of Ethiopia will be taken, let there be no making of mistakes about it. She will fall before the crocodile moon, and her carcass will be jealously apportioned. But my friends are not interested in Ethiopia per se. They are not even interested in Eritrea. These states are merely stepping stones toward...Fairer Pastures."

A note of softness, of awe, came into Franco's voice. "And I have been promised my own pastures, Mister...Vane... Cristian...it is only due to our deep and abiding friendship that I now reveal what I do—

"Franco's future stands far beyond this miserable port. And when I speak it you will know it is also your future, and that we were destined to become partners fast and final.

"The entire country of Eritrea will soon be merely an outlying territory of this new creation of my very powerful friends. Ethiopia will be little more. My friends will need a strong man to run this territory, and are impressed with my job here." He tipped his head. "Do not let her dreary face dismay you. *Massawa*," he said impressively, "is a military and administrative site, not a tourist trap. Beneath her surface she is running quite smoothly, thank you, but only because of my ruthless attention to detail. Example: when I first took control of this port a scant three weeks ago, the underground economy was a complete embarrassment. Some workers were spending as much as fifty per cent of their income on the procurement of qat leaves. Qat, if you have yet to experience it, produces a mild sense of euphoria when chewed. The user becomes addicted, loses interest in politics, fritters away whatever he may have saved. Think of it! Fifty per cent of one's earnings devoted to a mind-numbing drug! I was outraged. But, after scrupulous investigations into the drug's trafficking and its users' psychology, I can tell you without too much humility that I was able to increase that percentage in some areas to as high as eighty per cent. My friends and I, just as do we two now, see eyes to eyes on these matters." He nodded conspiratorially. "We know that no man of wealth and power achieves such a station without manipulating a few addicts and breaking a leg or two here and there. Great power breeds great cunning, and...great friends.

"I am warning you now, my great and special friend, that your sorry little farm in the desert will be crushed by this huge coming wave, and all your charges splattered like cockroaches under a steamroller. But not with Franco on your side. I will guarantee you complete protection. More than that! With my connections you will be able to expand indefinitely. So do not scowl, my dear, dear friend. This—" he waved a hand, "all this is not merely the dream of a pipe; it is a future certainty. The world can be ours!

"But right now," the colonel concluded in a cautious voice, "Massawa is in turmoil. The great wave is building. For our sake, the goods of these warehouses and yards are being held for safekeeping aboard that monster cargo ship. And aboard that ship they will remain, until you and I have signed our pact. Only then will my friends be certain you are one of ours, and not an agent of the American government." His expression became hurt. "So you see, Cristian, your partner is in a touched situation. He has to put up a strong face with his still-suspicious friends by holding our wares in this miserable harbor, which must seem a hostile act to his future co-ruler. But know that, when we make our bid, your wealth and my influence will be a combination unbeatable. We will reign as we were meant to reign. And we will be invincible." He spread his hands. "These things, good and bad, were made to be. They were made so the moment your hungry blue eyes fell upon this plump, waiting land."

Franco tore off the top page and tossed the memo pad with its remaining blank leaves onto the coffee table. It was a closing gesture. He folded the page delicately and, observing Vane man-to-man, placed its secrets securely in his breast pocket, saying, "For my eyes only." He patted the pocket, thumbed home its snap.

Franco bowed and stepped away from the stool, his smile retreating as he melted back into the shadows. "Take your time," said the smile. "Study this offer in private. When you are ready, send a courier to Massawa. He will be royally received. Be prepared to be impressed." The smile dangled in the darkness like a dirty yellow bulb. A gloved hand showed dimly, forefinger extended and thumb cocked in the universal gesture of a pointed handgun. "Allah and Visa," said the smile, "baby." The smile went out.

Vane sat quietly for a spell, listening. Though the warehouse was echoing still, he could tell the colonel had exited the premises. It was as if a cold front had moved on.

He grabbed a Coors, twisted off the cap, and shoved the bottle in his mouth before the beer could foam over. Warm or not, it was liquid ecstasy in that frying pool of light. Vane chugged it down. He then slit open the pack of Marlboros and lit one, placed it on the ashtray and let it burn. After a minute he picked up the memo pad and cigarette, tapped ashes onto the top blank page, and very gently rubbed the ashes into the paper. He blew the remaining ashes away, tore off the top page and held it against the light. The pen's indentations, revealed by traces of ash, read:

> *Pissing bullets* (gun then is?) (*!!!!*)
> *Putting peas on pansies* (accomplishes what?!?)
> *Dogs eat in jungles* (which jungles where?)
> *Rich American boys are fed corn* (why? How much?)

Vane crumpled and tossed the page as he strolled back through the warehouse. He could see the cooking Land Rover framed in the access doorway, with Mudhead hunched to one side in the passenger seat. He heralded his approach with a heaved sigh, but the slouched white bundle remained motionless. Not until he reached Isis did Mudhead attempt to sit upright. Failing, he shook his head sharply, once each way.

"Bossman still driver."

Vane climbed behind the wheel and watched the African staring into space, his throat arched and his face expressionless. In a minute Mudhead held up his right hand, purple and massively swollen behind the knuckles. "Mudahid Bossman right hand man," he explained sourly, sweat rolling down his face. "So soldier break Mudahid right hand. Warning to Bossman."

"Ah, Christ. Man, I…just hang in there, buddy. I'll get you to a doctor."

Mudhead shrugged his left shoulder. "Mudahid already see doctor. Military doctor. Doctor watch close when soldier break hand, so doctor know how re-break hand just right." He sighed hugely. "Lucky Mudhead."

Vane looked away. "How bad?"

"Plenty bad."

Vane hit the ignition. "All things considered, right hand man, I think we're getting out of here cheaply enough." He took the same route back and tore through the blockade. With nowhere to turn, Vane found himself hurtling up the road like some young punk in a hot rod. Eventually he noticed a bug in his rear-view mirror. The bug became a motor scooter. Vane pulled over and killed the engine as the little Vespa hurtled past. The scooter made a hard U-turn and gently motored back. The rider, grinning under his goggles, handed him a stuffed lunch bag, revved his scooter twice, and shot back to the harbor.

Vane opened the bag curiously. Inside were a dozen prescription bottles, a handful of disposable syringes, and several vials that were certainly morphine. The 'scrips were Percodan, codeine, and Tylenol 4. "Happy Ramadan," he said, and handed the bag over. "Looks like you're gonna be facing Mecca for quite a while."

Mudhead groaned as he peered into the bag, but half a minute later his good hand was digging. Vane checked out the back seat, on the off chance he'd been left a beer; Mudhead would need something to wash down the pills. To his surprise he discovered two cases of Lowenbrau, cartons and cartons of cigar-ettes, and a variety of snacks: nuts, jerky, trail mix, chips. A Coleman ice chest was stocked with cubes. There were even packages of local sweetmeats with unreadable labels. The gas gauge showed a full tank.

"Funny guy," Vane muttered, grabbing two bottles. He warned Mudhead to go easy on the Percodan, fired up Isis, and respectfully kept his eyes on the road while his friend worked morphine into a syringe. After a deep breath he guzzled his own beer and handed Mudhead a follow-up. A mild overdose might be just the thing.

Chapter Ten

Xhantu

Old Road was rough on Isis's suspension, torture for her injured passenger, and murder on her driver's nerves. Vane had driven hard for ten minutes with an expression cut in stone. Now his knuckles were white on the wheel, his head scrunched squarely between his shoulders. His feet danced on the pedals at the baritone yelp accompanying each spine-jarring crash. Half his attention clung desperately to the rough distractions of the road. The other half gradually accepted the unthinkable: he was heading home empty-handed. When he finally acknowledged it, in his heart as well as in his head, the realization was like running into a wall. Vane's entire body went rigid. His ramrod arms slammed his back against the seat. His feet hit the brake and gas simultaneously.

The resulting sidewinder stalled the Land Rover facing south. A low cloud of hot dust rolled over them. Mudhead, tripping but still in pain, leaned into the swirling haze and heaved.

Vane hollered something unprintable, punched the dash,

kicked the firewall. He threw out a shoulder trying to tear off the side-view mirror. Finally he fired Isis back up and spun her through a radical arc. When she stalled again he sat glaring at Massawa, adrenaline clouding his vision. He'd lost it. *Everything.* He howled out his anguish and restarted the engine. Vane grittily steered the Rover homeward. He halted and childishly revved the engine in neutral, facing Mamuset and failure.

Loser. Just like always. He jammed into first and whirled round and round in a broadening circle; cursing Franco, cursing Massawa, cursing himself. Isis died again, this time facing a wide empty desert in the eye of a fading dust tornado.

Mudhead kept right on spinning. "No...more...Boss... ma..."

Vane repeatedly pounded his forehead on the wheel, spewing a different four-letter word with each impact. The poundings tapered to palliative contacts. Vane massaged his temple on the wheel until his nose caught on the horn plate.

"Now what?" he muttered.

Mudhead leaned out the side again. When it was over Vane hauled him back in and grabbed a couple of beers. The African shook his head and shoved a handful of ice in his mouth.

"How's the paw?"

Mudhead raised the mangled hand, now swollen to the girth of a football. His eyes were streaming. "Better." He eased it into the ice chest and poured out a mouthful of Tylenol, then decided to go for the beer after all. He nodded a few times at the endless waste.

"Mecca's behind you."

Mudhead half-turned. "Whatever. Bossman remind Mudahid nod right way tomorrow." He knocked back the caps and sucked the bottle dry.

Speaking as much to himself as to his partner, Vane mumbled, "I can't go home without supplies. I just *can't!* There wasn't enough on those trucks to get everybody through the day." He slowly motored along, still mumbling, letting the machine drive itself. "It's mine...*mine*...that fu...that...damn that rip-off! I've got to get it back...*got* to...maybe if I called... maybe if I just...no, no, no, they'd never break through in time."

He wasn't the only one rambling. Mudhead's rap was all about masks and caves, pools and dwarves. That would be the morphine talking. Vane shook his head hard as he drove, trying to toss out the grim image of a crater filled with dead. The stupid Afar trusted him way too much; they'd probably die waiting on him. The doctors and volunteers would be hip enough to beat a retreat in the buses and trucks. They might even try to organize some kind of rescue work through the government. But it would be too little too late; Mamuset would end up like Preston's death hole. Vane briefly pondered a cash ransom for his goods, knowing Honey would bend the Banke as far as he demanded. In the same breath he acknowledged the stakes. Franco wasn't after money. He was after Cristian Vane.

"*What*," he wailed, "what do I effing *do?*"

Mudhead did his best to answer, using babbled narrative about some nonsensical desert shaman better able to address the pangs of Vane's conscience. After listening a while he decided Mudhead wasn't out of his skull after all, but was in fact describing in some detail a sightless wise man, or spirit-healer, who lived in the Danakil in a big underground stone house.

Once he had a few beers in his bloodstream, Vane was able to embrace the idea of meeting *Xhantu*, Mudhead's fabulous wise man. It was that or go out of his mind. Mudhead described the wizard's lair as situated some thirty miles southeast of Mamuset. There was plenty of gas in the tank. It wasn't yet ten o'clock. He followed Mudhead's basic directions automatically, his mind half on the desert and half on his friend's respectful tale.

This is the history Mudhead related, in broken English so drug-laden Vane got a contact high just trying to follow:

Xhantu was born in Cairo in 1905, the illegitimate son of a wealthy industrialist widower. As a child, the future blind seer survived a mild flirtation with the polio virus, along with the first taste of what would become chronic bronchitis. These diseases produced a stunted, hobbling boy who broke out in fevers at the least change in weather. He was far too sickly for adventure, and far too subdued for friends.

On his tenth birthday he was kidnapped by elements of

Al-Shalek, then held for ransom through six long terrible days. Over that period the father was rigorously pressured by the Egyptian government to stall; the State Department was convinced the group harbored a member of the terrorist organization Allâh Râm Allâh. Each day the kidnappers produced evidence of greater tortures inflicted upon the son, rapidly driving the father to depression, to drink, and to madness; their final ploy being a threat to pluck out the boy's eyes if payment was not made on that sixth night. The hysterical father, fortune in hand, was apprehended halfway to the dropoff site by a chilly contingent of military police. Flanked by Army jeeps, he was escorted home clutching a stamped and endorsed State Department certificate assuring him the kidnappers were all but captured, and his son a heartbeat from release. When a courier arrived the next day bearing a package containing the boy's eyeballs, the father took his own life with a single pistol shot through the roof of the mouth. The following evening triumphant Egyptian police stormed and torched the kidnappers' hideout. Burned over sixty-five percent of his body, the boy survived a year of intensive care in a Port Said hospital and, upon his release, was adopted by an American husband-and-wife team assigned to a dig at Menat Khufu.

He was a hideously deformed child. The mouth was a lax aperture, the nose and ears burned to shapeless nubs, the facial skin like red rubber slag. Refusing to speak a word, he was considered mute by his adoptive parents and their friends, though specialists could find no evidence of long-term damage to organs of speech. Through thrashing fits, he made plain his refusal to accept prosthetic eyes, eye patches, or half-mask. Once the shock and horror had abated, the new mother and father came to love him just as he was, gaping eye sockets and all.

Xhantu's parents belonged to a brilliant circle. Their awarded home in Cairo University was the focus of long and regular get-togethers featuring physicists, historians, linguists, and philosophers. The boy was spoon-fed the English language. He was tended like a precious alien weed. He became the passion and darling of all: these good people attained their highest pleasure tutoring him in their various fields, by way of lectures bursting with affection, erudition, and wit. The young student would sit quietly in their midst, his cocked head ratcheting voice-to-voice. Rather than regale him with bedtime stories, his parents took turns reading aloud the Great Books of the Western World, followed by volumes of the Encyclopedia Britannica in alphabetical order. A coddled prisoner throughout his teens, the young man was halfway through the W's when he simply walked off campus and out into the real world, never to return.

He felt his way as he went. As a teen he'd compensated with a passion for the tactile; tenderly fingering and toeing clothes and household objects, attaining greater sensitivity through experience. His supreme interest was in fabrics of complex weave, and in intricate curios brought in as presents by friends of the family. There was much to explore in the streets and storefronts of Cairo.

This strange eyeless beggar eventually made his way into the desert, surviving Egypt, Sudan, Kenya, and Ethiopia by drifting tribe-to-tribe, dispensing Western wisdom in exchange for supplies and small handmade articles of great intricacy. Over the decades he attained a mythical status and the common appellation Xhantu, a polyglot description meaning, roughly, "Sees Blind."

When he reached extreme old age he was given, by grateful Amharic pastoralists, a female albino dwarf camel and a prized two-wheeled laminated wooden cart. The old man was then ushered, with great honors, into the Danakil to die, his little red cart brimming with victuals, treasured personal artifacts, and scores of many-faced items ceremoniously donated by emissaries from tribes as distant as Tanzania and the Congo.

The thirsting camel, named Pegasus by Xhantu, pulled cart and master up a rocky table and down a spiral chimney into a labyrinth formed by underground rivers last active during the late Tertiary. Pegasus drew Xhantu through a great cavern to a small artesian pool, and thereafter the two lived peacefully in an abutting cave, the camel growing old while Xhantu ordered his learning into extended meditations. When supplies were low, the quirky little spectacle of camel, cart, and blind man would be seen meandering tribally, dispensing and collecting. Xhantu's home became a kind of shrine, where carefully-screened tribesmen and the occasional city-dweller were directed for counsel and tutoring. Mudhead himself came upon the sage this way, referred by a frustrated mullah during his stormy Ramadan withdrawal. Having learnt of the old man's penchant for the tactilely complex, Mudhead arrived with an elaborately engraved bamboo-and-ivory abacus. The gift was an instant hit with the sage.

Xhantu advised Mudhead to flow: if he was moved by something, he was to move with it. If an ideology ran against his grain, he would be a fool to spend his life attempting to conform.

The sage wanted Mudhead—indeed he wanted all healthy individuals—to focus on Virtue, believing there would be much less Vice in the world if Vice was much less trumpeted. "Vice" meant all qualities attractive to the sensual, or reactive mind, as opposed to those ideals appealing to the analytical, or objective mind. Aware of the flaws inherent in even well-meaning pursuits, Xhantu directed seekers to not embrace religions and philosophies whole, but to embrace their *Ascendant Virtues*. He worshipped the abstraction "Virtue" as the masses worship the abstraction "God." He simply felt no need to anthropomorphize it.

Mudhead, winding down his story in the bouncing Land Rover, rolled sluggishly with the terrain, his broken right hand still submerged in ice. He appeared free of pain, but the bumpy ride and overmedication made him certain one minute and lost the next. Eventually he began to recognize landmarks; outcroppings and depressions that, to Vane, appeared identical to their background. Then, in the absolute middle of Nowhere, he suddenly rose half out of his seat to indicate a strange little snowflake balanced on a rounded, flat-capped rocky rise. Through his binoculars Vane made out a scrawny white camel, perhaps three feet high at the shoulder, perched leaning on a stepped shelf. In the lenses it was no larger than a hamster. Mudhead waved his good hand at a pass in the rocks, and Vane hammered on through to a barely navigable foot trail. The trail continued up the rise, rolling and twisting to the summit. It was one of those natural courses that seem ingeniously designed to test a young man's courage and equipment, and Vane was no exception to this call. He revved the engine hard, his palm itching on the gearshift's crown. In response, the camel's tiny white head popped out above the shelf. Vane clearly discerned the pink of its eyes. It began making little barking sounds, like an asthmatic Pekingese.

He hit the path full-bore, stomping accelerator and clutch like double bass drums, ever on the lip of disaster. After a complete circuit, the path ended twenty feet above where they'd started. Mudhead opened his eyes and caught his breath. In a minute he swung back his good arm and grabbed a bag of sweetened dates. He opened the bag with his teeth. "Bossman," he gasped, "carry goodie box." Vane hefted the remaining beer under one arm, the box full of cigarettes, snacks, and sweetmeats in the other. The African approached the little camel crooning, honey-dipped dates overflowing his outstretched left palm. "Hello again, Peggy. Peggy remember Mudahid?" The camel dropped her head. Her nostrils quivered while one eye metronomically followed the gently rocking hand. "Peggy good girl." The muzzle stretched forward, the lips writhed, the dates vanished. Mudhead patted her nappy white head. "Party time now, sweetheart. Bossman bring Oreo."

Vane had to mind his fingers while shoveling Pegasus Ho-Hos and Ruffles; the animal was in a state of gustatory ecstasy. When at last he turned away he was just in time to see his friend being screwed into the ground. He walked over curiously and peered down. Mudhead was gingerly descending a rough spiral staircase in the rock. The interior appeared inky black, but as Vane followed him down the darkness gradually dissolved, becoming a restful twilight at the swept stone floor. The caverns they were nearing were immense; the cave he and Mudhead now occupied was more of an antechamber, leading into the black depths of a much broader hall to their right. Numerous small ceiling fissures illuminated the cave, emitting slender beams that struck the walls and floor at various angles. The men waited patiently, letting their eyes adjust. Someone, Mudhead's sage apparently, had draped the rock walls with colorfully dyed tapestries, and arranged native artifacts and objets d'art upon a series of homemade tables and shelves scattered amid furniture created out of old crates, straw, and blankets. Vane found himself closely admiring a Karamojong ceremonial headdress of human hair and ostrich feathers, a few oddly-stitched cloths from Madagascar, and an ornate divination staff from Mozambique. There were funerary figures, necklaces, an Angolan thumb piano, a Maori talisman, even an intact Maasai shield. All works had been showcased for their intricate nature, and were very carefully kept. A far corner contained a small thatched hut modeled on Amharic homes, but with an outsize door cut in its facing wall. Vane, reminded of a doghouse, remembered the little albino camel and smiled. There was an oddness about the texture of the thatch. On closer inspection he perceived that fibers had been closely braided, and the braids interwoven. The amount of painstaking work involved struck him as mind-numbing.

"A nasty fracture," piped a voice behind him. "Or perhaps merely a bad sprain?" It was the voice of a wizened child.

"Whole hand broke," Mudhead grunted. "But scooter-man bring magic bag. No more pain."

Vane half-turned to see a figure so tiny it might have been a bit of washing tossed on a chair, almost smothered in an undersized version of the Afar sanafil. The little man's deformed fingers were exploring Mudhead's swollen hand, seeming to hover rather than contact. Despite his friend's straightforward description, Vane was absolutely unprepared for the monstrosity he was facing. Xhantu's gaunt hairless skull and mooning eye sockets were exactly reminiscent, minus the toothy grin, of the skeletal remains popularly portrayed on pirate flags and poison labels. As the old man rose delicately the intrepid American, much to his dishonor, instinctively retreated a step. A hand like an anorexic spider found his forearm. Vane forced himself to look down, directly into that taut, ruined face. In the dimness the dark orbits seemed as prominent as a fly's eyes. He wouldn't have been surprised to see a pair of wispy antennae waving inquisitively.

"Bad news and good," came the tiny voice. "You bring a friend." Turning back to Mudhead, the sage swiveled his whole frame rather than just his head. He couldn't have weighed more than sixty pounds.

Vane self-consciously rummaged through his pockets

171

Microcosmia

and came up with his beloved Swiss Army knife. He nudged it
forward until it brushed the back of Xhantu's hovering hand.
"Um, this is a gift. From me."

The warped hand revolved until Vane's knife was cradled in the creased old palm. Xhantu's head ratcheted in a
heavenward arc, his chin thrust toward the tool, while his other
hand inspected the knife's every curve. His fingertips studied
the emblem dreamily. Long yellow nails found, extracted, ex-
amined, and repositioned the implements one by one. "A most
intricate and considerate token."

The man from the States relaxed. "Vane. Cristian Vane.
I'm from the States."

"Ah."

"Bossman big problem Eritrea."

"Ah?"

"No." Vane shook his head. "Uh-uh. Not with the
country directly. My problem's one of her renegades. I really
don't think the Eritrean government knows what he's up to."

Grimacing deeply, Mudhead carefully wagged his
broken hand. "This matter war!"

"*Ah!* And, Mr. Vane, what is the nature of this rap-
scallion's offense?"

"Stole all my goods. Everything. Warehouses stocked
with food and supplies, soil regenerators, parts in plastic, steel,
aluminum. You name it, he glommed it."

The sage silently clapped his hands. "So it is you! Mr.
Vane, I have received much news of your endeavors. Intriguing
news, inspiring news. It has become one of my favorite treats to
humbly envision your great work in its completion."

Vane sighed histrionically and muttered, "Then get comfortable." He checked himself. "Sorry, Mr. Zantoo. I don't
mean to be rude."

Xhantu inclined his head toward a central arrangement
of overstuffed homemade furniture. "Please."

Vane buried his butt in blankets and straw. Mudhead
passed round the beer and snacks. Their tiny host gushed politely over the goodies and gratefully sipped his Lowenbrau.
Pegasus came clattering down the spiral chute at the sound of
Mudhead ripping open a two-pound bag of Chips Ahoy. She

172

stopped just short of bowling him over, nipped the bag from his good hand, and vanished inside her little thatched house. The visitors laughed. Xhantu smiled uncertainly. The ice was broken; Vane explained his situation between swallows.

Xhantu had no need to ruminate. "It is imperative you retrieve your supplies at once. Were this a matter of pride, or of property for property's sake, I would doubtless counsel otherwise. But this is not about you or your goods, nor is it about your vile colonel. It is about your many dependents, and about placing responsibility above ego." Xhantu's head rolled back and his gummy mouth fell open. Suddenly he was smiling like a child digging into ice cream. "What a marvelous operation! How audacious! To in fact construct a Utopia from scratch— and with mathematics for a foundation! You are a rare man, my friend, a rare man indeed."

Vane shrugged uncomfortably. "Well, sir, not everybody gets my opportunity. If I'm a rare man it's because I'm a lucky one."

The sage shook his head, still marveling. "And even rarer for possessing the gift of humility. Such a gift is not shared by small men. A truly small man, in your most enviable position, would be interested in others only for their capacity to be dazzled."

Vane shrugged again. He shifted about in his seat while carefully sweeping straw back under the chair's fleece blanket. A schoolboy called on to speak, he froze dead in place and studied his clasped hands. The sage appeared to be deciphering each awkward realignment of human tissue. When he spoke again it was with the exaggerated clarity of a guarded therapist. "That small man would strut and preen. The universe would pale by his ego. He would shower his mother with jewels, impress his friends with gifts of expensive automobiles, and make certain he was never seen without a curvaceous young starlet on his arm." He cocked his head in the manner of a man listening intently. "You like automobiles, Mr. Vane, and lovely young women? Have you no mother to impress?"

Vane looked back up. "Some. Yes. And definitely no. This is all incidental to my problem, Mr. Zantoo."

"I would venture a guess—and please do not take offense—that you also have no deity to impress."

"All…" Mudhead mumbled, slumped in a loveseat-sized heap to Vane's right, "everything…dust in wind."

Vane ignored him. "I'm not stupid, sir."

Xhantu nodded respectfully. "May I then assume your philanthropic project serves as a surrogate for some or all of the above? And that, in your magnanimity, you are relieving yourself of the guilt often accompanying tremendous wealth?"

"Not a bit of it," Vane said flatly. "It's the right thing to do under the circumstances. Stick me in the unemployment line, and I seriously doubt I'll be dreaming so big."

"And these people in Mamuset? Do you not feel great compassion for their plight? Do you not take their hurts to heart? Could it be that they represent family to you, and that their happiness redounds to your self-esteem?"

Vane got to his feet. The prying little monster was beginning to bug him. He said brusquely, "I just really don't know," and grabbed a bottle from the case cradled in his unconscious friend's lap. He aggressively popped the cap with an opener on his key chain. "I *guess*." After two minutes of furious contemplation he said equably, "If so, then no more so than any other population in any other part of the planet. These people are no more important to me, intimately, than I to them." He nodded and took a long drink, nodded again. "The principle's the thing."

"Then *sir*," the sage said gravely, "it would appear you are afflicted with the dread disease microcosmia."

"How's that?"

"It is a sickness," Xhantu said, "or perhaps a mood. A life-mood. It means abhorrence of the microcosmic mentality, or, more accurately, abhorrence of taking worldliness seriously. Do not bother looking it up, as it is not a plaint of the herd. It is what eats away at sensitive, intelligent men repulsed by the meaninglessness of the real world. Such unfortunates are born with wounded souls. Rather than lock horns over possessions real and imagined like normal, healthy men, they pass their lives brooding and dreaming, allergic to the crowd. Microcosmiacs are, by definition, compelled to extrapolate." Xhantu paused for emphasis. "It is one of the great tragedies of life, Mr.

Vane, perhaps the supreme tragedy, that a man cannot know all that men have learned. The human mind is a near-infinite reservoir, capable of almost continuous analysis and retention. There simply is not enough time. One might learn a simple fact concerning a minor culture during an undistinguished epoch, and his mind, always active and venturous, will dissect that item, and erupt with unlimited related questions and possible answers—enough new self-generated input to send his poor brain forever reeling into shifting realms of light and shadow. But with what delight! No greater gift could nature provide her poor student than the ability to ruminate, to dwell, to *envision*.

"There is a kind of projector, Mr. Vane, far more wonderful than any in your famous Hollywood, that exists within the crania of all creative and ruminative men. A man successfully freed from the bondage of worldly concerns is a man sitting before a glorious and ever-changing screen, with speculation nestled in his lap like the most domesticated of Siamese. Greater, far greater, than *knowing* is the ongoing tremor of *wondering*. Once one has learned to wonder, one can do no else."

Vane suppressed a yawn. "The wealthy, Mr. Zantoo, ponder no less attentively than the poor."

"Touche," Xhantu said. "Relax, Mr. Vane. Your wealth notwithstanding, no one is accusing you of being rich. Rich men are never afflicted with microcosmia. They are far too preoccupied with profits and losses. No matter how high they may ascend on the ladder, they are always looking up to see whose rear end they must bite in order to claim the next rung, then looking back down to see whose teeth are testing their own precious behinds. No, my friend. You are poorer than they." His head drooped sadly. "That top rung could be yours."

Vane had to pinch himself to remain standing. It was so dark and cool in the cave—for a moment he had the disturbing feeling Xhantu was trying to mesmerize him with all this underground psychobabble. He struggled to remain on-topic. "I've seen what people will do for money, sir. I may be a fool, but I'm not a masochist."

"Microcosmia," Xhantu hummed, swinging an erect forefinger to the left, "is an illness as real as masochism." He swung that same forefinger to the right, then brought it to his lips, his voice dropping accordingly. "Perhaps the sufferer," he whispered, "has witnessed an act of cold-heartedness too intense to appreciate maturely. Or perhaps this individual, of a sudden insight, has realized the full measure of his insignificance in the universe. He has been...*jolted!*" Vane's eyes popped back open. "The damage," Xhantu declared, "has been done!" Again his voice fell, and again Vane's eyelids drooped. "Now the microcosmiac becomes progressively moody, and his basic urges go by the wayside. His ego withers. He grows very ...*soulful*." For a while there was nothing to be heard but Mudhead's snores. Xhantu resumed speaking in a conversational tone, as though no pause in his monologue had occurred. "Those broken by microcosmia, Mr. Vane, are our genuine artists, our genuine philosophers, and our genuine philanthropists." He shrugged. "If they are in my corner of the world, they eventually come to me."

Vane shook himself. "Sir, the only thing genuine about me is my stupidity. I'm a big-time loser, even with every card going my way." He sighed deeply. "But I didn't come looking for anybody. This trip was totally spontaneous."

Once more the sage cocked his head, this time until it was nearly parallel with his shoulder. "Spontaneous..." he muttered. Then, speaking as much to himself as to Vane: "You really believe this." For a moment he was lost for words. "Sir ...you are no loser! Your actions speak for themselves. You possess a priceless quality, a quality the crowd can ape but never carry. Mr. Vane, you are a man of vision."

Vane barked with laughter. "Vision? Catch me on a bad day, Mr. Zantoo. Better yet, watch what happens when I get my hands on a certain bombastic Eritrean pirate."

"You sell yourself short." Xhantu folded his hands behind his back. As though encouraging the shyest of prodigies, he explained, "You are no ordinary man. An ordinary man would not *reach*.

"The ordinary man, sir, exists as the voluntary prisoner of a bubble defined by his senses, in a universe stretching precisely as far as his eyes can see. It is a flat universe, covered by a dome alternately painted black and painted blue. If he moves a mile, if he moves a thousand miles, the dome rolls right along with him. Time is an event that began upon his birth, and will continue, notwithstanding a minor speed bump called Death, into a groundlessly assumed, yet blindly and wholly accepted, hereafter. Humankind is an odd assortment of ingrates. A very few, the Good Ones, are familiar. They are to be prized, trusted, and protected. Very many more are misguided strangers, ignorant of our ordinary man's intrinsic superiority. They must all be reminded, ad infinitum, that they are either guests or trespassers in his bubble."

Vane folded his arms across his chest. "Mr. Zantoo, each man is a prisoner, one way or another. Maybe of his circumstances, maybe only of his imagination. And a man's bubble can be anywhere. It can be a crater in the desert." He briefly released one arm for a casual cave-wide gesture. The sage's face followed the movement like a cat's. "It can even be made of stone. We're all ordinary men. The entire planet's a bubble; the same old program year to year and culture to culture. There truly is 'nothing new under the sun'."

"*Ah!* But there are flowers rare and sublime! There are *individuals*, Mr. Vane, who do not run in place; men dissatisfied with the status quo. Men who realize that an existence devoted to appetites and egos is an insult to the gift of life. And, on excruciatingly rare occasion, fate produces an individual positioned to exalt that gift."

Vane unfolded his arms to make a damping motion with his hands. "You're embarrassing me, sir. I'm very sorry to disappoint you, but I'm not that aspiring man. Nor am I a particularly inspired one."

"I am not disappointed. Your openness and modesty fully embrace my expectation." He turned and, proceeding with extreme confidence, drifted across the cave's floor toward the arch leading into the main cavern. "Come with me."

The cavern was vast as an indoor stadium, but with a ceiling averaging only a dozen feet above floor level. It was wonderfully ventilated, the rock actually cool to the touch. Scores of narrow ceiling flues created a crazy cathedral laced with thin columns of sunlight standing at various angles. The floor dropped off at the east wall, producing a deep stone hollow containing ten feet of clear water. The pool's surface was lit by a pair of these flues, the beams poised like crossed swords.

Vane found himself nodding with an envy strange for a billionaire. "Mister Zantoo, I tip my hat to you. A water hole in the middle of the desert in a dark cool cave. You've got it made." His nod went on with increasing vigor. "Yes sir! Yep. That's how I want to go out, man."

"Pardon?"

"When I die. Just submerge me in the dark surrounded by endless stone, a zillion miles away from everybody."

Xhantu inclined his head. "Consider your place saved. But do not be in such a hurry, my friend. There is something I would like you to experience first." Turning his back abruptly, he led Vane through the cavern into a gulf that grew deeper with each step, proceeding fearlessly while his guest inched along behind. They crossed the great chamber to an arch like the gateway to Hell. The blackness beyond was so profound Vane instinctively hit the floor.

Slowly swiveling his body, Xhantu addressed the dead space above his eager young disciple. "There are times, Mr. Vane, when the wind comes howling and moaning through these chambers from somewhere deep in the caverns. Clearly it originates without, on the lip of the Highlands where hot and cool air collide.

"At such times the chambers respire, and the air funneling up the fissures behind us produces tones like those of a gargantuan organ. They are for the most part capricious and fleeting, but occasionally idiosyncrasies of current and bore will produce a startling *vox humana*. It is a lonesome voice, Mr. Vane, patient and grieving, as old as its Cambrian womb." Vane, feeling the rock floor beginning to tilt, nauseously rose to his feet. The little sage's body language seemed to be questioning the motion. He was now a ghostly outline, visible only due to the fuzzy haze created by the nearest flues.

Vane shivered in the bottomless darkness, fighting for balance and listening to the silence. Finally he mumbled, "It's …it's beautiful."

"Yes." The ghost folded its hands neatly at the waist. "Think about all this colonel expressed. He is obviously a megalomaniac, and megalomania is the exact opposite of micro-cosmia. Therein lies his weakness. He is a molecule, a little self-adorned balloon ready to be pierced by the plainest of pins. He sleeps fitfully, for the world is crawling with traitors and sham flatterers, all scheming to usurp his unique wonderfulness. They are jackals. Their eyes gleam in the withering savannah of his dreams."

"That's my guy," Vane whispered.

"Do what you have to do. Go about your business knowing that, as a man of vision, the decision you make will be correct."

"But how will I know—"

"You will know."

Chapter Eleven

Massawa

The café was spotless.

Old Harbor's rhythm was in all things; in the practiced ease of tarbooshed waiters, in the exotic laughter of a dozen melding tongues.

But now and again activity would cease abruptly, and an icy silence envelop the scene. In the inner ring of tables, walnut-faced Algerians would lean to poker-faced Moroccans, who in turn leaned to hatchet-faced Egyptians. Their whispers would radiate to the outer ring. The signal would be passed by Nigerian traders, Somali tunny fishers, and Eritrean soldiers, who responded by tapping their respective timepieces, fish hooks, and military knives. The whole circle would close in, until the obscenely fair stranger was sure to break.

But the American would continue sipping his mint Darjeeling, at the same time shrugging deeper into his lame disguise. Vane was outfitted in that full-sleeved, deeply hooded, body-length garment known as *djellaba*. His clean pink feet were shod in cheap rubber sandals. The hood's dingy gray confines only accented his race; those peeping blond locks and that perpetually peeling nose belonged to Capricorn, not to the equator. A leper would have looked less out of place.

Vane could only shrink so far. When the tension became too great he'd tear his gaze from the tiny cup to manfully meet his grizzled tormentors' eyes—only to find them apparently lost in the day's small comforts; nuzzling bowls of thick black coffee, playing dominoes, watching ships ply the harbor. Again he'd lower his eyes and peek between the lids, looking like a monk in a whorehouse. Vane was waiting, desperately, for a certain blind beggar to come tapping through the crisscrossing camels and jeeps; a granite-faced, single-winged beggar who'd be right at home with the flies, the Third world desperadoes, and the half-naked ragamuffins.

The sun was just grazing the skyline when the prayed-for tapping sat him up. Vane watched his beggar shuffling up the crumbling street, a pine cane chopping a path through the dancing hooves and darting shins. The old man's head was bent as though from a lifetime of mindless prostration, a bleached tarboosh riding high on his woolly gray crown. Vane threw a handful of birrs on the table's dainty lace and stomped through the patio's mihrāb-shaped entranceway. In the street he was swallowed up by a black wave of beseeching humanity. He swatted his way through the scrabbling hands.

The blind beggar must have caught a promising nuance in the passing American's gait, for he immediately turned and began tapping in pursuit. Vane cursed him and his family, and all his forebears and all their stock. But the beggar persisted, matching Vane's towering insults with increasingly booming praises of Allah and Muhammad. The pair argued down a stinking harbor alley until they'd reached a well-shaded alcove between two leaning outbuildings. There Mudhead removed his tarboosh and extracted a fat white envelope. Vane thumbed the stacks of crisp new Franklins quickly: a hundred bills in each banded stack, five stacks in all. The topmost bills bore the distinguished stamp of Banke Internationale. Also in the envelope was a cable from Denise Waters, informing Vane that, per his broadcast request, one Mudahid Asafu-Adjaye had indeed been flown directly from Kahreb to Addis Ababa, had been photo-graphed extensively, and had his fingerprints, dental work, and body scars scanned. With these vital statistics and Vane's signa-ture, the glum African was eligible to embrace unlimited funds directly from Banke Internationale, or small sums through a Honey agent dealing solely with the air courier. Mudhead, now sporting a small wrist-and-metacarpals cast and sling, had been jetted from the Ethiopian capitol and dropped off at the border. Left to his own devices with a sack full of local coins and bills, he had managed to get himself transported from the border, first by bus and then by crop duster, to the desert outside of Mas-sawa. The plane owner's sister's eleventh cousin on her father's side thereupon provided Mudhead with a sturdy little donkey and half a dozen runners. These scouts, all children, had scur-ried ahead on camel, bicycle, and foot, locating Vane with uncanny perspicacity and passing back directions for a harbor rendezvous. The entire operation, half-assed as it must have ap-peared to Honey's link Tibor, took only slightly over seven hours and went off without a hitch. Pleased and eternally sur-prised by his saturnine second's efficiency, Vane stuffed the stacks under his djellaba and followed him back out the alley.

Mudhead banged his cane metronomically, hammering out a path to a particularly decrepit section of Massawa. Here ancient brick buildings grew together like weeds, broken-down streets deteriorated to dank alleyways sloping into pitch. In the deepening twilight only a few lamps flickered fitfully. But he knew where he was going; he'd been here only half an hour a-go, before rejoining Vane.

With whispers and Hamiltons he'd sought out the har-bor's ugliest brigands, all the while smacking away hands like flies. Those tens gave way to twenties and fifties as he bought his way to Massawa's squalid heart, the one part of Old Harbor feared even by Franco's well-equipped soldiers. Here lurked the guerilla-like, barefoot adults and children who, with daggers and Molotov cocktails, worked to undermine the military autho-rity holding sway over every family-run business on the Red Sea's African coast.

At the filthy funnel's bottom, the dark street terminated in a depressed cul-de-sac containing a hatbox-shaped structure with a dirty glass face lit by three golf ball-sized bulbs. The place appeared to sag with the street, as if all north-facing matter were being drawn into its caving belly. Movement to either side accompanied their approach: shapes on the right that rolled quickly downhill, shapes on the left that hiked back slowly, closing the gap behind.

"Nice going, Mudhead. You just got us mugged. Big time."

"Bossman not worry. In shadow only watchman. Big fish bottom sea. Shark circle, not bite."

The collapsing building turned out to be an old movie house with a deserted lobby. A single yellow bulb partially exposed a mess of mildewed carpet and peeling film posters. There was a title in Arabic sprawled across the theater's cracked plastic marquee. Vane nodded upward.

Mudhead replaced the dark glasses with his wireless spectacles. "One Who," he translated awkwardly, "Terminate Two."

"Terminator 2? In Arabic?"

The lobby doors cracked apart. Sounds of shouting and gunfire blew out. A small brown man slithered into the paneless booth. He scowled up at them. The cheeks under his bitter black eyes were covered with smallpox scars. One wing of his nose had been eaten away by syphilis. The mouth was a lopsided wound, whitely scarred at the corners as though by a pair of yanked fish hooks.

"Two," said Vane pleasantly, flicking his thumb along a stack of bills. The little man watched the bills whir up and down before slithering back out. A momentary squeal of burning rubber, more gunshots. Vane grew aware of a heavy presence at his back. He smiled at Mudhead and nodded. "After you."

A hard command in Arabic stopped them dead. They remained perfectly still while two pairs of hands thoroughly patted them down. Vane's hood was pulled back. The stack of bills was plucked from his hand, the envelope lifted from beneath his cloak. He and Mudhead were propelled by fists on their spines.

Rather than feature a glass snack stand, as in American theaters, the lobby contained a grouping of small tables bearing urns, cups, and various boxes of African and Arabian teas. Vane got the impression that intermission was a gathering, a social function. The only recognizable word, stamped on an ancient steel dispenser, was *Pepsi*.

The two goons, large for Eritreans, wore cheap suits and white kaftans with a red dot on either side of a solid black vertical line. One stepped ahead to hold open the right-hand door while the other walked them through. Despite this man's forceful guidance, Vane and Mudhead repeatedly barked their shins as they stumbled down the aisle. It was nighttime on screen. A poker-faced Arnold Schwarzenegger was explaining to Linda Hamilton the complexities of computer-versus-human warfare while driving a trashed police car. Their voices had been dubbed over in Arabic, and were completely out of sync with the lips. Hamilton's voice sounded like Minnie Mouse, Schwarzenegger's like a cab driver about to go postal. The audience consisted of only one member, sitting raptly in the center seat precisely midway between screen and lobby. Projected light caught the intricate gold brocade girding his snow-white fez.

Upon reaching the row directly behind this man, a goon took Mudhead's elbow and walked him to the far aisle, then turned him about and walked him down the seated man's row. Vane's guard propelled him from the opposite side, until he and Mudhead were seated beside the man in the fez like competing girlfriends. The goons took seats directly beside their captives, arms draped around the backs of their chairs. It was all very close, and all very uncomfortable. The tight knot of five stared silently as bullets were plucked from Schwarzenegger's synthetic back.

Vane felt a tickling at his left shoulder. He carefully rolled his head until he saw a stack of bills dangling six inches away. The man in the white fez pinched the stack gently and held it under his nose, his eyes remaining on the screen. He thumbed the new bills delicately while inhaling their fragrance. His eyes closed, and he appeared to shiver. He thumbed the bills again, muttered something to Mudhead's guard. The guard looked back at the projection room and made a chopping motion with his left arm. The screen went dark immediately, but the house lights did not come up. The theater was now lit only by the thin strip of light separating lobby doors, and by a pair of tiny exit signs, one on either side of the screen.

The man in the fez returned the stack to the dangling hand. The hand disappeared. The man in the fez rose primly. He was of less than average height, mustached, wearing light slacks and a dinner jacket. That was all Vane could make out in the dark. The man cleared his throat. The guards rose as one. After a moment he cleared his throat again, this time with emphasis. Mudhead and Vane rose tentatively. The five men filed out to their right in a tight chain, turned left down the aisle, and marched quietly to the exit corridor.

The group halted in the corridor. Mudhead's guard reached into the pleats where the curtain and wall met and pushed hard. There was a muffled rumbling. When the rumbling ceased the guard pulled aside the curtain to reveal a narrow passage. The five men edged into a large room behind the theater's screen. Seconds later the place was lit dazzlingly. Vane's envelope was returned. Both guards exited into the corridor. The section of wall rumbled back.

Lounging in the room were perhaps two dozen men, from scrappy teenagers to grizzled seniors, dressed in robes, in rags, and in street clothes. Many were barefoot. They wore turbans, skullcaps, or knotted towels. Their eyes were hungry black pools.

The room's interior was a mishmash of tables and mats piled high with a wide variety of weapons and combat paraphernalia. There were Sten guns and M16s, bazookas and flamethrowers, German 9mm submachine guns and hand grenades, boxes of dynamite, flak jackets, flare guns. Lining the rear wall were bucket after bucket piled to overflowing with bullets of all calibers.

The man in the fez snapped his fingers. More than a simple signal, this was a quick but intricate display, almost a riff. The men and boys obediently moved back against the rear wall.

Vane fingered novelties as he browsed, his eyes gleaming under the floodlights like a kid's in a candy store. Out of a box of odds and ends he plucked a bossed green minaret-shaped spyglass, pressed it closed, pulled it open, peered through the eyepiece at the shifting faces. "Far out." He focused on Mud-head's glaring mug, then swung the glass by its leather cord and placed it upright on the table. "Tell him we'll take it." Again he dug through the box, producing a ship's compass, a broken old pocket-timepiece, and a small, elaborately engraved throwing knife. On a floor mat he discovered a pair of authentic knee-high goatskin moccasins in good condition. "Tell him we'll take it all." His eyes fell on a heavy spiral-bound mass, its deep red cover broken only by a broad black diagonal line and thick Russian characters.

"Come here, Mudhead." Inside were exploded diagrams of what were certainly spy planes and attack helicopters. Text was in Russian, Chinese, and Arabic.

The man in the fez snapped his fingers like castanets. "Glass-e-fyed," he lisped.

Vane nodded, whispering, "Can you decipher this?"

"Sloppy Arabic. But easy read."

"Then tell him we'll take it!" He stomped to a central table covered with stabbing weapons, brushing aside rusty bay-onets and a chipped cutlass to expose a *jile*, the fifteen-inch dagger worn by ancestral Afar warriors. The blade was curved and extremely sharp; a sweet tool. He raised it to his eyes and smiled.

The man in the fez snapped his fingers in a wavy, mes-merizing pattern that concluded with the forefinger tensed hor-izontally like a bowed arrow. Out of the bunched beggarly fig-ures came an old man with a false eye of solid gold. Deeply etched into that orb's polished face was the legend *al-Wakil*, ensuring its security against theft by a follower of Islam. This man reached below the table and came up with a sensitively-worked, brass-ribbed calfskin sheath sewn into a heavily-bro-caded sash. Gold Eye demonstrated how the jile was sheathed, and how the sash was worn about the waist and right shoulder. Vane smiled again. From then on this man was ever at his heel, wordlessly assisting his shopping while the man in the fancy fez watched politely, hands folded at the waist.

At last Vane moseyed over to Mudhead. "Ask him if this is the best he can do." The man in the fez slowly rocked his head side to side, listening closely to Mudhead's translation.

His reply took forever.

Mudhead turned back. "Massawaman get whatever Bossman want. Anything. If price right any quantity. If price right rush order. Massawaman guarantee this. Police issue. Military issue. No order too big." He gestured at the tables. "Small stuff here. Massawaman get remote bomb, police van, tar heroin, sloe gin, fast woman."

"Tell him thanks but no thanks. Just ask him about boats. Anything seaworthy."

Mudhead translated again. This time the man laughed, and appeared to speak glowingly. Mudhead nodded. "No Massawaman not have boat, or not know someman have boat. Father, brother, uncle, son." His hand swept the room. "Seaman."

Following Mudhead's gesture, Vane's eyes fell on a few wooden steps melting out of an unlit corner. He raised an eyebrow. "This place has an upstairs. Ask Mister Congeniality what he's hiding."

The man in the fez didn't wait for a translation. He snapped his fingers all over the place while jauntily leading his guests and men up the gently winding steps. The loft was crammed with larger objects: winches, intact and partly dismantled jet skis, gutted outboard motors in waist-high racks. The room smelled heavily of grease and fried motors. Ropes and cables hung from the walls, along with spear guns, crossbows, gas masks, and grappling hooks. The men stepped around the equipment carefully.

Against the far wall stood a series of rolling clothes-racks. These racks, tightly pressed together and draped with protective sheets of clear plastic, bore military uniforms of every rank, interspersed with camouflage field wear and various articles of Middle Eastern dress. Under Fez Man's rock-hard gaze, Gold Eye delicately peeled the plastic sheets aside. Vane casually thumbed through the articles until he reached the black silk robes of a Turkish sheik. He was flabbergasted. With the utmost delicacy he slipped it from its rack, cradled it in his arms. The material flowed over his forearms like water. When he looked back up his eyes were wet with awe.

The man in the fez was one big smile. He snapped his fingers urgently. Gold Eye hopped behind the racks and reappeared a moment later wheeling a full-length mirror.

Vane removed his jile and slipped the robes on carefully, tied the fringed sash at his waist. The robes fit as though tailor-made. Gold Eye's hands appeared in the mirror, holding a matching black silk turban with the girth of a medium-sized pumpkin. A vacant silver inset, its six prongs like seizing talons, was centered in the turban's stiff bulbous face.

There came a single snap of fingers, dramatic as a whiplash.

Gold Eye looked down grudgingly. One hand vanished under his kaftan and reappeared holding a serrated three-inch throwing knife. In a breathtaking motion that made Vane's knees cross, Gold Eye slipped the knife beneath his robe, slit a leather testicle pouch, slid the knife back out and returned it to the kaftan. His free hand now supported a beautifully-faced, deeply luminous sapphire. Gold Eye brought the turban to his mouth. The man had precisely two teeth left in his head, a lower molar and an upper canine, and he used these to bend opposing prongs over the inserted stone. He then crowned Vane like the homecoming queen. The American put on his jile and stared raptly at his reflection. He tried on his shades, modeled himself at different angles, propped his head so that the overhead floods shone dramatically on the magnificent sapphire. Finally he spun around, his mouth hanging, to see the whole room grinning. The man in the fez gave him two thumbs up. Vane, fighting back tears, turned to Mudhead. "Tell him," he choked, "tell him it's time to talk business. Ask him if he knows Franco's routine."

At mention of the name their host clenched his fists. His mouth worked soundlessly, his eyes fixed on Vane while Mudhead explained their plan. Slowly his features softened. His response was muted, but with sharp inflections. Mudhead nodded over and over.

"Bossman make friend. Bossman need, Bossman get."

"Excellent." Vane stepped up crisply, handed over the envelope. "Tell him this is just for starters."

The man did not look at the envelope. He merely handed it back and bowed deeply. After a passionate speech he threw his arms around the American and hugged him like a long lost son.

Vane squirmed out. "What in Christ's name did he just say?"

Mudhead was nodding vigorously. "Praise Allah, Bossman! Money no good here. This matter war!"

"Tell him I'm honored he's on my side."

After the translation the man bowed again, but this time the room froze. He and Vane stared hard at one another, for the longest time. Finally the man in the fez snapped his fingers in a complicated series of clusters, his eyes still locked with Vane's.

Gold Eye slid over. The two spoke back and forth with the urgency of jackhammers. They ceased abruptly, stared crazily at Vane. An instant later they were at it again. Once more they stopped to stare.

"Why," Vane whispered, "is my stomach fluttering? What the hell are they jabbering about now?"

"Massawaman discuss Bossman."

"I can *see* that, Sherlock. And if they stare any harder, I'm gonna start blushing like a schoolgirl."

Mudhead clucked and shook his head. "Bad move. Mudahid advise Bossman try more John Wayne, less Shirley Temple."

The men ceased their bickering. A gentle smile lifted the corners of Fez Man's moustache. He faced Gold Eye and the two bowed formally. Fez Man glided up to Vane and Mudhead as Gold Eye drifted back to the scruffy group of lounging men and boys.

The man in the fez addressed Mudhead and Vane alternately. The silver in his smile caught the light of floods as he sadly nodded and shook his head.

"Don't tell me," Vane muttered. "There's been a change in plan."

Chapter Twelve

Old Harbor

The first sign of a weak enemy is a relaxed guard.

The tug should never have slipped past Old Harbor's cruising sentries. She shouldn't have reached *Scheherazade* at all, but she'd almost rammed the ship when a deck spotlight lit her up like a deer in headlamps. Within seconds, a hundred flashlight beams were crisscrossing madly on the water. There was an urgent clatter of firearms. Suddenly dozens of men were barking down in Arabic. The brightly-lit little man with one eye barked right back up.

The ensuing verbal dogfight stopped on a dime. Gold Eye stalked into the cabin and returned with a bound Cristian Vane. The stumbling American rolled his head against the light, cursing his captor up and down, using both English and in an ingenious, spontaneously created pidgin Arabic. Gold Eye, jabbering viciously in return, manhandled him across the deck.

Vane bellowed up, "Not without my man! I can't understand a word you freaks are spewing. I'll sit right here all night if I have to." To make his point, he deliberately dropped on his rear. Gold Eye howled in frustration. He kicked Vane repeatedly while shaking his fist at the clipped voices pounding down like rain. Two diseased-looking characters ran out of the cabin and tried wrestling Vane to his feet, but he tangled his legs in theirs, butted their faces with his head and knees, rocked side to side and back and forth until a single rifle shot pierced the night. Everybody froze. Gold Eye's assistants scrambled to their feet and dived below.

From behind the light came a cool command. Gold Eye hopped into the cabin, reappearing a minute later with an unbound Mudhead, his crippled hand hugged to his chest. Gold Eye really tore into him, screaming up and down. The African glumly dropped his eyes.

"Bossman get up now."

Vane could only glare.

They hauled him upright and walked him to the tug's stern. Gold Eye released him and plunged a hand under his kaftan. The cloth binding Vane's wrists was severed.

A dropped line was secured to the tug's rail, followed in half a minute by a dirty rope ladder. Gold Eye prodded Vane up, with Mudhead dragging the rear. Once on board they were surrounded. Two ranks of facing soldiers simultaneously formed a rifle-spired tunnel five feet wide. Down this bore moseyed a slender, darkly handsome man wearing an open coat bearing the stacked chevrons of an Eritrean army major. He'd been interrupted: a delicately embroidered bib was snagged on a brass button of his shirt, brown flecks of Moroccan *tajine* clung to one corner of his mouth. He studied Vane up and down in a shower of flashlight beams, slipped off the bib and tenderly dabbed his lips, then watched like a hawk as an orderly very carefully folded the bib and placed it in a satin-lined cedar box. His eyes slid back.

"The American, Va'en. Interesting attire." He turned on his heel. His men followed automatically. "You will not need your interpreter here. Or do I flatter myself? The occasional literate informs me I speak the American well."

"Mudhead's coming along anyway," Vane mumbled, wondering if that 'attire' comment was a crack. "He's way more than a mere translator."

"This is kosher," said the major, watching Vane closely.

"Whatever."

The major sighed. "Such a vexing contrast this must be for you. One moment you walk in the fire of neon and jewels, the next you tread one of the smelliest, dirtiest vessels any man was ever forced to haunt." His eyes swept the ship systematically as he spoke. His face twisted with distaste. "Among the foulest, least-cultivated specimens…" He appeared about to spit, but his vanity caused him to grimace and swallow.

The men were forced to step side to side as they navigated the sprawling mounds of foodstuffs and soil nutrients. Several times Vane saw shadows scurrying between piles. A healthy disgust, and a jealous regard for his doomed property, made him halt with his fists clenched, ignoring the rifle barrels sticking him like pins. "Don't you know there are *rats* on this ship?"

"This," the major replied distantly, "is no fault of mine. I do not do the recruiting." He gestured his men along with a bored forefinger-flick. His nose crinkled as he ambled, for *Scheherazade* stank, as bad as Port Massawa and worse. Yet she was no simple overblown garbage scow; German engineers had fitted her with four tremendous frigate screws for fast unprotected Mediterranean runs. "Mind your robes around these pipes," the major warned. "There are occasional projections."

The "pipes" were enormous sections of rusted flanged steel tubing, eight feet in diameter by twenty feet long. The lengths were secured with frayed cables, and stacked in tier-formation upon rolling jumbles of straw. In settling they had taken out cabin walls, caved in sections of deck, and crushed yard upon yard of piled canned goods. The major waved his hand airily as they proceeded alongside, randomly drawing additional soldiers. "Your escort intimated that you might find some of the goods aboard this swamp bucket familiar."

"Not some. Most."

"And you have come to reclaim these goods? And found it convenient to be bound and dragged aboard in the process?"

"As you say, I was escorted."

The major popped a long Turkish cigarette into a silver-tipped, hyena bone holder. "An indulgence of mine," he explained while lighting. "I am not one of these men who blindly *baa* to their Ka'bah, refusing every sophisticated pleasure in life. Ordinary rodents," he sniffed, "have more sense than ordinary men." He offered Vane a smoke.

"Not one of my indulgences, I'm afraid. But thanks anyway."

"So? A pity. But certainly you are no stranger to the many delights of the palate, and to the manifold pleasures of...the flesh?"

Vane stopped dead. The whole group halted with him. Again with the pricking rifles.

The major went on hurriedly, "I am certain that the sweets of this world, for a man such as yourself, must be virtually limitless. And such is the market that, even in this forsaken toilet Eritrea, a discerning shopper might daily squeeze—ah... the fruit more tender."

Vane said nothing.

The major waved his cigarette nervously, creating a crazy shooting star with a serpentine tail. "Although the produce here," he managed, "is certainly of an inferior quality."

"*I*," Vane said icily, "wouldn't know."

"Of course not. Of course not."

The major worked himself back together, regaining his haughty mien through the practiced act of leading his men, barking, "Your captor—this soiled old ignoramus with a bauble for an eye, apparently feels your name, in America at least, would command a handsome ransom. However...you are not so well-known here." He spat out a lungful of pugnacious Arabic as he strolled. The man with one eye spat right back.

"He *wish*es," the major snarled, "to see General Franco a' Muhammed en Abbi—as though Massawa's frightfully busy commander exists merely to do the bidding of water spiders."

Vane turned his head sharply. "*General?*"

"Yes. Apparently General Haile Mdawe Mustafu suffered a fatal accident on a visit to Massawa this very afternoon. His personal plane seems to have set down on a fuel spill before crews were able to close the runway. Sparks ignited the undercarriage and the plane was instantly consumed by flames."

"You should watch those fuel spills."

"The problem is already remedied. All personnel involved have been disciplined and removed to remote posts. Muhammed en Abbi was immediately awarded the vacated rank." The major was struck by a funny thought. He nodded at Gold Eye while jocularly nudging Vane. "He thinks he is in Washington." The major pronounced the capitol *Woe-sheen-town*. "He thinks he is soliciting his congressman, who will introduce legislation into the...into the..." The major was cracking himself up.

"The House," Vane said absently, wondering if his below-deck perishables were rotting as they strolled. The whole ship smelled vilely. "We Americans just never seem to get it."

Even in the act of recovering from his laughter, the major whipped round and strafed Gold Eye with godawful abuse. Gold Eye's responding barrage made Vane's head spin. Mud-head translated impassively. "Everyman agree."

"Good," said Vane. "I'd hate to see these guys argue."

"We *agree*," the major said witheringly, "only that this dog is truly a dog. Although he brays like a beast of lesser repute." He rolled the tension from his neck. "But he is not entirely stupid. He has learned that Muhammed en Abbi has designs on a...partnership with you, sir. This is no great secret. The general speaks long and often of his plans." His nose turned up. "But this...this monkey wrench seems to think the general is easy prey for a blustering half-witted showman, believing he would pay any sum rather than see his future partner eliminated." The major shrugged. "It is of no moment to me."

There was a sudden commotion at their backs. Gold Eye shoved a handgun up Vane's spine so that the barrel rested at the bottom of his skull, buried deep beneath his turban's billowy nape. Nine rifle barrels immediately surrounded the principals.

"It is," Vane gasped, "of considerable moment to me."

The major addressed his men with a passion incomprehensible to his silk-clad prisoner. Rifles were lowered grudgingly. Using Vane as a human wedge, Gold Eye now plowed through the knot of useless soldiers. After ten yards' progress he stopped to deliver a half-shouting, half-wailing diatribe.

The major turned to Vane. "He demands access to the helm. I have *explained* to him that the pilot of this vessel is a *civilian*: in charge of nothing! This fat steamer is a commercial vessel impressed during wartime; the hoariest of tramps. I have also *made clear* that General en Abbi is utterly inaccessible at this point, and that *I* am the man he must address." The major's mouth turned south. "He is uninterested in these data."

Vane nodded with care. "I had trouble with him too."

The major stared coldly. "There is a gun at your brain stem, sir. Your future can perhaps be measured in minutes, rather than in witty comebacks." He reprised his nonchalant stroll. The group followed closely.

"Do I," Vane grunted, "detect a note of anxiety? Could it be that this scurvy little bastard's got your number? Could it be that a certain light-footed major's head will roll if Goldie here makes good on his threat?"

"He never should have boarded with a firearm. I blame myself. And, though speaking with the helm will do him no good, he simply will not be persuaded otherwise. So he will have his way. He will meet with the wheel, and discover that the man is indeed as mindless as he. I do not know what he will think of his situation then. He will surely see himself a cornered brute, and I deem it likely he will, out of frustration alone, blow your clever fair head off its mounting. I do not know. My sole concern will be to soar free of the pulverizing volley certain to follow."

"Out of the frying pan," Vane gasped, "and into the fire. Because once you've successfully flitted free, you're gonna have some real explaining to do. Believe me, I know where your general's head's at, okay? My corpse will guarantee yours. I'm a lot more important to Franco than you might think, *sir*— far more important, believe it or not, than you. So, as a very partial commentator in all this, I very seriously recommend that you take very serious pains to keep me alive."

"Recommendation noted."

They reached the wheelhouse. Except for a few patches of bluish light, the interior was dark. The major glared. Without another word he stormed inside.

Hard yellow light burst out the wheelhouse doorway, followed by the sound of heated Arabic, a smacking sound, more shouting, and several more sharp reports. A disheveled man wearing a slapped-on ensign's cap staggered out, the major right behind him. This man's shirt was open, his feet bare, his black hair a sweaty tangled mess. A three-day growth covered his cheeks and chin. But the story was best told by his blood-shot, unfocused eyes.

"As I said," the major spat, shoving the drunken man from behind, "a civilian!" He pushed him right up to Gold Eye, cried, "*Here!*" and flew into a wild verbal Arabic ride.

Mudhead translated. "Moron, meet moron."

Vane's captor threw back his head. The gold eye appeared about to pop from its socket as he pointed the gun straight up, screamed "*Allah Akbar!*" and pulled the trigger.

It was a flare gun.

For an interminable few seconds everyone involved instinctively watched the tracer rise and level off, their jaws hanging. Vane and Mudhead hit the deck.

A moment later night had become hellish day, and the Red Sea was seething. Small outboards and a fan of jet skis converged on the massive ship like ants on an upturned beetle, emitting bursts of machine gun fire that quickly scattered the standing soldiers. Kneeling behind the rail, the Eritreans fired back in systematic spurts while the spotlight sought small craft popping in and out of its hard white pool. Vane stared mesmerized at Old Harbor aboil, reminded of savages circling a wagon train. To either side, soldiers rose to shoot, ducked to reload, rose again.

The major rolled across the deck and came up running. He sprinted straight into the wheelhouse and ran back out waving a megaphone. After a short squeal his voice boomed a flurry of commands in Arabic, sending crouching figures dashing shadow-to-shadow. *Scheherazade's* lights were killed one by one. From somewhere on the roof, the ship's searchlight pierced the heavens. The light was righted and began sweeping the harbor. A moment later a mounted machine gun erupted. The jet ski riders approached from all sides, crisscrossing recklessly, firing from shotguns, from Uzis, from hunting rifles and handguns. In one spontaneous rush the searchlight was shot to pieces, even as two jet skis and a motorboat were blown right out of the water. From the docks rose a complex wailing of sirens.

The second sign of a weak enemy is tunnel vision.

Even as opponents were duking it out to port, half a dozen small fishing craft were clinging quietly to starboard. In all the racket no one heard the grappling hooks striking true on the guardrail, no one saw the spiders slinking up the ropes and rolling aboard. No one saw them making their way along the deck, sliding like grubs over the broken sacks and heaped crates. And, embarrassing to say, not a single defender was prepared for the attacker's knife pressed to his throat. Each captive timidly obeyed the whispered command to lay down arms.

Truth be told, even the dashing major was taken aback when he gallantly rolled, megaphone in hand, directly into a pocket of highly paid pirates just itching to cut his tender official throat.

The battle, perhaps fifteen minutes in execution, was over in two shakes of a lamb's tail. Mudhead translated as Vane ordered the humiliated soldiers lined along the guardrail. The major shook off his grungy captors and coolly marched up the deck, his head held high.

A couple of horn blasts came off the water, and a moment later deck lights leaped into play. The port gangplank was lowered. A derrick swayed in the dark as the battered lifeboat holding Vane's little armory was hauled up the side.

Way down the deck an approaching form phased in and out of the swaying light, at last becoming a swaggering septuagenarian barely four feet tall. The little man's dirty white beard was so long it trailed over a shoulder, his dirty white robes so long they swept the deck left and right as he strode.

"This…" Vane muttered, "*this* is the 'great and mighty mariner' I paid top dollar for?"

Mudhead quite naturally used Vane's sarcastic tone as part of his verbatim translation, and the baldness of this effrontery made Gold Eye almost chew the African's head off. He glared singly at Vane, then turned back with an expression of intense adoration. The stranger came right up to Vane, looked him up and down, cocked his head and walked on, his bare feet making tiny sucking noises. With an undisguised scowl for the helmsman, the dirty little robed figure stepped inside the wheelhouse as if he owned it.

The major stood smartly at Vane's elbow, unable to conceal his embarrassment as he glared at his men's squared backs. "It must come as an exceptional thrill to best such a worthy adversary." He produced a cigarette, paused and raised an eyebrow. "You would not begrudge a final request?"

"Go ahead. It won't be your last."

The major lit up casually and took an urgently needed lungful. "Then I pray you are not one for shackles. My men, lightning-quick brutes that they are, might erupt with unbridled indignation at the sight of their beloved leader in such a debased state."

"Don't worry. Even though I think chains would become you."

Vane had three of his crew walk the major and previous helmsman to the gangplank. He and Mudhead watched as they were kicked aboard an oarless rowboat containing two dead and three wounded soldiers.

Scheherazade shuddered stern to stem when her two great anchors, embedded for nearly a month, were torn free by winches. A moment later there came another, deeper shudder, as her immense screws bit into the sea with German precision. Aft waters appeared subjected to a feeding frenzy. With a subterranean explosion, *Scheherazade* lurched forward.

"Here comes the part I don't like," Vane breathed, watching lights stream away from the docks. "I sure hope this guy at the wheel doesn't have an axe to grind."

"No suicide run, Bossman. Strict cash procedure."

Vane nodded. "And away we go."

Chapter Thirteen

Aseb

The night was uncomfortably warm; even the slight breeze created by the ship's motion was a blessed relief. The little wedge of rowboat became a chip, became a spot, became a speck surrounded by converging outboards. While Mudhead barked Vane's instructions over the major's megaphone, lights on board were extinguished one by one, leaving only a wry yellow slat from the wheelhouse. All forty-eight captured soldiers were spaced against the rail on their rears, hands clasping ankles. Each of Vane's men sat facing three prisoners apiece, a confiscated rifle across his knees.

The lights on the water dispersed, then slowly reformed as an arrowhead. The white tip of this arrowhead ate into *Scheherazade's* wake, creating the impression of a lace-embroidered black fan with a dozen silvery ribs. The sirens grew fainter and fainter still, until there was only the rumble of the screws and the silence of immensity.

Mudhead drifted out of the wheelhouse, his face passing

from deepest black to imperceptible as he moved beyond that one slice of light. The white teeth showed dully. "Twelve knot."

Vane shook his head. "Tell him faster. It's going on two hundred miles to Djibouti. My math isn't so hot, but it doesn't take a rocket scientist to see we won't be outrunning anybody. And pretty soon the big guns'll be showing up." Almost before the words were out of his mouth a pair of lights appeared in the blackness above Port Massawa. "Those'll be choppers!" Vane called. He drew the minaret-spyglass to his eye and pulled it open. "Despite what Franco said about 'intelligent weapons,' there can't be anything modern around here on short order." Squinting into the eyepiece, he noted the positioning of body lights and placement of rotors, then checked and double-checked his sightings against the Russian manual under Mudhead's flashlight.

"Apaches! Good old American Apaches! Viet Nam vintage. Black market purchases. Got to be; America wouldn't be selling to Eritrea. We've still got strong ties with Ethiopia and Djibouti." He browsed the diagram with a forefinger, muttering along while Mudhead deciphered the Arabic, "They'll be armed: four rockets apiece, thirty-millimeter turrets." Vane raised his spyglass again. "There's only those two showing. Tell What's-his-Face to kill the engines. I want him sending a distress call." He paced neurotically, braked mid-stride, threw his arms in the air. "I've *got* it! Damn, I'm good! Here's his message: the captured soldiers, in an attempt to take back the ship, have disabled all engines. Their guys and ours are engaged in close combat below. The ship's on fire and in danger of going down. At last report our guys were all cornered amidships— how on Earth do I do it? Now listen, Mudhead, you've got to rehearse with him. Go over the message, go over and over and over it—until he gets it straight! But whatever you do, don't let him make the call until I give you the word."

Mudhead's eyes rolled in the dark. Vane saw him raise and flick his hand—more a tossing of forehead-sweat than a proper salute—before wearily making his way into the wheel-house. A minute later the screws locked.

He returned to find Vane perilously giving directions by sign language; he'd reduced the guard by half, and the dismissed men were staring back fiercely, not certain which way to point their rifles. "*Order* them," he said, smiling unpleasantly, "to pick their four fastest." Mudhead did so.

There was much arguing, much shoving, much slapping of faces. Finally four were pushed out of the group; three youngsters and a lean old man.

Vane placed his hands on his hips. "I want these four to go through this ship, grabbing anything expendable that'll burn. That means packaging, pallets, and crates—tell them to stuff it all in these pipes and to send it to blazes with flares." He paced impatiently while Mudhead translated.

The selected four exchanged looks. Without a word, they sprinted noiselessly through the piles and drifts. Vane halted imperiously and rocked on his toes. "Ask the rest of these idiots if they can handle stingers." At Mudhead's translation their heads snapped up. The eyes burned with eagerness.

Vane led his crew to the stocked lifeboat, a battered old forty-footer now suspended against the rail by winch cables. The men rooted through the piles like naughty children, each e-merging with a stinger and an assortment of handguns. Vane's smile was strained. He swung his flashlight across the shining faces, saw the eyes glinting redly in the passing beam. "Tell them to put the extra weapons down. I don't want any nonsense. No cowboys."

Mudhead translated with exaggerated deference. A gnarly old man cut him off. The entire group rose. Mudhead muttered from the corner of his mouth, "Massawaman want rest pay now. Not like outlook."

Vane's whole face contorted. "I *knew* it! A pirate is a pirate to the quick. Say no and mean it. The deal was half up front and half when this is over. It's a long way from over."

A handgun was cocked.

Vane smiled broadly, and spoke through his teeth. "Okey-dokey. Pay the scurvy Third-world bastards. But first tell them we'll need to divvy it up in private."

In an alley created by a splintered cabin wall and leaning crates, Vane flicked on his flashlight, doffed Mudhead's cap for him, and removed a flattened stack of bills. Once he'd switched off the light they grew aware of a low red glow; the runners were lighting scrap doused with diesel fuel. He thumbed off a wad. "Go hit our touchy little skipper and the runners."

Vane settled with his men, grabbed a rifle with infrared scope, and found a box of shells on the lifeboat's floor. He led them around the deck, seeking access to the ship's highest level. Stairways and ladders were backed to the roof with miscellaneous cargo, all tied down with cables, ropes, rags, and bungee cords. The men leaped heap to heap in the jerking beam of Vane's flashlight.

The islands' roofs were vast badlands of split and leaning cargo. Vane stood looking over the dark dreamy sea. The wide fan of following lights appeared motionless. The helicopters were still a long way off. The night was brilliant with stars, the sea air running cool and lean beneath the night's heaving heat. Just to port, a dirty dark cloud was leaving a low puffy tail. Vane turned to his men with his heart in his throat, his magnificent silk robes billowing. He pounded his flare gun against his chest and shook his head dramatically, indicating that no one was to fire unless he gave the signal. This order was not well-received. Several figures pointed their weapons straight at his fat turbaned head. One squatting shape hawked and spat right between the rich boy's authentic knee-high goatskin moccasins. They turned and filtered into places of concealment like cockroaches. Vane trembled all the way down to the deck, but by the time he'd reached the wheelhouse he was back in command.

"Mr. Mudahid, we're dealing with a bunch of damned Barbary dickheads! Order their little poster boy to make that call."

Now smoke was pouring to port, in long black plumes. Cherry sparks flashed in lazy arcs, occasional prominences lit up heaving piles of trash. Mudhead rejoined Vane at the rail. They stood side by side, watching the Apaches slowly close the gap. In the darkness the men were reverse images; the African a headless ghost of white robes, cap, and sardonic suspended eyes, the American a floating pasty white face propped and cropped by black silk. Mudhead gave Vane the scoop:

The helm's distress call, through argument, displays of incompetence, and panicky outbursts, was gradually taking effect. *Scheherazade's* pursuers were now half-convinced the pilot was entirely incapable of handling the crisis, and interested solely in rescue. This was excellent news. Vane leaned against a wheelhouse doorjamb and peered in, nodding gratefully while rubbing together his thumb and adjacent fingers in the universal gesture for money. The bearded steersman returned the nod and continued transmitting, but his patter seemed directed more toward invective than entreaty. At length a calm, familiar voice could be heard, carefully iterating "Va'en" at the middle and end of the transmission. Vane, leaning inside, pointed at his own head with one hand and made the throat-slitting gesture with the other, indicating he wished to be reported dead. The pilot nodded and smiled, his eyes gleaming with sweet anticipation. He went on muttering into the transmitter.

Vane walked Mudhead to the rail. "So what do you think?"

"Wait time." Mudhead looked Vane dead-on. After a minute he appended in a whisper, "Mudahid counsel patience," and stared out to sea. "Walk soft."

Vane winked cannily. "But with a big stick."

The ivory eyes rolled back, annoyed. "No stick! Walk *soft.*"

Vane lasted all of thirty seconds. "Wait, *hell!* This is taking forever. I'm gonna go check on my property. If you see any movement up there, just sing out and I'll come running." He stared into the darkness for a space, then gently pried off his turban and handed it over. "Watch Sophie for me. I mean, don't get me wrong; it's not like I don't trust these guys or anything."

He picked his way around the deck cautiously, expecting the worst—knowing the worst. But he wasn't about to surrender to the obvious that easily; he had to sift through vibes and vestiges, had to see for himself. A pile of molding flour, peppered with rotten apples, onions, and pears, removed all but the most stubborn remnants of his denial. Little or no care had gone into basic preservation. Perishables were scattered about in heaps and clumps, piled in crevices amid strange hulking machinery, or stuffed unprotected between perilously stacked boxes. Individual items had been left to roll around the deck, eventually catching on greasy parts and broken parcels. And in one cul-de-sac, at the end of a haphazard passageway created by opposing cliffs of teetering crates, Vane noticed a particularly nauseating odor. His anger escalated as he approached, his curiosity over-taken, step by step, by a single black realization: Franco had simply stored; he'd just dumped—*the son of a bitch hadn't even used refrigeration!* In a blind rage Vane began smashing at a greasy wooden panel with his jile. The stench intensified. With tears in his eyes he went berserk on the panel, at last hacking out a football-sized hole that spewed forth a stinking swarm of flies. He dropped his jile and threw his hands over his face, retching, even as the whole section of floor gave way and sent him plunging into pitch.

It was a short fall, only two or three feet. All he knew was that he was on his back, half-buried in putrefied meat, flies buzzing around his waving arms, flying into his mouth, crawl-ing over his face. Frantic, he struggled to sit upright, pushing with his elbows and heels, yelling and coughing while he slipped and slid. Vane squirmed onto his hands and knees, al-ternately plopping his hands in and out of the slime as he fought to keep his balance while reflexively backing away. His skin was crawling, and not only with horror—every inch of exposed flesh was covered with maggots! Vane screamed hysterically, swatting his face and body. But he only buried himself deeper. His little panting screams became one continuous shriek that didn't end until a pair of black hands, popping down through the jagged aperture like God Almighty, slipped under his arms and hauled him out into the sweet night air. Mudhead couldn't contain him; Vane was freaking out of his mind, rolling side to side like a man on fire, slapping himself silly. At last he jumped to his feet and ran. If he hadn't been suddenly tackled from the side and rear, he would certainly have leaped the rail into the cleansing sea fifty feet below. The little helmsman, snapping in Arabic, tossed a bucket's worth of gasoline on him, immed-iately followed by a bucket of fresh water from Mudhead. Then water was hitting him from all sides. Vane lurched to his feet. Coughing and sputtering, he staggered to the rail, dropped to his knees, and puked his guts out. He hung there for the longest while, his hair and robes drying in the breeze. Finally a snootful of acrid smoke snapped back his head. He raised himself by the elbows.

"Wait time over, Bossman." Vane felt his turban set squarely on his head. When he reached his feet Mudhead handed him the jile and bowed. "Big stick."

He looked himself up and down. There wasn't a trace of fumes or vermin. "Gas?" he coughed. "On silk?"

Mudhead fingered the material. "No problem, Bossman. Plenty water, plenty fast."

Vane sagged against the rail until he was roused by his twitching nose. Black smoke had all but obscured the port horizon. He ordered Mudhead to have the captain kill the radio. "I just want those damned helicopters off our tail, man! This has to be a rescue job, not a military operation!" Inspiration hit him. "What are the odds of getting one of these soldiers to transmit that the situation's under control? Maybe some of our boys would temporarily donate a few bills to persuade him." He licked his lips. "I'm plumb out of cash."

"Odd zero both way."

"So you're saying Eritrean commanders aren't particularly fond of renegade soldiers?"

Mudhead's expression was fixed. "Wrong, Bossman." He carefully placed his hurt hand's thumb on the rail and used his other hand to mimic the turning of a thumbscrew. "Officer like bad soldier very much." He looked up meaningfully. "Officer crazy about Americaman."

The sky lights shifted.

"Okay," said Vane. "Show time. Tell those boys to stoke the flames with whatever they can get their hands on. I want way more smoke in the air." Mudhead loped off. Vane scraped about until he found a piece of plywood large enough to lean against the wheelhouse doorway, cutting the escape of light to a sliver. He knelt at the rail and peered through his rifle's night scope. The thing was beautiful: when focused away from the helicopter's running lights, he could make out details of the lead Apache's undercarriage while it was still over half a mile distant.

The helicopters initiated their searchlights, and the abrupt blast of white light almost knocked him over. The dead wedge of outboards shot to life. Just like that, the copters were right on top of *Scheherazade*, splitting wide, passing to either side—one a hundred feet overhead, the other low on the water, trying to penetrate the heaving black smoke with their beacons.

Vane kept the high bird in his glass as it hovered overhead and slightly to starboard, while trying to keep his other eye on the low copter's back. It was impossible to hold a bead long enough for a clean hit, but there was one crazy moment when the pilot's goggles and helmet were right in the palm of his hand. The low copter's second circuit drew a concussion and tracer from the roof. Immediately the overhead chopper laid its turret into the spot, ripping a trail across the heaped cargo and taking out one whole side of a cabin. There were screams amidst the billowing debris, followed by a shot from a second stinger that took out the low Apache's tail rotor and sent the copter spinning into the water. The other chopper, veering hard, was promptly blown out of the sky by a furious volley.

A chorus of cheers was quickly drowned by a hail of machine gun fire off the water. The ship's screws bit into the sea. Vane, crouching behind a mound of salt water-hardened Portland cement, took careful aim at a hunched soldier wrestling a hurtling outboard's wheel. He'd never fired a weapon in his life, and for thirty seconds was stone-paralyzed as he watched that intense black face bumping in and out of his sight. Vane caught his breath and squeezed the trigger. He needn't have worried; he was a lousy shot. The soldier didn't even blink.

A snap-and-squeal was repeated twice. In horrifying slow motion, one of the heated pipes swung out over the side and began rocking with the ship, the rhythmic scream of metal on metal growing more pronounced as the arc widened. A zipper-like roll of snapping cables, and the pipe went straight down, followed by seven others. They hit the sea like bombs. As the ship lurched side-to-side, the loose pipes on deck smashed into cabins, rolled back, and took out the guardrail. Four more went over, sending up great resounding founts that capsized three outboards. The rest of the boats came on with a vengeance, veering wide, racing and weaving, their occupants shooting all they had. But *Scheherazade* was impervious to small fire, and her pursuers fell back into the old pattern one by one.

Eventually an amplified voice commenced hailing the

ship in Arabic. Vane carefully studied a flag-bearing inboard at the arrowhead's tip. The speaker's face was hidden behind a bullhorn. Ignoring the monotonous calls, he urged Mudhead to get more knots out of the helm. Sooner or later reinforcements would arrive. And this time they'd be coming to take the ship out.

Yet the passing hours brought no sign of Vane's predicted lion. The boats maintained their flotilla-like aspect while that patient voice droned on and on, gradually driving everybody crazy. Now and then a bored pirate took a potshot with a stinger, but the man with the horn never missed a beat.

By three a.m. *Scheherazade* had passed over a hundred miles of coastline without a sign of retaliation by air or sea. Other than the occasional wink of a lighthouse, the world was black; other than that damnable droning voice, the night breath-takingly still. The outboards stuck behind the big ship with their lights killed, never once breaking formation.

But when the false dawn made a ghost of the Saudi penin-sula, with Djibouti less than sixty miles away, the little flotilla came alive. The outboards circled furiously, taking shots at any-thing moving. Vane ordered his men to remain in the shadows, so as to frustrate the pestiferous pursuers with a formidable show of indifference. And in time the boats fell back. Mudhead translated as the lifeless monologue resumed: the pirates' situ-ation was hopeless. Eritrean law was merciful. "Wrong both count," he concluded.

Yemen's coast grew more distinct in the east. Not far ahead to starboard, the port of Aseb was winking in a red stream of sun. They were nearly out of hostile waters; Aseb's military base was now the sole hurdle between Vane's wares and Dji-bouti. He searched the coast for the inevitable jets until his scope eye was burning and bleary. But all Aseb produced was a battered gray PT boat, popping into sight long after they'd passed the base. When it finally drew near, the smaller boats ignored the cargo ship and gathered round like whelps.

Vane stared and stared through his spyglass. "Damn it! They're priming the mounted machine guns. There's crates of ammunition up the yin-yang. My guess is they plan on just shooting the deck to pieces." He saw an officer on the patrol boat accept the bullhorn from the previous handler. The message that came across the water was all Greek to Vane, but it raised a chant of defiance from *Scheherazade*'s mangled roof. The next thing he knew, the patrol boat had kicked and was tearing their way.

Bullets shredded the deck and cabin walls, zinged into space, ricocheted off the steel pipes. The lifeboat, bursting into flames as its onboard ammunition detonated, hung burning for a few seconds before shrieking down the side. The ceaseless barrage minced every pirate on the roof's edge and fifteen feet beyond. Vane and Mudhead were completely buried by an avalanche of debris. Above the lustily revving patrol boat, the Arabic voice calmly repeated its commands.

Vane dug himself free. "Get 'em up!" He threw his arms wildly. *"Get 'em up!"*

The closest defenders looked his way and nodded. Each man banged his rifle's butt on the deck to get attention down the line. The pirates one by one prodded their prisoners, whispering nastily. The Eritreans got to their feet nervously and stood facing the water, hands clasped behind their necks. Thus shielded, Vane's men rose at their backs, kicking their captives' legs wide apart.

It was nearly full daylight now; bright enough to catch the expressions of the pursuers as they stared up in wonder. For the longest time no one made a move. Then the little torpedo boat, no more than a hundred yards to port, rocked back and forth, champing at the bit. The rush was on. With complete disregard for their countrymen, the gunners opened up on the deck. The captured soldiers went straight down. But when the storm of bullets had passed they lurched to their feet, wailed to Allah in unison, and leaped into space. Vane could hear their breaking ankles smack the water far below.

A single outboard pulled forward cautiously while the PT moved back. The receding amplified message seemed directed at the ship in general, and from the tone Vane had to assume it was a truce call for the sake of rescuing the dozens of soldiers flailing below. He dug about until he found a dirty towel to wave overhead as a white flag. The remaining men on the roof, watching curiously, scooted back out of sight. Vane turned to face the approaching enemy and waved both arms generously, his black silk robes billowing and retracting like the animated cartoon wings of a crime-fighting crusader. The outboard motored right up to *Schererazade*'s hull. Vane, leaning clean over the rail, did his awkward best to direct the rescuers to bobbing and drowning bodies. When the outboard was stuffed he clutched the mangled rail with relief, blessed the Fates, and waved the little boat away to safety. A moment later it had been pulverized by a quartet of stingers. Vane staggered from the rail in horror, sickened by the spray of blood and debris. He turned to the roof, waving his arms side to side, shaking his head frantically. The next thing he knew bullets were zipping all around him. He scrambled between heaps and listened to the laughter on the roof.

Now the amplified voice was in butchered English. It was obvious the speaker was repeating, word for word, what came over his radio's receiver.

"Krees-chun Vah-een! Krees-chun Vah-een! Puhleez turneenk auf engeenz now. No moer warneenkz. No moer...no moer—" There was one fragment of a clipped exchange. "No moer...*gam*-eez! Teez American Pee Tee bot eez ar-med weet tree torPeedoz weet woerhedz kapapa...kapaboo...kapa...*bull!* auv seenkeenk yoer vessehull. Yoo well hav gain-eed nahteenk. Yoo well hav loss-ed *evra*teenk!" A short snarl of Arabic, and the voice came back, "An puh*leez* lit me upAllahjiz foer teez eegnuh-runt harf-weetuhd babbaboohun hoo eez speekeenk foer me now. Heez stoopeeduhtee eez troolee minah boggleenk."

Not needing a translation, Gold Eye got right up in Mudhead's face. At last Mudhead nodded dispassionately and turned. "Massawaman say torpedo plenty serious business. Say Bossman best make deal fast."

Vane, wracked by all the death and indifference, cried, "Or *what?* We'll have us a good old-fashioned mutiny?"

Caught in the middle, the African slowly raised his hands above his head. "Mudahid only messageman."

"Then *give* him a frigging message! Tell him he can change sides any time he wants. The idiot's useless now anyway." He stormed into the wheelhouse and began wrestling with the radio, still refusing to believe he'd lost all control. The little pilot glared, slammed the ON lever into play, and smacked the ignorant American's hand back and forth while indicating switches.

Vane hardly noticed him. "Um..." he said into the phone. "Um, Mayday, man. Mayday, Mayday, Mayday. Or...is that only aeronautical?" He pinched the bridge of his nose, closed his eyes, and forced himself to speak slowly and coherently. "This ship is under attack and I need to know what to do. I am an American. I am not supposed to be at war with anybody. A whole lot of people just died who didn't really have to. If someone else in this part of the world speaks solid English, please let me know. I am maybe half an hour out of Djibouti, in Eritrean waters. A number of motorboats have been dogging us all the way from Massawa, plus there's this PT out of Aseb." Vane shook the phone in frustration. Nothing but dead air. "They...are...*threatening* this ship!" He hammered the phone on the console. "Is anybody picking up on this? *Talk* to me, man. We're a cargo vessel, with no real means of defense. Now *look*, I'm gonna need some kind of super-relevant advice here. Okay? The guy at the wheel is a total cartoon. Hello, Djibouti! Hello, Djibouti! I need an English-speaking operator." He punched knobs and switches until the little captain jumped all over him in Arabic. Vane shoved him back with a forearm. "*Is this on?*" he screamed. "Do you have the slightest freaking idea what I'm trying to *do* here, creep? We're going *down*. Distress call. Djibouti. Not far little country no bad soldier." He tried broad hand gestures. "You *free* in Djibouti. Free! No more be nasty little pirate. Big bonus from shouting American. Oh... *please*. Would you just *help me* with the *goddamned distress call!*"

The helmsman reached up and slapped Vane flat across the face. He then repeatedly stabbed his finger at a blinking red light on the console. For a moment Vane was stupefied. When the crimson veil lifted, he found himself staring down insanely at that filthy little gnome. Unaware of his actions, he grabbed his spyglass and raised his arm to strike.

The captain didn't flinch. With his eyes welded to Vane's, he slipped a hand under his robes, extracted a Walther P-38, and placed the tip of the pistol's barrel squarely on the tip of the American's pink peeling nose.

"I paid for that," Vane gasped. "It's mine. Now you just put it down or give it back."

The man literally steered Vane by the nose, marched him backward through the doorway and out onto deck. His black eyes blazing in the morning sun, he used the gun's barrel to forcefully thrust Vane onto his rear. Staring down venomously, he propped the plywood sheet against the jambs and hopped back inside.

"Vah-een!" came the exasperated voice. Vane, scrambling to his feet, was knocked right back down as the captain threw all engines into the red.

"Vah...*een!*"

Vane raised his spyglass, saw a rail-thin Algerian officer staring back through binoculars. The man was having a tough time keeping his balance. At last he set down the bullhorn and pointed his left arm toward Yemen. Vane followed the arm with his glass until he came upon a blurry white blister. He adjusted focus.

The object was a bound cluster of disabled boats. He swung back, saw the PT kick, and clearly made out the turmoil of launch. Vane followed the torpedo's telltale wake of air bubbles for a ways, then returned to the drifting white blister. Suddenly his spyglass became a kaleidoscope. He had to back off on the focus to make out the descending plume of water and debris. The blister had been excised. He swung the glass back to the officer, who was watching him with two fingers held high, indicating two torpedoes remaining.

"Totally unnecessary," Vane called across the water. "I think we've got the picture." He ran a hand back and forth under his turban as he paced. "I wish we had *something* to intercept torpedoes. Then those guys would wimp out and we'd be home free." He drew his jile and stabbed a few crates. "Any one of those steel pipes, dumped over the side at the right time, could absorb a warhead...but *Jesus*, man, that would just turn the pipe into a battering ram!"

"Vah-een!"

He waved an arm for silence. "Or would the torpedo home on the greater mass of the ship? Are they triggered magnetically or on impact?"

"*Vah-een!*"

Vane glared in the direction of the voice. He didn't need his spyglass to get the picture. The PT kicked, flashing her sleek belly as the long gray tube leaped from its rack. It was amazing how time actually seemed to halt. Every man on deck froze in every particular but one, mesmerized by the arrow on its silent underwater flight. *Son of a gun*, Vane's mind chattered, *it's radio-controlled. No! It's attracted by the motion of the screws!* The gray streak disappeared.

And all aboard were flat on their backs, listening to the concussion singing through the hull while the ship pitched like a rocking horse. A geyser showed to stern and vanished.

Vane shook Mudhead off. "See if we're taking on water!" He ran into the wheelhouse, where he found himself looking straight down the Walther's barrel. "Peace," he tried. "Allah be Akbar." Vane turned nonchalantly. The console showed three propellers out of operation, leaving a single screw to limp *Scheherazade* along.

The little pilot, after expectorating a particularly jangling mouthful of Arabic, aimed the Walther at the ceiling and fired twice. The pair of concussions was much louder than Vane had expected. Cannon fire. He pushed out his palms instinctively and very slowly raised his hands. The captain raved and reiterated, jabbed the gun at Vane's belly and face, threw back his head and howled. He shook the radio's phone menacingly, then thrust it and the pistol in Vane's face.

"I already *called!*" Vane shouted, tears in his eyes. He gradually lowered his arms until he could indicate the captain with one hand and the phone with the other. "*You* call. Me no speak Arab. *You* talk Djibouti. Say S.O.S. You comprende S.O.S.?" He drew the letters in the air with his nose. "Ess. Oh! *Ess!*"

The captain veered the pistol a hair and fired, nearly taking off Vane's head. Vane went down, rolled, and kept right on rolling; across the cabin's floor, through the doorway, and out onto deck. He came up running for his life, quickly disappearing behind a dung-capped mountain of bleached flour. His right ear was ringing wildly, but the other picked up a scuttling to his left. In that ear he heard Mudhead yell, "Hull okay, Bossman! Propeller history."

"Vah-een!"

Spitting out every four-letter word he could think of, Vane fumbled his spyglass from his robes and stared long and hard. The grinning officer was standing rock-steady, watching right back.

"Enough!" Vane cried, and motioned Mudhead into a huddle. The African, after listening incredulously for a few seconds, stalked off and returned with the night-scoped rifle. Without taking his eye off the officer, Vane laid the barrel on the rail and pointed it straight at the final torpedo's head. The skinny officer's grin collapsed. He spoke rapidly and, still watching, handed the bullhorn to one of his men in exchange for what looked like a Mauser. Squaring himself, he aimed right at the hot blue sapphire in the fat black turban.

"Jesus!" Vane swore. He very carefully waved the barrel to the side a few times, motioning the officer away from the torpedo. Keeping his weapon trained, the man just as carefully shook his head. Now the sweat was trickling out from under Vane's turban. In a dream, he dropped the spyglass and transferred his vision to the scope. There was some unseen puppeteer in charge of his actions, causing him to very slowly, very gently arc his rifle upward until his sights were fixed precisely between the binoculars' absolutely motionless lenses.

Not until the actual sound arrived did Vane realize a bullet had just ripped into his upper left chest. He was amazed to find himself lolling on his back in Mudhead's arms, in shock, watching his black robes run red. In no time he was growing cold. His consciousness began to drift. He rolled his head until he was looking back into Mudhead's eyes. "Glass," he dribbled. Mudhead, in an otherwise unthinkable act of compassion, tore off his snow-white tarboosh and pressed it against his master's wound. His other hand found the spyglass and held it to Vane's right eye.

The officer was still grinning. Without pulling away his binoculars, he took a step to his left to tenderly pat the final torpedo, itching in its rack. When he raised the hand he was showing only the forefinger, indicating this was the one. With the last of his strength, Vane raised his right hand in response, exhibiting an erect middle finger. The officer threw down his binoculars.

Vane's arm dropped like a stone, but he never felt it hit the deck. He was already so far gone he'd become detached, and had begun watching the world as a cinematic event. Colors were sharply defined. All action was taking place in slow motion. And nothing, but nothing, made a lick of rational sense. For instance, the Red Sea shouldn't be parting: that hallucination was straight out of DeMille. Also, the little PT boat, in complete control of the situation, shouldn't be rearing and turning about, and the fan of outboards shouldn't be breaking formation to hightail it back to Aseb. That dramatic and gratifying image would be the final tease of a dying man's ego. And, sure as shooting, a huge gray whale shouldn't be surfacing midway between *Scheherazade* and her fading pursuers. That was pure Disney. The whole scene seemed flaky, and kind of funny to Vane, but it also struck him as totally nick-of-time cool. In his gathering delirium he actually hallucinated the surfacing gray whale magically morphing into a surfacing gray submarine. His jaw fell while he watched a billion diamonds cascade off the illusion's broad smooth hull. None of these events produced sound: it was a silent movie. But there was a synced soundtrack issuing from a speaker just behind him, featuring what sounded like a for-once very human Mudhead, mumbling gratefully in Somali over a broad background of jabbering pirates.

The submarine was the most beautiful thing Vane had ever seen; both deadly and protective, her impenetrable armor and subtle contours suggestive of an elegant, wonderfully composed sea serpent. While he watched, hypnotized, wavy crimson tracers began arcing around her, spiking and sinking rhythmically with his pulse, narrowing at the middle, showering at the peak. The outline of this strange disturbance became humanlike, and then quite feminine; its flanks now extending, now bending to fold about him in a cosmic embrace. A pair of bright level eyes grew amid the electric tresses, and beneath these a wide pouting mouth. It was the saddest mouth Vane had ever imagined. The eyes were only for him.

He was paralyzed by all that beauty; couldn't lift a finger or wiggle a toe, couldn't feel Mudhead holding him up or hear him speaking in his ear. Vane knew it was fundamentally wrong to meet his mother like this, at the close of his life; it was cruel and unfair—as cruel and unfair as the icy numbness weighing his limbs, as wrong and as alien as the very un-California sea. And then, as the horizon was swept up in a great fireball of pomegranate-colored light, he realized the world was anything but cruel. Only a benign nature would produce something so lovely.

Chapter Fourteen

Kid

Vane's emergency surgery aboard a U.S. submarine on maneuvers off Madinat ash-Sha'b, his surprise entry into the Gulf of Aden on a pirated ship under Eritrean registry, and his subsequent ignominious removal from said ship via winch on a jerry-rigged stretcher of broken pallets and dung-covered rags, were, taken together, Honey's worst nightmare come true, but the Foundation jumped on it so quickly, and with so much attitude, that its prime interest left the hospital three weeks later facing little worse than a tough lecture and chilly interview. After sitting for two grueling hours in the American ambassador's office like a schoolboy in detention, Vane, his shoulder in a plaster cast and his left arm in a sling, was interrogated by three nameless men in suits, who permitted him to return to the Danakil on the condition he permanently keep his nose out of Eritrea. They were surprisingly cool on the whole *Scheherazade* issue, and frankly skeptical of his account of Franco's plans, but boy, were they ever pissed about his black market purchases.

And they took his neat warships manual, and refused to give it back. Vane slunk from the office, sulking, unable to shake the feeling he wasn't considered mature enough to run around the Horn of Africa unsupervised.

Denise Waters, his guardian angel, got right to work on new warehouses and a friendly corridor, using Mudhead as Vane's personal financial go-between. She fought for peace, fought for time, fought for Vane; directing trifles to Washington, routing important calls to beleaguered bureaucrats in Addis Ababa.

Vane's former employees, like the rats they were, threatened Mudhead into wringing the rest of their pay out of Honey's Djibouti courier by way of Banke Internationale, grabbed the cash, smuggled out the stingers, and disappeared into the frying shadows of Duomoa, one of the hottest and most desolate cities on Earth. Mudhead, his loyalty to Vane grown profound out of the tragedy, clung steadfastly to the night-scope rifle, the minaret-shaped spyglass, and his master's crusty-trusty jile. Long hours were spent delicately repairing the beautiful robes of flowing black silk. The salvageable foods, supplemented by a massive, highway-robbery buyout in Tedjoura, came the long way; south by rail on the Djibouti City-Addis Ababa line. Some fifty miles down the track, where Honey began earnest construction on the Vane Depot, the goods were loaded onto surplus troop transports for carriage over the desert to Mamuset.

With his newfound responsibilities and awesome capital power, Mudhead really came into his own. He hired hundreds of pastoralists to pave a single-lane road through the desert, and hundreds more to work the Danakil end, while the daily parade of supplies made its way by ATV and camel train. Although this ninety mile road was completed, amazingly, in less than a month, it was all too slow for Mudhead. He demanded more out of Tibor, more out of Honey, more out of his rocketing employees. The Depot was erected with dizzying speed, using both lumber imported by rail and whatever material the drought had spared. In time the Vane Depot would become a major landmark and oasis; a bazaar-like stopover in the middle of nowhere for weary travelers on the DC-AA line. Waters supported the development with a Mamuset Ready Fund, stocking the Depot's strongbox with birrs, francs, and dollars. Mudhead, during Vane's absence a man of near-superhuman stature, made regular flights to the Depot with Kid and his favorites, who fought savagely for a chance to ride in the plane until the problem was solved by selecting only the best-mannered. The youngsters were sent from the Depot with survival packs containing coin samples to entice Afar, Amhara, and Tigriya pastoralists. Others left Mamuset by camel, while still others were dropped off at strategic spots near sites yet occupied by skeleton tribes. The incentive—paid labor and adoption into Mamuset—was a strong one, but tribal recruits were few, for to many such a life-saving course was tantamount to defection. Scouts had better luck with nomad groups, who obediently and listlessly trudged to the Depot as if it were one more watering hole. They then trekked, toting stamped picks and shovels, to temporary crew sites, or to permanent marked-off sections in the desert. Once employed, they put their backs into it sunup to sundown, camping on their half-mile sections jealously, chasing off supervisors driving section-to-section with food and fresh drinking water. Sides of the developing road were marked by flagged stakes, each section including a turn-out space for opposing traffic. At the outset these stakes were in many places arbitrary, clambering along slopes and into gullies.

Mudhead intended the new road to be a model of construction, and a vast improvement over Vane's original Mamuset Highway. The African had learned a great deal during his months as Vane's second in command, but had always frowned on the easy-going, aesthetic approach. Mudhead's workers, driven to exhaustion and proud to a fault, took seriously every aspect of their jobs. Even in the dark they could be found single-mindedly chipping away at hillsides, filling and tamping depresssions, tidying perfectly straight borders. And, once they'd begun to personalize their sites, those roving supervisors, climbing out of jeeps with parcels and flashlights, approached the pickaxe-wielding workers at great peril.

In this manner—with limitless energy and immeasurable pride—a clearly definable pass was created with astounding rapidity. Crews spanned gorges not with suspended or vaulted bridges, but with dynamite and biceps. Great boulders were rolled into these gaps or blasted from their walls, to be cemented with any stone that could be ported. Amhara and Afar vied to outwork each other, sometimes with a viciousness that would have certainly panicked Vane into declaring an immediate holiday. But Mudhead, knowing better, encouraged segregation by grouping these ages-old competitors on opposing gorge-sides and putting them to work racing toward the center, realizing that, upon each impending violent clash at points of convergence, the competing teams would simply rush back to begin the next level. Those completed spans were then packed with dirt. Terrified steamroller drivers were taunted across every inch. And the moment Mudhead's crew laborers had cash in hand, they began stoically walking the new road back to the Depot, where they patiently applied for more work.

Both Depot and road were regularly monitored by Ethiopian officials, and constantly wondered over by passing fares. It was only natural that imaginations should embroider upon observation, and that those imaginations should be further fired by rumors and gossip. One day, just before his friend was scheduled to be released from the hospital, Mudhead paid a visit bearing a Los Angeles Times *Column Left* article pulled off the Internet. Vane had been persistent news in the gossip rags since his eccentric father's death. He was rumored dead, in cahoots with the Mob, partying in the Aegean, and searching for Morgan's treasure with super-sophisticated equipment. Rumors only slightly more accurate popularly vilified him as a swaggering E-gyptian overlord using thousands of slaves to construct a monolithic idol to himself.

This heartless, flamboyant character, assembled from gossip originating half a world away, had earned the paper nickname *Kid Rameses*. Apparently the Times had purchased, from at least one of these rags, information considered reliable and newsworthy. The article described how Cristian Vane, perennially-soused continent-jumping billionaire playboy, had recently been involved in a shootout while running drugs on the Red Sea. The article wasn't sure how the escapade correlated with rumors of secretive doings on a farm in Ethiopia, whether he'd been growing cannabis or poppies there, or even if the pampered American adventurer, now kept under wraps in an inter-

national clinic for strung-out rock stars, had survived the rela-
tions-straining Red Sea battle.

Vane stewed for days over this swashbuckling criminal
image fabricated by the sensational press. Fortunately he had
constructive distractions that continually forced him to refocus.
In moments alone he thought only of Mamuset's new Highway,
of his great responsibility, and of the enormous lesson he was
still in the process of learning. That old guy in the desert was
right: ego's a monster. When it comes to seeing the big picture,
the worst thing you can do is get bogged down in your micro-
cosm's details. Designing Mamuset had been possible from a-
far; micromanaging the completed project was another animal
altogether. And as Vane got better, reality found new ways to
wear him back down. He tried to run his world from bed, but
remotely keeping the peace between squatting workers bordered
on a full-time job. Supervisors were in and out of his room all
day long. Again and again he was pushed to arbitrate fights
between Afar and Amhara crews over rights to work as little as
a few square yards of earth.

A similar bullheadedness possessed those individuals in
charge of half-mile sections. Once their jobs were completed
they became entrenched; refusing to be relocated, distrusting the
asphalt-runners and threatening the rovers. While awaiting
steamrollers, these workers grew meticulous with their plots,
smoothing the new road surface ahead of the crews, cleaning
stakes and trimming flags. As soon as the rollers became apparent as articulated heat waves, these men positioned themselves as human barriers. Not until they were paid in full on the
spot would they relinquish their sites. When that last birr kissed
their palms they took their camels offroad and began the long
trek back to apply for work.

Homecoming was tough for Vane.

The worst part was his pre-dawn cruise with an over-
competent second-in-command, in a gift-laden Isis, on a road as
smooth as polished glass. A thousand crew workers and section
laborers proudly lined the way, each man waving a custom-

made welcoming torch. But Vane, weary of ordering Mudhead to flash the Land Rover's brights in response, slumped gloomily in his seat and nursed his battle wound with the dignity befitting a returning commander. Mudhead didn't brag, or in any manner acknowledge his success—he seemed light years above that sort of thing; and that was *another* thorn in Vane's craw. The CO's initial compliments quickly tapered to grunts of approval, then to surly silence. Who were these people *really* waving at? By the time they'd reached the new Onramp, Vane's mind was made up. He tore off his sling and used it to buff his turban's sapphire, fluffed out his fresh-as-daisies black silk robes, and rose majestically behind his microphone while the citizens of Mamuset were being wakened by a chord like thunder.

For some reason the Afar appeared none the worse for his absence. Rather, they embodied Mudhead's description of loyal dogs; patiently guarding the house while awaiting Master's inevitable return. But Mudhead's analogy involved behavior in a world of tooth and nail, against readily identifiable foes engaged in clearly defined assaults upon territory, propriety, and, ultimately, upon principle. That analogy did not embrace unknowable assailants cropping up in the dead of night, nor did it include the senseless dismembering of women, children, and animals. *That* kind of assault, on both body and soul, produced a much different reaction in the Afar—a very African reaction.

One tranquil night, not long after that uncomfortable homecoming, Vane was lying flat on his back in an open field, watching the stars clumping and dispersing pyrotechnically while the plastic earth played with his shoulders and heels; nibbling here, massaging there, rolling over his ankles and wrists like warm water—clamping, gently but firmly, on his throat and limbs, tenderly pulling him down. He might have been swallowed without the least resistance, had not the exquisite peace been broken by a single electrifying scream. Vane tried to sit up, but the clamps only tightened. With all his strength he raised his head and forced his eyes wide.

An entirely naked, brightly painted savage leaped up just beyond his splayed feet, screaming insanely. The savage's flesh, wherever unpainted, showed jet-black; its ivory-white eyes, lacking both irises and pupils, took up fully half its face. Vane somehow tore himself free and rose weightlessly, in slow motion, all the while struggling to free his lead-heavy *jile* from its sheath.

That strange screaming face transformed as it approached; first becoming a black leopard's mask, then a scarab's pinched mandible, and finally the rock-hard face of Mudhead, burning with deceit. As Vane watched, gaping, Mudhead's face morphed into John Beregard's spewing death mask, which in turn became the self-despising, negative-image face of Cristian Vane himself. Still screaming, the savage *reached*, its yellow nails like curling bamboo shoots.

The jile was anchored to the ground. Veins standing out on his arms and forehead, he snarled and strained until he'd torn it free, then swung the dead weight in an arcing motion, lopping off an arm before the jile's tip, passing its zenith, fell like a shot to the ground. The savage *screamed* at its spurting stump, leaned in hard, and slashed at Vane's face with its remaining claw. Again throwing all his will to the task, Vane swung his jile in a counter-arc, chopping off his assailant's other arm at the elbow. The savage came on. Vane totally lost it; backpedaling while swinging the weapon side to side, screaming in return, hacking off one leg, hacking off the other. But the limbless monster continued to advance, a lurching, gory trunk swinging four gushing stumps. With a final effort Vane swung his jile like a Louisville slugger, cleanly decapitating the thing. The headless torso flopped around for a minute, jerked violently, and stopped.

Vane was done in. He stumbled up to the settling head one frame at a time, saw his own dismembered hand drift off to lift it by the hair, saw the head turn under his fingers, scream maniacally, and bite down hard. Vane dropped it and staggered backward, and that still-*screaming* head pursued him like a bloody flesh ball, its eyes now huge empty sockets in a wildly contorted face. Vane saw it as through a camera's blood-spattered lens, bouncing erratically as it neared, growing larger and larger until its gnashing, spewing, *screaming* mouth filled his vision.

He sat bolt-upright, marinated in sweat. The ghastly

wash of a full moon was seeping between his Domo's wide-open gills, capping the furniture with a fuzzy white veneer. He held his breath.

A scream tore across the still night like nails on a blackboard, followed a moment later by two others a hundred yards apart. Mongrels, howling in response, were immediately muted by owners, leaving only the nervous grunts of camels and cattle. To Vane, still in that half-conscious realm between slumber and full wakefulness, it all seemed an extension of the dream. He focused his senses. Half a minute later the screaming was renewed.

He'd just swung his legs off the bed when his door burst open to reveal the black-and-white ghost of Mudhead, hunched in a skewed rectangle of moonlight. Vane fumbled on his robes and, barefoot, stumbled up the Steps on his friend's heels. From their vantage on Top Step, Mamuset's dully glowing Streetlamps created a false impression of security and serenity. It was dead-quiet.

"Why," Vane whispered, "isn't anybody moving? Who's been doing all that screaming?"

"Visitor," Mudhead whispered back. "Mamusetman now stoneman. Try no-noise hide."

"Hide from what?"

Another shriek, perhaps a quarter-mile away. The response, much nearer to their right, was quickly followed by a few seconds of commotion inside a Domo. Complete silence. Mudhead bent to his tripod. Vane, for some reason compelled to tiptoe, pulled his Massawa rifle from between the Big Clock and Grid Map. He spun off the wing nuts that secured the binoculars to their mounting, balanced his rifle's barrel just above the trigger guard, and crouched to peek into the night scope's blood-red unreality. Mamuset was a shantytown in Hell, the distant East Rim a dead ridge on Mars. He swept left to right, very slowly, until a pair of screams gave him a fix. A lanky black figure came loping out of a Domo, something in his hand glinting dully. Vane's free eye squinted. The man, painted head to foot, was naked except for a thatch skirt, a massive necklace, and an oversize mask made up to frighten. A second later the figure was lost from view.

"Not one of ours."

"Three…" Mudhead counted, "…four. Now two more on Street. Run crazy."

"Let me see." Vane peered into Mudhead's mounted binoculars. Thermal imaging produced bright-line features vacillating from startlingly clear to irksomely muddy. The digital processors that made night detection possible created an artificial, two-dimensional image interrupted by a near-continuous vertical shift. Trying to control this shift only produced spikes, abstracted from moonlight, that broadened and shimmered with the least vibration. But Vane was able to locate his original culprit, and at least four others running Domo to Domo. He picked out a definite pattern: black form runs into Domo brandishing some kind of sword, scream of terror, scream of triumph, distant answering cry. He stepped back to his rifle, and found it slippery in his hands. Vane heard his voice say, "Sorry, Mudhead."

"Sorry why?"

He took a very deep breath, trying to imagine his next move as a harmless, video game experience. "I don't know. Maybe saying it first will make this easier." Squinting into his eyepiece, he focused on one of those big ugly Halloween masks and froze. Just as its owner opened his mouth to scream, Vane simultaneously squeezed the trigger and slammed shut his eyes.

The shot, coming as it did in the razor stillness between screams, snapped and reverberated through Mamuset like the crack of a buggy whip. He briefly opened his scope eye, saw the mask jerk back and disappear. Vane's face twisted into a god-awful grimace, and for an instant time screeched to a halt. Then dogs were barking hysterically, and Mudhead was shouting beside him. Vane sagged, his trembling fingers releasing the rifle as though it were a hot frying pan's handle. The gun fell butt-first between his big toes and he jumped back three feet.

"Real money shot," Mudhead said appreciatively. "Man down. Otherman run to Rim." He stepped aside. "Quick look." Vane shook his head, his hands gripping the hard knot of his stomach. "Okay, Bossman. Stay put." Mudhead melted off the Stage. In two minutes Isis's horn was sounding on Stage Street. Vane pitched down the Steps and toppled into the passenger seat. Mudhead threw her into first.

By now every dog was howling bloody murder. Mud-head, guided only by his impression from the Stage, hurtled a-round corners to a Domo indistinguishable from its neighbors. In the front Yard of that Domo a few Afar were curiously creep-ing past Vane's hard-flung, very spattered kill. Most of the population remained indoors.

"Cowards," he mumbled, looking everywhere but down.

"Not coward. Afarman fierce fighter. But fight man, not spirit."

Vane peered at the sprawled body. The top half of its head was a bloody plateau. "Looks pretty solid to me."

Both men knelt. The Afar trickled out of doors. A femi-nine wail poured from a Domo across the Street. A pair of oxen smashed through an adjacent Yard. Somewhere children were chanting a family member's name. A light crowd grew around the costumed American and his grim African friend. Mudhead picked up the dead man's bloody machete by the fat of its blade, turned it in his fingers and gently set it back down. Vane lifted a corner of the mask with his thumb. It was heavy and quite large, secured by skull-and chin straps. A strangely familiar design: sharp horns, pointed tongue, long fangs, wild eyes. Underneath, what was left of the face was in repose and unpainted. He kept pushing the mask until the mess above the brow was covered. Vane's initial adrenaline rush had passed, and he was gradually acknowledging something reserved for blue-moon fantasies: he had just killed a man.

"Recognize this mask?" his mouth asked.

Mudhead stood up. "Not Africaman."

"You're sure?"

"Hollywoodman."

"What?"

Mudhead toed the painted horns and fangs, the clumsy thatch skirt. "Hollywood." He nudged the multi-layered bone necklace. The resulting clatter was certainly plastic. "Holly-wood." His big toe traced the swirls of body paint. "All Holly-wood."

Vane lifted the machete by its handle. "And this? This is Hollywood too?"

"This," Mudhead said somberly, "Port Massawa."

"You think?"

"All," Mudhead extrapolated, "message Mamuset. Port Massawaman mean send Bossman scare."

"But why not just take me out? What's the point in killing innocent people?"

"No." Mudhead shook his head. "Bossman still long way understand Africaman. Slow terror important. Quick death no big deal. Revenge long sweet feast. Dead Bossman," he said, performing an abruptly-halted ballet with his fingers, "no more dance for Port Massawaman." He watched a wave of black spiders scurrying up North Rim and nodded to himself. "Mudahid bet doughnut Massawa truck wait outside. Mudahid up bet one: Port Massawaman only tickle. Next time many more. But not Hollywoodman." His ramrod forefinger directed Vane to the smashed face between them. "Next time real deal." He peeled a mat off of Isis's floor and draped it over the face.

The dark sheik, rising slowly, found himself the awkward nucleus of a very primitive, very curious crowd. "Damn it, Mudhead, you're right! A troop of Cub Scouts could take this place." He appeared to gain confidence in standing erect. "Nobody pushes C.H. Vane around, man. *No*-body!" He whooshed back a step, imagining himself a swirling, philosophic Zorro. The crowd did not whoosh with him. Vane tucked in his butt and pulled snug his wilting robes. "Mr. Mudahid," he said with dignity, "I'm deputizing you." The word seemed so out of place he felt compelled to address his people. "In America," he said expansively, "to deputize means to bestow certain powers on the spot. *Anybody* can be a deputy. It could be you, or you. Or you! That's because in America, man, nobody, but *nobody* is better than anybody else!" His words trailed off. "It's a democracy," he tried. The ring of faces waited. Vane deflated like a black toy balloon, mumbling, "Actually, it's more of a democratic republic."

Mudhead glared, turned, and delivered the most abrasive monologue Vane had ever heard. The crowd tightened with him, standing tall. It was a short speech. Mudhead turned back.

"Everyman understand. Tomorrow Afar fist rise with sun." His normally reserved expression became frankly sardonic. "Democratman," he said, sweeping his arm, "bring Boss-man equal share Massawaman heart." He inclined his head. "Unum."

Vane looked man to man. There must have been a hundred standing around him now, waiting. It was like being surrounded by strings of black ping pong balls with white-painted eyes. "Okay then," he said, nodding snappily. "Okay! If you guys need me, I'll be in the War Room."

Daybreak found Vane pacing the Stage like a caged beast. He hadn't slept a wink; mentally repositioning bugs, tossing and turning through fantasies of valor and praise. What was it he'd told Mudhead...he'd said a rich man in this part of the world could equip a private army. It was just a matter of shifting Denise into high gear, and maybe throwing a few bones Tibor's way.

Right after Strauss he began the militarization of Mamuset, repeating the manual of arms hourly. The Afar dutifully mimicked his actions, using wooden pallet ribs in place of rifles, while Mudhead barked out commands in Saho. With great ceremony Kid was made Site Sergeant, and permitted to wear Vane's turban during drills. Site Sergeant Kid was the most thorough instructor imaginable, swaggering Square to Square and Street to Street, inspecting pallet ribs dawn to dusk and making sure every Afar male moved with speed and precision.

Vane was finding himself. He plagued the Foundation with calls; at first beseeching, then commanding. Within a week Mamuset's mail plane took Mudhead to the Depot, where a Honey agent produced a wicker basket full of American cash. Mudhead, flown at ground level over a terrain familiar only to lizards, was put down in the outskirts of Massawa. The cold black soldiers in dark glasses paid scant attention to another basket-toting beggar inching down a crooked little street into a crooked little cinema.

For the next eight days drills were interspersed with rampart construction, a seamless process featuring chains of human worker-ants continuously porting miscellaneous material up Streets and Inner Slopes in order to fashion Rim Bulwarks. A typical Bulwark was roughly the size of a railroad car—basically a skeleton of bound wood ribs stuffed with debris and covered by a staked canvas tarp. Each Bulwark supported a standing aluminum ladder, that its flat roof might be accessed by marksmen. Bulwarks were separated by a space of twenty feet. In those spaces Mamusetans quickly built thatched Guard Posts, sturdy little huts modeled on the circular Amharic wattle-and-daub homes. But they differed from those solid-wall traditional homes, in that each Post utilized a single high broad window yielding a 180 degree desert vista. A Guard's status was hard won and jealously sought. Posts were communally provisioned and universally envied; provided with, thanks to Vane's hyper first-day spending spree, high-tech surveillance equipment, Post-to-Post "Intercoms," and personal Nissan pick-up trucks. Vane intended they also be provided with semi-automatic weapons, flare guns, and manually-operated sirens. Rim Road was quickly hewn, along with a series of steep Inner Slope ramps. Only the Mamusetans' near-maniacal industriousness made it all come together so quickly. A casual observer would have seen countless crews busily attacking solid earth with the most basic of tools, with improvised wedges and levers, with bare hands. But unlike members of paid or compelled crews—pacing themselves or relaxing the moment the crew boss had passed—these workers approached their tasks passionately; wrestling for positions, shoving one another to be first to break a stone or fill a hole.

In the middle of construction Mudhead arrived on Vane's old An'erim-Massawa Highway, riding shotgun in a tractor hauling a forty-eight foot, kemlite-lined Dorsey reefer with a malfunctioning refrigeration system. The trailer was backed into Dock, where Mudhead joined Vane, Kid, and a pair of strong pickax-wielding Afar. The driver unlocked the door and the Mamusetans rolled it up.

A blast of white cold burst from the trailer. Inside was a solid wall of frozen food: two whole sides of beef and three cheese wheels in bas relief, with chickens, pork butts, and lamb shoulders cemented in haphazardly. Everything was coated by a thick ice glaze.

"Now," Vane said, addressing the two adults, "one guy on each side and start breaking away toward the middle. We're cutting a corridor." Halfway through Mudhead's translation Kid stepped up to show his stuff. He bowed and saluted Vane sharply, clicked his bony ankles together, performed a dizzying about face, and snapped out an order. The two adult Afar produced their pickaxes at parade rest. In a brisk, efficient move, the Site Sergeant snatched one in each hand. Without further ado he began assaulting the ice wall, swinging both pickaxes insanely.

The men all jumped back, battered by flying chunks of frozen meat. "Wait!" Vane called out. "Damn it, Kid, that's an order!" But Kid only swung with greater ferocity, grunting and yelping as he alternated swings left and right. Soon a jagged niche appeared between the sides of beef. Kid attacked this niche wildly, metal ringing on metal, occasionally embedding one pick and using the other to smash it free. When the first side of beef broke away it took a 3 X 5 piece of the trailer wall with it. Kid, with this advance, went berserk, all the men backing off for their lives as his pickaxes became whirling, slashing blurs. Five minutes later he staggered out into their embrace, his arms shaking out of his control, both tools solidly embedded. But he'd managed to clear a walkway through almost four feet of ice-locked meat and bone.

The two adult Afar left the pickaxes embedded. They fatigued the ice wall by rocking side to side on the handles, one man's weight on each. A large section containing the second side and a wheel began to give. Vane and Mudhead stepped in to assist. Kid and the driver kicked out chunks sliding on the trailer's floor. With four strong backs on it, the section immediately tore away. The men used their feet to shove the marlin-sized mass out onto the hot concrete platform.

The rest of the wall came away in substantial chunks. The hackers now encountered a barrier of wood and earth over Styrofoam slabs; actually one end of a huge mass surrounded by a foot-wide space stuffed with newspaper. This mass stood on a knee-high bed of pallets. Everything was iced over. The men used the blunt heads of their pickaxes to smash the ice veneer, then tore out all the paper and packing they could reach. The Styrofoam, wood, and earth came away easily, exposing stacked oblong crates wrapped in skins, canvas, and cloth.

The Afar wrestled off the top crate and eased it to the floor; it was quite heavy. Each crate measured four feet long by three feet wide by two feet deep. The trailer held eighty-four in all. Vane lifted out the lowered crate's recessed top panel. Packed in straw, and wrapped in oilskins, were thirty-two M16A2s, laid butt-to-barrel. Vane plucked one out by its handle. He blew off pieces of caught straw and balanced it under Kid's rolling eyes.

"The official rifle of the United States armed forces. Two thousand, six hundred and eighty-eight of 'em, if the head vulture can be trusted." He laid a hand on Mudhead's shoulder. "Mister Asafu-Adjaye, you done all right. And the rest of the stuff?"

"Siren, flare, more magazine come later. No problem search."

"Excellent!" Vane posed menacingly with the rifle. The Afar grinned uncertainly. "It's time to bring Mamuset into the so-called civilized world! Ring up Utility Squares! Roll out the pickups! And once these guns are stocked you can tell my people to lose their sticks. From now on they're using the real McCoy!"

From that moment on progress was smooth and practically effortless. While the Afar men were learning to handle their numbered weapons individually and in regiments, their women and children were training in a reloading exercise that rhythmically swept them between arbitrary field stations and Bulwarks. This maneuver, the *Ripple*, would come in handy down the road. Throughout training and drills, revolving Utility Square commanders distributed ammunition, graded results and passed them to Kid, who was incapable of being pleased. And so gun-happy was Kid that Vane forbade the use of live ammunition during target practice. This drove Kid crazy. After a day of unbearable peace, he enlisted all the children of Mamuset to smack wood blocks together whenever men mock-fired their weapons. This drove Vane crazy. He retaliated by blasting rock music during drills, but succeeded only in further jazzing his manic Site Sergeant.

Soon Rim Road was completed, and all Posts and Bulwarks fully erected. Vane's ammunition, hand-crank sirens, and miscellaneous materiel arrived at night by camel train.

The weeks passed. And as Mamuset rediscovered its center the punctual daily drills deteriorated to weekly random drills, much to Kid's, and to the population's, chagrin. Vane a- gain stressed cultivation, exercise, and education. Rifles were assigned to numbered spaces in Utility Squares, just like any other implement.

The big scare was over.

For the first time a real lassitude descended on the cra- ter. There were always new projects, always new problems, but interest plummeted with the passing of war fever. Days grew increasingly long, the Afar correspondingly less energetic.

And out of the great peace came a great boredom. Men tinkered, rather than worked. Greater free time meant greater leisure time. With leisure to bicker and side, the sense of purposeful community dissolved. The crater suffocated while Vane, resplendent in flowing black silk, grew impatient and crabby, pacing the Stage and alienating himself with petty out- bursts and amplified asides.

He refused to acknowledge that the fabric of Mamuset was fraying, though in private he prayed long and hard for something to shake up the place. But, needful as he was, when the explosion came it caught him completely off guard.

Chapter Fifteen

Rebecca

The bomb arrived without warning, without warhead or fins, without a protracted heart-stopping scream of descent.

It came instead on Mudhead's black magic carpet, in a dusty Ford Explorer almost sagging with superfluous chrome. Magnetic signs on the rear panels certified media clearance. Decals portraying the logo of some tacky periodical were plastered all over these signs, on both bumpers, and across the upper windshield. A toy American flag hung from the radio's antenna, toy Djibouti and Ethiopian flags from the grille.

The Explorer, having majestically climbed the new On-ramp onto Ridge Bridge, halted adjacent to the Stage facing the Big Clock. The passenger door swung open. A very long, very supple leg oozed out like honey from a hive, and a tiny, spotless hiking boot hovered for half a minute. The brown knee bent. The perfect thigh extended…and extended…until it seemed every sidelong Afar eye must bulge and explode. But at the moment of truth an impeccably folded hem caught the sun, and out stepped the most beautiful California bunny Vane had ever seen.

The abrupt insinuation of this goddess threw him completely out of whack. In the first place, as a healthy young man months removed from titillation, he was instantly aroused. In the second, as a man of vision attempting to stand for something profounder than instant arousal, he was instantly deflated... Cristian Vane had been groomed for failure from the moment that cold-hearted, skinny white whore had—Vane was *outraged* (albeit quietly, and with great dignity)...a spoiled, near-naked Western wench had come to parade her privates in front of his innocent multitude, to treat Mamuset like the French Riviera on a fat summer noon.

Not only that, she was *press*—and the level of press that had, for way too many years, portrayed him as a clueless prince. Vane hated her, immediately and absolutely. Right away he knew *They* had found him. Somehow. Those ruthless, fabricating parasites had reached across two continents and an ocean to further mangle his name. It had to be that whole silly Kid Rameses business.

Of course she was gorgeous. They wouldn't have sent a plain woman; not to shatter the guard of a conceited, paranoid billionaire playboy. Vane probably had a stable both fair and dark, probably went through beautiful women like Kleenex. He might even be keeping ranks of innocent young boys hopped up on drugs and promises, if there was even a scrap of truth to the rumors. Who knew what went on in a lawless, backward country, where the remedy for an atheistic fatcat's raging libido was only a voodoo dance away?

Then there was all that adrenaline-junkie malarkey; the dope dealing, the treasure hunting, the shootouts on the Red Sea. Vane was a dangerous man, and a secretive one. He'd certainly view the conquest of attractive blondes as a challenge as natural and appealing as narcotics and gunplay.

But the airbrushed model *They'd* sent, now performing a sound check in the shade of her sensible parasol, was obscenely beautiful. She was far too perfect for weariness—or for genuine sweat, for that matter; only the daintiest beads of amber clung to the down on her nape and arms. Skin too perfect to burn, lips too perfect for paint, a figure too perfect for support; she stood poised without posing—sensuous, sleek, and silky, but way too perfect to care. And either she'd mastered the subtlest applications of makeup, or, even in this dark and diseased part of the world, every part of her perfectly sculpted face blushed the rose of ultimate health. The capper: a spun-gold ponytail, cheerily catching the merciless sun, wagging behind a cute little denim cap with a shocking pink press badge.

She was an *erotic angel*. This uncomfortable contradiction posed a real problem for closet misogynist Vane: by not typifying the classic slatternly dumb bombshell, she made it difficult to justify his natural contempt. He ogled her peripherally as she leaned in to retrieve a large suede bag. Catching herself holding this bag like a purse, the woman slung it over her shoulder and playfully tossed the parasol to a driver obscured by glare. The door closed. Vane looked away nonchalantly. The Explorer, relieved of its dazzling cargo, motored back across Ridge Bridge and rolled to a rest.

The man in black turned to face his unbidden guest, bracing himself for the chirpy greeting and pretty extended hand—but the blonde woman walked past him and stood looking over the community, her hands on her hips. She extracted a video camera from the bag, looped its strap around her neck, and brought the camera to her shoulder. It was the smallest, sleekest instrument of its kind Vane had ever seen. A tiny red jewel appeared on its front panel. The woman panned left and right.

"Cristian Vane," he tried. "I run this place."

She said through her teeth, "So I've heard."

Backing off a notch, Vane studied her unobserved while she panned. She was his age; maybe a bit older. Early thirties. But from different angles, and at different approaches of light, she could pass for her late, mid, and early twenties. There was even one scary moment, when she lowered the camera to study the community critically, that a freak of sun revealed a tender golden teenager with wide-set emerald eyes.

"Can I help you with something?"

"Just looking." She swept an arm above the wide field of aluminum cottages. "So this is where you keep your people?"

Vane's expression locked up on him. "Why did I just get the impression you used the word 'people' as a euphemism for slaves?"

"Then what do you call them?"

"I don't call them anything. They live here. I live here. The damned donkeys live here."

"One big happy family." She swiftly raised the camera and directed its lens at his face. The red jewel lit up.

Vane threw out a hand and the woman lowered her camera. The red light disappeared.

"Perfect. Now I'll look like some hit man hiding his face as he's escorted from court. Is that what you came for?"

"Mr. Vane. It is the policy of M & S to respect the rights of its subjects. We don't print photos without permission. So if there's a problem, perhaps we could discuss your druthers, preferably somewhere off of this hotplate."

"S And M? What sort of enterprise do you work for, anyway?"

The pretty nose crinkled in annoyance. "*M & S*, Mr. Vane, *M & S*. Movers And Shakers." She wagged her head. "I realize you're cut off from the real world out here, but surely you receive *some* news in *some* way. Movers And Shakers is just the biggest, just the glossiest, just the fastest-growing alternative news magazine in America. I write a column: *Rogue Bulls*. It's a very successful column. I mostly work out of our main office in sunny California. You remember California, don't you, Mr. Vane? California definitely remembers you."

Mr. Vane bowed and gallantly swept his robes, but his tongue betrayed him. "You'll forgive me, my dear, but I'm afraid my company removes me from the worlds of movers and shakers, nor have I time for the pleasuring of lovely young ladies, um, Miss?"

Her eyes burned. After a minute she muttered, "My name is Rebecca King, both professionally and casually. And I'm here on *business*, Mr. Vane."

Vane said quickly, "Look. I'm not a flirt. I'm actually quite uncomfortable around women—" He caught himself. He'd almost added *especially pretty ones*. His eyes toed the dirt. "It's just that I'm not really all that sure what you expect me to say here."

"Try being honest. And don't embroider. But don't be e-vasive, either. We'll get along just fine." She reached back, slipped the band off her hair, and removed the cap for a couple graceful shakes of the head. Aureate cascades billowed, fell, whipped side to side. The tresses rolled like water over her shoulders and down her back, continuing to flash at the least movement.

"*So...*" Vane hemmed, "...tell me. How do I come off in the States? Or need I ask? You weren't exactly gushing when you got here."

King pulled an enormous pair of sunglasses from her fanny pack. The massive lenses did nothing to diminish her beauty. "There's a dichotomy," she said shortly. "There are exactly two breeds of Vane-watchers. There are the ones who think you're a virtuous lunatic, and the ones who're sure you're an evil genius. The latter far outweigh the former."

"Why 'lunatic'?"

"Because it doesn't make any sense the other way. No sane man *steps down* in life." She folded her hands behind her back and took a longer look around. "It may be the world's oyster," she punned, "but it's your pearl." The sun leaped lens to lens as she varied her gaze. "Mr. Vane, please don't get me wrong, but I'd like you to be just as honest with yourself as you're very definitely going to be with me. Consider: every healthy criminal *knows* he's unfairly accused. Just as his mother *knows* he's a 'good boy.' Just as everybody *knows* everybody else is at fault. We're all victims, and we're all good people. We're just misunderstood. By the same token, we're all certain that everybody else is less scrupulous than we, and that the most successful people are ipso facto the least scrupulous. Suspicion fosters fascination, and vice versa." She held out her hands, twisted one around, and peered through the frame formed by her thumbs and forefingers. "In our commercial system the strength of a celebrity's appeal is directly related to his mysteriousness. Our uncertainty makes him *sexy*. We, the soap loving public, want dirt on our latest bad boy, and we're willing to pay up the yin-yang for it. A kind of *gratification* comes from the piling on of this dirt. But, like the gratification that comes from sex, the bashings become increasingly inadequate. We want stronger stuff—sensational stuff, graphic stuff. It becomes harder and harder to get off, and, Lord knows, we'll never be truly satisfied until the ungrateful son of a bitch is lynched. Now I'm warning you, Mr. Vane. You'll face interviewers a lot tougher than me, so you'd might as well come clean right here and now. People will forgive you for being human. Just don't lie to them. It insults their intelligence."

"What makes you think I'm a liar?"

King tore off her shades and raised a hand sharply. "Look, you've got a lot of charges to answer, okay? One way or another I'm coming out of here with a story, and with an interview on tape." She circled him critically. "Try thinking before you open your mouth. There's a simple approach to this business, Mr. Vane. Forget you're a big shot. Instead, try to imagine yourself a viewer:

"You're Joe Anybody, sitting in front of the tube in your two-bedroom apartment, sharing the sofa with dog hair, a Banquet frozen dinner, and your calorically-challenged wife. Now cut to a news blurb leaping across the screen. The set's speaker grabs you, overpowering the squalling of the kids. The blurb's about that freaking egomaniacal tabloid billionaire who refuses to go away. What's his face? Oh yeah. That celebrity jet-setter Vain Somebody-or-Other. You've hated him at least as much as you've hated all those other philandering, dope-snorting superstars, who run around publicly gallivanting with supermodels and super agents and more supermoney to burn in a giddy week than you'll see in your miserable lifetime. And there's that spoiled California superprick again, all ready to dole out another emotional mugging. What'll be his latest escapade? How shiny his newest plaything? And how common, boring, and unhappening is he gonna make *me*, Joe Anybody, feel? Well go ahead, you lucky dumb son of a gazillionaire. Emasculate me some more."

Vane had simmered long enough. But before he could open his mouth to protest, that hand was back up like a crossing guard's.

"*Stop* gushing about your golden life! *Don't* give Joe the luxury of hating you personally. But don't be self-deprecating, either, and don't try to sell him on your love of the arts and humanity. Your father's ghost won't go away that easily. *Try* to not smirk or sneer. *Do* let Joe know if you're cooking up something super-dastardly, but never, *ever* be super-specific." Her green eyes went gray. "And don't you little-girl me or I'll hang on your gonads until you sing like a patriot. Peacocks always do. And when they sing off-key I just *squeeze* until they get it right." The shades went back on.

"Are you done?"

"You're being pre-interviewed, Mister Vane. You've got lots and lots of explaining to do. Laying the groundwork can save us needless stops and starts."

"You're not pre-interviewing me, lady, you're killing me."

"Rebecca."

He looked down and took a couple of deep breaths. It was already way too late to go for a natural, comfortable relationship; the roles were all messed up. But Vane wasn't about to be bullied or berated by some blonde bimbo with a video camera. They walked with affected casualness, like awkward first-daters. He kicked a stone off Ridge Bridge. "It behooves me to be a gentleman, *Rebecca*. However, there's a kind of etiquette we share around here. I'm afraid your...hostility...might be misinterpreted by these basically trusting people."

"I should be humbler in your presence, Mr. Vane?"

"Cris."

"So you're saying, Mr. Vane, that they might be confused by Master's sudden show of submissiveness?" She looked around. "Just where is the House of Pain, anyway?"

"Ah, for Christ's sake."

"All charges are alleged, Cristian Honey. Even Joe Anybody's knowledge is a media-filtered thing. But it doesn't matter. He hates you already. Just like he hates all the plum-perfect talking blonde heads like me...who also represent the unattainable, and who thereby mock the drought of his dreams."

Vane ground his teeth. Not only pretty and acerbic, but smart. An insidious and unfair combination. "Ms. King—"

"Rebecca. Miss."

"All...right! Now just what the hell am I charged with?

I'll gladly defend myself, or plead no contest, or even non compos mentis, if that'll clarify for you. But I *honestly* have *no* idea why *you*, and why *Joe Anybody*, and why *God Almighty*, for that matter, *are so freaking pissed at me!"*

This little display of passion got her attention; King knew, from long experience, that the sensitive-celebrity type is no stranger to psychotic outbursts. But she'd come for a fight as well as an interview. She cleared her throat aggressively and hurried through her words. The tactic worked well for her; the longer she extended her verbal flow, the ballsier she grew. *"Mr. Vane*, maybe you aren't aware of just what a luminary you've become back home. Now, some celebrities have their fifteen minutes, while others possess an indefinable quality that gives them lasting appeal. A man of mystery, such as yourself, attracts rumors the way a magnet attracts iron filings. You're like a personality assembled by an Identigraph: gossip-mongers slap claims on a general impression until the compleat scoundrel is exposed. Okay? The general impression of Cristian Honey Vane is Spoiled Godless Pervert. That's the reputation you've carried, like it or not, accurate or not, since the public's first view of the little boy at the famous Vane mansion's snazzy gates back in '72, being led from a godawful-pink limousine by some bleached, beat-up witch in a slinky black dress. *That* was the original snapshot the public had to go by—you, Morticia, and money. And this was just when your father's fancy lawyers were fighting off all those freaky charges of hush shenanigans involving Guatemala's State Department. Journalistically speaking, I cut most of my teeth on archival images of *that* convoluted fiasco. Little Richie Rich and his nanny whore, in a loony palace run by a faded, probably treasonous old basket-case. What a gammy group." She took a deep breath.

"Throughout your life there've been other snapshots, of you and your crowd. There are pictures of shifty sycophants, rumors of lewd parties, stories of venal shadows flitting between the police station and the mansion.

"And the headshots of growing master Vane invariably reveal a morbid, friendless, media-shy enigma. Reasonably attractive, but with an expression that could curdle blood. A man without a soul.

"After your father died, the tabloid press pushed the man-without-a-soul angle to the hilt. Your disappearance couldn't have been timelier. Now every Vane-watcher could toss a sin and have it stick on an initial impression: traitor, gun runner, drug kingpin. Womanizer, pedophile, or outright fairy— it didn't matter. If it titillated, if it infuriated, it was you."

They walked back in silence. In the Big Tarp's shade Vane said, "You're going to savage me, aren't you?"

"We'll see."

"Miss King, you're obviously shrewd enough to realize what's truth and what's garbage. And you're absolutely right. I'm a made-in-the-shade rich boy who never had to punch a clock or dig a ditch." He faced the community and spread his arms so that his black robe's sleeves swept back dramatically. "But now take a look around you. Forget Joe Anybody. Forget your assignment. Forget the way people see you and me. You're a journalist; you're trained to observe. Take it all in. Let your eyes bask in the neon and glamour, let your camera linger on the frolicking playgirls and endless buffet."

"I *said*," she returned nastily, "*alleged*. Rumors, Mr. Vane, are only rumors, but they make up a major part of the business I'm in and, believe it or not, they're founded in fact ninety-nine percent of the time. I've never in my life met a genuine philanthropist. Especially of the rich celebrity ilk."

"Then maybe you're just jaded by your job. If you really knew me, if you really knew what I've been through, you'd realize that that class of people makes me as sick as it makes you. Maybe sicker. But go right ahead and describe that great Vane motive for me, so I can understand it too. Like I said, I've never once punched a clock, and I'll never have to. Yet I'm up every day with the sun. No weekends, no holidays. You're absolutely right, Rebecca. I don't *have* to dig ditches." He showed her his palms. "But go ahead and count the calluses anyway."

"So what's your angle, Mr. Vane?" She thrust forth her chin. "Why are you hiding in Africa? Enquiring minds want to know."

"I've been asking myself that same question lately. But look, Rebecca—"

"Miss King."

"Miss King. Look, Miss King, you're free to walk a-round and videotape all you want. Consider the place home. There are cool drinks in Cellar, and an assortment of refreshments to choose from in Basement. Many delicacies are made right here."

"I think I would like to interview one of your tenants first. I think I would like to interview..." she swung a finger round and paused on an elderly man combing his camel, "*him*. Or would you prefer to screen him first? Let me forewarn you, sir: I have earned a reputation for brutality. Many of my subjects even consider me something of a bitch."

Vane raised an eyebrow. "The Devil!" He blew out a breath. "Okay. But go easy on him. Like anybody else here, he can do drills, man Bulwarks, and build a damned fine Square. There's not much more you'll get out of him."

"So if these people can't speak for themselves, I am to assume the only source of information is their noble leader? That's it?"

Vane wagged his chin sadly. "Water, water," he said. "Everywhere."

King tilted her head, and the corners of her mouth slowly turned up. "Mr. Vane, when it comes to information, I am a human divining rod."

He cocked an eyebrow. "A divine what? Oh...*damn* it! There I go again. My most effusive apologies, Miss King. You were looking for what? Information? There are no secrets here. Come with me. I'll give you the grand tour."

"What about Mitchell, my driver? He will certainly parch in the car."

Vane depressed the transmit button on his radio. Mudhead, at arm's length facing Mecca, turned at the squeal of feedback. He kept his eyes down lest he be blinded by the golden display of flesh at Vane's elbow.

"Rebecca, this is Mudhead. He's an all-around go-be-tween, a wizard with a needle and thread, and practically the only other person this side of Gibraltar who speaks English. Mudhead, would you please assist Miss King's driver while I show her around? His name's Mitchell. Get him some shade and a drink or three. Jack Daniels would be nice."

Mudhead bowed deeply and slunk away.

Vane led her down the Steps, offering his arm at the base. King, smiling sourly, used the projected wrist as a peg for the strap on her camera case. Vane looped the case over his shoulder and followed her around eagerly, awed Mamusetans lining their way like parade goers. Heads popped up grinning as they walked Domo to Domo. He saw more than one thumb raised high. "They're all the same," said Vane proudly. "Mostly families. You won't find anybody bound and gagged in a closet, if that's what your editors are expecting. These people understand very little English, but they're friendly and eager to please. And they seem to like you."

King ran her camera over the beaming faces. "I'll admit I expected worse."

"You should've seen this place when I first got here." He pointed west. "Fields are that way. All kinds of grains. We're even developing rice paddies on West Rim's tiered inner slope. There's plenty of water, which we import via pipeline from a river south of here. These domiciles receive their living water through PVC running under their properties. Main lines run beneath Streets, so that there's actually a pipe grid corresponding to the roads. Everybody helps everybody here, Miss King. There are no disputes about water lines and property rights. That family there probably put almost as much effort into building their neighbor's place as their own."

"So no wild parties? No drug deals or harems?"

"It's all very dull, Miss King. I'm almost embarrassed to admit that life here is anything but wild. We eat, we work, we do drills..." Now Vane, for the first time, looked upon his creation as an observer. It was with an almost paternal pride that he turned smiling on Rebecca, even as a boy no older than twelve ran by waving an M16.

King blew it. "You—you *fraud!* You're letting children have access to guns? My God! They were right about you!"

"Who was...who was right?"

"I want to know what's going on here, buddy, and I want to know *now!*" She looked at the innocent faces around her, gone in an instant from sunny to scared. "To what end are you using these people?"

For a moment Vane saw red. Every expletive for female ran tommygunning through his head. "They're *not*," he spat, "being *used!*" The Afar shrank back, bewildered. "I busted my ass and broke the bank to make this place the best home they've ever had. I took a bullet, okay? Do you hear anybody crying about how terribly he's suffering, man? Huh? Do you see anybody fleeing? For Christ's sake, lady, quit painting me as the heavy, willya?"

"Armed children? You call that a good home?"

Vane threw up his arms. *"It's not even loaded!"*

The crowd broke up, but King didn't budge. "Why the weapons, pal? I'll find out! Don't think I won't!"

Vane stared out at the Bulwarks, controlling his breathing. How to get rid of her...did she ever shut up...he clenched his teeth and jammed his knuckles in his eyes. Finally he said dully, "There's this guy, a general in control of Port Massawa. He's got designs on using me to expand his power. A Franco Somebody-in-an-Abbey. It's a long, long story, but he's already spilled blood here. And boy, is he gonna get it when he comes back."

King shook her head. "You're an amazing man, Mr. Vane, an amazing man. You really *don't* keep up on the world, do you? Franco a' Muhammed en Abbi died in April."

Vane blinked at her. "Dead?"

"Very. He'd been putting together a personal assault force. At least that's the gist of it from Reuters. He was meeting with his top men in a hangar stocked with explosives. A small plane did a nosedive into the hangar and put der general into orbit."

"How about that."

"The new man in charge of Massawa has completely cleaned the place up."

"How about that."

King studied him clinically. Vane appeared dazed by the sun. She turned up her nose and panned the Bulwarks with her camera. "About those fields."

He shook himself. "No poppies. No hemp. I'm sorry, Miss King, but it appears you've traveled a long way to cover a story that doesn't exist."

"All stories aren't necessarily sensational, Mr. Vane. I'm afraid you're going to have to accept my interview. Like I said, I'm not leaving here empty-handed." They strolled back to the Mount. "If you're self-conscious about being filmed, we can work with Mitchell. He's an expert lighting-and-makeup man. A magician. He can make you look like George Hamilton if you want. And I'm not hard on a subject if I like him. It's only the posers who get reamed."

"And," Vane asked carefully, "do you like me?"

She considered. "Personally? You come across as an o-kay sort, I guess. A bit high-strung. Professionally? I've certain-ly met men more charismatic. But they're the ones who always turn out to be weasels. Charisma's developed over a lifetime of personal drum-beating." She stepped back. "The Darth Vadar get-up will work fine. I might even enjoy this."

"What about your own charisma?"

"Me? Skin-deep. Not many men get beneath the sur-face."

"I've been told that patience and persistence are vir-tues." They had reached Bottom Step. "We can go back up the Steps to your car, or you can reach it from the road. Tell your friend we won't be needing his expertise." Rebecca smiled thin-ly and turned on her heel. He watched her walking along Stage Street, his eyes, like every other male's, melting on her pert tail. Vane continued to stare while climbing the Steps. "How does nature do that?" he asked Mudhead at Top Step.

"Allah master sculptor. Westernwoman master tease." He tapped Vane's temple with a forefinger. "Nature in here."

"I want you making yourself scarce while I'm being in-terviewed, Mudhead. You look like a Zambian waiter. Speaking of which, be a good lad and run down to Cellar and Basement. Bring up some Egyptian beer and baklava. Let her get a taste of what life is like here. How do I look?"

"Like blushing donkey."

"Excellent." He thought for a minute. "If I face the com-munity I'll be in shadow. That'll look cooler, but it'll be all me. If I face the Wall the community'll be a great background, but I'll look like a crowned jack o' lantern."

"Lousy movie."

"It's just an interview. Now go get the popcorn, damn you. And don't do any thespian work for us. I'll give you a ring if the script calls for a loitering mummy."

Mudhead peered over his spectacles. "Bossman no actorman. Never buffalo cameralady." He vanished down the Steps.

Vane called after him, "Who said anything about buffaloing anybody?" and began positioning chairs around the table, pulling two as close as possible. He kicked back so that he was half in shadow with ankle hooked casually on knee, adjusted his turban forward slightly, buffed its precious stone with his silk robe's sleeve. Vane pulled the headphones off their Wall hook and set them on the table's corner, heaping the long spiraling cord to coil rattler-wise before trailing off the edge.

And she strolled across Ridge Bridge looking like a runway model for exclusive camping wear, sporting an olive leatherette cross-harness, stylish canvas-and-denim camera bag, and elegant matching case. King tested the table for stability, said, "Good," and removed a mount from the case, screwed the video camera onto the mount, and levered the mount down. She then placed a miniature monitor on the table, adjusted its angle, and attached a coaxial cable between the camera and monitor.

"The camera will be on you, but I can pan and zoom with this." She showed him a small keyboard with joystick, and plugged the keyboard into a port on the camera's rear. "Nickel-cadmium batteries. Don't be alarmed if it seems to move on its own." The camera swiveled on its mount as she demonstrated the remote. Vane could see the instrument's iris dilate and contract. "It has a condenser microphone. Say something."

"You look stunning."

"No good. The pickup's hollow. The level's all wrong." She stepped up with a tie-clip microphone. Vane sweated as she fumbled with his flowing robes. Her knee rested against his for an excruciating half-minute.

"No wires?" he managed.

King didn't miss a beat. "On every move you make." She studied a tiny meter on the remote. "Go ahead."

"Go ahead where?"

"Check."

Vane blinked. "Check what?"

"Mr. Vane, what motivated you to set up this enterprise?"

He squirmed a little. "It's not all that simple."

"Start again. Mr. Vane, what brought you here, to the
Danakil Desert in Ethiopia?"

He rolled his shoulders and cleared his throat, stared
uncomfortably at his perched foot. "It seemed like a good idea
at the time."

"Don't avoid the camera," Rebecca said. "Try to relax
and be conversational. Don't mumble. Speak clearly and with
conviction. Start again."

"Wait!" Vane said, as Mudhead's starched white cap
popped into view. The African was balancing, on a silk-covered
tray, six bottles of beer in a Stonehenge arrangement. Nestled in
the center was a small plate of powdered cookies. He slunk up
to the table with his head lowered as though fearing a beating,
carefully slid the tray between them and bowed almost to the
Mat. "How else dirty servant," he whimpered, "please mighty
Bossman?"

The golden hand moved on the joystick, the camera
swung to face the recoiling server.

"Ah, Christ," Vane groaned. "You'll edit that out, won't
you?" He glared at Mudhead. "Or maybe he can perform his famous burning man dance for you."

Mudhead clasped his hands under his chin and backpedaled down the Steps, bowing energetically all the way.

"He's a very good subject," Rebecca said, smiling at her
own pun. The woman seemed to glow even in shade.

Vane pounded down a beer. "Start again," he said. The
camera swung round. He looked out over Mamuset.

"When I was a kid I always thought life was pretty
meaningless. I'll admit that Father's wealth gave me certain advantages." He took a deep breath. "I understand that people
watching this will probably think I'm a shallow guy, and that all
my actions come from being rich, or are *re*actions from a guilt-
trip *about* being rich. So be it. I've got a boatload of money and
a bushelful of time. Circumstances couldn't be any better.

"Ask yourselves: if you were in my shoes, what would

you do? Buy a different-colored Lexus for each day of the week? Erect palaces in Naples, in Papeete, in Bordeaux? How long before you crashed to a state someone I once knew defined as *ennui?*

"I had an epiphany. Not long before I came here. Like all insights, it was the cumulative expression of countless thoughts, feelings, and memories. Impressions. This particular epiphany placed my life in context with the Big Picture. I saw myself as one of billions. There were billions before me and billions more to come. Given all that, there's not a damned thing a man can do to make a difference. But he can make a statement. For what it's worth. His very existence should be a statement, an attempt to exemplify certain principles which, I believe, are universal."

"Okay," Rebecca said. "I'm going to cut here. Mr. Vane, you're not being asked to pontificate. Nor is the watching public going to be all that interested in the tribulations of privilege, or in your billions of epiphanous whatevers. We don't want to expend endless tape on your childhood memories, or on your adult philosophy." She held up a hand. "Not that you're not a fascinating man. Believe me, you are. But you're rambling, you're digressing. What M & S sent me here to capture is the real skinny. *Why* you came here. *Why* you're doing all this. Not your moods, not your life story. We can make that Part Two. But it *won't sell* unless we know *why* there was a Part One. The big apology should come *after*." She fanned her perfect face. "Tell you what. Let's take a break."

"Before we've even started?"

"Before we've even started. This is my fault. Part of the pre-interview should have been an explanation of the ground rules. M & S is looking for a story, not a confession." She helped herself to a beer.

"I'm *not* confessing! I don't have a damned thing to apologize for! And I *am* telling you why I came here, and *why* I'm doing what I'm doing."

"You've told me nothing," Rebecca said coldly, and for a moment Vane despised her. "You haven't mentioned a single name, or a date; not a friend or an enemy. This is already the least visual interview of my career."

"Look, lady, why would I be doing all this if I was even half the skunk you seem to think I am?"

A shadow darkened her eyes. "Didn't I just ask you that? Isn't 'why' the operative word here? Jesus." She inhaled deeply. "Take a minute or two to get your story in order. We'll start all over, at Frame One. But please this time just answer my questions directly. Everything else will be cut anyway." She wiped a slender forefinger across her perfect lips. "*Mmm!* Good cookies!"

Vane got to his feet. "I don't have a story. I don't know why I'm here. This interview's a total bust." He opened another beer, stepped to the shade's lip and looked over the community. All the little Domos were baking in the sun. It struck him that the heat kept things very quiet. He could almost hear his heart beating. For just a second he had a wild hallucination, a gorgeous vision of shade trees lining Streets and Squares. Tamarinds, elms, sycamores; a broad canopy of cooling green. Saplings by the thousands. Better yet, young and mature trees imported in planters. Then, within Squares, peaches, apples, oranges, avocados. It could be done. Shipped, freighted, trucked. Mudhead's sweet road was waiting. Vane's vision vanished quickly as it came. He wiped his moist palms on his thighs and walked back to his chair.

The golden woman fanned herself, looking, somehow, radiantly bored. "Then maybe we'll try the philosophical angle. Maybe we *can* salvage something. Editing can work miracles, Cristian, but you've got to have some meat before you can fillet. Now give me half-profile." She unscrewed the video camera from its mount and hefted it, peered into the viewfinder. "So when did you get the idea to start all this, Mister Vane?"

He took a swallow of the dark, bitter beer. "It was the day my father died. He wanted me to run his empire, fully expected me to. Watching him die was the first blow of the day. Not because it hurt. Because it *didn't* hurt. Does that make any sense?"

"This is your show. Go on."

"I had to kick out all those people who'd been living at the Rest. It felt right to do it, because they were leeches, but later it struck me that I'd not only disrupted the lives of dozens of people, I'd removed myself from the one thing I'd ever had resembling a family. Then there was this woman who was masquerading as my mother."

"That would have been the skinny Elvira-type?"

"I had to dump her too. Suddenly I didn't even have a mother. I took off in the Lincoln. While driving I got a call telling me the man who had raised me had just had a heart attack. I was now all alone in the world. My father's company was in my ear telling me I had all these responsibilities and my head was about to explode.

"I guess I had some kind of nervous breakdown. I got drunk and staggered around the beach for days, balancing suicide against genocide. Either would have suited me fine. I went to my father's funeral and drew a blank. I only know I woke up in his big old crypt half-frozen and sick as a dog. But the situation sobered me. I felt I had to do something positive and meaningful with my life. Something that wasn't all about me. I knew I wasn't ready to die."

"A mature decision. So, Mister Vane, could we conclude that this place is your attempt to rebuild a family structure in your life? And would it also be fair to assume you're subconsciously filling your father's shoes as empire builder?"

Vane turned to stare at her, his eyes blazing.

"That's good," she said, "with all the little houses stretching out behind you. Tell the camera about the little houses, Mr. Vane, and all about the little people who live in them."

"Some other time."

King sighed. "All right, all right. Take five." She shook her head. "It's probably not fair of me to come barging in here expecting you to perform on cue. Relax a bit and figure out what you really need to say." She began stuffing equipment back in the matching carrying case, saying incidentally, "I'll be staying over."

Vane paled. "You see our accommodations."

"I'll make do. Is there any way out of here on my own? I don't want to keep Mitchell if he's not needed."

"There's a small plane," Vane said absently. "Piper Cub. Comes out of Addis Ababa. Brings us our mail and minor supplies. The pilot will do Djibouti if he has advance notice."

"That's fine, then. A 360 with you out of the picture, please." Vane hunched on the Mat while Rebecca did a slow pirouette, coiling in place as she turned, then reversing the motion. She carefully repacked her video camera.

He shook his head. "They'll be safe here."

Smiling faintly, King slung the packed cases over her shoulders, clipped them to the leatherette harness, and walked back across Ridge Bridge to the Explorer.

Vane slammed on his shades and stepped out into the pitiless sun. He fired a fistful of pebbles at his Domo across Stage Street. Who invited her in the first place? Why did her distaste for the rich and famous have to come off as something so *personal*? And why couldn't he stop thinking about her?

Twenty minutes later she came padding back to the Stage using Mudhead for a pack mule, her equipment cases now looped over his shoulders, an extra-large case dangling by its strap from his neck. On one shoulder was a folding cot, on the other a rolled sleeping bag, and, on his bowed black head, a cute little snow-white safari hat. King glided alongside, gently teasing while shading him with her parasol.

Yet it was all downhill from there. Vane grew increaseingly awkward during interviews, King correspondingly impatient. In a tacit compromise, she took to filming him from a distance as he went about his daily business. Their tension was contagious, echoed in a hundred raised voices of the normally complacent Afar. But that night, dining on Top Step, the mood was much mellower. There were just so many stars.

Looking down at the twelve-volt haze, King said levelly, "I think I've got enough to satisfy my editors. If today was any indication, it's a pretty constructive, non-threatened little world you've got going here." She sawed a tiny triangle out of her flatbread, nibbled it down with her perfect teeth. "Maybe I owe you an apology for the interviews, Mr. Vane. I was operating on a preconceived notion, and I was biased."

"Cristian."

That same wan smile. "I still have to write my story, so I still have to throw that little three-letter word at you."

"Which word?"

"*Why*. I'm still trying to find an angle."

Vane looked away. "Spiritual thing," he said presently, and pushed back from the table. "I just can't understand how this can be so obvious to me and to no one else. Wait till it's over, *Rebecca*. Wait until your eyes can see what's in my head."

"I'm not blind, *Cristian*. But maybe your motives need explaining. Because maybe no one else can afford the luxury of creativity in a pure form. The rest of us have deadlines, and mouths to feed that are dependent on our meeting those deadlines. Sure we're skeptical of those who have all the advantages."

"To quote Joe Anybody."

"Look, Cristian—"

"Cris."

She looked down and shook her head. When she looked back up her eyes were burning. "I'll tell you something, man. I do my homework. And I always end up knowing more about my subjects than they know about themselves. For instance…oh …I'll bet you didn't know your papa was investigated by the CIA, did you? Yep. Seems he got in a jam in Guatemala and offered the patent on a certain microchip to the government of that sad little country if they'd only reunite him with a dancer he'd fallen in love with in an American bar in Peseta. A place called Rosarita's Red-Hot Cantina. She was a stripper, billed as *Li'l Pink Honey Pot*, who performed a very popular routine involving foot-long pork sausages and pink whipped cream. Her real name was Bonita Alvarado, and your old man knocked her up, old as he was, crazy as he was. When he learned she was pregnant he showered her with sausages, honeycombs, and cinnamon jelly beans. He pursued her through term, and in the process fell wildly, fell blindly, fell idiotically in love with her."

Vane said quietly, "A stripper."

"Contempt for the rich and famous," King went on brutally, "is universal. It's pure envy, of course, but it's real nonetheless." She patted her lips with a monogrammed hankie, sawed off another miniscule wedge of flatbread. "Now, there's a difference when it comes down to doing a job. Then one has to dissociate one's feelings from one's work. Take my job, for example. It has nothing to do with my tastes. I'm hired to come out here and get a story, and to be utterly objective in the process. I'm a tool, a journalist. Not a groupie, not a therapist." She took a petite sip of her Zinfandel. "On my days off, on my own time, I'm free to hark back and take a subjective approach to the whole matter of Cristian Honey Vane. Then I can love him or hate him, be sensitive or indifferent."

Vane stirred his *injera*, spooned a large chunk of chicken from the spicy stew. "And what do you think your objective take on this place'll be?"

"Expect a positive piece. I'm guessing people will be pleased with what you're doing, especially in contrast with all the headaches that make up the straight news back home."

"And...what's your subjective take on Cristian Vane, the man? Just for curiosity's sake."

She rang a fingernail against her empty glass. Vane, guessing he was being tested, offered a crooked smile and filled the glass halfway. He was about to set the bottle back down when their eyes collided. He raised the bottle and continued pouring until the glass was brimming.

"Generous guy," Rebecca said. "Hides a big heart behind a typical show of macho indifference. More sensitive than he'd like to admit." She drained half the glass in a single draught and grimaced prettily. "Clumsy with women; thinks, like most insecure men, that females are impressed by displays of confidence and chivalry. E for effort." She finished off the glass.

Vane poured the last of the bottle into his own glass and drank it down. He stood up, said, "Excuse me," and nonchalantly stepped off of Top Step. Once he was out of view he scampered down the Steps, rousted Mudhead and sent him for two more bottles and a tray of date pastries. By the time Mudhead made it back, Bossman and Cameralady were dangling their bare feet off of Top Step, remarking the Domos and stars. Vane snatched the bottles and corkscrew and shooed the African off.

He popped a cork. "Pardon me while I grab the glasses."

"Forget it," King slurred. "Manners don't become you." She hiccoughed. "And I get sick of having to be dainty all the time." She took the bottle by its neck and knocked it back.

Vane raised an eyebrow. He popped the cork from his own bottle and swallowed deeply. "Awkward with men," he said, and nudged her playfully. "Tries intuitively, like most beautiful women, to control them by appealing to their egos. Knows they'll strut without realizing their strings are being pulled. It's all a dance. Both sides. Silly-ass minuets."

She took another gulp. "Hogwash. I don't need to win your affection. And why do I get the feeling you do your dancing alone?"

"Probably," Vane bristled, "because you believe that garbage you write."

"That's the spirit, tough guy. If you're going to win me, you'll do it with bayonets, not with violins."

He snorted. "What makes you think I'm trying to 'win you'?"

King's answering grin was lopsided. "Oh, come on. Just drop the masks, okay? What straight guy doesn't want to win a pretty woman?"

Vane shook his head. "You know what? You've got one humongous ego for a skirt, and one hell of a lot of nerve. Nobody can read anybody else's mind."

"Nobody needs to." She really kicked the bottle back. "Listen, Cris, there isn't a woman on this planet who doesn't know exactly what's going on in a man's head whenever he's within hailing distance. You guys get silly, you get solicitous. Flirtatious or standoffish. Doesn't matter. You *change*. You stop being the simple headlong weenies we've all come to know and love. Let a man get a peek at some leg or a whiff of perfume and he's totally transparent. Laugh at one of his dumb jokes and watch his testosterone go through the roof. Suddenly he's Goofo the Clown. Tell him he's strong, cute, smart, sexy. Whatever. The fool's dancing on cloud nine." She took a gulp and rocked against him. "So don't tell me about humongous egos."

Vane rocked right back. "And don't you flatter yourself. Men aren't as simple as all that. It's not easy surviving this world without the benefit of scents and paints and a cornucopia of specialized undergarments. Talk about masks!"

They leaned against each other, then leaned heavily on the wine, drinking furiously through ten minutes of electric silence.

Finally Rebecca belched sweetly. "How you must...suffered. But no mask here. All real; underneath, on top too. What you see...what you get."

Vane looped an arm over her shoulders. King oozed right out. "Figure speech," she said. "Where's ladies' room? And after that, where in hell guesthouse? I'm...done."

"Sorry," Vane mumbled. "No ladyroom. This's first time entertained actual *lady*." He pointed at a common outhouse just off the Mount. "H'ever, *if* you can manage, there's a not-so porta potty right...down...there! Septic tank under thatch roof. Like Afar temp'rary house. No slight 'tended."

"Cute," King said, wobbling to her feet.

"Very!" he called after her, and closed his burning eyes. When he opened them again she was coming up the Steps, fighting the last few. "Even stumble well," he gassed. "'pologize 'bout fusillyties, but royalty come...rarely."

"Beatsa squat hole anna palm fron'." She stared at him. "You're drunk, *Mister* Cristian! I don' trus' you. Not at all."

"Good call." Vane forced himself to his feet. "Sleep my place," he sprayed, pointing at his Square. "I'll sleep...here." He winked ghoulishly. "See? I'm...harmless after all."

Rebecca hurled down her gear. "I'm fine!" She tried wrestling her cot out of its bag, tangling everything hopelessly.

"Help," Vane said. "I'll." He stumbled over.

King was instantly sober. She indicated her pretty brown knee. "One more step and you're a eunuch."

Vane wobbled there, disappointed and hurt. "Welcome!" he pouted, before pitching headfirst down the Steps. He had fractured memories of Mudhead hauling him to his feet and leading him inside, and then of that same white-swathed, barking black creature binding the Domo's gills for the night. He remembered fighting the African for some reason, and finally being thrown on his bed like a bundle of dirty laundry.

Any amount of night might have passed before the door swung in and that damned golden statue was eclipsing the Stage lights. It had to have been at least a few hours, for most of Vane's drunk had been replaced by hangover. He saw the goddess clearly, though she should have been no more than a gold-tinged silhouette in a white-light nimbus. His imagination supplied the details. Her figure rounded off the throbbing glare, tapering in bottlenecks and sweet amber fields. Her hair, perfectly mussed, shimmered in a tight corona that crackled with random prominences. "I came to apologize," the goddess said. "Also, sleeping on that folding cot is a lot like sleeping on a folding cactus." She began to unbutton her blouse. Vane's jaw dropped and his mouth worked soundlessly. "You don't have to say anything," she whispered. "Anyways, I'm in no mood to argue." The blouse slid from her shoulders in a flash of gold. King kicked shut the door and stumbled to the bed.

Chapter Sixteen

Solomon

Vane paused, a hand glued to the upper edge of the Cub's door, urgently seeking the perfect parting comment. It wouldn't come, wouldn't hang, didn't matter. He and she'd spent an excruciating day behaving like burned-out marrieds; walking together but well-apart, addressing anybody but each other, avoiding eye contact. Neither could break the silence with anything meaningful, and only when they were separately involved did they resemble happening human beings again. Only then did proximate adults resume their daily activities. Only then would teens run wrestling in the Streets.

King directed those adults and teens to a fault; demanding unrealistic poses and expressions, getting in everybody's business, getting in everybody's way. Time and again Vane would overreact, rushing to their defense and exacerbating the tension. After these mini-explosions the Afar would slink around like children avoiding squabbling parents, and by mid-afternoon it was plain they'd all lost their fascination with the golden lady. It became increasingly difficult to photograph a Mamusetan. The human ring grew cooler and wider, until her position and demeanor resembled that of a bull in an arena. Everybody prayed the plane would arrive on schedule.

She spent most of the day in Mudhead's Domo, alone with her notes. When the Piper Cub finally arrived, the Afar came out in droves to see her off. It was a curious scene. Vane and King led the procession like bitter opposing dignitaries. By the time they'd reached the little airstrip they were surrounded by a mob of over three hundred absolutely silent Mamusetans. As the nervous pilot eased open the door Vane looked back guiltily. For a moment he was sure the Afar believed they were about to be abandoned.

The last thing he could think to say was, "You'll make it a fair piece, won't you?"

And she'd spat out, *"I'm a journalist!"* and wrestled for control of the door. After a pathetic little tug-o'-war, she'd torn it from his hands and slammed it shut. The Afar stared at the receding plane until it was lost to sight.

Vane shuffled back to the Mount in dead silence, a hunched figure in mourning black. The crowd opened before him as he neared, closed behind him once he'd passed. The Afar watched him climb the Steps with feet of cement. Returning to their personal Squares, they picked up right where they'd left off, for by now they were habituated to routine. And, while the Stage remained unoccupied for the whole of that day, the clockwork of Mamuset resumed as though no break had occurred. No one acknowledged Vane's lapse in leadership, and no one was stupid enough to kid him about the perfect lady. From the moment the little plane was swallowed up in the huge African sky she ceased to exist.

When the first mature trees rolled up Onramp, morning temperatures were flirting with the century mark, the Awash pipeline was being fitted with a series of reflective aluminum skirts, and the political map of East Africa was in a state of rapid flux. The assassination of Hassan Hassan-Salid in Mogadishu had drawn a terrorist response in Kenya's National Assembly. As a consequence, Somalia's western border was squirming like a worm. In the Ethiopian pale of Adwa, Eritrea had turned a skirmish into a bloodbath with the introduction of state-of-the-art weapons, promptly taking a bite out of the old Ethiopian border north of Mamuset. Additional forays to the south brought an Egyptian presence into the Republic of Djibouti; the tiny country was fast becoming an international wishbone. Due to American clout, the Foundation's new corridor was tolerated clear to Suez, although several navies were testing the Red Sea with escalating audacity. Honey now contracted directly with Djibouti in oil and copper, while agents bought up hides for the new leatherworks right in Djibouti City. Toe by toe, the Foundation approached its master.

The trees—sycamores, black oaks, maples, and birches—were shipped through Suez in 7 x 7 banded planters to the free port of Djibouti, moved by rail to the Vane Depot, and from there brought into Mamuset by tractor in standing groups of eight, their branches bound and sheathed in canvas.

First to arrive were sycamores, some reaching as high as forty feet, hauled with great ceremony to sites decided by lot. Because of this unsystematic method, certain Streets were heavily lined with sycamores, while others had comparatively few. Cristian Vane, with the bitch and the blueprint out of his system, was a changed man; a man happily surrendering mathematical practicality to the aesthetic. A wholly symmetrical community, he now stressed, was a community without personality. He recalibrated the site's entire routine like a madman, making up the rules as he went along. Over three hectic weeks, seven thousand adult sycamores arrived in a near-continuous train. Sections of PVC were diverted to allow for root growth, plots of 2,560 cubic feet dug from Street, Square, and Intersection. Every nutrient critical to a sycamore's well-being was worked into soil imported from nurseries around the Mediterranean, that each tree might take root in a carefully controlled microenvironment. And, at the end of those busy three weeks, Vane invited the five thousand-plus participants to file by on the Stage, where they could individually marvel over the broad canopy now filling the crater like a deep green mist. With the wide sun lighting their upper leaves, the foreign-born sycamores, obscenely vital in the midst of all that dead, dry desert, looked like they would burst into flame at any moment.

After the sycamores came the oaks and birches, the immature maples and elms, the soapberries, chestnuts and cherries—broad-leaved trees able to weather drastic changes in latitude, elevation, and temperature while providing maximum shade and beauty. The specialists had been up front: with proper care and a preemptive approach, plants indigenous to even radically different climates could thrive in a Mamuset-like environment, so long as certain critical criteria were met and maintained. That environment must be jealously controlled: Mamuset would have to be treated as a tiny, very vulnerable nursery in an immense, very thirsty wasteland. The site's salinity had to be reduced. Spot-floodings, combined with religious tilling of the soil, would effectively flush clumping salt deposits. The area's natural drainage would take care of the rest. The kicker here was a need for regular, massive, and hugely expensive applications of lime.

But at this stage money was truly no object. Honey was busily committing suicide; dissolving holdings and reneging on contracts as it diverted major funds to Djibouti and West Yemen oil fields. Thousands of acres of East African farmland were bought up and converted into horticultural stations, an apparently nonsensical move bailing stockholders referred to as "Earthworm, Incorporated." These fields were utilized for the spot-cropping of everything from asparagus to yams, Ticonderoga to violets. The Honey Oases, viewed from the air, gave a solid impression of chessboards stretching into infinity.

Routines in Mamuset became traditions. Streets were night-flooded by Rotating Sector Hands, and each morning fiercely competitive "volunteers" trekked Square to Square wrapping saplings in gauze to spare the young phloem from sunburn. Tossing handfuls of water on these saplings became a good-luck gesture for adults and a game for children, copied Sector to Sector. Vane organized Yard Socials, ordered every Square carted a fruiting citrus, and promoted Sector contests for injured, or otherwise "orphaned" tree specimens. Through a marveling Mudhead, he told the Afar of an American folk hero named Johnny Appleseed, and distributed to every Square packs of miscellaneous seeds. Then, having grown ever more whimsical with the project's continuing success, he almost embarked upon a harebrained idea to ring the crater with live doums, dates, and palmyras. The Afar, healthy and happy, would cheerfully have devoted the rest of their lives to it had not Mudhead talked him down. The African knew matching Vane's fancy would require countless palms, and present a mind-numbing irrigation problem, so Vane compromised, producing a gorgeous crescent of fronds radiating from either side of the Onramp entrance. These palms were "local"—bought from nomads, uprooted and dragged by camel over hundreds of miles.

The limitless supply of fresh water made desert miracles possible. Mamuset became an orchard, a forest, a jungle—but in the process the project created its own challenges. Strategic Field Squares, flooded to produce watering holes, over time seeped together into a series of small lakes, occasionally turning Field Quads into marshes. Nothing could have pleased the Afar more. Over one dizzy October week the entire population turned out with wheelbarrows and spades, constructing a highly personalized labyrinth of shallow canals that wended dreamily through the community to the sluice gate at Delta. Afar Fieldhands planted elm saplings and young willows on the banks of these canals in quilts of bluegrass and native purple pennisetum, while community elders delighted in building quaint little ornate bridges of varnished teak and mimosa. Vane stocked ponds with goldfish, introduced ducks and geese into the system, and then, over the course of two long magical weeks, trucked in a vast assortment of birds; everything from humble little sparrows to gaudy birds of paradise. Power over his environment made him giddy and wildly generous; Vane was easily sucked into an explosive, psychedelic decorative phase, considering plants for their exotic beauty rather than their nutritive value, favoring the ornamental over the practical. Dawn lectures became soft and sentimental. Weapons were out, birdhouses were in. The copycat method had evolved incrementally: now Rotating Sector Commanders, repeating translated Stage instructions reverberating from Utility Quad speakers, instructed blocks of Squares from plant-choked, garlanded and festooned Mini-Stages. One morning the population would be transplanting snapdragons and blood-red celosia, the next day everybody would be constructing rattan trellises while studying Japanese creepers and climbing vines. Gardens were erupting, Domos evolving into quirky inns. Before he knew it, Vane's efficient martial project had degenerated into a funky little Eden.

The great shade saved everything—cooling the air, cooling the earth, cooling the water in buried pipes. Afar women supplemented the natural shade with sewn canvas canopies suspended from branches, incidentally producing huge sagging Square-to-Square Shade Halls. Connected Halls eventually grew into a series of ramshackle tunnels. With Vane's encouragement, seldom-used Intersections gave way to miniature meadows and bayou-like bathing oases, while great sections on either side of Bisecting Way (the wide road separating Streets and Fields beyond the Ridge) were worked into experimental gardens and nature trails. In random spots the combination of heavy foliage, standing water, and human eccentricity produced hidden pockets that were quite dark, perennially damp, and occasionally even *chilly*. In these secret glens were lush stacks of staghorn fern smothering stalks of clumping golden bamboo.

And one day the Cub's pilot showed Vane a photograph taken during a noon pass. Between the photo's hard white margins lay a raw sienna waste surrounding what at first looked like a petri dish overflowing with green. The Grid was barely recognizable. But, under closer scrutiny, Fields appeared as collections of variegated squares, Shade Halls as tiny tents in an endless park, lakes as bright blue puddles in a quicksilver maze.

Vane's sapphire flashed like a signal lamp in the sun. He stood erect and handed his spyglass to one of a dozen scrabbling children, having counted over twenty camels trudging up Onramp in the rising heat, their riders slumped with heads down, as though dozing. When the train finally reached the gateway of flexed and entwined palms, not a single rider appeared aware he was entering, or that Vane and the children were darting side to side to avoid being trampled. The camels filed under the Arch and crossed Ridge Bridge to the Mount with Vane running alongside waving his arms. When he reached the Big Tarp he kicked the fifth in line and yelled, *"Hey!"*

The entire train pulled up, nose to butt. The man on the lead camel jabbed his brute in the hindquarters. The beast roared and pitched forward, kneeling on its forelegs a moment before reclining fully. At this signal the whole line went down like dominoes, each animal with its own distinctive echoing plaint. Four men near the middle hopped off and ran to an elaborately dressed-and-groomed camel. The elderly rider, wearing a bright orange cape and headdress, was eased to a standing position. He looked around dazedly. Another rider ran up and handed him an intricately woven acacia basket. The old man, embracing this basket possessively, looked around until his eyes fell on the queer black-robed sheik wearing the fat black turban with the blue precious stone. Flanked by his four assistants, he tottered over and handed Vane the basket while staring up out of pleading rheumy eyes. Vane peeked inside.

In the very center of the basket, on a soiled bed of bright orange cloth, were a black infant and a puppy, both covered by flies and ants. The infant, wretched in rigor mortis, had died of dehydration brought on by diarrhea. His family's prominent tribal status was revealed by the paint on his forehead, by a pair of onyx anklets, and by a swath of fine cloth around his midsection. The puppy was a mangy little skeleton, just as black as the infant, its eyes rolled up and its jaw hanging at ninety degrees. A leather leash ran from the infant's granite fist to the puppy's throat. Foam frothed around the puppy's mouth as its lungs labored for life. With a start Vane realized it had been strangled to prepare it for accompaniment with the dead baby.

He pulled back violently, flies following his head away from the basket. Suddenly he was shaking all over. Quick tears found his eyes. *"I'm not God!"* he screamed. "Now *get the hell out of here!"*

The elderly man, studying him meekly, bowed and backpedaled, the basket held firmly against his chest. He and his retinue returned to their beasts.

"Wait!" Vane sobbed. He snapped his fingers and Mudhead puffed over. The two huddled. Mudhead ran back under

the Big Tarp and returned with handfuls of birrs, francs, and dollars. Vane plucked out the puppy, removed the leash from its neck, and cradled the animal in his arm. He crammed the bills in the basket.

The old man's face fell. He pulled out the bills and handed the basket to a random pair of hands. His assistants, supporting him by the elbows, allowed him to very slowly stoop until his knees touched the Mat. Vane got down beside him. After carefully laying out the bills in a circular pattern, the old man gently disengaged the puppy from the cradle of Vane's arm and placed it on the Mat in the circle's center. This done, he righted himself without assistance, and with great dignity was escorted back to his gorgeously-dressed animal and lifted aboard. As the lead camel's driver jabbed it in the rear, the beast angrily roared to its feet. In a reverse of the original motion, the camels all struggled to their feet, roaring nervously one after the other.

Vane watched for a respectful nanosecond, then scooped up the dog and dashed down the Steps to his Square, kicked open his gate and ran puffing through his garden. He placed the puppy on his bed and dropped to his knees. Outside, the bravest children snuck through his gateway in twos and threes. Tiptoeing through the garden, they leaned up against his Domo to eavesdrop through the gills. They heard Vane speaking urgently inside, and their eyes met and flashed. Although his words made no sense, the tone was unmistakable.

"Come on, man, don't die on me! You're not gonna let me down too." Vane was applying pressure against its tongue to open the air passage. The puppy's mouth foamed harder. A leg gave a shuddering kick, and immediately the animal went into body-length spasms. Its jaws convulsed and froze. After a terrible little croak, it began kicking its rear legs frantically. A moment later the legs went stiff and a great sigh scattered the foam from its mouth. The head jerked straight back.

"No!" Vane commanded. "It is not going to happen. I forbid it! You are not permitted, under any circumstances, to expire!" He fanned the puppy desperately, massaged its throat, moved his face up close. "I said *no!*" he whispered. "Nobody gets out of here that easily." Vane pushed the puppy's belly in

with his thumb and cleaned its mouth with the little finger of the same hand. He then leaned forward so that the puppy's entire head was in his mouth and blew softly. The puppy kicked. He pulled away, pushed its belly back in. The animal gagged and struggled violently.

"When I *said* no," Vane muttered, "I *meant* no." He mouthed the puppy's head again, blew harder, backed off, pushed the belly in. The puppy kicked all four legs wildly and froze. "You can fight me all you want, but you're not getting away from me." A steady breath and push. "So *breathe*, baby. Breathe and get used to it." The tiny puppy flipped as though spring-loaded, dragged itself a few inches across the bed and vomited for all it was worth.

Vane fell back on his bed, and he might have been talking to himself when he said, "Just rest and get your strength back up. You'll need it." He wiped his lips clean, rolled his head and stroked the shuddering creature. "Because you're a Vane now."

He didn't remember kicking off his shoes or closing his eyes, but it was dark, and a squeak by his side indicated he'd rolled on the puppy. Vane swung his legs off the bed, lit a candle, and ran a hand over his face and hair. The dog was curled into a ball, trembling nose to tail. He touched its belly and the puppy squealed again. The belly was warm. "Good sign," he said, tenderly stroking the puppy with one hand while gesturing globally with the other. "I don't know if you saw any of the other people here, but they weren't always so strapping. Hell, when I first showed up they weren't any bigger than you." He very gently placed a fingertip in an ear and carefully probed. "But look at 'em now." The puppy shuddered. "Seems clean enough." He checked the other ear.

"Around here we start at the beginning." Vane popped the lid off a plastic bowl on his nightstand and brought back a finger coated with mildly seasoned goat curd. "We run a tight ship. Everybody eats." He ran the finger around the puppy's mouth, then stuck it inside. The puppy gagged and recoiled, but a second later was licking the finger eagerly. "Welcome to Mamuset," Vane said. "It ain't fun, it ain't easy, and it ain't always pretty. But it's the Vane method." He scooped another finger's worth. "And damn it, it works."

On one weekly aerial run in July, the supplies included, along with the delicacies and regular mail, the May edition of Movers And Shakers magazine. Vane and Mudhead went through it in Mudhead's garden over cigars and beer. Sure e-nough, Mudhead's groveling Top Step pose was the centerpiece of a two-page mosaic of tiles. It was the African's proudest moment.

A caption beneath the shot pointed out that the gesture was all in fun. The article itself was surprisingly honest, and in places even complimentary, defending Cristian Vane against all slurs. Vane was described as a basically decent and com-passionate man, but with an annoying flair for the theatrical. King couldn't help psychoanalyzing her subject. Vane was a well-meaning person, and a constructive and energetic man, yet he was way out of touch with reality, and unable or unwilling to offer a single believable reason for his altruistic behavior. She hinted more than once at guilt over his astounding wealth, and at a schizophrenic response to his fractured upbringing. The Afar, featured in a dozen cozy photographs, were described as happy and healthy overall.

Miss King also documented her frustrating attempts to get corroborative information from the famous Honey Found-ation. A Denise Waters, represented in a most unflattering photograph, was described as abrasive and highly protecttive of her distant boss. Just writing about Honey must have soured King, for she concluded her article with a dark spin on the big question: How would it all end? How long would the desert crater last before the globetrotter grew bored, collapsed under the weight of his own ineptitude, or simply left for greener pastures? King wondered what would become of the poor people left behind. Would they leave the way they came, or would the crater become their resting ground? Had the strange black-draped figure, caught looking depressed and confused in frame after frame, in reality built a desert graveyard?

Vane tacked the photo spread to the Wall for the delight

of curious children. In the interest of clarification, he had the mail pilot take a wide-angle shot from the Mount, showing hundreds of healthy Mamusetans posing in the Streets. Deep in the distance, the miniscule figures of men stood shoulder to shoulder on East Rim below its Bulwarks, appearing to perch on the green clouds of sycamores. Wisps of cooking fires were frozen between trees, jays caught in flight, children captured chasing delighted dogs. Camels yawned at the camera.

In the foreground sat an expressionless Cristian Vane in flowing black robes, winking black turban, and broad mirror shades, a cigar in one hand, a banana daiquiri in the other. Vane's four months-old mutt Solomon, perched awkwardly on his master's lap, watched a pair of snow-white rabbits bounding through a garden. To Vane's left, in clerical collar and top hat, a grim-faced Mudhead knelt holding a tray overflowing with bills and coins. To his right posed a grinning Kid, holding a thatch umbrella over the seated master. Nestled in his right arm was an M16, its nose pointed meaningfully at the camera.

The photograph's inscription read:

> *Dear Rebecca,*
> *Wish You Were Here.*
> *Kid Rameses*

Chapter Seventeen

Tibor

It was that golden hour of day when the world seems to slow; when work is done or slated for the morrow, when east-leaning shadows grow heavier even as one peers. At this hour men are prone to easy discourse, and domesticated animals, picking up on the murmur, find their eyelids beginning to weigh.

The music of an early whippoorwill whistled between the gills of Vane's Domo, for a tantalizing second seeming to mimic the strains of Ravel's *Bolero* on his boom box. Lateral shadows had snuck across his desk, leaving his Mamuset memoirs half-illuminated. He adjusted the manuscript to catch the light. Vane was tempted to press on with his *Microcosmia, or The Man Who Broke Honey*, but it was that golden hour of day when intellectual pursuits move to the back burner. Vane was bored, his mind wandering no less resolutely than those slats of light and shadow. He finished off his kirsch in a quick swallow and lit another cheroot. Solomon, nudged accidentally, shifted gears in his dream and nestled closer to his master's feet. The dog was a healthy, handsome yearling who loved children, hated camels, and was embarrassingly jealous of his master's affection. Vane stretched to his feet and ejected the CD, switched off the player. He stepped over Solomon carefully, but the dog, like all dogs, was attuned to the whims of his owner, and leaped to be first to the door.

Vane scratched Solomon's eager punkin head as they made their way through the clutter. Over the last half year his Domo had deteriorated to a chaotic museum-garage, bursting at the seams with miscellaneous gifts. There were dusty portraits by children, long-stale pastries prepared by Afar women, piled baskets and mats, utensils from faceless Mamusetan artisans. There was even an oversized, sun-dried stick-and-mud statue of Solomon, called by the children *Saumun Vahn*, to reflect his master's name. Vane was known as *Khrisa Vahn*, and Mudhead, by association, as *Muh-Muh Vahn*. Gifts were generally just heaped in corners and stacked along the walls. When space grew too dear, the stuff was toted across his Yard to Mudhead's and stored before being moved to Warehouse or Basement.

Vane's place, due to his continuous experiments in creating the ideal bohemian Domo, was without a doubt the most exotic home in Mamuset. Certain innovations, such as his erector shelves and collapsible woven partitions, had been adopted by neighbors. Other imported ideas, such as the rock garden and mood lighting, made no sense to the Africans, and remained mesmerizing features of his revered residence. The Afar had by degrees, and almost apologetically, covered their Domos with thatch in deference to their customary homes, then secured their solar panels atop these new thatch beds. Vane, picking up on the idea, tied thatch on his own roof and found it to be excellent insulation. Vane's pad was ever dark, cool and airy, aromatic with gifts of baked goods, with spices, with incense and potpourri. The grateful Afar had insisted his Yards receive the finest specimens of trees and birds, and in quantity. As a result his Square was part arboretum, part jungle.

Now Vane donned his turban, threw back his flowing black robes, and drew open the door. In two steps he and Solomon were swallowed by his garden—the master of Mamuset was way behind in his Yard chores. A pair of trellises were sagging under the weight of African marigolds, the storage shed was shifting over the avocado's roots. Grass and weeds had almost eradicated the inlaid rock path leading to his front gate. Spider webs glistened in rare shafts of sun, wasps whirled in and out of a particularly dark space between trunks. His orchids were flagging, and one corner of his backyard was a marsh over a broken pipe. As he did every day, Vane swore that today was the day he'd get around to it.

Solomon was off like a shot through the Yard. Worthless, half-asleep on her pad, caught the black streak out of the corner of her eye, but wasn't quick enough to evade another nip to the bottom. Her head lanced out, the great incisors snapped, and Solomon began dancing side to side excitedly. Vane pounded his fist twice on the back of the camel's neck. Worthless rose with that old, irksome series of roars and hisses that meant Solomon was just asking for it.

Worthless was the grudging possessor of a gorgeous polished crocodile hide saddle, a gift from the Banke's president. The saddle had sheaths to hold the spyglass and jile, along with snap pouches for pager and walkie-talkie. Vane was proud of it, and dependent on it, for he'd failed to master both the blanket and the bareback method. It was possible to loop great saddlebags over grooved bosses, and so use Worthless as an agile supply vehicle. Vane did a daily round of the Rim, bringing treats for the Guards and their children.

Having warned off Solomon, he was leading Worthless to the front gate when he was startled by a puff of sparrows bursting from his neighbors' trees. They shot into the sky whirling, joined a different flock and just as abruptly dispersed. Watching agape, Vane noticed dozens of distant flocks spiraling in all directions, soaring and plunging, breaking apart and converging. This phenomenon struck him, even then, as somehow ominous. Still staring, he kicked open his front gate and stepped out onto Stage Street. His Square's front chain link fence, overgrown with creepers, was sagging with rose garlands and the usual mounds of gifts piled high. Vane sampled curiously, running his hands over a few unfamiliar bulges while Solomon and Worthless sniffed alongside. He saw that Mudhead had toted a couple of jugs of homemade beer from Cellar and deposited them on either side of the gate. Vane stuffed a jug in each saddlebag, then broke a large chunk off a date and honey cake, took a bite and passed the rest to his animals.

A big eye appeared behind a pile twenty feet along. Solomon went down on his belly, his rear end oscillating as two other children peeked around the first. There were a couple of squeals. Solomon barked delightedly. Worthless shied and the children ran off giggling, Solomon running circles around them.

Vane filled the saddlebags with flatbread, fig jam, and sweetmeats, then pounded Worthless twice on the back of her neck. She knelt and he mounted awkwardly, carefully positioning his moccasins in the stirrups, still determined to become an adept camel rider on these daily rounds. He rode clumsily along the shady side of Stage Street while Solomon bedeviled Worthless. Other dogs and camels responded to their familiar barks and roars.

The Mount's east face was covered with velvet rosettes, patches of scarlet African violets, and a great variety of succulents. No protocol existed for Stage access, and, since camels were notoriously skittish on the Steps, dozens of wending and intersecting paths had been stamped into the slope. Vane let Worthless pick her own way while his dog bounded up the Steps to avoid being pricked. Under the Big Tarp's shade he pulled out his spyglass and took a long look around his paradise. Lazy tails rose from cooking fires, here and there a strolling figure appeared and disappeared between the trees. He took the Stage Ramp back down and clopped up Bisecting Way clear to North Rim, waving heartily to children while nonchalantly clinging to his ride's scruffy mane. The Rim was now Mamuset's most neglected area; Rim Road had fallen into disrepair, Inner Slopes were a canopied riot of wildflowers, impatiens, and blushing mums. Tranquility had completely lowered Mamuset's guard, making the siesta more a pursuit than a pastime. Field workers moved languidly, avoiding the sun, while Guards, constantly found napping at their Posts, faced only effusive apologies when wakened.

Vane, in his theatrical getup and casual ways, unconsciously encouraged the general lassitude. Occasionally he and Mudhead threw a surprise Ripple, wherein squads of defenders in the beds of pickups raced to man Bulwarks, while flanking arms of ammunition-toting women and children scampered up the Inner Slopes behind them. But lately these drills had been lackluster and abbreviated. It wasn't that the Afar weren't into it; they still came running at the wail of a siren. The fault was solely Vane's. He'd become lazy and distant, was putting on weight. The fact that his sole turn-on was writing his memoirs made him admit, sometimes to himself and sometimes in unintended asides, that the project was complete. And so he flirted with ideas of moving on.

Now, with his mind adrift on a lovely dying afternoon, he was completely caught off guard by the faraway cry of a hand-cranked West Rim siren. He urged Worthless into a cock-eyed gallop along the overgrown Rim Road, his adrenaline up for the first time in months. But the desert was dead as far as his glass could discern. Vane rang the Stage and waited impatiently, watching a number of running bodies in the Streets. After a long minute Mudhead reported, *"Runner."* That was all. Vane focused away from the desert, tweaking his spyglass. Finally he made out a flailing speck on Inner West Slope. He jabbed his walkie-talkie's transmit button.

"Why isn't he using the Ramp?"

"Big hurry. Run straight through Guard."

"I'll be there in two shakes." Vane clung like a woman as Worthless galloped erratically, avoiding Solomon's teeth, and by the time they'd reached the Stage he was a breath away from losing it. Solomon chomped Worthless a good one just as she was kneeling, which put her nauseous rider down hard on his tailbone. Mudhead helped him up and over to his Eyes. They watched the runner staggering between patches of alfalfa and millet, only to be brought down kicking by workers leaping out of the grain. A crowd quickly grew. Vane and Mudhead saw the tacklers rough the man up and interrogate him one after the other. Finally an old man addressed the crowd excitedly. Two Afar thereupon hauled the runner upright. They walked him a ways, but that tackle, after all his exertion, had just been too much. He dropped like a dead man. Immediately he was hoisted by four workers, one on each limb, and trotted toward the Mount. Four others took over after a few minutes of hard pacing by the original quartet, and the pace was redoubled. In this manner the dangling man was passed along between Field Squares, wrestled and mauled up the Steps, and deposited in a pile of arms and legs.

"Bring him in the shade," Vane said, directing with his hands. The panting men heaved the runner under the Big Tarp, where he kicked like a dog having a nightmare. Mudhead nudged him with a foot. The runner jabbered softly and his eyelids fluttered. He tucked his hands between his drawn-up knees. Mudhead tried him in basic Saho, in Amharic and Tigrinya. He was surprised when the man responded to a hailing in Ge'eg.

"Falasha," Mudhead muttered, shaking his head. "Come long way."

Vane drew a Bowlful of water and splashed some on the man's face and hair. At the shock of wetness the runner opened his eyes and sat upright, took a few sips and nodded gratefully. Mudhead crouched to question him. He remained hunched, his hands dangling off his knees, for the longest time.

"Well?" Vane said.

Mudhead didn't move.

"Well?"

"Falashaman," Mudhead said quietly, "run many day. Stop only small sleep." He sighed and shook his head resignedly. "Falashaman famous run long haul." He looked up. "Bossman famous all Ethiopia."

"Tell him I'm flattered. Now let's get him something to eat. He's all skin and bones."

"Come long way," Mudhead repeated. He rose, removed his spectacles and wiped the lenses on his robe. Such a move was offensive even for a reprobate; he was clearly distracted. Mudhead replaced his spectacles and looked thoughtfully at the northwest horizon. He walked over to Top Step, let a foot hover. Casually he began his descent.

"Wait a minute," Vane said. "Where're you going?" Mudhead disappeared in eight-inch sections, one Step at a time. When the top of his cap had vanished Vane walked over and looked down. "Mudhead."

The African either didn't hear him or ignored him completely. Vane pursued him Step for Step, repeatedly calling his name. When Mudhead reached Stage Street he turned like an automaton and paced south.

"Mudhead!" Vane caught up with him and draped an arm over his shoulders. Mudhead went straight down, as if a supporting wire had been cut, landing heavily on his rear. Vane sat opposite. "What's bugging you, man? Why'd you take off like that?" When Mudhead looked up, Vane was surprised to see his friend's eyes glistening. Mudhead's mouth trembled. He pushed himself to his feet and walked back the way he'd come. Vane caught him at Bottom Step and shook him by the shoulders. *"What did he tell you?"*

Mudhead's answering stare was blank. He turned and began climbing the Steps.

"Jesus!" Vane lunged after him. At Top Step he pushed him down and held him down. "Tell me, already! What'd he say?"

"Locust," Mudhead said matter-of-factly. "Plague. Falasha see from Ras Dashen. Plague out of Sudan. Eat everything crazy. Nothing stand, manyman die. Never such swarm."

"Oh...man," Vane said, rolling his head. He nodded and sighed. "I'm just so sorry, Mudhead. Really." He sat hard and squeezed his friend's knee. "You...you had friends in Sudan?"

Mudhead turned to gape at him. "No," he mumbled at last, "no friend."

"Still a shame," Vane said. He gestured broadly, searching for words. "This country's a monster. But I guess people have adapted to it. Over the ages, I mean." He added philosophically, "Where I come from you can die from a bullet and never even know what hit you. Death," he said, spreading his arms, "is death." He shook his head sharply. "Forgive me, Mudhead; I'm rambling." He studied the back of his hands. When no response came he stole a glance.

Mudhead's eyes were burning at the sky. "Death," he echoed, "death."

Vane stood up. The horizon was spotless. He patted Mudhead's shoulder. "Buck up, buddy. I'll get us a weather report."

In twenty minutes he had the score out of Addis Ababa. The swarm, one of the largest ever observed, had crossed the

Red Sea from the Saudi Peninsula in early March, impelled as a natural consequence of the drought's broad cycle, and by now had devastated the east coast of Sudan. Sudanese planes cooperatively provided information to Sudan's southern neighbors, but ceased tracking, as per United Nations directives, at the border. The latest report was a week old. Vane was dryly informed that the swarm's progress would be monitored by an office of the National Game Reserve in Gondar, and that that office would fax relevant data to another in Dese, and so on, until the swarm had made its way into Somalia or Kenya. The culled information would be ordered into a synopsis and correlated with prior swarms.

Plagues of desert locusts, Vane was told, were natural and inevitable. They were cyclical events in Africa and Saudi Arabia, as given and irrepressible as storms. No real preventive measures were taken, no institutions meaningfully devoted to their future eradication. They were the hand of Allah, and were taken in stride.

Vane, getting nervous, had his call transferred to the Game Reserve in Gondar. Gondar reported the swarm's position as presently south of Eritrea's capitol Asmera. It was a tremendously destructive movement, taking out fields, villages, and tribes in sporadic barrages greater than any military drive. Vane learned that this swarm's direction was determined by March wind currents, and could only be altered by meteorological events such as pounding rain and overwhelming crosswinds.

No rain was foreseen any time soon. Winds were steadily moving south.

All things considered, the hand of Allah was heading straight for the Danakil, and would soon be passing directly over Mamuset.

By now Vane's blood pressure was rising. He again rang the capitol and got on to Honey liaison Muhammed Tibor. The cold, thick voice informed him that there was little to be offered in the way of aid or advice. Tibor apologized without a trace of compassion, explaining that the country was at war. Vane would have to use his own measures to evacuate the site. He then offered to connect him directly with Honey over the diplomatic channel.

"Do that," Vane grated. "And while you're at it try hooking me up with somebody who gives a damn."

There was an excruciating hour of dead air. During this period Vane paced with increasing misery while Mudhead flogged him with tales of uncontainable insect frenzy and ravaged populations. His palms grew clammy as Mudhead described the desert locust's uncanny sense of smell, and how frenzy was biochemically produced when food was sensed by any part of a swarm. But formidable as Mudhead made these creatures out to be, Vane wouldn't accept an inevitable apocalypse. A pest was only a pest, he argued, and Mamuset wasn't some lame tribe of superstitious stampeding savages—it was a cooperative, productive entity trained as a fighting machine. Surely brains and teamwork, combined with cash and connections, could kick ass on a bunch of dumb grasshoppers in the twenty-first century.

When the new voice came over the speaker, identifying itself as belonging to one Professor Essahal of Dire Dawa University, Vane sprinted across the Stage and switched from speaker to phone receiver. "Right to the point," he puffed. "Tibor wouldn't have connected us if he didn't think you could help me. You're familiar with these bugs?"

The voice was heavy and pedantic. "*I*," it sniffed, "sir, *am an entomologist specializing in the physiology and migratory patterns of acridids.*" There was an impatient sigh. "*Our campus is indebted to Mr. Tibor. This is why you and I are speaking together now. But I have a full workload, and the hours are short. So...as you say, 'right to the point.' I do not mean to be rude.*"

"That's good of you," Vane said through his teeth. "So how can I stop these insects before they reach my property? What should I do?"

"*Stop them?*"

"Kill them, turn them aside, lure them elsewhere. What do you guys do when you want to stop a swarm?" Vane could have sworn he heard a truncated laugh on the other end. "This isn't funny, professor."

"*Of course it is not. Sir, there is no way to deter a desert locust swarm. You will perhaps appreciate my natural reaction to the naiveté of your question."*

"Fair enough. But the question remains. Rephrase it any way you want. What can I do?" He bit his lip. "Professor As-sahol, I'd like you to understand that I'm so wealthy it's beyond scary. With a single transmission over this radio I can draw on Banke Internationale whatever sum is necessary to meet my purposes. You can't tell me that in these modern times the technology to break this crisis is unavailable at any cost. I'm dead-serious."

The response was cool. *"I am certain you are, sir. And I am not laughing."* There was a pause. *"What did you have in mind?"*

Vane matched the pause, then said evenly, "Sir, you're the expert. I'm just the money man." He waved a hand irritably. "The obvious thing is an aerial drop. Crop-dusters. I have an ETA on the swarm of thirty-six hours, so there's still time to catch it in flight with some kind of pesticide. You're the one who would know the right stuff to drop."

The response was so emotionless it struck Vane as supremely bored. *"Sir, you know not whereof you speak. Aerial application of pesticides is a tedious process, commenced only after extensive surveys and botanical assessments. It consists essentially of dusting* plants *in a large, commercially viable crop area, for the sake of minimizing damage to neighboring quadrants. Malathion and carbaryl are commonly used. The ac-ridids ingest the poison during crop consumption, and in most cases achieve demise before they can produce greater damage. The poison is, in any case, fatal to the crops, and is never one hundred percent effective on the insects."*

"Okay, professor," Vane said slowly. "Call me stupid, but why can't the Malathion and other stuff be dropped directly on the swarm? Why can't these bugs be killed in flight?"

There was a long, hollow break, occupied only by a pinging echo. Finally Essahal said, as though with an effort, *"Mr. Vane, judging by our knowledge of the extent of this swarm, it would be physically impossible to address it fully with the entirety of the Park and Wildlife's air services, were there even a poison developed for such an application. Additionally, you would encounter problems in simple physics. These pesticides used on acridids come in both powdered and highly granulated forms. Their manufacture takes into account that this fine, dry product will be carried over wide areas and adhere to the relatively moist surfaces of leaves and stalks. The product currently available is almost as fine as talcum powder."*

"O-o-o...*kay*," Vane said with great control. "So why won't it stick to the relatively moist bodies of grasshoppers?" He clenched his free hand repeatedly while listening to the professor suck air. It had seemed an obvious question, so he'd had to ask.

"Sir," Essahal said gently, as to a child, *"plants are* stable. *They do not jump, they do not fly, they do not migrate. The turbulence created by millions, perhaps tens of millions, of frenzied acridids would serve only to dispel airborne dust. The beating of their wings would have the effect of a hurricane on a field of dandelions."*

"A liquid, then," Vane groped. "Gasoline maybe?"

"No such application exists." The professor was thoughtful. *"The physical reaction would of course be different. Distillates of petroleum, heavier than air, would at first be dispersed. The cloud would be swept upward only to fall again, be thrust forward and back...a mist would develop, finely coating the acridids. The vapors would certainly affect their respiratory systems adversely, but to what extent I cannot say."* There came a sound Vane recognized as a pencil tapping on a desk. *"An interesting proposition for a lunchtime discussion, but now is not the time. Such an application does not exist."* Another pause.

"Professor," Vane said very directly. "You've explained what won't work. Tell me what will...please."

The tapping was resumed, then the slow careful voice. *"No such application exists."* A tremendous sigh. *"Mr. Vane, I sincerely regret the failure of your experiment. I wish you the best of luck in your future endeavors. However, the time is really pressing and I have much work of my own. Good day, sir."* The line went dead.

"Good day?" Vane whispered. He replaced the receiver and turned away.

"Egghead always busy," Mudhead remarked.

"Get Tibor back!" Vane walked over to Top Step and

studied the northwest sky, hands clasped behind his back. He raised himself with his toes, relaxed. It was a typically clear, searing afternoon. Fragments of the just-concluded conversation nagged him while he tried to visualize a zillion ravenous locusts. In an instant his mind was made up.

"Tibor back."

Vane forced a few deep breaths, strode under the Big Tarp and switched to Speaker. "Tibor, pay close attention here! Drop everything and listen like your life depended on it. If you do me right, I'll make it possible for you to retire before the weekend. I want you to ring up every business that can perform aerial drops: crop-dusters, firefighters, Park and Wildlife. Whatever. While you're dialing, hook up with Denise Waters, the bank, and the Depot. Tell Denise I want complete and instant access to the bank's deposits. When you get hold of these plane owners, don't haggle with them. Just meet their demands. Buy whatever they've got. They won't rent them out when they learn what I have in mind; the hoppers and holds could be damaged. Okay? Top dollar to all owners and pilots. Then get hold of the military and see if they'll give us a hand. After that, ring up every gas station and every refinery and work some magic. I want all the gasoline you can get your hands on, *pronto*. And anything stronger you can find that'll mix with it. Talk to the chemical men, call the factories. Time is everything. The money *is not* an object. Did you catch that? Write it down, Tibor. Underline it, put it in all caps, and relate it that way to Honey. Then secure some hazmat trucks and arrange an airstrip loading zone. Get everybody on their horses! Once you've got the timetable—"

"*Stop!*"

The word came like a pistol shot. "*I have been handling your affairs,*" Tibor snarled, "*for going on two years, and I have yet to raise an objection. It has been my policy to keep my thoughts and feelings to myself, but I am telling you right now, Mr. Ever-loving Vane, that you are the absolute* limit. *The living end!*"

Dead air.

Vane purpled. "Abandoned!" he howled. "Deserted!" He kicked over a table and three chairs, ripped the Big Clock off the Wall. "Betrayed!"

It seemed another entire hour elapsed before that familiar peal sang on the radio. Vane hurried over. "Go."

"Cris?"

"Miss Waters! What did Tibor tell you?"

"Enough. You've got some kind of emergency, and you're after gas and planes. What's the story?"

"Okay, listen very closely and try not to interrupt. Time's the big factor here. Time and you." He explained the situation calmly and intelligently, laying out his plan with confidence and careful attention to detail. There was the longest pause. Vane banged on the receiver, suspecting a bad wire.

Suddenly Waters screamed, *"Get out of there, Cris!"* There was a sound of random manic activity. *"You're* not *thinking* clearly, *baby!* Let *your project* go. *You can start it up again next year, somewhere else,* anywhere else! *Everybody knows you did your best."*

Vane ground his teeth, realizing he was dangerously close to losing his final bid. "I...I guess you just wouldn't understand, Denise."

"Then explain it to me! *Tell me why one of the richest, luckiest, most eligible men in the world would commit suicide in an African desert, half a world away from the ones who love him."* She was hyperventilating.

"Take a deep breath."

"Why do you think I've clung to this job for so long, Cris? Why do you think I've perched here in this gilded cage, monitoring your progress, handling your affairs, guarding you against enemies you're not even aware of?"

Vane blinked, sincerely confused. "Perhaps," he said quietly, "you could fill me in."

"Not to watch you die in the middle of nowhere, darling. I'm not going to let that happen. I don't care how pigheaded you are."

"Miss Waters," he said levelly, "I'd like you to conference me with Saul Littleroth. Can you do that right away, please?"

"Not until I've had a chance to prep him."

"Miss Waters—"

"Now you *take a deep breath, Cristian Vane! You'll wait your turn."* There was a whispered curse. Half a minute later the voice said professionally, *"One moment, sir."* The ether flickered with echoes and pings. A distant droning phased in and out while Vane seethed.

"Cristian?"

"It's me, Saul. I don't know what's gotten into—"

"Now you shut your mouth and listen, boy! *I should have whipped the pants off you when I had the chance. You are without a doubt the most irresponsible, fatheaded person I have ever known."*

Vane drew back from the radio. "Is everybody but me having a nervous breakdown?"

"I'll break you down," Littleroth swore. *"Just as soon as I get my hands on you. I've been patient all this time, and I've protected your interests at home, because it's my job. But this is the end of the dance. You're simply too immature to be let loose on the world. Denise is contacting your mail plane now. Hop aboard and get out of there while you still can."*

"There are over five thousand people here with me, Saul. It's a small plane."

"They'll deal with it the way they always have. They've lived for ages in that damned desert. They'll get along just fine once your little garden's gone."

"Are you finished?"

"I'm just getting started."

"Good. Saul, I want every detail of this conversation recorded."

"Done. That was my first move."

"Denise, I want this call recorded on your end, too. Both records are to be time-stamped, copied onto floppies and hard disk. Transcribed, signed, notarized, sealed. Copies are to be held independently by both parties on this line. Should any of these conditions not be met, this order is to be considered legally null and void."

Denise sighed. *"Alright, Cris. We're on."*

"Go ahead," Littleroth said, speaking very clearly, very carefully. His voice came across like a sound-check.

"By this transmission I, Cristian Honey Vane, officially

relinquish my position as chief executive officer of the Honey Foundation in all its offices domestic and foreign. That position is hereby awarded to the Foundation's very able presiding officer, Denise Waters. I declare myself sound of mind and body, and not under coercion.

"Denise, you are now in full command of Honey's assets; lock, stock, and barrel. I admit it, you guys; I admit it, I admit it. I'm not cut out for responsibility. Saul's right, and you're right. I'm a walking disaster. For Christ's sake, Saul, is any of this legal?"

Littleroth grunted. *"Nothing's finalized, Cristian. What this record demonstrates is that you are unfit to manage Honey by proxy."* He hesitated. *"We won't pretend any longer that your position is anything other than symbolic, if that's your wish."* Littleroth sighed hugely. *"Why was everybody expecting this call? And why do you always have to be so abrupt?"*

"Is this cool, or isn't it?"

"You have the legal right to release any or all of your interests to anyone you choose."

"Well, I've made my choice! And now maybe you two can start pulling Honey out of the red."

"Why not discuss some options first?"

"You'd have to be here to understand," Vane said.

There was an undertone of excitement, of envy, in Littleroth's response. *"You're* really *facing a plague of grasshoppers?"*

Vane drew his jile and turned it flashing in the sun. "Desert locusts." He attempted to throw back his robes, but found he was standing on a hem. Vane knelt and very carefully rubbed out the smudge.

"What's it like?"

"The feeling?" He stood erect, puffed his cheeks and blew out the breath. "It's immense! Insane! Fantastic! Unreal!"

"Listen to him!" Denise said.

"Cris," Littleroth said quickly, *"get out of there. Now! I watched you grow up, boy. I was one of the guys who made sure nobody took advantage of you. And I saw a young man with tremendous potential, not a loser gobbled up by grasshoppers in the armpit of the world. Now listen to me, son. Get yourself a*

sleeping bag and a good bicycle. Wheel around the world and see and feel all the wonderful, all the real things Denise and I will never see and feel. Fall in love, fall out of love. Win and lose and start all over. You've got the stuff to make a real go of it, boy. Don't let your heart mess up your head. Wire me, or wire Denise, whenever you need cash, and we'll be right on it. Live, Cristian! Don't be a sentimental ass."

Vane jumped right back at him. "It's not sentimentality, Saul! I'm being practical. I've done a lot of growing up since I've been here. I've built something, I've made it work, and *I'm not giving up on it!* I...I talked to a scientist about this, Saul, an entomologist at Gabadube University, and he said I was practically a genius. My idea is not only right-on, it's groundbreaking. We went over and over this for hours, you guys, and he *guaranteed* me it'll work. The desert locust can't breathe in a gas-air medium. I mean, think about it. Could you?" He had a sudden brainstorm. "What's the name of that stuff you spray into carburetors to make engines start quick? Paris used to use it when the Lincoln was cold. Ethel Somebody..."

"Ethyl ether?" Littleroth wondered.

"Yeah! That's what that bug scientist called it. He said my idea would work a thousand times better if it was mixed in with regular gasoline. Completely cuts off the insects' oxygen supply."

"Cris," Denise said quietly. *"Do you know how strong that stuff is? It's liquid dynamite."*

"What of it? Noboy'll be hanging around smoking, if that's what you're worried about. I'm not crazy, Miss Waters. We're as good as out of here. But I'm not just passively surrendering everything I've worked for to a bunch of goddamned grasshoppers! If this stuff'll kill 'em before they get to my place then it's worth any expense to me. I can always come back later, clean it all up and start over. But I want something to come back to! Don't doubt me on this, Denise. I *will* start all over; I'll start from scratch if I have to. But why *should* I? And why *shouldn't* we make these drops to save the trees and gardens? Do you want to go through all that again? The purchases, the shipments?"

Littleroth cleared his throat.

Denise shot, *"Don't help me, Saul! I can see whose side you're on. And don't waste any more breath trying to reason with him. He's not listening. He's got a martyr complex. It's not his fault, and he's not even aware of it.* Shut up, Cris!"

"I didn't say anything."

"You were going to. You were all set to make a lovely politically-correct speech about doing the right thing in a wrong world. You were just about to try to make us all feel not only guilty, but downright evil because of your project's demise." She was stuttering.

"Oh, come on—"

"Shut up! Shut up and listen." Waters took a deep breath. *"Before I'll agree to anything, I want to know you're out of there."*

"You've got it. But, Miss Waters, the clock."

"The clock is stopped. I want your word."

"Can you pull it off?"

"Mr. Tibor said the contacts are open for petroleum and equipment, as well as for a variety of volatile chemicals. The man was quite busy while we were waiting to be put through. You're lucky to have such an efficient person on your side."

"Don't I know it!" Vane gushed. "Me and good old Tibor are just about as tight as tight can be. God bless him, and God bless you too, Miss Waters."

"Cristian?"

"We're evacuating everybody right now, using pickup trucks. I'll call you the moment I reach the Depot."

"Cristian..."

"I give you my *word*, Miss Waters; my solemn, inviolable word. I swear on my life. I swear on my mother...*besides*, it's *my* money, and *I* can use it any way *I* feel. That has nothing to do with Honey, right, Saul? Isn't it mine?"

"Shut up! I'm the boss now, Cristian."

"Denise," Littleroth tried.

"You shut up too, Saul!"

"You may be the boss, Miss Waters, but you're not *my* boss. Like I said, I quit."

"Isn't this just childish," Littleroth said.

"Yes, it's childish. It's childish because I'm dealing with

children. Believe it or not, Cristian, there are people who love you, people who would be horribly affected it anything bad were to happen to you."

"Name two."

"Childish," Littleroth muttered.

"Grow up! Stop being so selfish all the time."

"Yes," Vane said sarcastically, *"mom."*

For a long cold moment the line was dead. "Denise!" Vane called into his mouthpiece. "Miss Waters!"

"Please don't do anything foolish," the voice said quietly. *"Think of the people who worry about you."*

"Name one."

"Cristian!"

Littleroth challenged them both. *"Why do I feel like an eavesdropper?"*

"Because you're as immature as this idiot. All you little boys with your little fantasies. Go on, Saul. Gallop off with him. Simply throw off your responsibilities and join Huck wherever he roves. Run barefoot, run naked, run innocent and free. Steal apples instead of serving clients. God knows I'd love to go with you. But some of us grow up, boys."

"I knew it, Saul! I *knew* it, man! I knew that I, immature little polliwog that I am, could make at least one adult decision in my life. And I picked the best person on the planet to take o-ver Honey."

"You did, boy," Littleroth admitted. *"My instincts were right about you."*

"Good luck, Saul."

"Good luck, son."

"Shut up, both of you!"

"You're breaking up, Miss Waters," Vane said, gradually moving his head back from the transmitter. "You're...going, girl."

"Cristian!"

"Believe in me, Deni...show me...care." He switched off the set and popped out the power cord. "Mudahid Asafu-Adjaye, I think it's about time you made one of those great speeches of yours I'm so famous for."

Mudhead bowed almost to the Mat. Vane returned the

bow and threw the lever activating Utility Square alarms. After the short triple beeps had died away he enabled all Quad Speakers. To the Afar gathering around the Mount he bowed deepest of all, then looped an arm over his friend's shoulders, flipped a switch on the motherboard, and steered Mudhead to the microphone. There was a short squeal of feedback. "Go a-head," he said. "Do me proud."

Vane sat on a three-legged stool with his hands pressed between his knees and began to speak. "After all we've been through together, it looks like we're all gonna have to shut down together. In a way we got lucky: we've got advance no-tice of a humongous swarm of locusts coming our way. We can't see the swarm from here, but airplanes like the one that comes every week have seen it from high in the sky, and know its course and speed. The men who talk to the airplanes have told me the swarm will be here some time tomorrow night. It will spare nothing, but, before we all 'achieve demise,' I don't see any reason we can't evacuate this place, working through tonight and tomorrow, using the pickup trucks. We've done so many drills it shouldn't be a problem."

Mudhead's translation into Saho tapered off. Other than the small noises of animals and children there was dead silence. With his hands clasped behind his back, Mudhead slowly turned around, his expression bored. "Mamusetman already know plague. Runner tell Fieldman. Fieldman tell boy. Boy tell every-man." A certain smugness lit his face. "Radio small deal."

"This isn't about your stupid pride, Africaman. It's about survival. I just spent all day arguing with everybody and his mother, trying to make this happen so nobody gets hurt. We're evacuating! ¿Comprende?" He glared at his motionless audience. "Excuse me. Am I stuttering? Why are all you bozos just standing there?" He rose dramatically, thrusting out his robes like great black wings. "Everybody pack up! You heard the man. Shoo! This fiasco's history." His only answer was a field of grins. After a minute he said out of the side of his mouth, "They're not going anywhere, are they?"

Mudhead shook his head. "Mamusetman."

Vane threw up his arms. "Idiots!" he cried. "I'm sur-rounded by idiots."

Mudhead nodded ironically. "Pretty amazing idiot."

The rest of the day was devoted to hammering out a strategy. Zero-hour drills grew increasingly tight and smooth, due both to the Afar's conditioning and to their almost blind obedience to the harsh translated commands of Mudhead. There was absolutely no indication of a threat on the horizon, but that night dogs were howling like banshees, the bird population was all in a flap, and bawling cats were taking to the rooftops and Fields. Goats bleated, camels roared, children screamed at the constantly rattling hatches and coops. Fathers sent boys and girls shinnying up trees to hand down nestlings, and before dawn the last birds took off, ditching paradise for Hell. Within the hour they were all back, lighting in the canopies and rebounding. It was a big desert out there.

When Vane opened the new morning with Strauss, he was surprised and elated to be standing before a perfectly clear sky. He spent half the day up on North Rim, pinching himself with one hand and gripping his walkie-talkie with the other, giving useless reports to Mudhead while wrestling with the idea of telling Tibor to call it off. Vane searched the horizon until his eyes were burning. A little after noon he noticed a wavy haze that gradually condensed into a thin dark line. The line wobbled at its flanks, appearing to thicken even as he stared.

That was enough. He immediately rang up all Posts. At the sirens' wail the Afar broke into a manic supermarket sweep, hurling everything salvageable into wheelbarrows and truck beds. Immature fruit was ripped from trees, leaves of root vegetables were hacked off for fodder, livestock and pets were rounded up and tethered indoors. Pickups were moved from U-tility Squares to Guard Posts, that Guards might have last-minute transportation to the safety of Basement and Cellar. The Posts wouldn't last five minutes in the coming storm. Upon completion, the Afar responded to a prolonged series of triple beeps by calmly filing into their Domos and firmly closing their walls and doors. Everything went without a hitch.

With little else to do but be out and visible, Vane devoted himself to Bulwark stops, unable to keep his eyes off the horizon. By three o'clock the dark line was a flat black flow. Occasionally grayish towers would rise a thousand feet and more, collapsing even as others rose. In this way the swarm came on; an unreal, deepening entity lunging in slow motion.

Four hours later the skyline was a heaving black shelf under the natural deep blue of twilight. Through his glass Vane could see dozens of swarm appendages appearing as independently flaring plumes; visible one moment, replaced by flanking plumes the next. The Afar remained locked inside their Domos, gills drawn. Only Vane, Mudhead, Kid, and the Guards were up on the Rim, watching the black cloud appear to compress itself as it approached. Soon it was so dense it completely obscured the world behind it.

While they waited they grew aware of the swarm faintly pattering, its numberless wings beating like a distant downfall. Vane, twirling his forearms, signaled a Guard to trigger the chain of sirens. He was just turning over his pickup when a black hand found his shoulder. Though Mudhead brought his face up close, he couldn't be heard under the sirens. At last he pointed upward. Vane leaned out. At around four thousand feet the fading sunlight was being reflected by a slow-ly banking particle.

In Mudhead's binoculars the object became a helicopter flying well above and ahead of the swarm. As Vane gazed, a pair of enormous pontoons dropped from its undercarriage and erupted like pods. Two waves of a pink-green liquid broke up in the air. Behind and above the copter came an old Air Tractor, and behind and above it another little plane, and another. Vane squeezed the binoculars until his knuckles were white. "Tibor!" he cried, watching the twin puffs merge into a single slowly expanding cloud. The closing Air Tractor cut its engines. A few seconds later a smaller, similarly-colored cloud plunged and e-vened out. Once clear, the little plane's engines were re-fired and the red gleam rose, banked, and receded.

Vane swung back to the initial drop, glistening in the setting sun, and saw that the blood-olive droplets were slowly spreading. He lowered his gaze. Through the binoculars, individual insects could now be made out in the swarm, popping a-bout in plumes that distended like flowing smoke and ash. High above and descending from the northwest, the long line of tiny aircraft blinked in the sun, veered deeply north, then swung ahead of the locusts to make their drops. So high were the planes that their loads, five hundred gallons and more, approached the earth only very gradually, buffeted by lofty winds and suspended by rising desert heat. The men on the Rim watched fascinated as each dully gleaming drop expanded to join a massive drifting island of dark greenish-violet mist. As further loads were absorbed, the mass gradually developed tapering limbs, and these fuzzy limbs, blood-and-bile against the glinting black swarm, descended as blown and battered shadow tentacles. The body of locusts couldn't have been more than a few miles away. The swarm's head was already being misted.

Vane pounded Mudhead on the shoulder. "This is where they get it!" he exulted. "The end of the ride!" For the benefit of the Guard at his elbow he shouted, "They won't be able to breathe! That godawful cloud is a mix of straight gas and Ethel Merman. When it gets in their little lungs they'll suffocate, they'll drown." He nodded excitedly. "They'll be dropping like flies any second now!" The Guard grinned and copied the nod, but as soon as Vane turned away he looked over at Mudhead with a completely perplexed expression. Vane strained against the binoculars until he thought his head would split. "They're really taking a soaking, you guys! They look like little rubies with that ruddy sun on 'em. Jesus, there must be a billion, ten billion of them." He sucked a deep breath between his teeth. Then for the longest time there was nothing to be heard but that otherworldly pattering of numberless wings. Finally Vane lowered the binoculars and squinted thoughtfully. "They don't die all that easy, do they?"

Mudhead grabbed his arm and shook it hard. "No more scienceman!" he said with uncharacteristic fervor. Vane didn't like the look on his friend's face at all. His eyes slid away guiltily. "Into house!" Mudhead snapped. "*Now!* Everyman! *Go now!*"

Vane angrily yanked his arm free and stared up through the binoculars, desperately searching for anything unusual—a break in the pattern, a show of sluggishness...*anything*. What he saw was tens of thousands of frenzied locusts smashing into one another, zipping in and out of view, so close they seemed almost in his face. Behind the frontrunners, countless vaulting insects flashed like sparks before the setting sun.

Like sparks…inspiration rocked Vane, ignited his brain, shook him like a wet dog. He dropped the binoculars and shoved Mudhead passionately. "Get in, man; get in-in-in-in *in!*" Mudhead backed away, regarding him strangely. After a sufficient pause he primly adjusted his white robes, walked with dignity around the front of the truck, and climbed in decorously. Before the door was halfway closed Vane had thrown the truck into first and taken off in a storm of dust and pebbles. "Tell the Guards," he hollered, "to ditch their Posts. Order them to man the Bulwarks instead. I want holes cut in the tops." Mudhead's mouth worked soundlessly. Before he could frame a sentence Vane had pushed the truck to the nearest Post and yelled, *"East!"* Mudhead leaned out barking instructions, hanging on with his left arm and pointing with his right. The Guard immediately sprinted for the neighboring Bulwark. Vane sped along to the next Post and screamed, *"West!"* Mudhead shouted the message while making chopping motions with his left arm. The Guard ran off.

Vane tore down a Ramp honking the horn like a lunatic. The Afar popped out of Domos and came running behind, leaping into the truck's bed recklessly. Vane fishtailed into a Utility Square and continued to hammer the horn while shouting himself hoarse. Mudhead, confused and unnerved, could only cling to the door and translate urgently. A dozen men and boys obediently grabbed pails and hopped aboard. Vane threw her into gear and made straight for the Mount. The nearest trucks, filling quickly with bucket-wielding bodies, fired up and raced right along behind him.

The Afar, leaping out before their trucks had slowed, hit the ground running and made for the tarp-covered gasoline tanker. Nobody pushed, nobody fought or fell; each man balanced his pail as it was filled and jogged back to a waiting truck without spilling a drop.

Once the bed of Vane's pickup was full he stalled in reverse, lurched in first, nearly stalled again. The men and boys in back balanced their pails frantically, using their cupped hands to scrape spilled gas off the bed even as their driver careened across Ridge Bridge with the other trucks close on his tail.

When Vane hit Rim Road he was so blown away he almost stalled the truck again. He drove weaving like a drunk to the bleak oblong silhouette of Bulwark NW14, the roiling, glistening spectacle filling his vision. A Guard stood on top waving his machete, looking like an animated scarecrow before a sky that was all locusts. Men leaped out of the truck and immediately formed a brigade up a ladder leaning against the Bulwark's flank. While boys doused the Bulwark's taut walls, the Guard ran back and forth along the top, pouring gasoline through holes he'd chopped in the canvas.

Vane watched the trucks pulling up down the line, saw the spiders scurrying up the tall ladders. He ran to a Post where he could observe from between Bulwarks, and found himself confronting a solid wall of insects, completely saturated and coming on strong. He scanned high with Mudhead's binoculars. The last plane was receding to the west, the final light in a string of miniscule jewels.

He dashed back to his truck, hauled up Mudhead and yelled instructions in his face while leaning on the horn. In thirty seconds the bed was full of black clinging bodies. Pickups along the Rim honked in acknowledgement and raced to follow the leader. Mudhead leaned out the passenger's window and coughed out directions in Saho as Vane sped along East Rim. The smell of gasoline was everywhere. They took a Ramp on two wheels, came down hard on Bisecting Way, and made straight for Stage Street. Other trucks, responding to the waved signals of Vane's bailing riders, shot into the community, the men and boys spilling out and sprinting for their Domos.

Vane hurtled round the Mount and straight into gutted Warehouse, taking out a stack of pallets and almost turning the truck on her side before stalling in a cloud of flour. The men staggered out coughing; Mudhead to a broad wood centerpost, Vane to a lethal pile in the corner. Vane commenced scattering boxes of explosives, miscellaneous chemical stores, and bits of broken machinery every which way, at last letting go with a whoop of triumph. That sound verified Mudhead's worst fear, and when he saw Vane hauling out the sealed crate of flares he dropped to his knees in horror. "No, Bossman!" he gasped "Not fire…" The apocalyptic vision was too much for him. Mudhead collapsed on a pile of damaged gills, hands clutching his chest. Vane backpedaled dragging the crate, and as he crouched over Mudhead the gangly figure of Kid appeared outside, creeping up between the truck's tracks. His black flashing eyes ran over the pickup, the men, the crate of flares between them. Putting two and two together, Kid ran inside, grabbed the dead end of the crate and helped Vane heave it onto the bed just behind the cab. He watched intently as Vane stumbled back to help his number two.

Vane had Mudhead halfway to his feet when he was arrested by the sound of shattering glass. Both men turned to see Kid spinning a pickax above his head and grinning wildly. The youngster cleared the remaining glass from the truck's rear window by swiping the tool side to side, jumped behind the wheel and started the engine, revved it dramatically.

"Not yet!" Vane hacked. "Guards first. *Stop!*" He sagged in the weight of Mudhead's embrace. *"God damn it, Kid, that's an order!"* Kid saluted smartly and threw the truck in reverse. He slammed it into a mound of loose fertilizer, jammed it in first and tore outside, barely keeping the truck under control. Still clinging, Vane and Mudhead ran wheezing up the Mount's west slope just as the pickup swerved out of view. They froze in each other's arms on the Stage, overwhelmed by the strangeness of the view. The entire northern sky was heaving with insects.

Something wet slapped Vane's face. He put a hand to his cheek and brought back a struggling locust, threw it down in disgust, stamped on it twice. The next thing he knew they were plummeting all around; bouncing off the Big Tarp, slamming into the Stage, instantly rebounding in the direction of anything growing. Vane bent to his Eyes in a dark driving rain. North and West Rims looked like fog banks dissolving in a blizzard. Behind this blizzard a black wave was crashing in slow motion. He scanned Rim Road rapidly, west to east, until he caught the little white truck reeling through the blur. A tiny red light appeared above the cab. A second later it was arcing toward a Bulwark's wall.

"Go!" Vane shouted. He shoved Mudhead hard. "Run like hell."

Mudhead fluttered down the Steps toward his Domo, slipping on flopping insects, while Vane watched Kid tossing flares as fast as he could reach back and grab them. Gas-soaked canvas caught immediately. Flames raced up the sides, danced along the tops, and then a strange, jerky strand of fire was leaping Bulwark to Bulwark. Landing locusts combusted and shot off like sparks in a foundry, blew away as fiery puffs, ignited pyrotechnically in random clumps and streaks. Silhouetted against leaping spires, the wriggly sticks of burning Guards ran staggering down the Inner Slopes.

Kid's weaving pickup slammed into a Bulwark and bounced away, red tendrils clinging to its side. An instant later the little truck was a fireball spinning down East Inner Slope. Right before Vane's eyes, the entire Rim blew into a swirling ring of fire. He pried himself from his Eyes and tumbled down the Steps to Stage Street, his body casting erratic shadows in all directions. He paused in the middle of the Street, unable to resist a last look. The Bulwarks were now a string of exploding firecrackers, hurling lightning-like prominences in all directions. Behind this intense display, the great wave of locusts was just breaking on the bright hoop of leaping flames.

Vane put down his head and ran, kicked open his gate and staggered through his front Yard in a vile downpour. And then all hell broke loose: locusts, exploding in pockets, shot into the crater as flaring pinwheels, radiated shrapnel-wise, flashed and passed. Those insects separated by a yard or more caught fire individually, while those coming down in tight groups went right back up like sparklers. Locusts in actual physical contact created zigzagging streamers and wobbly arms.

A tower of flame rose out of West Rim. Another appeared to the north. Vivid red veils swayed back and forth, momentarily spiking at points of particular intensity. Then, in one great spewing ejaculation, the entire Rim became a broad envelope of flame. Overhead, a cloud of tiny meteors shot past in a dazzling rush, their moist smoke tails dropping to drag through the trees as long wavy ghosts. Suffocating in a hot noxious fog, Vane shielded his face, was knocked on his side, groped to his feet and was knocked right back down. He scrambled to his knees and pitched headfirst through his front door, pulling a cloak of smoke in behind him. He slammed the door, his eyes and lungs on fire. The door flew back open. A heartbeat later a hundred lunatics were hammering on his roof.

Worthless and Solomon lay huddled in a far corner, trying to escape the inrushing smoke. Vane was overcome by coughing. On his knees, he swam blindly through the acrid fumes and lunged into the huddle.

Jus outside. a torrent of flaming locusts spattered and skidded on the walk. The last thing Vane remembered was choking on a mouthful of fur in a jackhammer hail. He and his beasts, competing for air, went spinning into abyss.

Chapter Eighteen

Worthless

To the Afar, Daybreak had become a near-religious e-vent; they saw sunrise without Strauss as Mamuset's death knell. Still they'd shown as a unit, their faces and bodies smudged, their eyes roughened by want of sleep. But there was no functioning equipment left to meet the dawn; everything was fried and mangled under stinking drifts of slag. The crater's floor was a deep dish of ash and carbonized locust carcasses, peppered with chunks of charred wood and blackened foliage. A burnt stench clung to everything. So much smoke remained in the air that the pocked hulls of Domos stood indistinctly amid the scarred trunks of birches and elms. It was thick enough to make dawn a miserable twilight. *Still*, the Afar had shown, and, when that first feeble ray cut to the Stage, they watched dumb-founded, standing elbow-to-elbow as their logy leader threw back his head and spread his singed robes wide. "*I,* " he cried to no one in particular, "am a freaking genius!"

Throughout the morning, Afar men ran their wheel-barrows up and down the Streets, halting to accept shoveled piles of locusts and running on. Stationed teenagers did the sho-veling. Women raked the bodies into piles. Tots with wet rags tied below their eyes used sticks to knock carcasses from the remains of trellises and shrubs. The men would hurry their full wheelbarrows back to Utility Squares, where drivers shoveled pound after pound of roasted vermin into truck beds. The dead locusts were then dispersed around the Rim and raked down Outer Slopes into a narrow encircling ditch. For miles beyond this ditch, the desert was carpeted with burned insects and crawling with scavengers.

The noxious shroud rose as the day heated up. Noses and mouths were covered less frequently, animals got underfoot with new vigor. After a good soaking, boys and girls climbed into trees. Once secured, they were handed up long poles. Hun-dreds of thousands of dead locusts were beaten from the leaves.

Vane's sense of triumph over nature was short-lived—his victory-ride around the Rim turned his stomach. Everything that could be burned had been burned. Thatch roofs were now peaked piles of ash, Shade Halls fire-eaten rags. Warehouse was a collapsed, reeking mess of dark hanging threads. Black rivu-lets, produced by the constant hosing down of charred material, were everywhere. Overall it was a gray and dismal world, but here and there flashes of color showed in devastated gardens.

What depressed Vane most was his Rim view of the yellow, sickly-looking treetops. It was difficult to objectively assess damage to the great saving Canopy, central as it was to the wonderful home he'd built. Even as he was staring, a couple of long poles pierced the ruined crown of a nearby higan cherry. The poles banged about crazily, accompanied by squeals of de-light. Fried grasshoppers rained all around. And then Worthless, hypnotized by her own plodding rhythm, was almost clipped by a sooty truck tearing along Rim Road, its bed full of grinning teenagers wielding shovels and rakes. It struck Vane then: the place would heal! Mamuset's only real casualties had been Kid and the Post Guards. The Afar were strong, experienced, and eager to rebuild. And even now, outside his command, that eagerness was running through the Streets, up the Ramps and over the Rims. Children, their little black heads bobbing and racing in the Fields, were scooping locusts into sandbags with competitive zeal. Oxen were dragging lakes and ponds. Burned patches of grass were being uprooted, tainted soil replaced with fresh. All at once Vane hated his memoirs. He'd been behaving like a retiree. He poked Worthless into a half-assed trot, his mind shifting gears.

First off, he'd have to prepare for another swarm. They'd been lucky; now it was time to be smart. He'd been a self-absorbed, arrogant peacock. But how to have known? Guns and grasshoppers...Vane thereupon determined to be equally tutor and student, to ready Mamuset for anything. It was time to get dirty. It would be old days again.

The ditch accepted its last locust and was covered over. Trees were pruned by adventurous teenagers, leaf by leaf, until the Canopy achieved its former luster. New thatch was laid on roofs, new equipment purchased for the Stage. The Afar patched and puttered, as focused as ever, determined to build a community more exotic and splendid than before. The weeks passed. Fields were revitalized, gardens restored with daily imports from the Honey Oases. But the new Warehouse, Big Tarp, and Shade Halls had to be erected out of salvaged patches, for, in the process of ordering fresh canvas through Army Surplus in Addis Ababa, Vane learned that supplies were being sewn up by the government. A very real war was taking place outside his little fantasy world.

Vane's failure to take his surroundings seriously perfectly illuminated his irresponsible nature. Anywhere you put him, he'd be out of sync with reality. Practically on the borderline of warring nations, and he'd been too busy studying insects and weather patterns to heed the approaching front—though he was warned almost daily by his capitol connections. Then one day, while ringing Tibor to be put through to Honey, he was shocked to learn he was on his own. A bomb-laden locomotive had taken out a terminal in Addis Ababa, expanding Tibor's State Department duties considerably. Now non-critical use of airwaves was flat-out denied; only a bona fide emergency would get Vane's voice across the Atlantic.

As time passed, it grew harder and harder to squeeze a-nything out of the capitol. Worse, the Vane Depot was being shut down due to a dynamiting of the tracks on the Ethiopian side of Djibouti's border. Goods ordinarily transported from Port Djibouti to Addis Ababa via rail were being trucked over-land by a complicated system of roads and passes. Aksum and Mekele, small but commercially important centers northwest of Danakil, had fallen to Eritrea without protest. According to Ti-bor, the Depression was all but surrounded.

Vane's final conversation with Honey's liaison came on the eve of the project's penultimate threat, but it had nothing to do with broadcasts and borders. It was all about drugs and sav-ages. Tibor told Vane that communication outside Ethiopia was no longer possible. He warned the American to pack up and seek refuge in the Republic of Djibouti, coolly explaining that Ethiopia was way too busy to support Mamuset once it came under attack. And he stressed the inevitability of that attack.

Fighting to the north and south was described as far more intense than Vane's peripatetic sources would have him believe. But what really got his attention was Tibor's descrip-tion of the Eritrean vanguard. The man drew a nasty verbal picture of a particularly bloody brand of guerrilla warfare, prac-ticed by rogue Somali and Kenyan mercenaries who attack without warning, and with a frenzied behavior reminiscent of the Berserkers during their European assaults. These mercen-aries are a loose company without discipline, and although they are provided the uniform of Eritrea's elite Port Guard, they swear allegiance to nothing higher than an ancient form of Kenyan demonism. Their only weapon is the machete.

They come at night, soundlessly and without preamble, assaulting their victims regardless of age or gender, spontane-ously and collectively morphing into adrenaline-blinded der-vishes of whirling steel. By way of response, their deeply super-stitious victims become frozen slabs of mute terror. This react-ion, according to Tibor, only further excites the assailants, who will not be freed of their murderous mania until felled by ex-haustion. Even then they will continue to hack and dismember the dead, howling all the while. These savages, Tibor explained, are fueled in their attacks by megadose injections of heroin and amphetamine, distributed through Port Massawa. It is these drugs, taken singularly in encampments and in combination just before an actual assault, that are responsible for initiating and maintaining their demonic religion's ages-old practice of seek-and-mutilate.

The addiction is sponsored by the Eritrean Army, which organization also provides this bizarre company, its most feared and effective weapon, with syringes and strike points. It is the job of these maniacs to soften up a target before the actual military strike. They proceed well ahead of traditional ground forces, but not because their superiors think they're such clever scouts. It's because they scare the hell out of the regular troops. And once they're up they will not take orders, or in any manner be put off their game. They are utterly merciless and entirely without remorse.

Vane was bugged enough by this conversation to renew drills in Mamuset, complete with target practice, mobile distribution fans, and that family-oriented, run-and-load maneuver, the *Ripple*. New Bulwarks and Posts were erected. The Piper Cub, sent on a Mekele reconnaissance flyover, returned with two bullet holes in a wing and one in the fuselage. Vane set up sentry shifts all around the Rim, fortified the Onramp, and hired wandering tribes of goatherds to sniff out the expanding Eritrean front.

But when the assailants showed they breached all defenses, and virtually without warning—only a single, quickly truncated siren's wail spoke for the dozens of throats slit in complete silence. The hopped-up savages, singly and in clusters, came rolling down the Inner Slopes like water. Relying on surprise and terror, they burst into Domos whirling steel.

They were obviously ignorant of the project, for these wildmen, some two hundred in all, were quickly lost in the unfamiliar crisscrossing jungle of Mamuset. Without leadership, and without anything tighter than mayhem for a battle plan, the savages, in their official Port Guard uniforms, red and gold berets, and Nike knockoffs, found themselves wasting precious wrath chasing individuals through the strange obstacle course of Yards, gardens, and Shade Halls. When an invader did halt, from exhaustion or disorientation, he was likely as not to find himself standing amid three or more Mamusetans with M16s leveled.

The Afar were not stingy with ammunition—some of the spot carnage taking place in secret garden pockets that night put to shame all the damage done by the savages' blades. Those who came in over West Rim found themselves nonplussed by a maze of open Fields, with nothing to take their bloodlust out on other than an occasional tethered camel or snoozing Field hand. Disastrously conspicuous in their frustration, they were picked off by treetop snipers one by one as they approached the community.

Vane could find no pattern in the muffled popping of rifle fire. Fearing a diversion, he called for a defense of the On-ramp, and in less than five minutes was heading a force of over a hundred armed men and boys making for the Arch. But by the time he reached that goal he was practically on his own. Only he, Mudhead, and half a dozen excited children remained to defend the Arch—the men had deserted en route to join the fighting in the trees. Vane raged mightily at this treachery, storming back and forth with his black robes swirling impressively, but it really didn't matter. Generally speaking, surprise attacks don't use the front door. The Onramp was deserted.

Vane's ego was the attack's most dismissible casualty; once their blood was up, the Afar had absolutely no use for him. Ditching the children with difficulty, he stormed back to the Stage, attached his night-imaging binoculars, and hunkered down to his tripod. Not a trace of activity on the Slopes; no sign of a continuing assault, no sign of a retreat. But there were cries of exultation leaking out of the trees, punctuated by volleys of rifle fire. The place was out of control.

Vane jumped in Isis, roared up a Ramp, and screeched to a halt at a Guard Post. He climbed out with dignity and panache, adjusted his turban, fluffed his robes, and strode purposefully to the Post's quarters. Inside he found the Guard and his family decapitated, dismembered, and mutilated in ways suggestive of great passion. Vane staggered back to the Land Rover and sat with the door open wide, his head between his knees. After a while, when he'd found his breath, he rolled down a

Ramp to Bisecting Way, motored along to Stage Street, and so on up to his front gate. For some time he sat idling in a fog, sick to the quick. At last he killed the engine.

Mamuset was as still as a cemetery. Vane gently opened the gate, tiptoed over to Worthless's pad and quietly hauled out her saddle. Solomon, seeing the camel move, shot from concealment and nipped her rear a good one. Worthless roared to her feet. Vane kicked back the dog and heaved on the saddle, walked her out the gate and mounted. The three moved uneventfully through the dark community until Vane noticed, perhaps a quarter-mile away, a rectangle of light spilling from a Domo's doorway. A few wraithlike figures could be seen scooting in and out of that slat of light, their arms encumbered by white bundles. When the Square was still again he steered Worthless into the front Yard, careful to guide her around hard surfaces that would herald his coming. He brought her right up to the side of the doorway, just beyond the spill of light. Both brute and rider craned their necks to peer inside.

In the room's very center, a mortally injured man lay on a thatch bed, attended by four smeared and bespattered women. Blood all over the place. The women, two kneeling on either side of the bed like nuns at prayer, were holding fresh rags against the bleeding man's wounds. Soaked rags were piled in a corner. Vane was painfully moved by their silent efficiency, but the preoccupied women were unaware of his bloodless suffering presence until Worthless, her nostrils quivering, snorted quizzically.

The women looked up as a unit, and as a unit glared. The scene froze like that, and threatened to remain frozen if someone didn't do something soon. Finally one woman rose and stormed around the bed to the doorway. Her eyes screamed at the startled man in black as she slammed the door in his silly pink face. Worthless stuttered and spat, shied, rocked up and down. With Vane holding on for dear life, she went running backward through the Yard, Solomon nipping her bottom excitedly. Once in the Street, Worthless turned face-forward, threw back her head and galloped wildly, Vane hammering the back of her neck frantically, his feet slipping in and out of the stirrups. He clung giddily for half a mile, and was positively relieved when a small crowd of men with flashlights ran out of the dark to intercept him. Although he couldn't understand a word they were saying, he felt the war excitement leaping man to man. Aiming their flashlights south, they hauled him off and hustled him down the dark Street. In a minute he made out a Streetlamp's glow on a functioning Utility Square, and heard a kind of chanting from what must have been several dozen voices. A little boy ran out of the Square to greet them, squealed with delight, and ran back in. Soon a knot of grinning men appeared. When they saw Vane they grabbed his arms and dragged him along joyously, like children urging a parent to their big Christmas surprise.

Gently shining in an eerie halogenous frost, a huge mound of cadavers and body parts spilled out into a wide ring of ecstatic Afar, each man brandishing an M16 in one hand and a machete in the other. The corpses had literally been shot to pieces; heads and limbs blasted off torsos, uniforms blown off bodies. Faces and guts were black gaping holes. Now the ring of men, for Vane's savage delectation, went ballistic on the pile with their enemy's machetes. Pieces of the dead flew in all directions.

That same little boy scampered flapping to the pile. He bent down, reached in, and ran up to Vane giggling deliriously. In his tiny fist was three fifths of an oozing black hand. Vane turned to stagger back and forth along the Street, at last stumbling into a Square's side Yard. He dropped to his knees in a bed of violets and was violently ill.

That morning Mamuset held its first communal funeral.

Forty-one Afar had died at the hands of the Eritrean vanguard, every one on the spot.

Two hundred and nine savages—the entire offensive force—had been killed outright, or by means as slow and agonizing as the Afar could devise.

Having learned, through Mudhead, of the victors' intrinsic need for further mutilation, Vane ordered all enemy body parts trucked to East Rim and hurled over the side. The lazy vees of carrion birds were making for the perimeter before the last head rolled to a halt.

The funeral was not arranged or conducted by Mamuset's founder and guiding hand; indeed, he didn't have a clue until Mudhead pointed out certain Squares where men and women were dismantling Domos while their children carefully dug up gardens. He watched through his Stage Eyes, fascinated, as the personal Square of each slain defender was systematically reduced to a blank patch of dirt. Even the Squares' trees were uprooted and dragged, along with every scrap of material, to Warehouse. There gills were neatly stacked, flowers potted, thatch rolled and tied, foundation concrete shattered, pulverized, and bagged.

The dead Afar were wrapped in hides and buried at the centers of these glaringly bare dirt lots. Their Squares were retired, the numbered tools placed neatly in corresponding Utility Square shed slots. The slots were adorned with personal items. Family members of the deceased were smoothly adopted by neighbors.

The entire operation, with all hands involved, took less than two hours.

Vane, again struck by his total uselessness, spent the morning in Warehouse dabbling with Inventory and trying to rethink his place in affairs. He didn't like being left out, didn't like being taken for granted. Not that he needed praise or gratitude or anything, of course; he was light years beyond that kind of stuff...but, alone there in that hot dusty cavern, he began indulging in retributive fantasies, imagining the Afar worshipping him as a great white god capable of wrath as well as wisdom. The oppressive atmosphere of Warehouse stifled him, the passion of these dreams wore him out. He shook off a large draping cloth and laid it on a pile of bagged potting soil, carefully smoothed his robes and got comfortable. Vane tilted down his turban to block the light, and was just drifting off when the compound wail of a dozen sirens snapped him out of it. He squared his turban and swept back his robes, unholstered his walkie-talkie and called Mudhead to the Stage radio. Mudhead reported the advance of Army vehicles from the northeast, still at a considerable distance. Now wide awake and dead-serious,

Vane made straight for Isis. When he reached East Rim he marched to the nearest Post and stood shoulder to shoulder with the new Guard, whose personal items were still being ported up the Ramp by his donkey, camel, and family. The Guard made a sweeping gesture while nodding with grudging admiration. Vane squinted and looked concerned. The desert was absolutely vacant. He placed a comforting hand on the Guard's shoulder and squeezed, nodding in return, then slunk around a Bulwark and peered through his spyglass.

Now he could make out a dark crescent in the waves of heat—a crescent that soon became endless ranks of troop transports approaching from north to east. Vane hopped back in the Land Rover and raced around to South Rim with only one thought in mind: *the Onramp!* The damned Onramp was a red carpet. The wild sound of his horn drew a scrambling crowd of M16-toting men and boys. Vane shot under the Arch, over Ridge Bridge and into Warehouse. There he transferred to a dirty white Nissan pickup while the crowd poured in behind him. He repetitively and emphatically lowered his arms, until the Afar obediently put down their weapons. But they were reading his broad hand gestures through the eyes of an eager fighting unit, and commenced cheerfully tossing cases of dynamite into the truck's bed. Vane sat on eggshells while they wrestled for spots. He drove back to the Arch like an old woman.

It broke his heart to blow the Onramp, but he knew the Afar would repair it, rock by rock. The blasts took a huge bite out of the ridge just where it became one with the Rim; nothing short of a company of hang gliders would span it. By the time the demolition work was done the enemy's trucks were fanning out to surround the crater, forming ripple-like rings, maybe a hundred feet apart. The nearest ring halted half a mile away. Soon a number of jeeps and trucks split ranks to drive up the Onramp the long way, parking crosswise at the gap. Vane stood watching defiantly from the Mamuset side, until a call from Mudhead got him back in the Land Rover and jamming to East Rim. Tiny in the desert, a single jeep had broken from the pack and was slowly rolling their way. East Rim was already lined with Mamusetan sharpshooters, atop Bulwarks and on the ground, their rifles dead on the approaching vehicle. Vane climbed a Bulwark, stepped around the prone bodies, and stood silhouetted against the sky, peering through his glass.

In the jeep were only the driver and a man sitting on the passenger seat's back, rocking all over the place as he fought for balance. This man, noticing Vane, slapped his palm on the driver's shoulder repeatedly while pointing with his free hand. The driver veered and made for Vane, stopping the jeep a few hundred yards away. The passenger stood on his seat and studied the billowy black figure through binoculars. He swatted the driver impatiently. The driver handed him what looked like a telephone receiver. The passenger disentangled its cord and waved the receiver over his head.

Still watching, Vane fumbled out his walkie-talkie and called Mudhead, who transmitted back as soon as he picked up the caller on the Stage radio. Vane demanded an English-speaking officer. Half a minute later he saw the man in the jeep nodding emphatically. "On my way," Vane said. He drove back to the Stage like a hyper teenager.

Mudhead was waiting under the Big Tarp, his expression closed. He handed Vane the receiver. "For you."

Vane caught his breath. "Cristian Vane here."

"And here, field commander Haile Muhammed Sai-erin. Sir, you are presently entrenched in territory occupied by the nation of Eritrea."

"Not the last time I looked. Mamuset is a tract legally purchased from Ethiopia state."

"I suggest you look again, sir. Your situation is entirely untenable. You are surrounded by regiments of the Eritrean Army, under orders to take this desert. You and your subjects will be allowed safe passage. It is our wish there be no casualties here."

"I think we got a taste of your intentions last night."

Long pause.

"Sir, if you are referring to this moat of gore...those men were not Eritrean soldiers. They were Kenyan nationals, hired to precede our forces as scouts against possible ambush. Their behavior in no manner represents the official policies of Eritrea, regardless of what you may have heard. If they were prey to a savage call outside our purview...well, it would ap-

pear they were unequal to that call. At any rate, they were little better than animals, and blasphemous ones at that. You have done both the Eritrean Army and the vultures a great favor."

"Don't make us do those vultures any more favors, commander. Way too much has gone on here to just passively pack up and march out. I don't expect you to understand that."

"Of course I understand, sir, of course. Your project has become quite famous in East Africa. She is known as The Desert Rose, and to storytellers everywhere Cristian Vane is pure Hollywood legend: the great celluloid adventurer. He is Charles Allnut, he is Captain Blood, he is Indiana Jones. You did not know this? Sir! Your exploits are followed with much envy and admiration. And your pirating of a major cargo vessel beneath the very nose of Massawa—cracking good! Ah, Mr. Vane, it would crush we lambs of Muhammad, may peace be upon him, to see harm befall such an original and creative man. Ours is a great tradition of honoring the independent and innovative. Having such a man perish at his peak would be a sinful thing, sir, a sinful thing. I will not countenance it! No! I will not have your blood on my hands. In fact, I will guard your life as though it were my own. To this end I give you my word. Accept my escort. Come parley with me and I guarantee you, Allah be praised, that no harm will come upon your fair head this day."

Vane ground his teeth. "But it's so very *hot* in the desert, commander. How much better to discuss the situation here, under these lofty green trees."

An uncertain laugh. *"My word, Mr. Vane! But how would that appear to my command? You are trifling with me, sir. Let us speak no more of this. Let us, instead, speak intelligently; as men more accustomed to grace than thunder."*

A thin wail began on North Rim. Seconds later, three others joined in from East Rim. In half a minute sirens were crying from all directions.

"It would appear," Vane said coldly, "that the first man has already spoken." He handed the phone to Mudhead and jumped back in Isis. He was really putting on miles. As he neared East Rim he made out the sound of gunfire, but the reports were far too clear to be coming from outside the crater. The Afar were firing! Vane floored Isis and tore up a Ramp recklessly, his heart in his throat. His people were defending Mamuset!

By the time he reached Post E17 the Ripple was already in full motion. East Inner Slope was a steady flow of women hurrying up to Exchange Stations with fresh rifles, then running back down with discharged guns to Load Stations for new magazines. The boys at Exchanges scrambled up ladders to the prone riflemen, often as not their fathers, with replenished rifles, grabbed the spent guns and scrambled back down. This operation was done with such ingrained precision that riflemen could exchange arms almost without a break in what seemed relentless triple-bursts of gunfire. Kid's swaggering leadership had been taken seriously: the Afar were hard-wired to fire.

And fire they did.

Vane, as he viewed East Rim's Outer Slope leaping with billygoats in fatigues, cursed mightily the enemy commander and all his forebears; while he'd been distracted on the horn, the inner ring of troop transports had been pulling right up to the Outer Slopes. These vehicles now shielded snipers, who occasionally hopped out to fire in volleys while their storming partners scurried for whatever shelter they could find. From his vantage in front of the Post, Vane saw over a hundred trying to make their way up the Slope in spurts as the second ring of transports roared forward.

But the Afar were only invigorated. Like drunken cowboys, they fired without hesitation, without fear, sometimes without aim. Fresh M16s appeared in their hands before the children could scoop up the hot spent rifles. The rattle of gunfire became a sonic blur; one long rolling wave of nerve-wracking detonations. Vane crept along a Bulwark's side wall like a man on a ledge, peeped over the edge and got a good look at East Outer Slope.

Soldiers on the way up were now soldiers on the way down, the earth erupting around them. They were dancing as if their shoes were on fire, all adrenaline and prayer. Bullets, whizzing about in an unbroken swarm, pulverized rocks into clouds of dust. The retreating men were being shot off their feet, shot in the air, shot as they tumbled. At the bottom, body parts from the previous night's butchering popped like corn. Trucks, their windows and tires already shot to pieces, were jerking and rocking from the constant metal hail while soldiers scrambled to burrow beneath them.

From flat on the Rim and from prone on Bulwarks, the Afar rose in unison, firing wildly in their passion, caught up in a sustained howl of bloodlust. Their women echoed this passion on the Inner Slopes, punctuated by screams from children. And the bodies on the Outer Slopes bounced and burst with the fury of the barrage, were lost in clouds of dust, reappeared flipping through the air, were blasted to pieces that again were lost in the dust. A hellish choir of sirens cut through the voices and gunfire. More sirens joined in, and then the Rim was a ring of screaming bobcats. The few trucks containing living drivers broke as one, driving on their rims over the dismembered dead in a desperate slow motion flight. These pathetically fleeing targets were shot up until roofs, hoods, doors, and fenders had been blown away.

The sirens and voices faded, the storm of gunfire died, and in less than a minute a profound silence embraced the crater. Vane might have been a cartoon painted on the Bulwark's side; the only things alive on him were his eyes, intently watching the Afar for the least movement. But all defenders were standing in a pose of complete attentiveness, staring out over the immediate desert like wooden Indians. On the Inner Slopes the women and children were sitting silently, almost reverently. Camels, oxen, and dogs, picking up on this new tension, reclined deeply, without a hiss or whimper. The stillness, the unreality of the situation, became so protracted Vane began to experience little panic attacks. Yet he'd been around the Afar long enough to respect their deep-rooted responses. So he remained there, splattered against the Bulwark, while his pink face purpled and his gray matter faded to black. The world was absolutely static.

Finally, on some subtle signal lost to Vane, the surviving soldiers jumped from beneath their trashed trucks and bolted across the desert. The Rim instantly erupted with fire. The sprinting men all dropped in their tracks. But this sloping hail of lead seemed it would never end. Vane watched sickened as the scattered corpses flopped about like fish out of water. The butchery ceased abruptly, and the first battle for Mamuset was history.

The Afar strutted back and forth, their blood up and their heads tossed high. When Vane had seen enough he peeled himself from the Bulwark and staggered back toward Isis. Before he could protest, a multitude of men and women had converged on him, lifted him on their shoulders, and carried him to the back seat on a carpet of cheers. He was placed standing on the seat with children clinging to his legs. A howling old man hopped into the driver's seat and fired the Rover up. Honking the horn insanely, he slowly drove through a crowd soon numbering in the several hundreds. As Isis crept along Bisecting Way it seemed the entire community was turning out for Vane's elevation to godhead. Men, women, and children ran down the Inner Slopes and across the Fields, burst out of the trees, locked the Land Rover in a roiling sea of heads and shoulders. And for one wild minute there his eyes were misting over. He was Caesar, he was MacArthur—Cristian Honey Vane was the bleeding Pope.

When he was himself again he raised his arms in a gesture for silence.

Those nearest responded with a deafening cheer. Vane shook his head sharply and lowered his arms by degrees.

The crowd went wild.

"Help!" he hollered into the CB's transmitter. "For Pete's sake!" Mudhead, watching impassively on the Stage, obediently switched on the Utility Square alerts. It took a few minutes for the triple-beeps to pierce the hubbub, but little by little the crowd drifted off to the Mount to catch Mudhead's translation of Vane's exultant transmission. *Mamuset*, Mudhead announced, had performed splendidly. Khrisa Vahn was proud. The cheer that went up shook the new Big Tarp, shook the leaves on the trees, shook the dumbfounded Army listening without. *But*, Mudhead went on loudly, what they had endured was only a skirmish. The Army would be back, angrier than ever, and this time with many, *many* more men.

Ecstasy.

Vane sat hard on Isis's punished upholstery, fighting back the tears as the cheering went on and on and on. Up on the

Bulwarks, the specks of dancing riflemen could be seen shooting into the air.

"Wasting ammo," Vane sputtered.

Mudhead reported back: these men were shooting the guns of butchered soldiers, salvaged by children on the Outer Slopes. The celebration leaned this way and that, perplexing to Vane in its exotic African ways, and when he finally broke free he found himself drifting home, confused by his emotions. But he was still too excited to sit. So he saddled up Worthless and clopped off to the Rim to watch the enemy buildup. It was far more impressive than he wanted to admit. All day long he rode round and round, and all day long a parade of trucks and caissons buttressed the growing web of troops and artillery. Soldiers set up canopies between the corner posts of their trucks' sidings, and in this artificial shade cleaned their weapons, took naps, played dominoes. Mortars and small cannons were wheeled through and locked down. And still the trucks rolled in. By twilight it was solid Army as far as the eye could see.

The Afar, entranced, competed for gawking space atop Bulwarks, piggybacking their children. That night they stood in their thousands around the Rim, scattering eerie shadows by the light of hundreds of tiki torches. The troops occasionally responded with lights of their own, idling their trucks with high beams blazing. When they grew bored they played with directional signals and emergency flashers, hoping to unnerve the defenders. Confused, the Afar responded by leaning their torches left and right, lifting them up and setting them down.

It was all very disconcerting for Vane. He slept fitfully that night, under the stars on a canvas mat at Top Step. His dread of the coming day pursued him into his dreams.

But at the crack of dawn he was on his feet and waiting, along with a breathless audience of over five thousand Afar, for Strauss's theme to peak. And when that first spear of perfectly-cued sun broke the horizon, it was accompanied by a rolling cheer that flowed across the crater and over its walls. Vane pounded Worthless to her feet and paraded around the Stage like a rock star, caught up in the growing blush of dawn. Only the radio's familiar chiming snapped him out of it. He knelt Worthless with an attitude, dismounted lustily and snatched the receiver.

"Yes?"

"You don't carry, by any chance, Blue Danube?"

Vane sobered. "Sorry. Wrong Strauss. Besides, we don't take requests from enemies."

There was a huge sigh. *"Mr. Vane, this whole business is a grave misfortune."*

"You can change your fortune."

Another sigh. *"I will concede that so far we have been mightily embarrassed. And I will share a piece of intelligence with you: there is nothing in our training to prepare us for a ground assault on a natural fortress such as yours. Be that as it may, you will certainly see that, with persistence on our part, your cause must inevitably be lost. Sooner or later your walls will be breached. Sooner or later your ammunition will be depleted, your stores of food and water exhausted."*

"Commander, our supplies, and our heart, are no less imposing than our walls. We are prepared to hold out indefinitely. I like it here, commander. And I'm looking forward to dying of old age."

"Mr. Vane, nothing could make me happier than to have you die of old age. But that will not happen here. Please command your subjects to remove themselves in an orderly fashion, and to distance themselves as a population from you personally, and from any of your underlings. Your palace will be spared, your retinue permitted to retain whatever privileges they have been accorded. You will be escorted in complete comfort, and with pomp sufficient to maintain your regal image. We understand the necessity of such impressions." A pause for emphatic effect. *"I am empowered to authorize your unmolested transfer to Massawa or Aseb, or to Djibouti by way of the Red Sea, or, in fact, to any amenable port that is non partisan in this affair. You will be generously remunerated for your losses and trouble. This offer is not a bluff. I am prepared to present certified proof of your guaranteed safe passage and compensation for title. The document is signed by President Saille-Halla, who feels your demise would not only be a tragic blow for him personally, but would perhaps not be taken all that well in those States whence you originate. The Afar will be released to return to their old*

ways. They will not be harmed. Our business is with the state of Ethiopia and that with rapist Negasso, not with you or these innocent people. I beg you to reconsider."

"Commander, at this point in the game I sincerely doubt anybody in here's actually paying attention to me. Your little gambit's stirred up one helluva hornet's nest." He thought for a bit. "Goodbye."

"Mr. Vane! Please do not abandon communications. I urge you to leave this channel o—"

Vane slammed down the receiver and whipped out his walkie-talkie. "Mudhead!"

"Bossman."

"I want you back up here on the radio, partner. And pronto. My troops need me."

From his vantage on the Stage Vane saw the door of Mudhead's Domo open and his friend emerge resignedly. The African stood with his hands clasped behind his back, his robes brilliant white against the variegation of his garden. He looked around as though appreciating it for the last time, lowered his head, slowly made his way up his new polished stone walk. Vane whooped in acknowledgment, waved his jile high, and mounted Worthless with a vengeance. Solomon got in two good nips before bounding on ahead.

For the very first time Worthless bore him with alacrity, almost with dignity. The confidence and enthusiasm Vane emanated radiated throughout her frame, made beast walk tall and rider sit high. They eagerly negotiated the prickly Mount, trotted regally along Bisecting Way, charged up a Ramp in a streak of black and tan. When they reached the top they found the entire Rim packed solid with Afar, standing shoulder-to-shoulder in silent awe of the vast military sea. Vane, having sufficiently clopped along with his turban held high, paused in his inspection to scan the enemy with his minaret spyglass.

What he saw was a massacre in the making.

Except for a respectable few hundred yards of empty desert surrounding the crater, the world was all trucks, jeeps, and troops. In that one naked instant all Vane's bravado revealed itself as pure homespun foolishness. He was forced to face his immaturity like a man, to admit that the only sane move would be to order the Afar to lay down their arms, and with the utmost haste.

Vane sagged in the saddle. He was in command of nothing. He didn't even know these people. Once again he was, if anything, in the way. A crazy, Technicolor idea came to him. His blue eyes blazing, he would majestically ride Worthless down the Outer Slope and across that vacant space to surrender Mamuset to the Eritreans. It would be an act of great character. Commander Sai-erin would be impressed, his men terribly moved. The Afar would drift back to their previous lifestyle, none the worse, to mesmerize their grandchildren with time-embroidered tales of the great white miracle worker.

And he? Detention, interrogation, some tough lectures. Honey would bail him out, as always. Vane glazed over. A minute later he was roused by a dull boom and passing whistle. A mortar shell exploded in the trees, begetting a great growl all around. He sat straight-up—it was that same glottal storm he'd experienced on Dock when surrounded by threatening drivers. Vane looked back to see the bristling Afar shoving one another for better views, every expression twisted by a rage that remained beyond his ken. There came a trio of detonations in the Fields, this time from launches in the desert outside West Rim. The Afar's common guttural expanded in response, rising steadily as the barrage continued, until the ringed men of Mamuset were a howling, flailing mob.

Worthless was squeezed to the very lip of the Rim. Her toes vainly sought purchase while her eyes rolled crazily at the desert below. Vane pounded and pounded her neck, trying to turn her against the furious press, but as the Afar's howling rose to a nerve-shredding scream the camel threw back her head and brayed right along. Vane finally yanked her around and they teetered, facing an oncoming wall of wide-eyed shrieking psychopaths. Worthless roared, reared, and spat in their faces.

"Forward, you idiot!" hollered Vane. "Go *forward!*" He whipped out his jile and poked her in the rump. Worthless bellowed, pounded her throat on the dirt, kicked her rear legs in the air. "Go, damn it!" Vane cried. "I…said…*go!*" He poked her again, very hard this time, only to find himself clinging to the camel's neck as she skidded backward down East Outer Slope.

Worthless, issuing a resounding plaint of terror and rebellion, was nevertheless able to turn face-forward without spilling. Half-stumbling and half-galloping, she hurtled down the Slope with Vane fighting for balance by holding his free arm overhead like a common rodeo cowboy. His jile caught the sun as it waved back and forth.

The bloodthirsty scream of the men on East Rim ceased, though the howl continued to rise elsewhere around the Rim—the result was much like a phase-shifted echo. Suddenly Vane was able to hear his and his camel's grunts and gasps clearly, along with the clatter of her feet and the excited panting of Solomon hurtling in and out beneath them. Overhead, the whistle of a mortar shell flanged with all the clarity of a sound effect triggered in a recording studio.

A great shout erupted behind them. Down the Afar came. Their running battle cry galvanized the entire community, so that men and boys poured out of the crater like ants out of an anthill. Upon hearing that cry, Worthless lifted her head and raced across the flat desert floor as if the Devil were after her. In seconds they were swallowed up by the sprinting mob.

Vane bounced along in the manner of a bobble-head toy, stammering commands and stabbing the air with his jile. He jerkily made out the first row of soldiers, kneeling coolly with their rifles leveled. He heard those rifles popping away, and he saw the first line of racing Afar drop like dominoes. And he saw the soldiers leaping to their feet, one by one and then in unison, as the wave came on without hesitation. The Afar screamed continuously while they ran, shooting without a trace of discipline. Their second line collapsed almost as handily as the first, but now the wave was breaking, and now the soldiers were turning to run for cover.

The Afar hit the first row of trucks as human battering rams. Vane heard isolated rifle shots, a young man's cry of anguish, and what may have been a Gatling gun. And the Afar went right out of their minds, shrieking and whirling and diving, firing with one weapon and cudgeling with another. Trailing youngsters and seniors, hunched like spiders, tore down the aisles formed by rows of parked vehicles, leaping on occupants with total disregard for their own lives, savaging the trucks and jeeps, smashing their windshields, shooting and pummeling the bodies. As horror took the disintegrating ranks, soldiers howling to Allah began dashing through the maze of vehicles in zigzagging spurts that became all-out runs, crowds of kicking and caterwauling Mamusetans hard on their heels.

Vane yelled and yelled until his throat seized; disoriented by all the action, yet exhilarated beyond his wildest fantasies. There wasn't a man in uniform who wasn't running for his life. He croaked out a string of gasping congratulations, poked Worthless jubilantly and continuously. The camel wheeled round and round like a turnstile as the thinning sea hustled by, giving her master an unrequested 360 of the battleground.

Dead and dying Afar lay mingled with butchered Eritreans; bodies were stretched out in the dirt, scrunched one upon the other, sprawled across hoods and seats. But there were still small pockets of violent activity between vehicles, where Mamusetans mercilessly tore into cowering soldiers. In the distance Vane could see the backs of pursuing Afar, and beyond them the backs of screaming Eritreans. The battle was won, the siege wholly blown. It was every man for himself.

The Afar continued to fire as they ran. When their magazines were exhausted they ran swinging their M16s, and didn't stop until they'd caught their hysterical enemies or collapsed. Even then, on hands and knees, they forced themselves on, coughing and gasping, pounding their fists on the ground.

Vane was flabbergasted. They hadn't just survived the Eritreans; they had defeated them utterly. He stood high in the stirrups as he spun, giving vent to an oscillating, shredded war whoop. He coughed, he wept, he waved his mighty weapon high.

Cristian Honey Vane went right over his camel's hindquarters and headfirst into the dirt.

Chapter Nineteen

Mudhead

Vane tentatively opened an eye.

The first thing he saw was Mudhead's expectedly glum, yet strangely distorted countenance—the whole face was extended like a muzzle and covered by a heavy red veil. Vane rolled the eye carefully. Someone, without a trace of taste or consideration, had up-and painted every gill in his Domo a dull crimson. It took Vane a whole minute to realize the air itself was red.

Mudhead's muzzle continued to project, the black lips rolling round and round. "How Bossman feel?" The voice was miles away.

Vane weighed his impressions. Oddest of all, his thoughts seemed to be swimming in his mouth. It wasn't all that unpleasant. Someone behind him replied,"Weird. How should I feel?"

Mudhead nodded. "Weird." Leaning forward in his chair, he showed Vane a small vial and syringe. "Present from past."

Vane nodded back, but his head didn't move. "What happened to me, man?"

"Bossman hero." Mudhead touched a finger to his own right ear. "Take bullet. Dead for sure." He heaved a sigh, placed his hands on his thighs and pushed himself back. The face flattened to normal. "Sorry all out purple heart."

The red room blushed deeper as Vane tentatively directed a hand to his ear. His head was completely bound up in gauze. "A bullet got my ear?"

"Direct hit."

"How...how bad?"

"Whole ear gone." Mudhead tilted his head. "Now you lopside."

"*What?* You're lying! Show me!" He started to sit up, and was immediately knocked down by a stomping nausea. An odd pain—dull with a sharp core—projected into his brain like a tentacle, fragmented, and passed.

Mudhead groaned and pushed himself out of view, reappearing a minute later with a shaving mirror. Vane gaped at his reflection. His head was a huge mass of cloth scraps wound up in half a mile of gauze. An area the size of a saucer was brown with dried blood. His eyes were puffy crimson caves, his face a pale, haggard mask. He tried different angles and various expressions. Slowly a smile cut the reflection in two.

"Bossman lucky. Can grow pretty blond lock."

"What? Where's my turban?"

Mudhead shook his head sadly, and Vane went paler still. He was just sitting up in protest when the room hit him in the face like a fist. Vane's fingers dug into the sheets. "What..." he sobbed, "man...what happened after I got hit? I seem to remember us...kicking ass...royally."

Mudhead now recounted the events succeeding Vane's triumphant exit from consciousness. He was patient; enunciating as best he could, repeating sentences carefully whenever his logy one-man audience lost contact.

To all appearances, the rout of field commander Saierin's regiments had been astonishingly thorough. The Afar not only embarrassed and butchered their attackers, they dispossessed them of their weapons and transportation. Having chased the survivors deep into the desert, the chanting victors tramped back to commandeer jeeps and transports, picking up fallen comrades and every usable weapon they could find. The Eritrean dead—and there were so very many—were left for the Danakil to do with as it would.

Four hundred and thirteen Afar had died, most picked off in that initial blind rush across the open space separating Outer Slopes and the first ring of waiting soldiers. Some were but children.

It was difficult to estimate the number of dead Eritreans. From the top of any Bulwark they, along with the ugly kites of swirling vultures, were all one could see. Vane's heroes drove every navigable vehicle around to Onramp. Those disabled vehicles worthy of salvage to any returning army were doused with their own petrol and set aflame. A dozen empty transports were then driven to the dynamited space and rolled in, one on top of the other. The indefatigable Afar, revisiting the constructive zeal they'd applied in the building of Mamuset, packed the space with boulders and loose earth until a perfectly serviceable bridge was created. Over this bridge the long line of trucks were paraded through Sectors to Utility Squares.

But first the community's fallen master was carried ceremoniously up East Outer Slope on his camel, somberly attended in a massive procession up Bisecting Way, and reverently delivered to Mudhead at Vane's Domo. After dressing the wound and administering the pain killer, Mudhead sat back to await the resurrection.

Vane proved a tough patient, hard to keep down. He wanted to see the battlefield, wanted accurate tallies, wanted to congratulate the victors. His exuberance and intoxication would eject him from bed like a Pop Tart, but his injury and attendant illness would knock him right back down. Mudhead fed him beer and Percodan, hoping he'd burn himself to sleep. Still, the African was worn out long before his boss.

By late afternoon the beer and high-strung behavior caught up with Vane. He curled up on his left side and closed his eyes. He looked dead. Solomon snuck up to the bed and very gently climbed on, knowing his master forbade it, and watched Vane sleeping until his own eyes grew heavy. Shadows crossed the floor. The room grew dim. Mudhead transferred his butt to Vane's favorite padded chair and let his eyelids kiss. His old bones were sore and his neck stiff, but the padding was generous, and for one guilty moment there he thought he might actually have dozed.

When he reopened his eyes the room was black, and Vane nowhere to be found. Mudhead creaked to his feet, loped outside, looked around the Yard. Worthless was missing from her pad. He flapped across Stage Street and labored up the Steps to the Mat, his old heart flapping right along. Mudhead bent over until his tarboosh brushed the Mat, his withered old palms resting on shaking knees. After a minute he grabbed a walkie-talkie and depressed the transmit button.

"Bossman?"

"Mudhead!"

"Bossman stay bed!" Mudhead gasped. "Play general tomorrow!"

"What? Come on up to North Rim and join the fun."

Mudhead slumped against the motherboard. "Fun day over," he wheezed.

"That's too bad. It's a nice bright night. You can still see all the bodies left out in the...wait!"

Mudhead waited. "What matter?"

"What?" There was a lull. *"It looks like we've got company."*

"What," Mudhead whispered, "company?"

No answer.

"Bossman?"

"There are lights on the northern horizon, Mudhead. In the air. Hang on for a minute while I get a bead."

Mudhead repeatedly paced the Mat. Finally he walked over to Top Step and searched the northern sky. Nothing but a billion stars.

"It's helicopters again. Guess they're gonna try that dumb trick one more time. Remember the Red Sea? Well, I sure as heck do! What? This time we'll have every rifle in the house on 'em." Mudhead sat gently, holding the walkie-talkie tightly against his ear. *"Six or seven in a line. They're coming fast."*

There was a break in which Mudhead tried several times

to call. When he picked up Vane's voice again it was muted and accompanied by static. It sounded worried this time, and a whole lot soberer. *"They'll probably try strafing runs. God, they're big. I'm gonna get everybody down off the Rim under cover of the trees."*

Slowly, dreamily, the sirens wound up along North Rim.

"Get below ground, Mudhead! What? They may be bombing. Get to Cellar or Basement and stay there until I come for you."

"Ten-four, Bossman!" Mudhead tucked the radio under his robes. He stood high on his toes, staring over the canopy of treetops. Now he could see a broken ribbon of lights approaching between the stars. Mudhead hoisted his robes and puffed down the Steps just as fast as his feet would carry him. He hurried to his left around the Mount and fell up against Warehouse, looking back over his shoulder. A column of light was burning through the night. Mudhead dashed to Cellar, hauled up the right hand door and tumbled into pitch. In his left hand the radio came alive with an enormous clatter of rotors. Finally Vane's voice sounded, *"Mudhead!"* There was a long wedge of silence. The hard thumping of air came again, much louder this time.

"They're in!"

The black rabbit darted tree to tree and Yard to Yard, not daring to trust the narrow plains of crisscrossing Streets. Occasionally he was startled by a singed camel or cow bursting out of the murk and stamping past. Occasionally, too, he caught the gray silhouette of a masked soldier treading cautiously through the noxious smoke. The stuff was everywhere, drifting in slow motion—diagonally as suspended leaning pillars, horizontally as thinning and fatting wisps. It tended to roll on the roofs of Domos, like an unctuous substance, before oozing off and gathering in depressions. All around these smoke-matted Domos, weird flames were clinging surreally to trees; metastasizing, popping and sighing, trickling down trunks and dripping to the ground.

Mudhead nearly collapsed at a Square's hedged boundary, his head swimming with fumes. Through streaming eyes he caught a commotion in the haze: down the Street came that same nightmarish mob, that same reeling wave of heads and arms that had pursued him halfway across the Sector. For a tense minute the wave was lost in drifting reek, and when it reappeared it was almost on him. Mudhead gasped enormously. He clutched his chest, turned, and staggered across the Square with his white robes trailing.

There was a hard change in the pursuing voices. The crowd halted abruptly, and a second later was pouring through the Yard after the slow flapping ghost. Mudhead burst retching onto a Street so dense with smoke it appeared fogbound. Overcome by fumes, he threw out his arms just as the howling mob came down on him. He was hauled to his feet. Mudhead promptly collapsed on his knees, was again pulled upright, and again collapsed. The shouting crowd scooped him up and roughly propelled him down the Street. Swooning, Mudhead was borne supine by his limbs; first as a limp bit of dragging backside, then as a cruciform slab high on the shoulders of the roaring tide. Burning leaves and branches rushed by above and on both sides, interlaced by shifting cords of smoke, as he was washed down a dark acrid tunnel to his doom. The blood beating in his head made that tunnel dilate and contract, made the mob's cries seesaw in his ears.

It didn't take long to reach the Mount, though to Mudhead it seemed the ride would never end. At Bottom Step he was set firmly on his feet and pressed upward, gasping and shaking. He managed three Steps and dropped. Mudhead was straightened back up and forced to climb, and by the time he reached the Stage he was wheezing desperately. Yet when he collapsed on the Mat it was not from exhaustion; the scene before him knocked him flat on his knees.

Vane's twitching body lay surrounded by his dead dog, comatose camel, and a variety of charred personal belongings. He was so badly burned his skin looked like red bubble wrap. His robes had been scorched away, along with his hair, toes, and eyelids.

Mudhead's hands trembled above Vane's chest. "Boss

...." he tried. He could barely breathe. "Boss..."

Vane's hand shot off the Mat and seized Mudhead's right wrist. Mudhead watched the lipless mouth writhe for a few seconds, then carefully brought down his ear. Finally Vane hissed, "Oh, Jesus." His eyes rolled up. "Not like...dear God, not like this." The hand dropped to the Mat.

The African rocked back on his haunches, adjusted his robes, and reclined onto his rear. He sat there like a man of stone while voices of the Afar pattered around him. Once his mind had cleared, his thoughts automatically converted to Saho. The Afar were confused and breaking up; some were heavy with grief, others full of fury. They had no one to follow, nowhere to turn. From the gist of their plaints, Mudahid Asafu-Adjaye realized that the monster was now in his lap. He pounded a fist, and in Saho snapped, "The thing is done!"

That quieted them.

An elderly man responded, gently, "They will come for him."

There was a disapproving murmur.

Another said, "They will find him here."

Mudahid snapped, "They will *not!*" and chilled them with his expression. He looked back down, leaned forward, and held a steady hand over Vane's eyes.

"Mudhead know place."

Every aspect of Vane's consciousness revolved around pain.

He'd stopped screaming when his body went into deep shock, but each time a bearer stumbled his head would jerk back, his mouth fly open, and his fried lungs emit a short hissing squeal. He watched himself stiffen and relax, stiffen and relax, from the viewpoint of a hovering observer. It was like having a video recorder, attached to a kite just above, transmitting an image back to its arching, silently screaming subject.

Vane was having an out-of-body experience. He'd been enduring it, with varying degrees of intensity, ever since Sol's first spear burned the top off the Danakil Alps and transformed the brilliant black night into a burning blue diamond. Throughout the whole morning he'd watched his body carried on a makeshift stretcher by rotating groups of burned dying people, all struggling to shade, fan, and otherwise comfort him.

Why wouldn't they let him die? How long could that pathetic creature continue to jerk and clench, arch and settle? Vane's detached awareness watched his body go through its motions over and over, until the horror of the thing became matter-of-fact. The afternoon sun bit into his welling skin like acid, made it cringe, crawl, and burst anew. And so he went on screaming without really screaming, jerking and clenching, out of his mind with agony. Just beneath him, the bearers lurched in and out of the camera's window, forcing themselves up a rough path that wound round an isolated rocky table. As the weakest fell trying to climb, the strongest worked double time taking up the slack. With a terrible lunge, the remaining carriers began a sickening left-handed ascent that ended in a wild ride over a flat baking shelf. The spinning sun blew outward, swelling until it took the entire sky. Then it was merely the central bright pinprick in an insane kaleidoscope filled with distorted, collapsing faces. A dark fist closed about Vane. He shook up and down, up and down, convulsing like a drowning rat as his wretched red husk was sucked into Hell.

Chapter Twenty

Wildfeather

It was easy as pie to track the Afar's little romp over the Danakil. Captain Wildfeather led his team of three auxiliaries— a pair of jumpy green privates and a pest of a photographer— alongside the unmistakable trail of over a hundred stumbling, rapidly expiring Mamusetans. Occasionally the photographer paused to take a series of snapshots and jot down some notes. During these little unscheduled breaks one of the soldiers would hang back a ways and glare while the other scanned the horizon. Wildfeather was always grateful for an opportunity to segregate himself, and so return his full attention to the desert floor. He was keenly aware of a constant pattern in the prints: while followers were continually kicking over the course of their leaders, there remained two sets of parallel prints that staggered along in tandem, always around three feet apart and made slightly deeper than the others by a shared burden. And though in many places it was obvious a straggler had collapsed and been dragged, it was clear this had been a one-dimensional, tightly-grouped exodus.

Wildfeather, part Yakima Indian and part Yukon Inuit, was well-versed in detection, assessment, and pursuit—had in fact earned his promotion to Special Forces by successfully tracking the infamous Wraith Brigade during Operation Desert Sabre. It was jocularly rumored that he could determine, through vestigial evidence alone, the age, gender, and political persuasion of a midget pulverized in a cattle run.

So Wildfeather was actually disappointed by the obvious tale-of-the-trail; they'd might as well have assigned a Camp Fire Girl. He was annoyed, too, by the absurdly paranoiac waltz of his assigned men, needlessly sliding and swerving to confound imaginary assailants, and by the intermittent load of the photographer, who was searching for *atmosphere* rather than evidence. Wildfeather long ago decided he wouldn't play this man's game; humoring him was like walking a dog that insisted on stopping to sniff every flower bed. Sooner or later you stop fighting the leash and start leaning on the lash. Or, as in this case, you let go and walk on.

Wildfeather paused to study an oblique line at the top of a lonely rocky table. The pillars of heat surrounding this groove would have thrown off an untrained observer, but for Wildfeather they only exaggerated the anomaly's nearly horizontal aspect.

"Mackaw!" he said loudly, without turning. "If you still want that Pulitzer, get your perennially dragging butt over here!" The two soldiers, instinctively tensing and crouching, swung their rifles in broad arcs. The photographer rushed up to Wildfeather, now waiting like a bored pointer.

"Yeah?"

"You see that funny slope on the table up ahead?"

Mackaw raised his digital camera, allowed it to self-adjust, and rapidly took half a dozen shots of a depression a hundred yards to the left. "Got it!"

"No, *Ansel*, I'm talking about that breach in the hard stratum. Notice how you don't see any heat waves above it? That's because the darker gray beneath is a source of ventilation. It's an opening in the rock, probably a cave's vent. Underground streams used to rush out below the Highlands, through these rocks and onto the dead terrain behind us. They certainly would've left a system of east-west caverns, perhaps a series of labyrinths."

Mackaw licked his lips. "You think that's where all those natives went?"

Wildfeather looked at him with distaste. "Not natives. They're people, just like you and me. You watch too many Tarzan movies."

"I'll get my lights set up!" Mackaw grasped Wildfeather's upper arm. "This is it, huh, Scout? This is what we've been looking for?"

Wildfeather used one hand to peel off Mackaw's claw and the other to grip him by the lapel. "Now listen, picture-boy. I've been real patient with you up to this point. But I'm not going to let you make a farce out of a tragedy. I'm not permitted to bitch-slap a civilian, and anyway it wouldn't teach you a thing. But I want you to stop being selfish for a minute and just listen."

All four men stood stock-still and perked up their ears. Half a minute passed.

"Nothin'!" Mackaw said. "This place is so dead I can hear my career dying."

"Exactly," Wildfeather murmured. "You saw the tracks of those people." He pointed with his rifle. "They went up this path here, almost as if they were storming the place. They must have been out of their minds after crossing this desert." The men clambered up the winding path until they came out on the table's flat shelf. They all stopped to crouch maybe twenty yards from the fissure. "Well, they went down that narrow chimney there, one on top of the other. It's a flue, a kind of blow-hole from back when those streams were interacting with molten rock. The whole perimeter of the Danakil is volcanic. And those people weren't some prancing merry file, you guys; they hit that hole like Gangbusters. See how it's all torn up around the opening? That was one helluva crowd, and it was mighty important for 'em to get down there in a hurry."

Mackaw gently shifted his gear. "So what?" he near-whispered.

"So show a little respect," Wildfeather said. "I'm experiencing a deep sense of the sacred."

One soldier rolled his eyes comically. The other grinned.

"I saw that," Wildfeather said. "You guys go ahead and laugh all you want. But you're gonna be yukking it up on the outside. You too, Mackaw. Until I give the go-ahead, you three are stationed back here. Willard, you and Barnes watch my back. Keep a sharp lookout for rabid Mau Maus, and if you see any suspiciously pregnant-looking Eritrean hausfraus, well, you just make sure you shoot first and ask questions later. Mackaw, I'm depending on you to record every mind-blowing moment of the madness while I'm gone. It's your job to save for posterity what only your genius can define. If you don't see me again, give my regrets to Broadway."

"Wait a minute," Mackaw objected. "You can't order me around. How many times do we have to go over this, Captain? I'm strictly civilian. I'm being paid to save this whole ordeal not only by *Life* but by the goddamned American State Department. I'm an independent observer and freelance photographer. Don't you forget that. It's just as important to my bosses that we find Vane's body as it is to your bosses. So if you're looking for more medals here you're gonna need me on your good side when you're posing."

"I couldn't agree with you more, Mackaw. You've got a real talent for sizing up a situation. That's why I know it'll be crystal clear to you when I tell you that, if you really *do* want to be on my good side, you'll stay back here until I say otherwise. When I signal, you are to enter *only* with Barnes and Willard covering your silly civilian front and rear. Until then, everybody stay well back from that opening." He walked quietly to the fissure and peered inside. The passage downward was nearly spiral and not too steep; a man of medium height could manage it without hunching. He stepped down, using his rifle as a probe. After about thirty feet of descent, Wildfeather came to a level floor. His nostrils twitched and his pupils dilated. Despite the excellent ventilation there was the strong smell of a charnel house. He was surprised to have not noticed it outside.

This subterranean world was wonderfully cool and dim, eerily illuminated by sporadic shafts of light emanating from surface fissures. Carefully laid out on the cave's floor was a broad miscellany of masks, figurines, and baskets. Most appeared damaged beyond repair.

Wildfeather knew not to trust his eyes exclusively. He aimed a flashlight and flicked it on and off—one, two, three, four—while swiveling on his toes. He was in a roomy cave leading into a much larger cavern. He froze. His fourth flash had briefly exposed a lurking shape to his right. Wildfeather kept his eyes trained on that spot, knowing that whoever or whatever he had lit would be dazzled, if only for a moment. He simultaneously pointed the rifle and flashlight while his body automatically went into a crouch. At near floor-level he snapped on the light and kept it trained. He saw an ancient, horribly disfigured little man dressed in a tattered sanafil tied on the right in the manner of Afar pastoralists. The man was sitting in the lotus position on an oval mat of interwoven acacia fronds. Wildfeather's beam probed the yawning eye sockets and distorted features before sweeping down to a ratty lump at the little man's side, where he saw the wretched figure of a rigid white dwarf camel, her feet bound so as to not be outthrust in rigor mortis. The sitting man had one hand buried in the camel's scruffy fur. The other lay upturned on his knee. The smell of the dead camel made Wildfeather grimace.

"Batsu wem ji' *Saho?*" he tried.

"Parle vu France?" the little man replied.

"Um...propos quelques...seulement?"

"Same here. But it's a lovely language."

Wildfeather's eyes narrowed further. He lowered the beam.

"Thank you," his host said. "Save your batteries. Speak with me a spell while your eyes adjust."

Wildfeather switched off his flashlight and slung his rifle behind his shoulder. He took another look around. "You live here, Mister...?"

The tiny man inclined his head an inch. "Xhantu of Outer Danakil."

Wildfeather found himself nodding in return. "Captain Marlon Wildfeather of the United States Army. I've been sent to locate and return to the States the body of one Cristian Honey Vane. He is reported killed by an Eritrean assault force advancing on Addis Ababa. That force was routed." Still disoriented, he absent-mindedly handed Xhantu a full-face photograph of Vane. "Oh!" he said, recovering. "Forgive me."

The sage slipped the picture under the folds of his sanafil at the waist and secured it with the sash. "You do not say! That, then, would explain the pell-mell flight of once-sanguine camel drivers." He tweaked his head to forty-five degrees off the perpendicular. "Eritrea is attacking Addis Ababa?"

"Unfortunately so." Wildfeather could now make out an enormous arched mouth in the rock, perhaps a hundred yards along. It was the source of that deeper coolness he'd noticed upon entering. He felt he'd been conservative in his previous assessment: immense underground rivers, not merely streams, had ages ago torn into what was once the Danakil Sea.

"This man Vane," Wildfeather went on, "was an American philanthropist and social engineer who decided to assist people of this desert rather than those who were hurting back home. He was disgustingly rich; he could have bought Montana if he wanted. Instead he bought a large tract of land northwest of here called Mamuset, and made it into a kind of kinky high-tech commune to show the rest of the world just how clever and generous the filthy rich can be." Wildfeather brushed the rock floor with one tip of perhaps the world's only pair of steel-toed moccasins. The rock was streaked and daubed with brown smears of blood. He swept his light. Smears also appeared here and there along the cave's walls. The trail of dried blood went down the chamber and through that gaping archway into the unseen.

"This Vane guy," Wildfeather said, "was outrageously successful. After some gossip magazine did a spread on him he became a real big shot back home; a household name with all the draw of a movie star or politician. Sure enough, people stopped hating him for being rich. Now he was both popular *and* rich. Other rich people caught on, and began gabbing about his operation and dressing down—you know, wearing sandals in their limousines, adopting refugees for photo-ops and so on. Now he's about to become a martyr. After that, who knows? Christ reincarnated?"

"You are very cynical, sir."

"The Eritreans napalmed Mamuset and turned it into a volcano. A shame, really. Not because the rich boy got his, but because all those poor people were actually a whole lot better off for a while there. Anyways, the survivors, hysterical and half-alive, took off through the desert. I guess they too had become cynical, Mr. Xhantu."

"That must have been a terrible trek," the sage said, sadly shaking his head. "No one could survive the Danakil."

"Oh, they survived all right. Most of them did, anyhow. They came in a single burned and bloody wave, and they knew just where that wave was breaking. They made a beeline for your door, Mr. Xhantu. They came down that chimney, burst into this chamber, and went kicking and screaming through that archway."

Xhantu nodded. "They were much distressed; that is true."

"Let's go see," Wildfeather said, "why they dropped by so suddenly." He helped the sage to his feet and they walked arm-in-arm to the arch. Wildfeather immediately halted at a blast of stench. He looped a small disposable nose-and-mouth mask on his face and offered one to Xhantu. The sage shook his head emphatically at the feel of a mask on his face, but Wildfeather insisted. Once they were both masked they stepped into the great cavern, whereupon Wildfeather's arm went out like a shot to block Xhantu's progress. The captain's eyes narrowed. At least a hundred burned and twisted corpses were laid out on the gigantic floor, each in a 5 x 5 square defined by lines drawn with soot. The soot's source was evinced in numerous imported charred items, now arranged in elaborate and decorative stacks against three of the cavern's walls. These soot-squares were marked wall-to-wall around a central, unoccupied square of identical dimensions. Most of the dead had perished in their personal squares, some prostrate, some in a lopsided sitting slump. But all faced the central square.

Wildfeather pondered the display critically, feeling the place, taking notes in his head. After a space he reached into a pouch on his belt, extracted a small flash camera, and took several shots from various angles. The click of the camera's mechanism cracked like a whip in the cavern. He then made his way along the west wall, occasionally looking back. The sage was close behind, adroitly stepping around the carefully stacked remnants, the delicate probe of his hand walking swiftly along the wall like a hairless tarantula. The whole setup gave Wildfeather the creeps. When he attained a point opposite the empty square he tiptoed between the bodies to the blank space and went down on one knee, clearly discerning a large smudge created by a slow seepage of blood and sweat. The smudge became a narrow smear that snaked between squares to the east wall. Wildfeather took several shots of the square and smear. The sage crept up behind him, his bare feet making tiny smacking sounds. The two stood side by side.

"Like a cathedral, perhaps?" the sage offered, his voice muffled by the mask.

"Nah. Cemetery on a chessboard. Man's surrender to mathematics." Wildfeather's cynicism fluttered bravely before plunging. "Y'know, I feel very small in all this."

"Perhaps this rich American you speak of was not so callous and manipulating after all."

Wildfeather stared. "Sir," he said quietly, "we are standing in the middle of an empty square that lies at the center of perhaps a hundred similar squares, each containing a deceased individual—from my observation members of the Afar group. The slow dissolution of their bodies in this cool chamber has reached the point of putrefaction. It's the source of this miasma, and the reason I have insisted upon your donning the breather. Judging by your deep familiarity with this place, and by your demonstrated ability to perceive the particulars of your environment, I am going to assume you are perfectly aware of our circumstances here. That said, I am going to request you be perfectly honest with me today, and save us both considerable trouble and embarrassment." He took a breath. "To what," he said, tracing the square's borders with the rifle's barrel, "do you attribute the significance of this single empty square?"

Xhantu nodded in acknowledgment. "Apparently, Captain, it is some kind of space meant to signify a pivotal presence. I am not familiar with the intricacies of the indigenous religions; my intellectual and spiritual leanings are chiefly Western. My guess is that it represents a focal point of some sort, perhaps a kind of hub, or heart. A center is very basic to most faiths, and many Afar have received varying degrees of Islamic instruction. Could it be, do you think, a space meant to represent Mecca?"

The captain grinned wryly behind his mask. "Okay, Mr. Xhantu. We'll play it your way. You've suffered enough without having to be intimidated by the United States Army." He tapped the tip of his rifle's barrel along the central square's borders and watched closely as the sage's face precisely followed the tapping sounds. "Now, the arrangement of these bodies is immediately reminiscent of the American's operation in Danakil. The floor's grid-like markings support that proposition. Furthermore, there are stains within this square that are highly suggestive of blood and sweat." He strained against the heaviest shadows. "Dead men don't sweat, Mr. Xhantu." Wildfeather's eyes swept the cavern, picking up details, at last resting on a nondescript, pencil-thin beam of sallow light. He was having trouble weighing duty against spirit. "Sir," he said, "forensic operations would be very hard on you here. It would be difficult, expensive, and time-consuming to run DNA tests, as well as to gather print and soil samples. But it is fully within my authority to quarantine you elsewhere for the sake of preserving the site's integrity."

"Then you are running late, Captain. I would have had plenty of time to sully the place were its forensic significance of any interest to me. What you are witnessing is solely the doing of these people you find dead about you. They arrived, as you have postulated, in a frenzy, many badly burned or otherwise injured. I cannot help but agree with your general assessment. Your description of their floor plan definitely resembles what I have heard of the site created by the American. I have never visited Mamuset; I learned of its specific arrangement in my wanderings tribe to tribe."

Wildfeather, looking directly at the sage, found the man's face trained dead-on his own. "Mr. Xhantu, the government and people of the United States of America are not going to be satisfied with an empty body bag."

Xhantu didn't budge. "Then you must search Mamuset or the surrounding desert. When these people appeared they bore at their fore but one man. They carried him toward the center of this cavern while chanting the name 'Mudahid' over and over in a manner suggestive of great grief. He was certainly dead or mortally wounded. It would be natural to assume it was he who occupied this central space, and his serum you have observed."

"Then where is this man Mudahid? And why would his body have been removed?"

"Sir, I do not know. I did not observe the goings-on subsequent to the hysterical arrival of these people. I was flung violently aside upon their entrance, and did not regain access and full control until all was silent."

"And how long was that interim?"

"The space of a week or more, Captain. Apparently they considered the passing of this Mudahid person a considerable loss; their grieving was absolutely prohibitive of my entry. The sound of that great grief commenced each morning precisely at sunrise, becoming weaker day by day. And then...silence. The people had starved to death, and thirsted as well. It is my impression they did not molest my reservoir; nor did they, indeed, depart from their spaces once ensconced. These, as I say, are merely my impressions. Other than salvaging what I could of my artifacts, I have left this place as they left it. I have walked well around the grid to secure water for myself and little Pegasus. In that sense, Captain, this place is pristine for your investigation."

"I appreciate that, sir," Wildfeather used his rifle to indicate the brown smudge at their feet, and then to follow it, lazily, into the shadows of the east wall. "Mr. Xhantu, I'm pointing at a dark stain. The trail of this stain leads off the grid, almost as if a body had been dragged away." He shifted his rifle over his left shoulder and took the old man by the hand. "Let's go." They stepped between bodies carefully. "This smear," Wildfeather went on, "runs resolutely to the east wall, although it veers constantly back and forth, as if the guiding hand took great pains to avoid impinging upon the dead. Now, Mr. Xhantu, on the supposition your haunts are not haunted, I'm going to postulate a very solid intercession here—I'm going to suppose the body of your Mr. Mudahid was dragged along...here...and here...borne sliming all the way to this depression, where it appears a fresh water pool, your said 'reservoir' resides." He crept partly round the rim, flicked on his flashlight, and looked into the pool calmly. After a minute he said, without raising his eyes, "Sir, I'm afraid I'm going to have to ask you to come with me. The United States government will financially provide for your move, for your placement, and for your comfort. I have been authorized by the Army to make pertinent decisions in the field regarding my mission, which is essentially to wrap up the matter of Cristian Honey Vane. In that respect I am empowered to issue commands, and to have two American servicemen stationed outside carry out those commands. I also have—" He was cut off by a low, grieving moan issuing from the far end of the cavern.

Wildfeather looked back up to see Xhantu's death mask trained on him. The sound rolled out of the labyrinth's bowels, swelling as it came; now steadying, now oscillating like a banshee in labor. Wildfeather shivered, from the heels of his moccasins to the bill of his camouflage cap. A steady breath of rock-cooled air played with his scalp hairs, made his ears perk up like an animal's.

The song of the wind came on, crying through twisted alleys, piping up pinholes and calling down wells; filling the cavern with a chorus that was as beautiful as it was plaintive. Then, for a few delirious seconds, the deluge of air was sucked out the dozens of scattered fissures, and the great cavern became a whistling, wheezing calliope. The strange music made Wildfeather's toes cramp, made his gonads go for his gut. The music just as gradually lost its multitonality, at last becoming the sound of a giant blowing into a bottle. Even that passed. The two men stood tiny in the fading echoes.

Wildfeather walked straight up to the sage. "Mr. Xhantu, I feel like a Humvee just did the hula in my head."

"Pardon?"

"Nothing worth repeating." They stood very close for a long minute. The sage spread his arms, and Wildfeather reached round and hugged him as a son would embrace his father. He patted him very gently on the back, afraid the little old man might disintegrate like a puffball in a breeze. When they pulled apart the sage seemed almost too frail for words.

"Captain," he said, "it would seem we are in a quandary."

Wildfeather clasped his hands behind his back and paced in a short circle. "As a soldier, Mr. Xhantu, I am trained to follow orders without question. Obeying my spiritual impulses while in uniform would be most unprofessional."

Xhantu bowed. "Just so. And I am certain that you, sir, are every bit the professional." He cocked his head. "Yet you know, Captain Wildfeather, at this juncture you impress me as a man with a chronic case of microcosmia."

"Microwho?"

"Nothing worth repeating."

They retraced their steps across the grid; the sage a study in quiet contemplation, the soldier every bit the seeker struggling with his deepest demons. Finally Wildfeather nodded emphatically.

"I'm ordering these caves burned out and sealed, that no future investigative body be exposed to the perils of mass putrefaction. The search for Vane's remains will be focused on Mamuset, and I will personally campaign for an intensive look into elements of the Eritrean Army, on the premise that said remains may even now be held somewhere obscene." At the west wall they paused. "I want to apologize, Mr. Xhantu, on behalf of my country, for this grave turn in your situation, brought about by one of her citizens who, spiritually at least, had no business meddling in the affairs of ancient, respected cultures." They followed the wall out the archway and into the antechamber. "I hope you will not be left with the impression that all Americans are so self-absorbed."

They stopped. "Not at all, Captain. And you need not apologize for the limitations of others. You possess qualities, both spiritual and intellectual, that are of the highest order." He turned to face Wildfeather as a master faces his disciple. "As a matter of fact, sir, you strike me as a man of vision."

Wildfeather grinned, embarrassed. "Nah. I'm as shortsighted as the next guy."

"And modest, too! Amazing."

Wildfeather cleared his throat uncomfortably. "Very

well, then." He pulled off his face mask. "I'll have my men re-move these keepsakes of yours, and I'll allow you to oversee their safe handling. I'm going to radio for a guarded truck, that you and your property may be securely transported to a base in Djibouti. Sorry, but things are still too hot in Ethiopia for now. I'll make sure someone from our embassy is there to discuss your options with you." He preceded the old man up the twist-ing shaft. Once outside, Wildfeather dropped his sunglasses back into place. "Mackaw!"

The photographer scurried up, sandwiched between Wil-lard and Barnes. The three men took one look at the sage and froze like rubbernecks at a pileup. Then Mackaw cried, *"Man!"* and raised his camera.

Wildfeather stepped between them and ripped the cam-era right out of Mackaw's hands. With a voice hot and cold he said, "You've got five minutes, and not a single minute more. Put on your breather. You are allowed up to the archway of the great chamber. There you will find an unpleasant scene worthy of many frames. Take all the pictures you want, but under no circumstances are you permitted within among the bodies. Wil-lard and Barnes will be accompanying you, and will make certain this last order is followed to the letter." He held out the camera. As Mackaw's hand lunged for it, Wildfeather pulled it back out of reach. They went through this little ritual twice more before the soldier allowed the civilian to re-appropriate his property with a modicum of courtesy.

A small hand lit on Wildfeather's forearm. He inclined his head and the sage whispered in his ear. Mackaw got two close-ups.

"Mr. Xhantu," Wildfeather proclaimed, "would like a private moment to say goodbye to his home. Go ahead, Mr. Xhantu. Take your time, but make sure the mask stays on."

The sage glided back to the entrance, and, white rabbit, disappeared from view. He paused to run a hand over Pegasus, then hurried across his antechamber and into the great cavern. Xhantu felt his way halfway along the west wall, turned ninety degrees, and tiptoed between the bodies until he reached the hollow.

He took a deep breath before extracting a picture

gripped in the folds of his sanafil. Slowly, methodically, he tore the photograph into ever smaller pieces until he had a little handful of paper shards. He made a fist and held the contents high above the dreaming pool. Xhantu unclenched his fingers, and his final thoughts of Cristian Vane fell like petals on the Nile.

www.ingramcontent.com/pod-product-compliance
Lightning Source LLC
Chambersburg PA
CBHW031058260626
47172CB00001B/117